PRAISE FOR JENNIFER PROBST

"For a sexy, fun-filled, warmhearted read, look no further than Jennifer Probst!"

—Jill Shalvis, *New York Times* bestselling author

"Jennifer Probst is an absolute auto-buy author for me."

—J. Kenner, *New York Times* bestselling author

"Jennifer Probst knows how to bring the swoons and the sexy."

—Amy E. Reichert, author of *The Coincidence of Coconut Cake*

"As always, Jennifer Probst never fails to deliver romance that sizzles and has a way of tugging those emotional heartstrings."

—*Four Chicks Flipping Pages*

"Jennifer Probst's books remind me of delicious chocolate cake. Bursting with flavor, decadently rich . . . very satisfying."

—*Love Affair with an e-Reader*

PRAISE FOR *A BRAND NEW ENDING*

"*A Brand New Ending* was a mega-adorable and moving second-chance romance! I just adored everything about it! Run to your nearest Amazon for your own Kyle—this one is mine!"

—*BJ's Book Blog*

"Don't miss another winner from Jennifer Probst."

—Mary from *USA TODAY*'s *Happy Ever After*

PRAISE FOR *THE START OF SOMETHING GOOD*

"The must-have summer romance read of 2018!"

—*Gina's Bookshelf*

"Achingly romantic, touching, realistic, and just plain beautiful, *The Start of Something Good* lingers with you long after you turn the last page."

—Katy Evans, *New York Times* bestselling author

all
roads
lead
to
you

OTHER BOOKS BY JENNIFER PROBST

Nonfiction

*Write Naked: A Bestseller's Secrets to Writing Romance &
Navigating the Path to Success*

The Stay Series

The Start of Something Good
A Brand New Ending

The Billionaire Builders Series

Everywhere and Every Way
Any Time, Any Place
Somehow, Some Way
All or Nothing at All

The Searching for . . . Series

Searching for Someday
Searching for Perfect
Searching for Beautiful
Searching for Always
Searching for You
Searching for Mine
Searching for Disaster

The Billionaire Marriage Series

The Marriage Bargain
The Marriage Trap

all roads lead to you

JENNIFER PROBST

Montlake
Romance

Published by Montlake Romance, Seattle

www.apub.com

Amazon, the Amazon logo, and Montlake Romance are trademarks of Amazon.com, Inc., or its affiliates.

ISBN-13: 9781542006101
ISBN-10: 1542006104

Cover design by Letitia Hasser

Cover photography by Lauren Perry

Printed in the United States of America

*This book is dedicated to
all the animal lovers, rescuers, and do-gooders
who believe every life, both human and animal,
deserves a chance.
And for my own fur-babies,
Lester and Bella, who are now at Rainbow Bridge:
Mommy misses you every day.
Thank you for making my life so much better by
rescuing me.
Finally, for my son Jake, who has begged me for years to
use the name Elmo in a book. Here you go, love. You
inspired me to create a worthy character, and I had a
blast writing about him.*

The greatness of a nation and its moral progress can be judged by the way its animals are treated.

—*Mahatma Gandhi*

Chapter One

Something was coming.

Harper Bishop shot up in bed, heart rocketing at full speed, and squinted into the shadows. Soft fur and flaming heat surrounded her, but her body was so used to the raging temperatures, she couldn't sleep unless she was surrounded in a wolflike pack. Her dogs muttered in annoyance and shifted even closer, not sensing anything wrong as the clock struck three a.m.

Slowly, her body relaxed. Probably just a crazy dream. With her canine menagerie, no bad guy had a chance of sneaking in, and everyone in town knew there was nothing to steal in her two-bedroom cottage unless they wanted a rescue animal.

She lay back on the pillow and stared at the ceiling. Her insides shifted again, as if sensing a storm rolling in. Sometimes she wondered if she was becoming more animal-like because of her company. But this primitive instinct stirring her gut didn't feel like danger.

No, more like a premonition her safe, orderly, protected life was about to unravel.

Her brother, Ethan, would understand. He'd once confided he'd gotten those feelings back when he was in the military, ready to jump out of a plane on a rescue mission. A prickling of awareness that his old life was about to change for good.

Biting back a sigh, she carefully extricated herself from the queen-size bed, where she barely had enough room to breathe, and padded to the kitchen. Moonlight trickled through the windows, and a soft spring breeze wafted in, caressing her bare skin. Figaro lifted her head from her perch on the top of the recliner and shot her a disgusted stare. Then went back to sleep.

Harper shook her head. Figaro never acted like a rescue cat. The black feline had been half-starved, rain soaked, and shivering in the bushes when Harper saved her. A few days later, the cat had claimed her space like the royal queen she believed she was, forcing the dogs to accept the new hierarchy. Harper's animals were like a bunch of moody teenagers, hating when their sleep was interrupted even though they got about eighteen hours per day. Harper counted herself lucky if she scored five.

Flicking on the light, she perused her choice of coffee beans, deciding on the special Kona blend she had shipped straight from Disney World. She watched the pot drip, sucking in the amazing smell of energy and life, then took her mug to the oversize leather chair—the one Figaro didn't currently occupy. Curling her feet underneath her, she cuddled under the worn afghan and settled in to watch the world slowly wake up.

Her mind drifted, touching on the various tasks that made up her day. Running one of the oldest horse-rescue farms in the quaint town of Gardiner was her passion, but extremely demanding. There was another horse auction to attend, where she'd be on the lookout for any abused or broken horses to bring back and rehabilitate. Three horseback-riding appointments for guests at the bed-and-breakfast on the property, which her sister, Ophelia, ran. One vet appointment for Stitch, who might have bruised her foreleg. And two buyer appointments she prayed would go successfully. God knew there were only so many stalls in the barn, and the more animals she was able to place, the more she could take in. It was a vicious cycle, often filled with disappointment and heartbreak, but she lived for the victories. Time had taught her how to wall her heart high enough so a loss didn't wash away all she'd worked hard for.

One animal saved in this world by her hand was enough. Sure, she wanted to rescue hundreds, but wasting worry and precious time on wannabe intentions only drained her energy. In the past few years, she'd been able to find more balance in her life. Everything was exactly the way she'd dreamed it would be.

She was lucky her siblings had joined her in running the family business after their parents passed. When her brother and sister had found their soul mates, she was even more thrilled the ones they fell in love with had stayed in Gardiner, allowing them all to be together. Watching them pair up was a happy and bittersweet experience. The family table had nearly doubled, and she was the single one. Yes, she was lonely sometimes, but she'd never focused on finding a partner because she knew herself too well. Knew she was set in her ways, stubborn to a fault, and would pick an animal over people every time. In fact, the few short affairs she'd engaged in had ended with a jealousy over her job that had nowhere to go except Splitsville, USA.

She hadn't been upset to see them go. Even with the benefits of sex, no man seemed to interest her further than a few weeks. It was as if she were built differently from other women. She was thirty-three years old and hadn't experienced even a twinge of a ticking biological clock. No desire to try on white wedding dresses, or pick out baby names, or dream of a man who could complete her.

She was complete all by herself.

Which was why she didn't need a strange voice rising up to threaten her perfect life. She didn't want something new rolling her way. Lord knew she had enough work, enough security, and enough happiness as is. So Harper did the only thing left to do.

She told the annoying voice to go away.

The sun eventually rose, and the coffeepot diminished to dregs. The dogs jumped out of bed to greet her with their usual enthusiasm of licking tongues, wagging tails, and adoring gazes. Harper reset her mind to tackle the day ahead, and soon the strange premonition evaporated and it was business as usual on the farm with no surprises.

Just the way she liked it.

♥ ♥ ♥

Something was coming.

Behind the cheerful sign welcoming him to the B & B, Aidan O'Connor stared up at the gleaming white and robin's egg–blue house sprawled across several acres, framed against the stunning backdrop of the Shawangunk Mountains. He was tired, hungry, and didn't smell so good after such a long trip—a nonwinning trifecta. The small town of Gardiner seemed like the perfect place to hide for a while, but his gut was stirring in a sudden, familiar way that screamed trouble.

He growled back at the voice in hopes of shutting it up. He didn't care if it was a million-dollar opportunity or an adrenaline-spiked long shot ready to hit. He was done chasing dreams and primitive instincts with a burning hope that only ended up kicking him in the teeth.

His plan to explore the New York Hudson Valley region while visiting the States had seemed like a good idea when he left Ireland for a change of scenery and a desire to reinvent himself. He was at a crossroads in his career and needed to get his shit together. Needed a fresh start. Needed to let go of the past and accept he'd never control the actions of others, only his own. All those awful, canned expressions he used to laugh about had suddenly become true gospel for him.

Unfortunately, the past few months looking for new opportunities had only solidified his failure and bestowed upon him the gift of depression and burnout.

He was done. Done trying to find the perfect horse to train. Done trying to woo snobby owners and sleeping in crappy hotels and dealing with daily disappointment. Done traveling to endless racetracks to pimp himself out. His wallet was almost empty, along with his hopes.

He was here for a damn vacation and nothing more. This place looked just about perfect, reminding him of home, where cozy stone cottages welcomed visitors to Kildare with the promise of a good Irish breakfast; clean, damp air; and blinding-green scenery. The spring flowers were in vivid bloom, and an aura of charm and warmth seemed to surround the inn he'd chosen from TripAdvisor. So far, it looked like exactly what he needed. Peace and quiet. No people to bother him. A horse-rescue farm on the property where he could ride for pleasure, not work. From the number of farm stands he'd spotted along the way, he bet the food would be decent and fresh here, too. He was already burned out on processed airport fare and fast food.

Aidan walked up the stairs, his one battered duffel bag slung over his shoulder, and watched a pretty, willowy woman with strawberry-gold hair step out on the porch.

"Mr. O'Connor? I'm Ophelia Bishop. Welcome to the Robin's Nest B & B."

"Nice to meet you, Ophelia."

"I'm sure you must be exhausted after your long trip. Here, let me take that from you."

"Thank you, but I can carry my own bag, umm—"

The owner's sweet smile contradicted her no-nonsense movements as she deftly slid the bag from his shoulder and transferred it into her own grip. "Don't be silly, I've got it. Come in. I have paperwork ready for you. There's tea and cookies, but if you'd like a light lunch, I have a few menus of wonderful places in town that deliver."

She swept him inside, and he was struck by the beauty of the interior, from its graceful, winding staircase to its smart antiques and soaring ceilings.

Ophelia walked to the French writing desk and began punching computer keys with a deft expertise, the large diamond ring on her finger flashing madly in the light. "You'll be with us for two full weeks. I placed you in the Imperial Room, which will give you plenty of the privacy you requested." She confirmed his payment and had him sign a few forms. "How was your trip?"

"I'm a bit knackered from the drive, but nothing a pint or a cup of tea can't cure. Your inn is beautiful."

She smiled. "Thank you. I'll make sure you have both beverages handy. I've also stocked your refrigerator with water and light snacks. We serve a full breakfast until ten a.m., and I can make any of your reservations for activities or dining. I already booked you a few horseback rides and noted you were experienced for the trail."

"Sounds grand."

"No dietary restrictions?"

He appreciated her thorough knowledge and willingness to help. "Nope. Though I seem to crave pastries in the morning. Is there a bakery in town?"

Her blue eyes sparkled. "Do you like scones?"

He groaned. "I'd eat them every day, if possible. You wouldn't tease a stranger, would you?"

She laughed and shook her head. "Never. Besides, once you stay at my inn, you're no longer a stranger. What part of Ireland are you from?"

"Kildare."

Her face lit up. "My mother was born there! She was the one who built this inn. I've always wanted to visit."

"You should. It's good to stand on the land your parents were from. And your mother built a fine place here. Is she here? I'd love to meet her."

"Oh, she passed away a few years ago."

"I'm sorry."

Ophelia smiled gratefully. "Thank you. I feel like she's with us every day, though. She taught me how to make her famous scones, and I make fresh cream in the morning to go with them."

"Oh, I'm going to like you, Ophelia Bishop."

"Not too much, I hope."

Aidan turned his head. The man at the bottom of the stairs regarded him with a mixture of amusement and warning, a look that claimed his woman with no apologies. Aidan grinned. Ophelia was an interesting woman, but there were no sparks. Hell, even if there'd been any, he never encroached on committed relationships.

"I'm strictly interested in the scones," he said.

Ophelia rolled her eyes. "Really, Kyle? The poor man just checked in and you're already beating your chest like some ape?"

"Baby, I prefer the visual of a sleek predator just reminding another alpha what the deal is."

Aidan choked on a laugh while Ophelia crossed her arms in front of her chest and glared at Kyle. "We're not in the Bronx Zoo." She turned back, her smile gracious and her face smoothed out. "I apologize, Mr. O'Connor. My husband is new at greeting guests properly. He may need further training."

Kyle leaned against the railing and winked. "I think you're right. The one-on-one lessons work best."

Hmm . . . a married couple who still seemed crazy about each other. A good fight was as much fun as a good tumble in bed, at least in Aidan's opinion. The air crackled between them, but he knew Irish women well, and he'd bet this one didn't surrender easily.

She tossed her head, her red hair glinting like a matador's cloak. "I'm glad you think so, because I signed you up for a class at the Culinary Institute in hospitality service. You'll be quite busy for the next few weeks. I heard they give tons of heavy instructions and homework."

Kyle's shocked face was enough entertainment to make Aidan's day. The lass ignored her husband's bubbling protests and pressed a key into their guest's palm with a bright smile. "Up the stairs, fourth door on the left. I'm here twenty-four seven if you have any questions. I hope you have a wonderful stay."

"Thank you, I think I will." This time, he was prepared and faster—snatching his bag up before she could protest. He headed toward the stairs, shooting Kyle a sympathetic look, man to man, but damned if his mood hadn't improved in just the few moments of being here.

Aidan walked down the hall, his muscles finally relaxing, when the voice inside him rose up and whispered slyly in his ear.

Something is coming. You better be ready.

He gritted his teeth and wished to hell he'd never listened to the voice when he was a young boy. Yes, it had helped forge a career he loved. But it had also ripped his life away, leaving him to pick up all the pieces and wonder if they could even be put back together.

Pissed off, he entered his room and answered the voice.

Fuck you. I'm done.

After that, it was quiet.

Chapter Two

Harper strode into the barn, wiping her forehead with the back of her hand before realizing she'd only managed to spread the mud to her face. Ugh, what a morning. She was dirty, sweaty, and a bit pissy—the perfect trifecta.

She dropped the saddle and bridle on the cluttered table and made her way down the stalls, her boots crushing stray debris and clutter that had no business in her barn. Ridiculous. The place was a mess, and she'd specifically told Owen his main job was to keep her barn clean. Drawing in a deep breath for patience, she suddenly stilled as the smell hit her a few seconds after her boot settled into a pile of mush.

She'd just stepped in horseshit.

As if sensing her bad mood, a few of the horses whinnied, sticking out their noses for a stroke or a loose tongue for a carrot.

"Sorry, guys," she said with a sigh. "Not sure I'll be able to ride today. We're still shorthanded, and our new helper is more interested in his phone than cleaning up the stalls."

She hopped outside and dragged her boot across the grass. She noted a loose latch on the outside gate, the messy spill of weeds encroaching on her paved lot, and a thousand other tasks she'd never be able to get to in twenty-four hours. After a few more swipes and a mental note to wash her boot off with the hose, she perused the whiteboard posted with horseback-riding appointments and checked the voice mail messages that had piled up in the past few hours.

Her heart beat faster as she listened to a potential buyer for Little Foot, a tame little filly perfect for the buyer's son. The rescue needed a family of regular riders to flourish, not a revolving door of bed-and-breakfast guests and workouts from the employees. Unfortunately, by the time she got to the thirteenth message, the buyer had backed out of the deal because Harper hadn't called her back, so she'd gone and bought another horse from a different farm.

Fuck.

She rotated her neck to work out the knots and began to scream her favorite word in her head. Normally, she had no problem yelling obscenities but tried not to lose her temper around the animals. They were too skittish and had dealt with enough crap in their short lifetimes. They didn't need their only source of stability to lose it in an old-fashioned temper tantrum.

She dragged in a breath, opened her mouth wide, and quietly shouted the word to the rafters. "Fuck!"

"Uh-oh. Bad day, huh?" Her brother, Ethan, stood before her. Damn, he was always able to sneak up on her with a stealthy grace that had served him well in the military. He had ginger hair like their sister, Ophelia, and seemed to be jealous Harper had escaped the Irish curse. Only Harper knew how hard she'd wished for glorious red locks instead of her boring dark-brown ones.

She rubbed her forehead, ignoring his knowing grin. Ethan was able to peg her mood in seconds, as if he were highly sensitized to subtle shifts of energy. He had the same talent with horses. Another reason the family had dubbed him "the horse whisperer" early on. "I want to fire Owen. He didn't check the messages, so I lost a horse deal. He never cleans the barn properly, and he's attached to his phone." Her finger jabbed in the air, pointing out the large pile of poop. "Plus, I stepped in shit."

Ethan quirked a brow. "He's nineteen years old—they're all attached to their phones. Besides, I can't send back Judge Bennett's own grandson."

She groaned. "We should have never taken on a kid who gets so drunk he vandalizes his own dorm instead of his rival's."

"You know the judge likes to give us a challenge. We took Chloe on last year, and look how she blossomed," he said, affection warming his voice.

Chloe was a twenty-year-old assigned to the horse farm last summer by Judge Bennett for a vandalism crime she never committed. She'd worked the stables and ended up becoming close with the family, including Ethan's fiancée, Mia. Now she visited regularly and had her own horse.

Harper gave a long sigh. "Chloe was different. She's smart. Not a dumbass."

Ethan chuckled, moving down the stall line to say hello to each of the horses. "He's just a kid trying to figure stuff out. I'll talk to him. Tell him no phone and to clean it all up."

She rolled her shoulders to shake off the lingering tension. "Thanks."

Her brother shot her a look. "You okay, Harp?"

She hesitated, not because she was averse to talking to Ethan, but because she couldn't seem to explain the real problem. The tension in her belly had only tightened over the week. The word to describe her state of mind was one she despised.

Unsettled.

She waved her hand in the air to dismiss his question and her odd thoughts. "Yeah, sorry, I got a lot on my mind. With John out for the next few weeks, there's tons to do." John was her full-time assistant and had been working the horse farm for years. He'd sprained his back and was under strict bed rest for a while. Thank God his wife loved to spoil him; Harper knew he was in good hands. "Seems like the work has been tripling, expenses are up, and good help is hard to find. There's a horse auction next week, and I wanted to be able to save a couple, but there's no room until I get some of our current stable sold."

The horse-rescue portion of the property was Harper's heart and soul, but not as profitable as the inn. Her dreams of expansion were still far from reality, but she believed one day she'd get the money. Besides rescuing horses from various auctions, rehabilitating, then selling them, she took on boarding and horseback-riding lessons. But with her dependence on volunteers and John unavailable, there was too much work with too few hands on deck.

"I know I've been spending a chunk of time away from the farm," he said. "With Mia's business trips, the bungalow remodeling, and the upcoming-wedding plans, I may not be pulling my weight. You shouldn't be stressed out."

Harper rolled her eyes and shot him a disgusted look. "That's just stupid. You have a partner now and you should be a team. And I'm not stressed out, I'm just indulging in some good old-fashioned whining. Don't you remember how Mom used to tell us it was a healthy way to blow off steam?"

Ethan grinned. "How could I forget? My problem is you've never been a whiner. If you weren't so damn stubborn about new hires, I'd get someone in here to help."

"I'm not stubborn. I just insist on quality."

He snorted and braced his hands on his hips. "Seriously? You nixed the last few I wanted to hire and gave me ridiculous excuses."

"One had never owned an animal! How could she possibly help on a farm with no previous ownership experience?"

"She had fish and parrots. Last time I checked, those were animals."

"And that weird guy with the unibrow?" she continued, as if he hadn't spoken. "He didn't like Flower. Everybody likes Flower."

Ethan gave a suffering sigh. "He only mentioned the mare seemed a bit high spirited and undisciplined. Which she is."

"He said it with an attitude, and I don't want anyone here trying to break her spirit."

"I give up. Since I'm the only one left you do trust, I certainly don't want to piss you off. But you'll need a chunk of free time if you want to begin training Phoenix for racing. It's a big undertaking."

"You've never cared before about pissing me or Ophelia off," she said with a smile. "Mia must be training you well." He rolled his eyes and she laughed. "I've been wanting to work with a racehorse for a while. Been researching training methods and possible riders. I should have enough money to enter him in a few races and see how he does." She'd deliberately been taking on more work and avoiding hiring another full-timer in order to pad her savings account for the investment.

Ethan rubbed his head. "Phoenix has come a long way, but I'm still not sure how he'll do on a track with other horses. He's sensitive. It took me a long time to get him to take to a saddle. Those bastards did some real damage."

Anger rushed through her. She'd rescued Phoenix when she visited a farm in Pennsylvania and knew immediately he needed help. He'd been tied to a tree, covered in filth, and obviously malnourished. His previous owner had purchased the Thoroughbred to make some money on the track, but when it didn't work out, Phoenix had been left alone to suffer, then readied to be sold for slaughter. Harper had paid the same amount to the asshole, reported him to the authorities for animal abuse, and taken Phoenix home.

The horse's fiery spirit had saved him, and after multiple sessions with Ethan, he was finally able to accept a rider. He was wicked fast, with an epic temper. Harper knew the moment she laid eyes on him he was destined to run.

"He's a fighter." Pride filled her. "He won't let anyone break him, and that's what he'll bring to the track. I just need to get the right team."

"You know I'll help with whatever I can. Phoenix deserves only the best." Harper knew her brother loved the horse as much as she did. After Ethan had returned from active duty with a blown-out knee, his own journey toward healing essentially mixed with Phoenix's as he taught him to trust again.

She grinned. "Thanks. In the meantime, if you can yell at Owen for me, I'd appreciate it."

"Done. Unless you want me to let Hei Hei loose on him again?"

Harper laughed, striding out of the barn. "Even I'm not that cruel, bro."

Her spirit lighter, she got back to work.

♥ ♥ ♥

Aidan looked up at the clear cerulean-blue sky and wondered how long he was going to survive.

With a groan, he got up from the rocker on the wraparound porch and decided to head out to explore the grounds. His vacation was technically perfect. He was alone with his thoughts, with plenty of time to figure things out amid a picture-perfect setting. Yet one thing was ruining the rainbow.

He was fucking bored.

Deciding to take the rear footpath that led toward the stables, he began walking and wondered if he should cut out early. The inn was top notch, and he enjoyed the quaint town with its gourmet cafés, lunch places, and shops. The local college added a dash of color and kept things young. He'd stopped at Tantillo Farms for their famous apple-cider doughnuts. Scheduled a midafternoon hike at Mohonk

Mountain House. He was going horseback riding tomorrow. Things were good.

Except they weren't.

Frustration nipped at his nerves, and he lengthened his stride. He should've known it wouldn't be simple for him. He'd been working since he was young, and the only time off had been at the local pubs or the occasional weekend with Rachael. Her name brought no sting, even after her betrayal. He almost wished it did sting. At least that would've proved why he'd stayed with the woman for almost a year. Instead, he mourned the loss of Kincaid's Crown the most.

The image of the horse he'd taken to the Irish Derby floated in his mind. A lucky gray. A massive beast with the heart of a warrior and stamina that kept him at the top of his game. It had been hard to win his affection, but once the horse softened, they'd bonded and become a winning team. He'd loved training him. Spending all his hours with horses was perhaps the only place and time he felt fully himself. He'd had everything he ever wanted.

Until it was all ripped away.

He wondered if the horse missed him.

Raw pain tore through his body. Did it even matter? He vowed revenge on the son of a bitch who'd betrayed him, but leaving the horse he'd come to love had been his only choice. Kincaid's Crown deserved to run his races, and the smartest move was to walk. Aidan had planned to start over. Rebuild his name and reputation on his own terms, this time, trusting no one but himself. Success brought wealth and power, and there were too many people who greedily craved more, until it didn't matter who they destroyed.

Even family.

It was a brutal lesson he'd learned well.

He'd truly believed this time, when success came, he'd protect himself, his reputation, and his fortune.

But not anymore.

The constant sting of failure threatened to crush him. He had nowhere else left to go. The money he'd put aside to travel and rebuild his career was almost gone. His belief in both himself and the future was no longer pure but stained with betrayal and a mocking knowledge that this time he'd lost.

It was over.

The woods enclosed him with soothing coolness and the scent of damp earth. Large, crooked trees crowded the dirt pathway and blocked the sting of sun and sky. The high-pitched chatter of birds and scramble of squirrels kept him company as he walked, and slowly he relaxed. He'd check out the barns and see how they treated their horses. He couldn't believe the horrors he came across when it came to animal upkeep, especially at so-called "rescue farms." Too many of them figured just taking in every damn stray was enough and ignored food, hygiene, and proper care. But Ophelia seemed to run a tight ship at the inn, so maybe he'd be pleasantly surprised.

The path led to a thick wall of brush, but he fought through the tight space and stepped out into the pasture. The mountains overwhelmed the skyline, allowing only a few fluffy clouds and nothing else. The large red barns, neat white fences, and shocking green hills reminded him of home. Horses roamed in the fenced areas, and some lounged in paddocks, lazily munching on hay as they sunbathed. Chickens ran free, seeming to actually play with two dogs—a black Lab and a mixed brown-and-white terrier—in a strange game of tag.

He poked around and spotted a trail of riders heading down the hill. Ophelia had said her brother, Ethan, was handling the horseback riding. Might as well investigate while he waited for his return.

Starting at the first stall, he peeked his head in, finding most of the horses in seemingly good spirits. Some stuck their noses out, while others lashed at him with searching tongues looking for a treat. He spotted none of the usual signs of abuse or neglect. Thank God. He didn't have it in him today to try to right another wrong.

He took his time exploring, making mental notes. Definitely not a professional barn for racing or breeding. Most of the horses seemed to be a mishmash of ages and types, so it must be strictly a rescue-and-boarding place, with the side benefit for guests of the inn to do some light riding.

He headed out into the second barn. A few stragglers filled up the stalls in the front, and the loft was full of various supplies. He found a bag of carrots and grabbed a few, fed some of the mares, then went to check out the last barn.

It was small, with the front stalls empty. He walked toward the rear, then jerked to a stop.

His gaze fell on a horse staring back at him with fire in his eyes. Pitch black, he blended half into the shadows, the only color a bright streak of white zigzagging across his face like a beauty mark. Ears pinned back, the horse's gaze narrowed, and he blew a hard breath out of his nose, as if irritated with being faced with a stranger.

Aidan moved closer. God, the Thoroughbred was beautiful. Not overly bulky, but with a muscled leanness that hinted at good breeding. What was he doing back here isolated from the others? Were they hiding him? Boarding him for someone specific? Or was he too much trouble so they decided to lock him away?

"Hey, *capalleen*. You hungry? How about a carrot?" he murmured, offering the treat through the rails.

The horse stared back, not blinking, his body shuddering with an intensity that Aidan had never seen before. He made no move to take the carrot, even when Aidan pushed it farther out.

"Stubborn, huh? Think I poisoned it or something? Or do you need to be wooed first?" It was rare when a horse didn't immediately take to him. This one had shadows in his dark eyes and a powerful force that made

17

Aidan curious. Offering a smile, he fell into a stream of Irish in order to woo him. The horse shook, turned around, and gave Aidan his ass.

Then let out a big fart.

Aidan chuckled. Well, damn. Talk about being dismissed. This was a challenge he had to take on.

He deftly unlocked the gate, stepped forward, and closed it behind him.

"What the hell do you think you're doing?"

He spun toward the voice, his gaze narrowing on the woman in front of him. His fingers guiltily dropped from the lock. "Sorry. I'm a guest from the inn," he said. "Just checking out your horses."

Pure irritation bristled from her figure. He studied her with interest, noting her staggering height—about six foot one—and the blazing sea-green flame of her gaze, filled with a suspicion that reminded him of the horse who'd just dissed him. Everything about her screamed simplicity, from her short dark bob and makeup-free face to her plain blue T-shirt, jeans, and work boots.

But Aidan had spent his whole life peering beneath the surface to figure out people and animals, to unearth the real stuff. And he bet there was a bucketful of secrets buried deep within the woman before him. They were entwined in her whiskey-smooth voice. Trapped in those mineral eyes. Hinted at with the defensive stance of her lean body. He wondered how long it would take for a man to get close to her. He wondered how many men had tried and failed.

Her arms crossed in front of her chest. "I'm sorry, but guests aren't allowed free access to the barns. I can make you an appointment for a horseback ride, though. Follow me."

He didn't budge, just leaned against the gate. "Already did that. I'm scheduled for tomorrow."

"We'll be happy to give you a tour then. I'll show you the way out."

Amusement flickered. She seemed quite intent on ditching him. First the horse, now the woman. Had he lost his charm along with his reputation? There'd been few horses or women who he hadn't been able to win over in his many years as a trainer, yet in the span of a few minutes, he'd lost two for two. "How come he's locked up all alone back here?" he asked.

She cocked her head and squinted. "He prefers it," she said shortly. "Now, I have to get back to work, Mr. . . . ."

"O'Connor. Call me Aidan."

"This way, Mr. O'Connor." She began to briskly move away. The woman was polite, but it was obvious she didn't have the patience or desire to interact with guests. Fascinating. Quite different from the warm, welcoming way Ophelia had greeted him. She'd also dodged his request to be addressed by his first name, choosing to keep her distance. It was probably rude of him not to follow her out, but he wanted a few more minutes alone with her. All that prickliness on the surface intrigued him. If she worked around animals, there must be more to her.

He just needed to dig a little.

He raised his voice, and she pivoted on her heel. "Why does he prefer it? Is he giving you a hard time? I'm good with horses. I'd be happy to check him out for you."

Her voice iced and her eyes heated. "I'm good with horses, too," she shot back. "I'm also quite capable of handling my barn."

His brow arched. "Thought Ethan was in charge."

She gave him a look full of distaste, like she'd smelled something foul. "Ethan is my brother and *partner*," she said between gritted teeth. "And he'd be the first to tell you that I'm capable of taking care of the stables without his help, or his presence."

He winced. "Sorry. Didn't mean to insult womankind with that comment."

Her smile was sharp and mercenary. "No need to apologize. You give yourself too much credit."

He laughed. She knew the fine arts of banter and power plays, all right, but something told him she hid it well. Yeah, she was a ball buster, but she did it so quietly it'd keep a man on his toes.

He finally understood they were all related and worked together. She must've inherited the Black Irish gene, since she looked nothing like her sister. "So that makes you Ophelia's sister."

"Yes."

He waited, but she said nothing further. Just looked at him with a suffering patience that made him want to stay longer. "And your name is . . ."

His prodding finally managed to unstick her tongue. "Harper," she spit out reluctantly.

"Charmed to meet you, Harper," he said with a big smile.

She grunted.

"Does your horse have a name, too?"

She gave a drawn-out sigh. "Are you going to be one of these pain-in-the-ass guests who drive the staff crazy because he needs constant attention?"

His lips twitched. "Why do I think Ophelia would yell at you for calling me a pain in the ass?"

"Because my sister received the gift of politeness. I didn't."

"What gift did you get?" he asked curiously.

"Fortitude. Helps me deal with annoyance." Her pointed glance told him he was one of her tests.

He'd never been so charmed by a female so ornery. He still didn't budge. She was too much fun. "Fortitude is important. But in my experience, charm will get you farther."

"I apologize, then."

He cocked his head. "For what?"

"That you received neither. I need to escort you out now. I'm behind schedule."

Tamping down a laugh, he acquiesced this time, giving her a nod and following her out into the sunshine. He watched the swinging curve of her ass and the graceful way her body moved, as if each motion was clipped for efficiency. He bet she was a goddess on horseback. There had to be a way to see her fly before he ended his time here. "Your horse turned away from a perfectly good carrot. Seems to have a bit of an attitude."

She slowed her pace so they walked side by side, allowing him to study her face. He caught the quick upward curve to her lip. "Phoenix doesn't like a lot of people and owns a terrible sweet tooth. You'd have to upgrade to a cookie in order to snag his attention."

"I like Phoenix already. He's smart. Can I ride him?"

She shook her head. He liked the way the shiny, straight strands of hair lifted and caressed her cheeks. She wasn't traditionally pretty—her features were too strong—but it was the type of face he could study for hours without getting bored.

His gaze slid over her pointy chin, high brow line, carved cheekbones, and a jaw that held a stubborn tilt hinting at trouble. Her thick lips were peach colored. Her lashes were lush and dark, emphasizing the snapping green of her eyes. She was a mixture of too many shapes and colors held together, yet the whole worked like a perfect painting.

"No," she said. "No one rides Phoenix except Ethan and me."

"What if I paid extra?"

Just like that, she shut down. Her cold gaze crawled over him, and a wall slammed between them. "The only thing I take into consideration is my horse's well-being, and I don't take bribes. The path back to the inn is that way. Have a good afternoon." She tipped her head and strode away without a glance back.

Well, shit. That hadn't gone well at all.

Aidan stared at her retreating figure. She really didn't like him. He'd never had that problem before. Of course, he was usually more focused on training a horse for a big race than on chasing a woman who disliked him, so maybe this was the first time he actually cared?

He wanted to spend more time with her. God knew there was nothing else to do around here. Might as well enjoy some insulting conversation with a sexy female until it was time to check out.

He stuck his hands in his pockets and began walking. Ethan was scheduled to take him riding tomorrow, but he'd love to have Harper be his guide. Of course, there was no way she'd volunteer after their conversation. But Aidan knew the perfect way to snag some quality time with her.

He whistled and prepped his plan for action.

Chapter Three

"What do you mean I have to take him riding?"

Harper stared at her sister, who held a steely-eyed determination that reminded her of their mother. She might run the inn with sweetness and light, but Harper knew intimately the fiery temper that red hair warned of. And right now, Ophelia was pissed.

"I cannot believe you were rude to a guest," she snapped, shaking her head. "Aidan told me what happened. He was devastated he'd offended you by going into the stables without permission. Why would you yell at him, Harp? Did he do something to piss you off?"

Her jaw dropped. "He was very pushy! Wouldn't listen to me when I told him to get out of my stable. Then he tried to bribe me with money so he could ride Phoenix."

Ophelia rolled her eyes. "That's his big crime? He saw a beautiful horse and wanted to ride him? What did we agree on when we took over the B & B? Do you remember?"

She blew out a breath in aggravation. This was ridiculous. "To back one another up?" she muttered.

Ophelia glared. "No. We agreed you and Ethan would be nice to my guests even if it was hard. I know both of you would rather avoid the social spotlight, but making the guests happy is the most important thing for me. Aidan almost checked out! But he specifically asked if you could lead his trail ride to offer you an apology. And you're going to give him what he wants."

Harper opened her mouth to tell her no. Then shut it. Ah, crap, there was no way to win an argument when her sister was on the warpath. It was better to get the whole thing over with. "Fine. But I don't like him. He seems like a know-it-all."

"He's a fellow Irishman from Kildare on holiday and deserves our best hospitality. Understood?"

"Fine," she said again.

"Good. I booked him and the Grayson couple for one p.m. today. Be nice." Her sister spun on her heel with her last warning.

Harper couldn't help it. She stuck her tongue out and immediately felt better.

"Juvenile, Harp," her sister sang without a break in her stride.

Yep. She was just like Mom.

Pissed off, Harper stomped back into the barn. She hated when her schedule was messed with, and now she'd lose a precious hour babysitting. At least it was a group ride. She could spend most of the time chatting the other couple up and keep a slow pace. No galloping for Mr. I'm-Good-With-Horses O'Connor.

The ridiculous small victory made her pause. Why had he gotten her so mad? She'd met a ton of annoying guests, and she was able to keep her game face on for the good of the inn. He wasn't the only one who'd ever ventured into the barn to poke around.

Sure, he was good-looking. He had a nice body. Muscular. Solid. His height was surprising—he was actually a few inches taller than her. A rare occurrence, as she towered over most men. Still, he was nothing spectacular, and he shouldn't have thrown her off.

Owen interrupted her thoughts when he trudged into the barn, a look of fear on his face. With his cherub cheeks, ruddy skin, and wild blond hair that exploded around his face in corkscrew curls, he looked like a surfer dude who'd gotten lost on his way to California. "Harper, that chicken is after me again. I need you to lock him up."

She sighed. "Hei Hei won't hurt you. He just likes to squawk and pretend he's the boss. If you ignore him, he'll go away. Did you clean out the stalls and refresh the hay and water?"

"Not yet. The chicken's been following me, so I couldn't. Hey, can I get off early today? I think I'm coming down with a cold. I have the sniffles."

"No, you probably just have allergies. The pollen count is high today. I'll bring Hei Hei back to the house so you can finish the stalls."

"I don't think allergies feel like this." He wrinkled his nose, sniffing dramatically and putting a hand to his forehead. "I may have a fever."

His phone lit up and he dove for it eagerly, his thumbs flying over the screen as he texted back and dropped out of their conversation.

"Big guys' night out, huh?" she asked innocently.

"Hell yeah. Dudes want to hit it hard, so . . ." he answered, trailing off as he realized what he'd said. His face fell. "Guess you got me on that one, huh?"

Damn, either he wasn't that bright or he just wasn't paying enough attention. "Listen, Owen, your grandfather wants you to do well here. You need to pay off the vandalism. Lying isn't helping anyone."

He gave her the perfect puppy-dog look, his baby blues wide and pleading. "You're right. Please don't tell him, Harper."

"Do the stalls and I'll consider it."

"Okay, but the smell sometimes makes me gag." He wandered off, still checking his screen.

She wondered briefly what the future held. The last time she'd gone to Bea's Diner, an entire family had spent their mealtime with their heads down, gazes glued to their phones. Family dinners at the Bishop farm revolved around chatter and laughing. Connection. She hoped Owen would begin to notice the beauty of the animals around him and appreciate the farm. Real joy existed beyond his Instagram followers. She'd like to show him that.

Shaking her head, she got back to work and did her best to stuff in as many tasks as possible until her fated horseback ride. The hours flew by, and she had just begun to pull the horses to prep them when the air seemed to thicken, reminding her of the tension before a storm exploded. She turned her head and met Aidan's gaze head-on, and everything inside her stilled.

"Hello, Harper."

Her belly did a long, slow flip-flop. Damn Irish brogue. What was it about a man with an accent that made women weak at the knees? Guess she wasn't immune, even though her clichéd reaction annoyed her.

Harper turned and swept her gaze over his figure. He wore casual faded jeans and a simple green T-shirt, which stretched over a nice set of muscles and broad chest. His hair was closely cropped, the crisp strands the color of straw. He had a broad, defined nose, arched brows, and full lips enhanced by just the slightest stubble. Tiny lines bracketed his eyes and mouth, evidence he liked to laugh. But it was his eyes that got her. How hadn't she noticed them before? The color of mysterious amber, a mixture of brown and gold that seemed to glow with a direct intensity. A woman could get lost in a gaze that deep. A woman could get found.

A woman could get into trouble.

Harper nodded a greeting and shook off her strange thoughts. "Ready for your ride?" she asked politely.

"Been looking forward to it." He strode close, reaching out to stroke Maximus, letting his fingers linger so the stallion could catch his scent. He hadn't been lying when he said he was good with horses. She caught it in his very aura, the sense of familiarity and comfort as he stroked the horse's flank and double-checked the fit of the saddle. His scent drifted to her nostrils. Clean and earthy. Like woods mixed with freshly cut grass. "Just us today?" he asked.

She almost gave another sniff before catching herself and stepping back. "No, we have another couple joining us."

"This fine one mine?"

She watched his hands rub the horse. They looked rough and hard, with a few lingering blisters. Working hands. This man didn't push paperwork around. "Yes, his name is Maximus. I'm assuming you're an expert rider?"

"Yes. Been around horses my whole life. They're family."

The simple words stirred her emotions. It was rare she heard men talk like that about animals.

He murmured something in the horse's ear, and Maximus gave a snort of pleasure.

A crazy flare of heat shot through her, and she deliberately turned her back on the lovefest to get the other horses ready.

She was losing her mind.

A few minutes later, Owen came into the barn, sniffling dramatically. "Harper, I think I am sick for real, and it has nothing to do with dollar shots tonight. I did one stall, but then Little Foot kept butting me, and when I didn't give her attention, she crapped all over and I almost threw up. Oh, someone also called and left a message about canceling a horse ride."

She clawed for patience. "The Graysons? For today?"

He snapped his fingers. Blond curls bounced around his face as he nodded. "Yeah! Those people. Can I go home?"

"Did you clean up the crap?"

His face fell. "Can't Ethan do it?"

"No, and we're short-staffed today. Just do that first, and then you can go."

"Deal." Owen skidded out.

"Please tell me that wasn't one of your top workers," Aidan said, staring after his retreating figure. "He seems to do a lot of *whingeing*."

She enjoyed the way the unusual word rolled over his tongue, and a laugh escaped her lips. "God, no. We take on volunteers and the occasional community-service project. This one's the latter. I promised his grandfather a favor, and I'm sorely regretting it."

"If some horse crap scares him, he's not likely to flourish here."

"I should've sent him to Ophelia. She would have gotten him in shape fast."

He cocked his head, studying her with those jeweled eyes. "Something tells me you're just as hard-assed. Bet it runs in the family."

She shot him a grin. "Maybe. Need any help?"

"No."

"Then let's go."

She saddled up smoothly, guiding Uncle Scar out toward the pasture. He was a spirited horse that liked to test limits, but she was in the mood for a bit of spunk today.

She checked quickly on Aidan, but he seemed comfortable and at ease. "Maximus is a bit dominant and likes to steal control. He tends to snack on the trail, and usually tries to open up when we get to the fields."

"Does he like long walks in the moonlight, too?" Aidan teased.

"Only with Flower. They're currently in a relationship. I can't take them out too much together because they get distracted making moony eyes at each other."

"It's a genuine Match.com here, huh? How many horses do you have?"

"About twenty," she said, leaning back as they climbed down a steep hill.

"Nice. Are all of them rescues?"

"Mostly, but we also board and offer lessons. I use the majority for trail rides, but I'm always looking to place them with permanent homes. The more I place, the more I can take in."

"How big is the farm?"

"Thirty acres of property and about a dozen working trails."

He whistled. "Big place. How long have you been doing the rescue portion?"

She glanced behind to check on him. Pride etched her voice when she spoke. "My mother taught me you can't ride until you can take care of your horse, so I was helping in the barns daily as a six-year-old. Took over the farm full time after my mom passed."

"Most don't have the stomach to do rescue work long term. No money. Lots of heartbreak. Little reward."

"Funny, I disagree. I'm pretty damn fulfilled. And if I save one, that's all the reward I need."

He was silent, but she got the sense he was examining her words. It had taken her a long time not to worry and analyze everything she said, which was another reason she'd gotten into a habit of speaking less. A shudder racked her body at the memories. In school, if she'd uttered the wrong thing, her peers had delighted in viciously teasing her until even answering a question from the teacher had made her nauseous, her head spinning with all the possibilities to keep herself under the radar. Returning home to her beloved horses was the only thing that had eased her. Animals needed only love, and there was never any judgment from them. Or cruelty.

The only sounds were the gentle creaking of leather and the wind in the trees. Her muscles adapted to the sway of the horse, legs tight, heels down, her body a natural extension of the saddle and the magnificent creature who allowed her to ride him. She soaked in the beauty of the mountains before her, then led them into the crooked paths deep into the woods. Inside, the tension dissipated, and her mind grew quiet again. The woods were her own personal church and heaven, reminding her there was something much bigger and more important working constantly; reminding her she didn't have the control she always furiously sought; reminding her it was okay to just be and accept what was.

"Ophelia said your mother came from Kildare." Aidan's voice broke into her thoughts.

"Yes, both our parents did. They settled here and built the inn first. The horse rescue came later. We lost our father early on, though. Heart attack. It was more of a working farm then, but our mother decided to concentrate mostly on the bed-and-breakfast portion for financial purposes. We lost her a few years ago."

"Ophelia mentioned that. I'm sorry."

"Thanks. I feel like she's here, though. Each time I watch a new horse blossom or see the guests happy at the inn, I know we made her happy."

He came up closer behind her. Twigs snapped. She felt his gaze burning into her back and shifted in her seat. She'd never felt as if a man was listening so intently to her when she couldn't even see his face.

She tried to redirect his attention. "What brought you to the States? Just a vacation?"

"Yes. I needed a change. I don't like to stay in one place for too long."

Was that a thread of tension in his voice or just her imagination? "A wanderer's soul, huh? My brother was like that for a long time. Traveled for years in the military. Now he's practically a homebody and happy."

"A woman, I'd guess?"

She turned and shot him a grin. "You guess right. He's getting married next year."

"What about you? Are you married?" he asked.

She shook her head. "Nope. You?"

"Nope. Too many places to see and horses to ride."

She rolled her eyes. "Spoken like a true man."

"No, I really meant horses. That wasn't some sexual innuendo."

That made her laugh. Who would've thought after her initial annoyance he could be fun to converse with? "Do you own your own horses back in Ireland?"

He didn't answer right away, and this time, she definitely sensed reluctance, as if he wasn't ready to let her know the full truth. He took his time, guiding Maximus to walk beside her. "No, I actually train horses. Work with them to coax out their full potential for racing."

Startled, she studied him, but his gaze was stuck on the path ahead. Maximus bent his head to snatch a treat, but without pause, Aidan firmly tugged the rein and the horse settled right back into his walk.

He was a real trainer? Holy crap, she might be able to grill him for information to help with Phoenix.

She opened her mouth to pepper him with questions, then shut it. No. He didn't seem to want to talk about that part of his life right now, and she respected a person's secrets. Being pushed by strangers to share personal things always pissed her off. "Sounds cool. Ready to gallop?"

He tossed her a wicked grin. "Thought you'd never ask."

"You signed the liability forms, right?"

His laugh was deep and rich, pumping the space with life. "If I fall, I won't sue."

"Good. Follow me, Irish." She kicked her heels and eased into a trot, then broke from the woods into a vibrant green pasture that spread out for miles. With a whistle, she let Scar break free and fell into a smooth, satisfying gallop.

He was right beside her, expert enough not to need to follow, and Maximus welcomed the challenge of the casual race. Clouds and sky merged and whizzed above, and she stood up in the stirrups, letting her body move with the horse beneath her. Maximus took the lead, and she caught Aidan's wink as he rushed by, but Harper loved a good competition, so she dug in and urged Scar for more speed. Hooves pounded the ground, kicking up dirt and grass, and she let herself soar.

The horses slowed together, both instinctively knowing when the race was over, and settled into a satisfying trot. Smiling, heart pounding, she glanced at Aidan to gauge his reaction.

A satisfied grin curved his lips. A few beads of sweat dotted his brow. Confident and tall in the saddle, his thighs pressed against the horse's flank, the sun turned his hair to spun gold, highlighting the toasty color of his skin. Amber eyes glinted with pleasure and something else, something a bit deeper that hadn't been there before. Caught off guard, she kept his stare, and her chest tightened in an odd ache.

"Harper?" The sound of her name lifted in the wind.

Blinking, she tried desperately to figure out what was going on. "Yeah?"

"Are you a wanderer or a homebody?"

In that moment, time stretched and pulsed with unspoken questions and a sizzling attraction she'd never experienced before. It had taken one solitary ride to figure out this man called to her—a man she barely knew, who was only here on holiday. He waited for her answer, but there was only one to give. "A homebody."

He nodded slowly. "I thought so."

The moment exploded with intensity, then faded away like fireworks turned into ash. She ripped her gaze away and turned Scar around. In a light tone, she joked, "Not bad . . . for a trainer."

His chuckle floated in the air. "Not bad for a girl."

She swiveled in the saddle. "Did you just—"

He flung his hands up in the air. "Just teasing you, love. It's obvious you were born to ride."

The quick surge of pleasure took her off guard, so she pretended it was nothing. "Ready to go back?"

"Yeah."

They walked the horses toward the woods. This time, there was only a thoughtful silence and the sense of something important drifting away, but it had been so quick, she didn't know how to grieve it.

Chapter Four

Aidan dismounted from Maximus and tried to wrap his head around the scene in the field.

Sure, Harper intrigued him, and he wanted to learn more about her. He figured she'd be a temporary distraction. She was fun to annoy and was different from any other woman he'd met. But that odd moment of connection between them? The way she looked at him and his chest got all tight and achy? That shit was stuff that happened in bad romantic movies, and he didn't believe in magic moments.

His question had been too personal and too intimate.

But it was her answer that haunted him. The raw pang of regret that hit him like a sucker punch was foreign. Almost like he'd lost something he hadn't even had in the first place.

Ridiculous.

He shoved the strange feeling aside and tugged off the horse's bridle.

"I can do that," she interrupted. "Guests just enjoy the ride."

"No, I like to follow through. He gave me a good ride, and he deserves my attention."

"Fine, but you better not tattle on me to Ophelia like you did the first time."

He arched his brow. "I'm not a tattler."

She snorted. "Yeah, right. You wanted to annoy me, so you told my sister I hurt your feelings. You knew I didn't want to see you again."

He gave a shrug. "I don't know what you're talking about. You were smitten the moment you met me."

Her laugh was genuine. "I thought you were an arrogant ass who knew nothing about horses but wanted to pretend he did."

"And you were wrong."

"I was wrong," she admitted. "About the second half. You do know about horses."

"And the first half?"

She tossed her head with a touch of playfulness. "Jury's still out."

He led Maximus over to the hitching pole and grabbed a brush from the rack, grinning. The easy banter between them was back, and any lingering tension had dissipated. Maybe it had just been a weird fluke. Maybe being back on a horse and riding for pleasure had affected him in a way he hadn't prepared for. She'd shared the special moment with him, so he'd transferred it to her. Made sense.

"I hope you don't mind me saying this, but you don't seem to have much help for a farm this size," he said, rubbing Max's rump.

"My full-time assistant is off the next couple of weeks with back strain, and my regular summer volunteers have all found real jobs. Ethan's schedule is a bit crammed with his fiancée's PR business, their upcoming wedding, and renovating a house, so we're just in survival mode right now."

The words popped out of his mouth. "I can help out."

She waved her hand in the air. "That's very nice of you, but we're fine. Can't have guests doing any work."

"No, I mean it." He shifted his weight and let out a restless sigh. "Listen, I'm bored out of my mind. I wanted some downtime but it backfired. I'm not talking nine to five here. Just a few hours. What do you think?"

"I think you're nuts. If someone gave me a vacation, I wouldn't offer to help anyone during it."

"I don't believe you. Has there ever been a time in your life you haven't worked?"

She leaned against her horse and shot him a look. "No, which is why I'd take the vacay. Besides, you're leaving soon. Why don't you explore the area? There're a million things to do around here. The strawberry festival is in Beacon this weekend. You'll have a blast."

He should drop it. Obviously, she didn't want his help, and what if that crazy energy field came back between them?

Strangely disappointed, Aidan finished up with Maximus and grabbed an apple from the bushel in front of the barn. "What do you do at a strawberry festival?" he asked.

The horse snatched the treat and chewed with enthusiasm, juice rolling out of his mouth, lips curled up in pleasure.

"Eat strawberries. They have great shortcake. And strawberry beer. Craft booths. Maybe they'll even give pony rides. Go enjoy yourself, Irish. You'll be back with your own horses in no time."

Her words flicked at him like tiny stings. It was ridiculous to feel dismissed. He had nothing to do with her life or her barn.

Already he could tell she was shifting her attention away, caught in the million tasks ahead. He knew the feeling well because that's how he'd lived his entire life: without apology or second thought.

He gave Maximus one last pat and stuck his hands in his pockets. "I'll let you get back to work, then. Thanks for the ride, Harper."

She barely glanced at him as she untacked Scar, fingers deftly removing the throatlatch. "No problem. If I don't see you, have a safe flight back."

Aidan walked back to the inn, realizing she hadn't addressed him by name. Not even once. He wondered why that bothered the shit out of him.

Maybe this vacation had been a mistake. The only thing downtime was giving him was a fucking breakdown. He should've realized work was bred into his genes, and trying to take a break did nothing but stress him out.

His mind sifted through his choices. For the past two months, he'd scoured the most popular racetracks east of the Mississippi and used up all his contacts to find a new horse to train. But there was nothing left for him here.

He couldn't return to Ireland with nothing to show for his time in the States. If he dug deep into his bank account and cut his stay short at the inn, he might be able to finance a trip to California and sniff out any possibilities. He might be able to work some odd jobs at Santa Anita. Hell, maybe he could be a consultant. Anything to keep money in his pocket and his feet by a barn. Best to leave New York behind and see if the West Coast offered a temporary solution.

Yes, that was the best decision.

He'd let Ophelia know he was leaving early and head out this weekend.

If only Harper weren't so stubborn about letting him help in the barns. It was easy to see she had too much to do and not enough people. Owen was useless, and with her brother distracted, there were too many horses who needed workouts, grooming, feeding, and—

The idea hit him.

Harper wasn't the type to ask for help, especially from a guest. Hell, he wouldn't, either. She was prideful, stubborn, and liked to do things her own way. Those traits were obvious at their first meeting. No, he'd made a mistake by giving her a choice.

He'd correct it immediately.

♥ ♥ ♥

The next day, Harper chugged down some Red Bull, donned work gloves, and began to attack her midmorning schedule. Already out at the stables by five thirty a.m., she knew it was a good time to tackle the workouts since the day's weather was a bit more seasonal and cooler for early June. She did her best to give every horse the attention and exercise they needed, but she always worried one would be neglected. Today she wanted to have some time with Phoenix and get a few workout sessions in so she could begin getting him ready to tackle the racing circuit.

She tacked up Flower, laughing as the sweet mare tried to nibble at her hair, and suddenly felt the air around her squeeze and charge. Harper looked up.

Aidan cocked his head and treated her to a slow, lazy smile. "You're such a pretty little lass," he said, his lilting, deep voice stroking her ears and other places. *Bad places.*

She ignored her body's horrifying reaction and concentrated on his words. "Are you kidding? Did you really call me that?"

Amusement glinted in his golden eyes. "No. I was addressing the horse."

She absolutely refused to blush.

Flower turned from her, stretching out to greet the newcomer who promised her sweet words. Aidan laughed and scratched behind her ears.

Harper shook her head, trying to regain her balance. "I'm sorry, there's no time today to schedule a ride. Ophelia never let me know."

"Not here to ride. Here to work. Are we doing workouts?"

She blinked. He was dressed in the same type of casual clothes he'd worn yesterday—jeans, a black T-shirt, and work boots. He was freshly shaved and incredibly virile, and she fought the sudden urge to move closer and get another whiff of his incredible smell. Damn it, he smelled better than Ophelia's freshly baked scones, and that was hard to do. And why was his height so sexy? She literally had to lift her chin a bit to look at him. "I told you yesterday guests don't work the property."

He gave a wink. "I'm not a guest. Just a volunteer looking to help out for a few hours. If you're uncomfortable with me riding, I'll muck the stalls. Or give baths." His gaze stabbed right through her. "Whatever you need, Harper."

A shiver raced down her spine. Oh no. She was not about to deal with this type of distraction today. The man had no right to invade her sacred space. "I appreciate it, but we're fine."

Flower butted her head against him in a demand for more stroking. "Aren't you a greedy little thing," he murmured. "'Course, I do love a female who asks for what she wants." He spoke the words to Flower but never broke his intense gaze with Harper.

Her mouth dried up, and she stared at him like an idiot. Finally, in an awkward move, she yanked Flower back from him and began prepping her to ride. "This may come as a shock to you, but I can take care of this farm by myself."

"Imagine how much better it will be with me here."

She shook her head, clamping down on the urge to laugh. There was something about his arrogance that came out charming—a rare feat for a male to accomplish, at least the ones she'd tried to date. "Thought you weren't a guest anymore. When are you leaving?"

"A few days. I'm here through Friday, and then I head to California. Gonna let your pride lose you two strong hands for the rest of the week and the opportunity to boss me around?"

She was saved from answering with the arrival of her rescue chicken, Hei Hei. Spotting the stranger in front of Harper, he stopped a few feet from Aidan, his beady eyes narrowing in on his prey.

Harper settled back to enjoy the scene. There wasn't a person alive who didn't freak out when they first met the Polish chicken. With his crazy white head feathers sticking up in the air, heavy red jowls, and gigantic mottled-black body, he looked like a monstrous mutated animal ready to attack.

Aidan stilled, his gaze swiveling to study the new visitor. "Harper?"

"Yeah?"

"What the hell is that?"

She smirked. "Meet Hei Hei. Hei Hei, this is Aidan. He wants to work on the farm with us. What do you think?"

The chicken cocked his head. Scratched his claws against the ground. And started to screech at the top of his lungs.

Was that a bead of sweat on Aidan's forehead or just her imagination? Harper knew the chicken was harmless, but she also knew Hei Hei had a hard time around men. He liked to intimidate and show them who was the real boss in town.

"What's he doing?" Aidan asked in a low voice.

"Probably getting ready to charge."

"Ah, shit."

With one last outraged shriek, the chicken took off toward Aidan in a mad fury. Even Harper recognized Hei Hei looked like one of those creatures from the *Goosebumps* movie. She watched to see if Aidan would run or try to fight.

With one smooth movement, Aidan knelt down to the ground, arms casually resting on his knees, and waited for the attack.

The chicken skidded the last few feet and bumped against his knees. Spinning around a few times as if confused, he began pecking at Aidan's feet, but when there was no fighting or loud voices, he began to settle. Lifting his huge head, the chicken studied the man before him, then slowly relaxed, brushing his feathers against Aidan's legs in a stroking motion.

Aidan's hands came down very slowly, and he began to gently stroke the chicken. "Good boy," he said in soothing tones. "What a massive, amazing creature you are."

Hei Hei clucked in delight.

WTF?

Harper stared in shock. The only male the chicken could stand was Ethan, and her brother had worked hard to gain Hei Hei's trust. Something inside her chest loosened, but she had no time to process it, because Mia and Ethan were walking up the path, hand in hand.

"Hei Hei, leave the poor man alone and stop—wait, what is going on? Is he being nice to you?" Mia asked, her eyes wide in shock.

Aidan grinned. "Guess so. What type of chicken is he? He's absolutely amazing."

"A Polish chicken. Another one of Harper's rescues, but he seems to dislike men. I've never seen him act like this before with a stranger."

"Except for Mia," Ethan noted. "Hei Hei fell in love with her the moment they met. It took him a while to gain her affection, but now I can't even try to come between them."

Mia laughed, gazing with adoration at Ethan. "What can I say? You both broke down my barriers with sheer grit, charm, and annoyance."

Harper's future sister-in-law was a city girl at heart who'd spent last summer at the farm on business and ended up falling in love with Ethan and the entire town. She now ran her PR firm from upstate and was a beloved fixture in their lives. With her stylish burgundy hair, sleek clothes, and designer shoes, she was not only gorgeous but also brilliant. Harper was lucky to claim her as family.

"I'm Ethan, and this is Mia. Are you a guest here?"

Aidan straightened up, giving the chicken one last pat. "Nice to meet you both. Aidan O'Connor, and yes, I'm a guest." He shook both of their hands. "I head out in a few days. I was just offering Harper my service on the farm. I'm a horse trainer from Ireland, so I'm familiar with the work, and honestly, I'm bored out of my mind on this vacation. I figured I could help out before I leave."

Mia smiled. "You sound like me. Vacations only stress me out."

Ethan's gaze sharpened with interest. "Horse training, huh? Did Harper tell you about Phoenix? Bet you'd have some good advice for us since—"

"I explained to Mr. O'Connor that we can't have guests working on the farm," Harper interrupted. She wasn't ready to share her plans for Phoenix yet. Aidan might have strong opinions or leap too fast to dismiss Phoenix's racing chances. This was a personal mission she believed in, and she wanted to be careful who she brought into her inner circle.

Unfortunately, Ethan didn't seem to notice her forceful change of subject. "Hmm. Usually, no. But with your experience and background, we could make an exception. We could use the help if you really don't mind. We've been a bit shorthanded."

"Ethan, I don't think—"

"Good, then I'll get to work," Aidan said. He shot her a look, his eyes squinting with mischief. "Any other animal surprises for me?"

On cue, Wheezy and Bolt appeared, running in circles around his legs and barking playfully at Hei Hei. The senior Lab and his best friend had lived at the farm for many years, and the horses enjoyed their company.

Mia laughed. "Just these goofballs. Harper doesn't usually bring her dogs here, but when she does, it's a free-for-all."

Aidan raised his brow. "More rescues at home, huh? How many?"

"Two dogs and a cat," she answered.

Ethan snorted. "This week. Her home is always open to anyone who needs it. She rescues helpless cases and rehabilitates them on sheer determination."

"Every soul—both human and animal—deserves a worthy life."

Everyone got quiet.

Harper shifted her weight, embarrassed at her sudden outburst.

Ethan's face softened. "Just like Mom used to say."

Trying not to squirm under Aidan's intense gaze, she reached under Flower and cinched up the saddle. "Well, if we're breaking the rules, we better start now. I need all the horses in the first barn prepped for workouts. Barn two needs to be cleaned. Ethan, the fence on the south side needs repair, and I told Allen to come cut the lawn and trim back some of the bushes on the trail. We need to be careful of bee nests, so let's schedule a sweep. Irish, if you can start with Flower, since she seems to have taken a shine to you, we can get this party started."

"Yes, ma'am," Aidan said.

Mia kissed Ethan. "See you later, baby. Come on, Hei Hei, let them get to work. We need to create some new marketing plans."

Hei Hei scurried over to Mia. With a quick rub of his feathers against her leg, he trotted after her in adoration while Wheezy and Bolt took off behind them.

Aidan scratched his head. "Mind telling me where these crazy names came from?"

Ethan snorted. "I'll let Harp answer that question. Thanks again, Aidan. I'm going to start on that gate." He tipped his head and walked off with a slight limp.

"My mother had an obsession with Disney movies," she said. Fondness threaded her voice. "When she began the horse-rescue farm, she got in the habit of naming all the animals after Disney characters. Ophelia and I stuck with the tradition. Ethan thinks it's ridiculous, but for us, it's a fun way to honor Mom."

"If it's something happy that unites you, it isn't ridiculous." She caught a flash of pain in his amber eyes before he turned from her. "Better get going. Don't want to get yelled at on my first day. Come on, *bláth*. Let's have some fun."

Flower pushed her nose into his hand, and he led her off to the fields.

Harper watched him, wondering what had caused his pain.

Wondering why seeing it had hurt her, too.

She buried the thought and turned away.

♥ ♥ ♥

A few hours later, Mia dropped by with sandwiches and called them to the picnic table.

Owen scurried over, looking warily around to make sure Hei Hei wasn't there, and peered at the pile of food. "Can I take a break, too?"

Harper lifted a brow. "You just got here an hour ago."

"But I'm so hungry."

Mia waved a hand, encouraging him to sit. "Of course, Owen, I got plenty."

"Thanks." The kid took a hairband from around his wrist and tied his hair back, then happily grabbed a hero and soda. "Man, I had no idea working with horses could be so stressful. Scar almost kicked me and gave me a concussion."

Harper's hand froze, sandwich halfway to her mouth. She tried not to bluster her words. "Wait—I told you several times not to walk on his right side. He gets spooked."

Owen frowned. "Thought that was Maximus. I get them all mixed up. There are too many. Can you make me a spreadsheet? That would be super-helpful."

Her fingers clenched. She was going to murder him. "Sure. I'll take a few hours and list every tic and hot spot for all of my horses in alphabetical order for your convenience. Anything else you'd like to request?"

"Maybe put each of their names on the stalls? I've seen stables on TV with these brass plaques. Could be a nice touch."

She ground her teeth together and prayed for patience.

Aidan shot her a look and seemed to catch her frustration. He jumped into the conversation. "Hey, Owen, what are you studying in school?"

The kid shrugged. "Communication. Figured I'd work in television or media. Me and my dudes started a YouTube channel, and we already have thirty subscribers. If we come up with the right stuff, maybe we'll go viral. That way, I can drop out of college and be a millionaire."

"What do you film?" Mia asked.

"Things that make people laugh. Once, we did this prank where we hooked up an invisible cable to a bike and put a sign on it that said

RIDE ME. When you tried to pedal away, you'd get yanked off the seat. It was pretty funny."

Aidan bit into his pastrami on rye in an obvious attempt to keep quiet.

"Chloe had a hard time her first year at SUNY New Paltz," Mia said. "She stayed at the farm last summer for her probation and ended up really loving it. Sometimes college takes a bit of adjustment. Finding the right friends and the subjects you're interested in. Do you like working at the farm?"

Owen munched on a potato chip. "Well, I kind of got assigned here after my screwup. I got drunk and, as a joke, tried to graffiti my friend's dorm, but it ended up being my own dorm, and it was either probation or community service. My grandpa was pissed and figured if I did some manual labor, I'd learn how to be a real man, as he put it. But I had this cool job set up at a vape shop that I missed out on, so that's kind of a bummer. I haven't met Chloe yet. Is she hot?"

Harper opened her mouth to tell him lunch was over, but Aidan interrupted. "Have you ever ridden a horse before?" he asked Owen.

The kid shook his head. "Nah, I'm scared of them. They're unpredictable."

Aidan nodded. "It's always good to be cautious when dealing with animals, but if you know and respect their triggers and fears, a real bond can form. I'm sure Harper knows which horses would be gentle. If you actually rode, you'd be more interested in what goes on at the farm."

Owen seemed to consider the offer. "Maybe. Not sure if Harper has time, though. She's got a lot to do, especially now with the spreadsheets."

Aidan pressed his lips together. "I can take you after your shift. If it's okay with Harper."

Three sets of eyes swiveled to look at her.

Ah, crap. She really didn't want to get further involved with a kid who didn't fit in here, or a man who pulled unexpected feelings from her. Then again, Aidan would be gone in a few days. Maybe riding a horse could give Owen a different perspective. "Sure," she finally said. "As long as it's in the pasture here, where we can all keep an eye on him. And I'd use Flower. She's pretty mellow and has a smooth gait."

"Sounds like a plan," Aidan said.

Mia got up with a sigh. "I'm going to take this to Ethan before he starves to death. See you guys later."

"Thanks for lunch," they all called out.

Owen stood and grabbed the trash. "Thanks for letting me eat, Harper. I'll refill all the water buckets." He trudged away, leaving them alone.

The silence seethed with an undercurrent of tension. What was this weird energy between them?

"You didn't have to offer him riding lessons," she said, desperate to break the strange mood. "He just wants to do his time here and move on with his life."

"Maybe. Maybe not. But I don't think you would've kept him on if you truly believed that." He wiped his mouth with a napkin and regarded her with interest. "You're a champion of lost causes. You just don't like to advertise it."

She snorted. "Trust me, I'm a realist. I don't believe in unicorns and rainbows."

"I think you know the odds are high, but you hope anyway. What I find fascinating is why you hate to admit it. Do you think it makes you soft? Or too vulnerable?"

Oh, hell no. He was not going to sit at her table and try to analyze her. She lifted her chin and glared. "You know what I find fascinating, Irish? The real reason you're taking this so-called vacation. Why are you desperate to work at an unknown horse farm to keep busy? Are you running away from something in Ireland?"

He jerked back. His face closed up, his gaze breaking from hers, and that's when Harper realized she'd hit buried treasure.

Her belly clenched. She wanted him to tell her the truth. But of course he wouldn't. They were strangers. There was nothing between them. They didn't owe each other anything.

It was exactly the way she liked it. Simple. Clean. The only way she knew how to lead her life.

She swallowed back the tinge of bitterness and watched while he stood up, poised to leave. Instead, he surprised her by swiveling his gaze back to meet hers head-on.

His jaw clenched. "You're right. Something did happen back home. I got my heart broken, so I came here to put myself back together again." A lopsided smile curved his beautifully defined lips. "Guess I was hoping to distract myself for the next couple of days. Horses are so much simpler than people. They don't know how to lie."

His words shattered in the air.

She tried to say something, but her throat choked up, so instead she watched him walk away, leaving her confused and longing for something she didn't know how to satisfy.

Chapter Five

It was better to avoid him.

After spending the morning introducing Aidan to all the horses in her charge, she'd kept her distance. The conversation at lunch had thrown her off. At this point, she figured she'd take the help he offered but not engage. Each time she did, the bond strengthened between them.

She sat in the small room that served as a makeshift office and groaned. God, she despised paperwork, and running this place was 50 percent administrative. The last three office assistants hadn't worked out, and she didn't have any more time or desire to train someone who inevitably left for college, found a better job, or just decided not to show up one day.

Excel sheets filled the computer, letters needed to be written and emailed, and the supply inventory was a tangled mess.

Pushing a hand through her hair, she tried to focus, but her attention kept wandering outside, where Aidan was instructing Owen on the basics of horse riding, walking Flower in circles, getting Owen used to the feel and gait of the horse. Their voices drifted in the breeze.

"Own your space," Aidan called out. "A horse is looking to be led. Heels tucked down, gaze focused ahead, fingers loose but firm around the reins."

"What if she gets pissed about something and throws me off?" Owen asked nervously.

"A horse can get spooked at any time, but if you're calm and aware, it's easy to regain control. I don't want you to worry about that now, though. Take a breath. Be aware of the both of you as one, moving together. That's the only place your attention should be along with your form."

"My ass hurts."

A chuckle. "Spine straight, tailbone tucked. Yeah, people who think horseback riding isn't exercise learn that's a myth. You work a lot of muscles."

Harper looked up again from her computer to watch. Lord, the man was hot. He moved like flowing water, smoothly blending one motion into another like a choreographed dance. Confidence oozed from his body, along with an intense energy, especially when his golden gaze lasered in. His biceps bulged and relaxed as he guided the horse, his hair reflecting in the dim shade like a halo.

She'd dated a cowboy once. He'd been on break from his horse ranch in Montana and stayed at the inn for a week. It hadn't taken them long to connect and fall into bed. They'd had only a few nights together, but Harper had liked the tough wildness of his body, the way he spoke about his home and his animals. It was a satisfying affair, with the end fully accepted by both of them. She thought of him sometimes but never to contact him. Harper understood they lived separate lives. She'd never leave Gardiner, and he'd never leave Montana. He'd been able to quench her loneliness for a bit, and for that she was grateful.

At first, she wondered if Aidan attracted her because of the memory of her own cowboy. But something was very different between them. The connection was beyond a physical attraction. He dug deeper, with his words and his intense gaze and his quiet power that captivated her. He was more dangerous than her ex-lover. Because with Aidan, she had a terrible feeling one tumble in bed with him would never be enough.

Who had broken his heart? A lover? Fiancée? She ached to know the truth beneath his quiet demeanor. But if he opened up, she worried she'd only fall deeper into the trap.

Better to avoid the whole mess. In three days, he'd be just another memory.

She refocused on her spreadsheets, and too soon he popped his head through the door. "Harper?"

She barely looked up. "Yes?"

"I'm finished with Owen. Is it okay if he knocks off for the day?"

"Absolutely. Thanks for taking him for his first ride and a good day's work. We appreciate it."

"Do you?"

The question forced her gaze to meet his. His sun-bleached brow quirked. "Of course. I told you that several times." Her voice came out a bit defensive, but she ignored it.

He leaned on the doorjamb, arms folded in front of his chest. "Your words don't match your actions. You seem to avoid me."

Her fists clenched in her lap as her heartbeat ramped up. "That's ridiculous. Listen, if you're not interested in coming back tomorrow, I completely understand. No hard feelings."

"Bet you'd like that," he murmured. "It'd be easier."

"You're talking in riddles," she said with annoyance. Usually, she was direct, having no time for false denials or game play. But he threw her off balance, and she didn't want to admit his presence affected her. She didn't want to admit he was right. "Would you like a handwritten Hallmark card to convey my real gratitude?"

"Maybe. Will you add those extra emoji hearts so I believe it?"

She couldn't help it. A smile tugged at her lips. She had a feeling it would be hard staying mad at him for long—his dry humor beckoned her to laugh with him. "I'm sorry. I just have tons of paperwork to get through, but I am thankful. And I hope you find what you're looking for in California. I'm assuming a horse to take on?"

"We'll see." His eyes became shadowed. "It may be time for a change. Finding a horse to train is difficult. There's a ton of factors to consider. Usually, the horse picks me, not the other way around."

She tilted her head with interest. "What do you mean?"

His shoulders lifted in a shrug. "Working intimately with a horse is like any relationship. There has to be a connection. I've learned forcing myself on a horse doesn't work. I'm usually guided to the next opportunity, and then I know it in my gut."

"What if the owner doesn't want to work with you?"

"Doesn't matter. Once the horse and I connect, all obstacles usually fall away, including a reluctant owner. I'm very good at getting what I want."

"Winning?"

His lips tightened into a firm line. "Sometimes winning is the only thing that matters."

She considered his words. She thought of Phoenix and how badly she wanted to see him run on the track, to watch him come into his true power and feel the glory of a win. The road was a long battle, and she was already drowning in work. Was it worth it? Could she really handle a professional racehorse and all it entailed? The finances alone could break her.

Aidan was right. Once she dipped a toe in that world, it was all about winning. What if she didn't have what it took to get Phoenix to the next level?

"I guess you're right."

He studied her, probing her expression. Slowly, the air began to crackle and hum, and that damn surge of heat threw her off guard. She sensed the focus had shifted away from horses. "I am, but I also never forget one important thing," he said.

"What's that?"

He gave her a sexy smile. "The first step to winning is getting yourself in the game."

She sucked in a breath. The challenge hung heavy in the air while tension whipped around them. Oh, it was a tempting game, but she refused to participate. Because he'd spoken the truth.

This game between them, she'd never win. She had a sense this man was out of her league—used to the art of flirtation, seduction, and walking away to the next challenge. Her? Not so much. She was too direct, and too focused on Phoenix to allow any distractions, as tempting as Aidan O'Connor might be, even for a night or two.

She turned away and refused to look at him again, choosing to ignore his last words. "Maybe I'll see you tomorrow." The dismissal was clear. She waited to see what he'd do with it.

The sounds of his footsteps retreating made her shoulders slump in relief.

♥ ♥ ♥

Aidan woke up the next morning and wondered if he should just stay in bed.

Two days left. He could go to Mohonk Mountain House for a challenging hike. Grab a few beers in town afterward and chat with the locals. Anything but show up at the barn to shovel shit and stare at Harper Bishop with moony eyes all day.

Humiliating.

He'd never been so sexually attracted to a woman who specifically did nothing to encourage male attention. Maybe that was it. She was so comfortable in her own skin, it was hard not to imagine what she'd be like in bed. With him. For one endless, perfect night.

She wasn't interested in a one- or two-night stand, though. Usually, he'd respect her decision and move on without another thought. But something about Harper intrigued him—gave him an itch he'd never experienced before. Spending more time with her was an opportunity he didn't want to pass up, even though she'd made her decision. His instinct told him he'd regret not using his last days here helping her on the farm, even if she did make him feel like a tangled-up schoolboy.

He glanced at the clock. Five thirty a.m. No one would be up now, and he craved a long, brisk walk and the reverent silence of a sunrise. He took a quick shower, pulled on jeans and a hoodie, and quietly made his way outside.

He walked the same path that had led him into the woods the other day. Shadows closed around him, and he used his phone's light to pick his way through until he reached the barns. Aidan caught his breath at the vision before him: the shapes of massive rock slowly being revealed by the crawl of the sun pushing itself above the horizon.

He settled himself on a large rock and let the natural beauty of earth soothe him. As much as he missed Ireland, he enjoyed the opportunity to carve out a new path on his terms. He'd been trapped in the same routine for too long, always balancing his goals with what his business partner wanted, what the owner demanded, and what the horse required to thrive. A delicate balancing act he'd juggled since he was fifteen. With his fortieth birthday approaching, maybe this was the right time to step away from horse training and find something else to fulfill him, not just temporarily but for good. God knew he couldn't take any more frustration and heartbreak in this field.

He was finally done.

His realization brought a touch of grief but also relief. He was so damn tired of chasing a horse, chasing a win, chasing a life. Maybe coming to the inn had been a good thing. Maybe he had finally achieved some clarity and could head to California and be open to different opportunities.

Sounds of activity rose from the barn. He wondered if Harper was up, starting her morning routine early to get ahead of the day. He wondered if she had trouble sleeping past 6:00 a.m. like he did, the call of a brand-new day too tempting to miss.

A flash caught his eye, and he turned his head toward the open pasture, where most of the workouts and training occurred.

Then caught his breath.

Horse and woman flew over the ground with such heart-stopping swiftness, he wondered if one of them had sprouted wings. Their silhouettes blended together as one, and the sound of hooves pounding rose in the air, along with a misty fog that made the entire scene feel like a dream.

Aidan stumbled to his feet. He squinted as more light funneled through and highlighted the rocketing forms. The horse took the turn with a combination of grace and strength, his legs stretching to cover more distance. The rider hung on, crouched in the saddle, leaning over the horse as if whispering encouragement in his ear. Unbelievably, the horse caught more speed, thundering forward. The horse's mane and the woman's hair flew behind them.

In that moment, everything inside him stilled.

Something is coming.

The echo of the mantra filled him with conviction. Quickly, he calculated the distance of the field and hit the stopwatch on his phone with a trembling finger. The horse reached the far post, and Aidan clicked the button, watching the seconds mount until the pair did the entire lap even faster than the first one.

Sweat dotted Aidan's forehead. He was on the verge of shredded nerves and an excitement he hadn't felt in five years, since that first time he'd laid eyes on Kincaid's Crown and sensed the horse was meant to win under his hand.

When he looked at the stopwatch and saw the evidence before him, Aidan shut his eyes.

Dear God, it was impossible.

But it wasn't.

This horse was going to be a champion.

This horse was going to change his life.

Harper eased back and began the cooldown lap. He imagined her throaty voice praising the horse on the run, practically felt her fingers stroking his neck in soothing approval.

The past and future melded together in an odd, fated melody. Minutes before, he'd been sure he was meant to move on and leave horse racing behind. He'd been making his peace with it. He'd been ready.

Now?

Everything had changed.

He fisted his hands and pressed them against his eyes. Did he really want to take on this horse right now? Was this a test and he was supposed to walk away? Or was this finally the opportunity and answer he'd been searching for?

Doubts and questions assaulted him. He faced the attack head-on, trying to find the quiet inside and connect with his intuition. He didn't know how much time had passed when he finally knew. Slowly, he dropped his hands and opened his eyes.

The road had led him right here, to this farm, to this horse. He was meant to be here and train him. He was meant to make Phoenix a champion.

Aidan dragged in a breath, knowing he had only one job to do.

Convince Harper to let him stay.

Chapter Six

Harper slid off Phoenix, breathing hard with excitement. His workouts were getting stronger, but it was time she got serious. It was time to get him to a racetrack and test him out.

He ran like a champion at the farm, but he had a boatload of issues to work on. He hated traveling and usually balked near the trailers, so it was almost impossible to load him in. He also disliked most other animals, preferring his own isolated company. The horse went full-on crazy when Hei Hei wandered into the barn, and had gotten into an old-fashioned alpha fight with Maximus when Harper had once tried to put them in the same barn together. Harper had read a companion animal helped calm many horses, especially with travel and strange racetracks, but so far, Phoenix wasn't having any of it.

She'd been studying horse training for weeks, trying to learn everything that could help. Yes, he did better with people now, but how would he react when he faced other horses on a track? Would he spook? Would all this work be for nothing?

Harper shook her head hard to dislodge the negative thoughts. No, Phoenix had the ability to run faster than any horse she'd ever seen and had the heart of a champion. She had to try. Not for herself.

For Phoenix.

Her gut whispered he was meant for this. Meant to run and be free. Meant for the glory of a win. Pure Thoroughbred fire ran through his veins, but it had been beaten out of him until he'd managed to either forget or repress his need to race. Her job was to get him there so he could make his own decision. Maybe his previous abuse had scarred him too deeply to race again, but she sensed he had survived for a reason. To thrive in the world he was meant for.

Time would tell.

If she could find enough of it.

She led Phoenix back to the barns while Baloo and Bagheera greeted her with barking enthusiasm. The dark-brown shepherd-hound mix and charcoal Standard Poodle had been with her for a few years, saved from a bad hoarding situation. They'd bonded and refused to leave each other, so Harper had ended up taking them both and never regretted it. Usually, she left them back at her place while she trained, but they'd seemed a bit anxious this morning watching her get ready to leave, so she'd brought them to the farm. They adored romping with Wheezy and Bolt but avoided Hei Hei, who scared them to death.

Phoenix gave the dogs a haughty glare, snorting with irritation as he stepped around them.

Baloo whined at the dismissal, shooting Harper a pathetic look. She laughed and patted his head, then got knocked over by Bagheera, who was jealous of the attention. In no time, she heard the echoes of more barks from Wheezy and Bolt, and then she was surrounded by four canines lashing her with tongues, completely thrilled by her very presence in the early morning solitude.

Phoenix pawed the ground and peeled back his lips with annoyance.

"Don't be so grouchy," she scolded him, trying to pet all four dogs at once. "They just want to be friends."

"He's a loner at heart."

Gasping, she spun around. The dogs caught sight of the new visitor and charged full speed.

Aidan welcomed them with a grin and open arms. She watched him with the dogs and tried to ignore the squeeze of her heart. She'd always been a sucker for a man who loved animals.

He gave each one his full attention, then straightened. The dogs immediately settled at his feet, recognizing an alpha and natural leader, panting happily as they stared up with adoration.

Damn, that was hot.

"You're up early," she said.

"Sleeping past six a.m. is a waste." He gestured to the dogs. "What are their names?"

She pointed them each out. "Wheezy, Bolt, Baloo, and Bagheera."

A frown creased his brow. "Disney again, right? I know *The Jungle Book*. Baloo is the funny panther."

"Bear. Baloo is the bear. Bagheera is the guardian panther."

"Aren't you going to run out of character names one day?" he asked curiously.

She grinned. "Doubt it."

"Isn't this the horse you wouldn't let me ride when I visited the stables?"

"Yes. And you didn't visit. You were sneaking around."

"Phoenix, right?" He said the name with a touch of reverence. Goose bumps broke out on her skin from the sheer intensity of his gaze. "Another Disney character?"

"No, not this one. Ethan named him. The phoenix rises from the ashes and—"

"Becomes whole. Yes, I know." A strange look flickered over his face. As if he knew something important she didn't. "How old?"

"Two and a half."

"He ever race before?"

She hesitated for a moment, then answered, "I think so. He'd been abused when I rescued him. My gut says they forced him too fast, probably hoping to get him trained early, and when he didn't perform, they beat him."

Aidan nodded, seeming to analyze her words. Why did he look like he wanted to pounce? His eyes glinted with a touch of greed as he flicked his glance back and forth between her and the horse. His hair was slightly damp from a shower, and he smelled like freshly laundered sheets. Soap. Spice. Mint.

Man.

He closed the distance between them, and her heart pounded in an uneven staccato. She tensed, gearing up for his nearness, but he moved past her and stood in front of Phoenix. Lifting his hands up, he let the horse catch his scent. Harper waited for Phoenix to rear back like he did with most strangers, but the horse stood oddly still, as if waiting to see what Aidan would do next.

"You're quite the beauty, *capalleen*," he said in his lilting voice. "They tried to break you, didn't they? Maybe with a whip. Maybe a hand. Maybe old-fashioned human cruelty. But you're too stubborn to let them win."

That magical voice gave her shivers. "What's that word mean?"

"*Horse*. Just sounds prettier in Irish." He kept his focus on Phoenix. "Does he have a sweet spot?" Aidan asked in the same tone.

She stared at him with surprise. "Yes, under the chin."

He curled his hand under and reached out.

Phoenix stepped back.

Aidan waited. His entire aura breathed calm and patience, as if he could stand there all day long until the horse was ready. Harper watched in fascination. Aidan tried to touch him two more times before the horse finally gave in and let him scratch under his chin.

Phoenix practically sighed in pleasure.

Keeping his gaze locked on Phoenix, Aidan spoke to him, telling him how strong and beautiful he was, and that he needed to be brave and keep pushing.

The sacredness of human and horse offering each other comfort and a level of trust broke through her, tearing down some of the carefully built walls she'd never even realized she'd erected. Emotion washed through her, tinged with pain, and she shook her head, trying desperately to process.

It took her a while to realize he was saying her name. "Yes?"

"What are your plans with Phoenix? Do you intend to race him?"

She shifted her weight, unsure of how much to tell him. She liked the way he spoke and handled her horse, though, and was beginning to wonder if she could use some of his advice as a trainer. "I want to. He loves to run like no horse I've ever seen, but he has issues to work through. I've been studying training methods. I'd have to enter him in regular races to see how he does and see if he can even qualify for the bigger stakes."

"With his speed, he'd qualify," Aidan murmured. "Does he spook easy? Have you tried breaking him from a gate? Has he raced on a dirt track or strictly turf? Have you run him alone or with a partner?"

The questions peppered her like a machine gun. Uneasiness gathered within. "No. It's still early, and I need to make sure he's comfortable before I push."

"Agreed. I think racing a horse too soon competitively isn't a good idea, but if you're shooting for the Breeders' Cup this fall, you need to push a bit. If you don't, he'll never be ready in time." The authority and knowledge in his voice made her pause. "He needs a strict regimen of training, from his behavior to everything he'll face on the course. He's green, and his past already has him at a disadvantage. He may not even be able to manage an official race."

She threw her head back and glared. "If he can't, I'll accept it. But we're going to try. Thanks for the pep talk—you should charge for them."

She went to yank the rein away, but he got in front of her, pushing his face close. A tiny muscle worked in his jaw. She spotted the creases bracketing his mouth and eyes, the sexy scruff hugging his mouth, the burning heat of his golden eyes as he stared at her, into her, holding her pinned. "I'm trying to get you to see you need a professional trainer for Phoenix. There's only so much you can learn and do in your spare time. Let me help you."

She blinked. "No offense, but I don't think two days of your training is going to make a big difference."

"You're right, it won't." He cocked his head. "So I'll stay. I'll train Phoenix. Get him ready for some stakes races and see if he gets enough points to qualify for the Derby next year."

His words hummed in her brain like an annoying pop song, repeating over and over. "You want to stay?" she repeated in disbelief.

"Yes. I've raced horses in the States, so I'm familiar with the rules. We'll need a jockey, but I know a guy who would be perfect. I'm not sure if you need to line up some investors at this point or if you have the money to cover salaries and the entry fees, but—"

"Wait a minute." She shook her head, trying to catch up. "This is ridiculous. I'm not going to allow you to take on my horse."

"Why not?"

His demand slammed through her. *Why not? Well, because. Because . . .* "Because I don't know you!"

He shrugged. "I can give you referrals. My contacts. You can search the web for proof I know what I'm doing. Harper, listen to me." He leaned in, and she was hypnotized by the sheer force of will practically seething from his figure. "This will sound crazy, but I get these gut instincts. These feelings that warn me of something big coming, and I've had this tickle nonstop since I got here. The moment I saw Phoenix run, I knew I was meant to train him. I'm asking for you to give me a try. Check out my references. Give me the next two days to get to know him. Talk to your brother and family. Because I can promise you one thing." His voice dropped to a sexy growl. "If that horse has half the heart I believe he has, he's going to win. And I can help you get him there."

Her breath stopped. She gazed at him and saw the sincerity and passion in every one of his gestures. She, too, believed in fate. Believed in the voices.

Something was coming.

The world tilted, and the roads diverged before her. Her first instinct was to reject his offer and go it alone. She was comfortable doing things herself. It was easier, allowing her to avoid trust issues, discomfort, and messy emotions. For years, she'd depended only on her family.

But this was bigger than all of them. Harper didn't know how to go about training a horse for the Triple Crown, especially one damaged by a past history of abuse. If Aidan was a professional, maybe this was an offer she needed to seriously consider.

The idea of spending nonstop hours together shook her core. He'd been at the inn only a week, and already her body peaked to attention in his presence. Could she handle a long-term working relationship without getting physically or emotionally involved? Could she trust him with Phoenix and her family? Could he really take Phoenix all the way? The questions whirled through her mind.

Slowly, she stepped back, needing the distance. "I don't know," she said honestly. "I need to think. Talk it over with Ethan. Look over your history."

He nodded. "Of course. Ophelia has all my personal information on file, but I'd be happy to sit and talk with everyone tonight. To go over things. Would that be acceptable?"

She nodded. "I'll let you know where and what time later."

"Good. I'll get started exercising some of the horses." He pivoted on his heel and walked away.

Harper looked at Phoenix. The horse was staring after Aidan's retreating figure with a touch of longing she'd never glimpsed before.

Or maybe it was her imagination wanting to see things that weren't there.

"Come on, sweets," she whispered. "I'll get you washed up and find some iced oatmeal cookies for both of us. I think we deserve them."

♥ ♥ ♥

She'd never find out.

Aidan refilled water buckets and feed trays while his mind combed over every detail of the incident with Kincaid's Crown. No one knew about it except his business partner and Rachael. Aidan had agreed to pretend to part amicably in order for it to be kept out of the news and off the internet. On paper, it looked as if he'd gotten his usual itchy feet and left to find a new opportunity. There should be no record of what'd happened after the Irish Derby to make Harper question his motives.

Unless he told her the truth.

Uneasiness clawed at his gut. The idea of beginning a working relationship with a lie bothered the hell out of him. Of course, it wasn't technically a lie—more like an omission.

But what if she heard him out and didn't believe him, deciding to reject his offer of training because she didn't trust him? Even worse, she could contact his ex-partner, Colin, for more information and rip open old wounds. Besides lying to Harper about what had really occurred with Kincaid's Crown, Aidan didn't want Colin to know about Phoenix. He didn't trust his ex-partner not to make trouble, especially if the man believed Aidan had sniffed out a potential champion.

Aidan had come to the States for a fresh slate. Telling Harper about his past wouldn't help anyone. He'd prove he was the best trainer for Phoenix. He respected Harper and her family. He'd work his hardest to give the horse the best chance possible to win.

Isn't that what truly mattered?

Now that he'd met Phoenix, he couldn't flee to California and look for a new career. He'd be forever haunted by the possibility of returning to Ireland as a king. As a winner. The opportunity of a lifetime had finally dropped in front of him like a damn Christmas present.

He couldn't screw this up.

A few hours later, Ethan came up behind him. "Harper told me about your offer."

Aidan regarded her brother. His previous military background was evident in the alertness that emanated from his figure. "What do you think?"

"I think it's worth discussing. Ophelia's making dinner for the family tonight at seven. Why don't you join us so we can all talk?"

"Appreciate it. I'll be there."

Ethan nodded and strode out of the barn. At least they were all willing to hear him out.

He worked most of the day with the horses, gave Owen another riding lesson, and went back to his room to freshen up before dinner. He was curious about the rest of the family and how they fit into Harper's plans to race Phoenix. Were they supportive? Would they be investing money with Harper? Or were they against trying to train a professional racehorse? Horse training was intense, and supportive family members made the process easier. It was important he figure out how each of them related to one another. He'd been known to turn down a job when the dynamics were too difficult to work with, especially if family members interfered regularly with his training process.

He showered and changed into khakis, a white button-down shirt with the cuffs rolled up, and leather boat shoes. Then headed down to the kitchen.

The scents of fresh meat and garlic hit his nostrils. He followed the smell down the hallway and to the back rooms, where guests weren't allowed. Peeking his head around the corner, he caught Ophelia and

Kyle laughing in the kitchen. The table was half-set with platters of an amazing array of food displayed.

Ophelia caught sight of him and waved him forward. "Hi, Aidan. I'm so glad you could join us for dinner. Do you like pot roast?"

He couldn't help the groan that escaped his lips. "It's my favorite thing in the world."

Kyle grinned. "Good, 'cause I made it. You'll love it."

Ethan walked in with Mia and rolled his eyes. "No one likes your meat, Kimpton. Stop bragging."

Kyle blew him an air kiss. "You know it's the best you ever had."

Mia shook her head and laughed. "Oh my God, guys, cut it out. You're scaring Aidan."

"It's okay. I grew up with three older brothers. There's nothing I haven't heard or seen," Aidan said. "Once, they told me stories about a crazed barn killer, then locked me up in the stable overnight. I slept with the horses, terrified I wouldn't survive."

"Dude, that's harsh," Kyle said, carrying out a platter filled with biscuits.

"But kinda funny," Ethan admitted. "Ever end up getting revenge?"

"Of course. When they were asleep, I snuck into each of their rooms and cut their hair. Let's just say the mohawk look wasn't flattering on any of them."

Kyle pointed at him. "I like you."

Ophelia placed a bowl of fresh peas on the table and sighed. "I will never understand boys. Now, let's sit down to eat. Where's Harper?"

"Right here."

Her voice squeezed him like a velvet vise, and a bunch of carnal images attacked his brain, throwing him off. What was it about her scent? She worked in a barn around horses all day long, yet when he got close, he smelled a spicy musk tinged with chocolate that turned his brain to mush. He narrowed his gaze and studied her, trying to figure out why this woman drove him a bit mad.

She'd changed, too, but still sported jeans, a T-shirt, and simple sneakers. Her hair was loose and fell around her face in a sexy disarray. No makeup. She seemed comfortable with simplicity. Refused to be pretentious about who she was. Was it the innate confidence that poured from her aura that attracted him so much? The sense of power of watching a woman who liked who she was and owned every bit? Her height would intimidate most people, but those Amazon legs and perky breasts were hypnotic.

Did she have a boyfriend? Girlfriend? A lover?

He immediately shut down those thoughts. He was looking to forge a business relationship with her. Any type of sexual attraction would need to be smothered so he could do the work needed.

Aidan wondered how many times he'd need to remind himself.

He took a seat, filled his plate, and listened to their easy chatter. The two couples were obviously close, with easy ribbing and genuine caring intertwined in their words. He learned Kyle, Ophelia, and Ethan had grown up together and been dubbed The Three Musketeers when they were young. He watched Harper under lidded eyes. She laughed and chatted with them, but there was a distance around her that told him that as much as she loved her family, she felt like the odd one out. Made sense. The couples were publicly affectionate, sharing kisses and intimate gestures that spoke of solid relationships. Being single in such an environment could sting a bit. Did she wish she had a companion to bring to the table? Someone who'd hold her hand, and kiss her fiercely when she needed comfort? Someone to laugh at her jokes and hold her when she cried?

"Aidan, why don't you tell us a bit about your proposal?" Ethan said, interrupting his thoughts. "Harper told us you'd like to stay on and train Phoenix for stakes races. What would that involve?"

He faced the curious gazes at the table. "I've trained horses in Ireland for the past decade and won many grade stakes, such as the Irish Derby. Some trainers like to get a horse ready to hit, then move to the next one. I tend to seek out a quality horse for a longer period of time. I think Phoenix is a winner. I'd like to stay on the property and train him for the next six months and see if we can win some races. The road to the Derby is competitive. I'm not sure if he'll be able to deal with the pressure, or even take to the horse-racing circuit, but I want to try. If that's what you want."

His gaze settled on Harper. She was listening intently, meeting his eyes with her own demands, as if trying to probe beneath his surface words for truth. "You really believe after seeing him run just once he'd be able to go to the Kentucky Derby? Isn't that a bit ambitious?"

"Yes." He couldn't help the confident smile that curved his lips. "With that type of speed and the right training, I think I could get him there. He's the right age. And I don't take on a horse I don't one hundred percent believe in. Do you?"

The challenge took her by surprise. She jerked back a little, wet her lips, and came back with her own challenge. "It's not all about belief. You should know that. I'm more interested in the long game here, and making sure my horse is comfortable and not pushed too hard. What if Phoenix doesn't take to the training?" she asked bluntly. "Are you going to drop him immediately? Will you make us pay whether or not he runs? How will your contract read?"

"We can negotiate, but if a horse isn't what I believed, I'm always prepared to walk and void the agreement. We can put in a clause about that. What I don't do is give up easily, though. Sometimes the best runners have difficult personalities, and they get stuck. They need time to get unstuck. That said, the horse's needs will always come first."

Harper lifted her chin and narrowed her gaze. "And if I tell you to do something you don't believe is good for the horse?"

His lips firmed. "I don't do it. The horse's welfare always comes first. No exceptions."

She nodded, her face softening. "Good."

"What would you need from us?" Ethan asked. "Money? Time? Marketing? We've never been in this position before. We've been strictly a rescue organization."

"I understand. In my eyes, that's a benefit, because you'll be open to my training and not question my every move."

Harper snorted. "Believe me, I'll be watching your every move, Irish."

He flashed a grin. "I'd be disappointed if you didn't. Gotta keep me honest."

"Are you?"

"Am I what?" he asked.

"Honest?"

A chill skated through him. He reached deep and told her the only truth he lived by. "'Truth speaks even though the tongue were dead.'"

Ophelia slowly nodded. "Yes, truth will always rise, even beyond the lies. I believe that, too."

His gut clenched, but he ignored the reaction and squared his shoulders. Best to return the conversation to racing and away from his past. "I'll map out the extensive schedule of training and races we want to enter him in. I'll work with him every day. I require room and board and a small daily living expense. The big money comes with a percentage on any wins Phoenix has."

Mia wrinkled her nose. "I'm really sorry, but would you be able to clarify the process for me? I'm good at betting on horses, but that's where my talent stops."

Aidan smiled. "Of course. I think it's important everyone here knows how this works. First off, in order to qualify for the Derby, a horse needs to accumulate points throughout the racing season. The season kicks off in May, but we'll begin racing Phoenix in August. Depending on the race and the stakes, first, second, and third place earn a certain number of points. They tally them up, and if Phoenix's total puts him at a high-enough ranking, we can enter him into the Derby."

Mia nodded. "Makes sense."

He held up his hand and began ticking off bullet points with his fingers. "Since Phoenix is young and has no real racing history, we'll begin by training him for a stakes race. There are grades one, two, and three races, with one earning the most recognition and money. I'd like to start Phoenix off with two lower-grade races at Saratoga. It's an important track and not too far from here. If he does well with those, it will allow us to enter him in higher-grade stakes and compete against a field we'll likely see for the Triple Crown."

"What are the bigger races?" Mia asked.

"There are a few. There's the Iroquois Stakes at Churchill Downs, the American Pharoah Stakes at Santa Anita Park, and the Champagne Stakes at Belmont Park. I'd plan to skip the first two and target the Champagne at Belmont, which takes place in October. Again, we'd avoid having to force Phoenix to travel far, which can be a bit stressful in the beginning of a racing career. After that, we'd shoot for the Breeders' Cup Juvenile at Churchill Downs. That goes off in November. It's a huge race and racks up a number of points for the Derby. It's quite difficult to get in to compete, though—a horse must win or place in a grade-two or -three stakes race."

"If he wins either the Champagne or the Breeders' Cup, will he qualify for the Derby?" Mia asked.

"We'd have a damn good chance," Aidan said with a smile. "If he happens to win the Champagne Stakes, we get a ticket straight to the Breeders' Cup, which is an amazing feat and would allow us to use the winter to rest him and continue light training until the spring. Then there're a few big races held right before the Derby. I'd focus on the Wood Memorial Stakes at Aqueduct Racetrack next April—again, it's local and a perfect time for him to compete. If he does well there, we'd get the opportunity to run in the Derby. Does that make better sense?"

"Yes. And let's say he wins the Derby. What happens next?"

"After the Derby, there are two more races to complete the Triple Crown. The Preakness, which is held at Pimlico in Maryland, and the Belmont, which is held in New York. If a horse wins all three, he's a Triple Crown Winner and goes down in history."

"A good goal to have," Mia said seriously. With that level of focus, it was easy to recognize that she was an ambitious, assertive business-woman who'd achieved success in a competitive industry.

"Playing devil's advocate, what if he struggles in some of these important fall races?" Kyle asked curiously.

"We can still have a shot in the spring if he wins some of the big stakes races, but if he's been doing poorly all fall and I've run out of options, I doubt we'd decide to continue. At that point, we can end the contract if both parties agree. Again, I'm negotiable on clauses and terms."

"How much will this cost?" Ophelia asked, sharing a glance with Kyle.

"Entry fees can get expensive. I'll also need to hire a jockey, so his salary and mine need to be covered. Vet expenses. And time for Harper."

She tilted her head. "What do you mean?"

He leaned back in his chair. "You're the heart and soul that drive this farm, but training a horse needs to be a joint effort, especially because Phoenix trusts you. I'd recommend you hire another full-timer or assistant so you're not overworked."

"I can step up," Ethan said.

Mia jumped in. "My PR business has been growing steadily, so I'm going to hire another employee. Ethan helped me out for a while, but he can return his attention to the farm."

"Plus, Chloe will be helping us out most days this summer on her break," Ethan added. "We should have enough hands for Harper to focus on what you need from her."

"How do you feel about that?" Aidan asked. He watched the bloom of pink heat her cheeks and wondered what she'd been thinking about. Was that a flash of guilt in her piercing sea-green eyes or his imagination?

"That's fine. Ophelia, would he be able to stay at the inn full time?"

Ophelia sighed. "I have weeks completely booked out, but I'm sure we can make it work if you're flexible, Aidan."

"I am. We'll need to put the jockey up, too, but we don't need much. I'm sure we can find a local hotel to use in a pinch." His muscles relaxed. The Bishops were on board and fully supportive in this journey, which made his job a hell of a lot easier. Satisfaction settled in.

Was taking a third biscuit too greedy? Definitely. Plus, it was the last one left. He really shouldn't. He'd already scraped his plate clean, eating every last shred of pot roast. He eyed the remaining biscuit with longing but decided he should be polite.

"Take it," Kyle urged with a laugh. "My wife makes the best biscuits, and she likes to see people enjoy her food."

"Aww, you like my biscuits, baby?" Ophelia teased.

"You can butter my biscuits anytime," Kyle responded with a growl, giving her a quick kiss.

Ethan groaned. "I just gagged. Seriously."

"You're just jealous you don't have the moves I do," Kyle retorted.

"I don't think I can do it, Mia. How can this joker be my best man with lines like that?"

"I taught you all the best lines, bro, and—what did you say?" Kyle broke off, staring at his friend with puzzlement. "Best man?"

Ethan gave a mock sigh, but his eyes twinkled. "Yeah, but now I'm starting to reconsider. You'd have important jobs to do. Plan the bachelor party. Get me to the church on time. Hold the ring. Escort Hei Hei down the aisle. You up to it?"

Aidan had never seen a man get choked up when asked to be a best man before. Hell, he'd never stayed put anyplace long enough to be a part of a wedding party. He had plenty of acquaintances. He'd won races with them, gotten fluthered with them, and bitched endlessly about the horse-racing industry with them. But when he moved on, he never kept in contact. Neither did they.

He wasn't close to his brothers, either. He loved them because they shared blood, but Aidan hadn't been home for years, and they rarely conversed. They all sent money to their mother to care for her, but no one visited for holidays. She was hard of heart, and the few times he called her, she was always brief and a tiny bit cold. He just didn't come from a warm, loving type of family.

But Kyle's reaction came from the heart, and damned if the moment didn't move him.

Kyle rubbed his forehead. Raw emotion leaked into his voice, which came out half-ragged. "Hell yeah, I'm up to it. I'd love to be your best man. I love you, bro."

Ophelia got teary eyed.

Mia put a hand over her mouth and sniffed.

Ethan muttered a curse, then got up from the table to give his brother-in-law one of those half hugs that men do to keep their masculinity in check. "You, too," he muttered, slapping him on the shoulder for good measure.

"While we're getting all weepy, I might as well finish us off," Mia said. She turned to Ophelia with a smile. "Would you be my maid of honor?"

Ophelia blinked, obviously stunned. "Are you kidding?"

"No. Do you not want to do it?" she asked worriedly.

Ophelia shrieked, jumping up and hugging Mia with mad glee. "Yes, I want to do it! Oh my God, I'm so excited! I'll make sure you have the best wedding cake in the entire world!"

Everyone laughed.

Aidan glanced over at Harper and froze.

Longing carved out the features of her face. A smile rested on her lips, and the light in her eyes was real and not fake. She was genuinely moved and happy for them. But he could also see she craved something that danced beneath the surface, trying to claw its way out.

She wanted.

And God knew he understood.

Staring at her from across the table made his insides shift, and he ached to cross the room, tip her chin up, and kiss her until all the empty longing disappeared and transcended into a different type.

A type that was satisfied in bed.

He coughed, trying to break up the moment before he did something he'd regret. "Congratulations," he said. "When's the wedding?"

"Next summer," Mia said, squeezing Ethan's hand. "You'll be invited, of course. If things end up the way we all hope, you may be joining this family table as one of us."

The words hit him full in the chest.

He didn't really know what the phrase meant. Had never felt he truly belonged anywhere other than a barn. He was closer to animals than people, and it'd never bothered him. God knew the only person he'd cared about like family had been his best friend, who'd ended up betraying him and destroying any type of softer emotion that had once lived inside of him.

He'd learned his lesson. No attachments but the open road ahead. If things didn't go the way he liked, he left, and no one got hurt. It was a good way to live. He'd always been satisfied and never sought more.

Still, he was touched by the genuine invitation in Mia's voice.

He forced a smile and stood from the table. "That's very kind of you," he said politely. "I'm sorry, but I have to go. Have an important call coming in from Ireland I have to take. Thank you so much for dinner. I can have some contracts initially drawn up, along with an estimate of costs to help you make a decision."

With a nod, he turned and left.

He didn't look at Harper.

It was better that way.

Chapter Seven

Harper gave a low whistle and approached Phoenix's stall. Her usual greeting was rewarded by the horse's perked ears and immediate attention.

When she'd first rescued Phoenix, he'd been like a hellion, ready to take on anyone who came near. She and Ethan had spent months slowly gaining his trust. Now that the foundation was built, she had a choice to make on the next step.

Should she hire Aidan O'Connor?

Reaching into her pocket, she removed an iced oatmeal cookie, smiling at the horse's low grunts of excitement and the curl of his lips that revealed his teeth in a goofy grin. He munched as she thought in the still silence of the barn, late at night.

Ethan had spent most of the day trying to convince her to accept Aidan's offer. Seems he and Kyle agreed after their dinner last night he was a man worth trusting. The contract he'd put together was fair. After researching the trainer's reputation and statistics, it seemed she was looking a gift horse in the mouth.

Pretty damn clever.

But she knew her decision to retain him for training Phoenix was more complicated than Ethan believed. A connection simmered between her and Aidan—full of danger and temptation. They would both need a sharp focus for the upcoming months, and being distracted by physical chemistry was a liability. Also, the expense would be a strain. The fees were large, but Mia was quick to remind them her PR business was thriving and amassed a large profit, so they'd have a decent cushion if things went to shit. Kyle's book was being turned into a movie, and he quickly offered up the advance. The inn was booked solid for the summer season, and no large repairs were needed anywhere on the property. It was doable.

It was possible.

But she didn't want to completely rely on her family's money. This was her dream and her responsibility to finance. She'd contacted the local bank to inquire about a loan on her house to help offset the fees.

There was one other loose string that bothered her. She'd dug deep to examine Aidan's career, searching for signs he was a man worth entrusting Phoenix with, and one question kept popping up over and over.

Why, exactly, had he left a successful business in Ireland behind to start over?

His background check simply said he'd parted ways with his partner after winning the Irish Derby with Kincaid's Crown. No details could be found. In their past dialogue, Aidan had hinted at a betrayal. Was it strictly personal? Or was his need to be free ingrained so deep, he couldn't physically stay in one location for too long? What would happen if he decided to cut them loose without warning—his wanderlust spirit calling him to a better opportunity?

Harper unlatched the gate and stepped into the stall. She slowly reached out and scratched under Phoenix's chin, studying those dark, expressive eyes that had seen way too much in his short two years.

He snorted, pressed against her, and achieved almost full-body contact. It was amazing how affectionate the horse could be once his barriers were removed.

She leaned her head close and muttered the words aloud. "Is this what you want, baby? Because if it is, you're going to have to be brave. We both will."

"I think you were both born for this."

Phoenix startled, rearing back at the sudden entry, but Aidan began murmuring nonsense in a soothing voice, and the horse quickly settled.

Harper's arms dropped to her side. "This is the second time you've snuck up on me. What are you doing up? It's late."

His brow lifted, but he didn't seem bothered by her prickly tone. "Couldn't sleep. I saw the lights during my walk. Why are you still up?"

He stepped inside the stall, and suddenly the space shrank between them. Harper tried to breathe steadily and act nonchalant, even though the energy in the barn pulsed with awareness. Her skin pulled tight and her tummy clenched into a silken knot. His straw-colored hair was mussed, and a crease line pressed into his cheek, confirming he had at least tried to get some rest. She wanted to reach out and touch his cheek, run a finger down his chiseled jawline to see if his stubble felt scratchy on her skin.

She cleared her throat. "I'm a night owl. I checked on the dogs and came back to clear my head."

Cognac eyes narrowed with interest. "Did you clear your head?"

"Not yet."

He nodded. "Why don't you tell me about the issues that are blocking you from agreeing?"

She blew out a hard breath. "Everyone else is on board," she admitted. "But some things don't add up for me. You owned an extremely successful training business in Ireland. Why did you leave after winning the Irish Derby with Kincaid's Crown? Are you really here on a vacation, or is there something more going on? Wouldn't you rather go back than take a chance on a green horse in a different country?"

Shadows flickered over his face. "Does it matter why I'm here?"

She waited a few moments, recognizing the sudden distance that abruptly surrounded him. Normally, she respected privacy and secrets. God knew she was an expert at hiding if she became uncomfortable. But there needed to be an openness between them if they were to go forward. "Yeah, it does. Because if we do this, I need to know my family will be safe. That Phoenix will be safe. I need to be able to trust you."

"You need me to do my job. Won't that be enough?"

She held her position with a stubbornness that was part of her genes. "No."

He let out a litany of Irish, and she bet most were swear words. He looked at the horse in front of him as if Phoenix held all the answers. "My business partner and I had a difference in opinion regarding a personal matter and decided it was best to part ways. We made an agreement he'd keep the business, and I'd be free to make a name for myself on my own."

She pondered his answer. A prickle of suspicion flared. "Did you *want* to walk?" she asked bluntly. "Or did you get pushed out?"

Demons danced in his eyes. Still, he answered. "A mixture of both. I didn't want to stay after some shit went down. I decided it was time to try American racing for a change of scenery. Spent a few months traveling, but no horses called to my gut. Not until Phoenix."

She refused to back down, knowing every one of his answers was critical to her decision. "And the money? I'm assuming there was a lot of money on the line after the Derby win. Did you prefer to just take your cut and hit the road? Is money the most important goal for all of this?"

"I earned a decent cut but not as big as you think. There was a lot of people to pay. Not gonna lie and say money isn't nice. So is winning. But is money the ultimate goal?" His gaze seized hers. "No. What mattered to me the most was Kincaid's Crown. I found him the same way I found Phoenix. It was simply meant to be."

A man who believed in gut instinct and fate was a man she could respect. Still, questions burned. "You've termed yourself a wanderer, so how do I know you won't drop us if a bigger and better opportunity comes along?"

His jaw clenched, but he answered the question. "The contract clearly states I can't just walk away for greener pastures. Besides, I won't want to if I'm training Phoenix. Because he's going to win."

Again, that touch of arrogance in his voice caused a shiver to race down her spine. Her last inquiry was the most important. "But will you put him first? Or is this an attempt for revenge on your partner, using my family to make your mark?"

His golden eyes burned. She caught a flicker of regret, but it was gone so fast she wondered if it was a trick of the light. "I swear to you, I'll make sure Phoenix comes first."

The vow was spoken with a naked truth that seared her soul. He couldn't fake that type of passion for the well-being of an animal he hadn't become involved with yet. Could he?

She had to believe Aidan would do the right thing if forced, and that was her priority. She couldn't hire a trainer obsessed with only money and glory, or everything later would become tainted.

She needed to take this leap, or she'd never know the true talent of her horse, and Phoenix deserved the best opportunity to race again.

"Good," she said. "Then there's one last thing to discuss."

"What?"

Sweat broke out on her body, but this was too critical to squirm from. It was best to face the problem head-on. "Us."

The air grew heavy with sexual tension. His bottom lip quirked, and his lazy gaze raked over her figure. He never moved, but he didn't have to. That gaze caressed every inch of her, over and under her clothes. She could only imagine the things he could do with no barriers between them. "What about us, love?" he drawled, his voice dropping to a sexy growl. "Am I part of the contract?"

She ignored his teasing and tried to attack the issue with bluntness and logic. "I want to be clear that we won't be sleeping together. We both need to be focused on Phoenix's training. Having an affair has the potential to explode into chaos and ruin everything we're working toward. Do you agree?"

He moved, shifting his body a few inches closer. Her back pressed against the roughness of the gate. His scent teased her nostrils, a combination of musk and spice and pure aroused male. Something about his quiet strength and confidence hit her straight in the gut.

And between her thighs.

Shit.

"You been thinking about us together, Harper?"

She licked her lips, then cursed herself when his gaze dropped to her mouth. Temper frayed at her nerves, reminding her the only way to face him was no-holds-barred boldness. "Yes. Have you?"

"Yes." The word struck like a bullet. "In fact, since we're putting all our truth out there, I should let you know I've been fantasizing about kissing you. And not just on your mouth."

Shivers crawled down her spine. Her nipples turned to hard, aching knots beneath her shirt, imagining that sexy mouth kissing and licking her breasts. Searing heat exploded between them. It took her a moment, but she gritted her teeth and rallied. "Again, not a good idea."

Another inch closer. His body heat practically glowed bright in the dim barn. Phoenix caught the swirling tension and snorted, shaking his head and taking a few steps back in the stall. "So no sex. No kissing. I'm going to assume that includes touching, right?"

Her body wept. Her temper ignited. "You like playing games, Irish? You want to get into my pants more than you want to race my horse?"

He braced one hand against the wall by her head, leaning in. She didn't flinch and tried to ignore the soaring freedom he made her feel by the confrontation. "A crude way to put it, don't you think? I'm just trying to make sure we don't cut off all options before we even try."

"There won't be any test experiment. We both need to commit to the only thing that matters between us." She lifted her chin. "Phoenix."

A muscle worked in his jaw. His breath came out jagged. "Is that what you want?" he demanded.

Her heart skidded and tripped over itself to keep beating. *No. But it's safer this way.* "Yes."

The word took all possibilities away, yet his lips were poised inches from hers. If he ignored her declaration, she'd send him away. If he pushed his advantage, she'd be unable to work with him as a full partner. He needed to respect her claim for distance.

Her mind urged him away.

Her body urged him closer.

"I'll give you what you say you want in exchange for one thing."

Disappointment crashed through her. It was over. There might be a kiss, but there'd be nothing further. "What?"

"Say my name."

She blinked, confused. "I don't understand."

The blistering heat of his gaze almost burned her alive. He overwhelmed her with his strong body, his breath mixing with hers, his hand just brushing her hair, his chest an inch from her straining nipples. "I want to hear my name on your lips one time before I walk away. Before we close this door between us." His voice dropped. "Just once."

Shock barreled through her. The demand was more intimate than a kiss. It was the acceptance that he already meant something to her, but she was voluntarily rejecting him. Speaking his birth name was the beginning of a relationship that would never happen.

A strange grief and pain tore at her insides, but she had no choice. She gave him what they both wanted in that moment. "Aidan," she whispered against his mouth. Her voice trembled over his name. Her tongue tingled with pleasure, and she wished she could moan the beautiful melody when he was deep inside her, when his mouth swallowed hers whole, when she screamed it as she shattered to orgasm.

He sucked in his breath, as if the pictures in her mind had seeped into his, and he closed his eyes halfway, his shaking body fighting both of their needs to surrender to the wicked temptation and leave the rest to hell.

Instead, he stumbled back, fisting his hands, and turned. "It's a deal. We begin tomorrow. Good night, Harper." He patted Phoenix and left the barn.

She wrapped her arms around her middle and fought the overwhelming urge to go after him.

Eventually, she was able to straighten, lock up Phoenix for the night, and return home.

His words replayed in her mind like a mantra, and the sweetness of his name on her lips lingered for a long time.

♥ ♥ ♥

Aidan surveyed the sprawling property before him. It'd be a decent workout track for now. He'd have a starting gate by the end of the week to begin practicing breaking out clean, but for now, he was about to make things a bit uncomfortable for the fiery horse.

Owen came up beside him. Peering over his aviator sunglasses, he stared at the empty field, where a worn dirt track wrapped around in an almost perfect mile. "What'cha looking at?" Owen asked in puzzlement.

"The training track," he responded a bit gruffly. Deep down, he thought Owen was a good kid. Unfortunately, his lame-ass work ethic and phone addiction were getting in the way of figuring out if he could actually help on the farm. "You finish rounds?"

He wrinkled his nose and looked glum. "Yeah. Little Foot wouldn't let me lead her in. Kept running away from me, so I ended up chasing her around, and then when I got mad, she blew a bunch of spit in my face. Disgusting."

"Harper told you not to yell at her, remember? She's young and a bit spirited, but if you'd stood your ground, she would've listened."

"Yeah, I forgot." He checked his phone and groaned. "I missed out on another outing at Splash Down Waterpark. My friend's been posting pics all day. They don't understand I'm stuck here."

Aidan shook his head. "Your friends convince you to vandalize your dorm?"

Owen shrugged. "We were all drunk. Didn't know what we were doing."

"Did they get community service, too?"

Owen shifted his feet. "Nah, their parents got them out of it. Paid the college off."

"But your parents didn't?"

"My grandfather is a retired judge and wouldn't let me walk away clean. He doesn't believe in payoffs."

Aidan nodded. "Sounds like a smart man. Trying to teach you that life doesn't give free rides."

Owen rolled his eyes. "Grandpa is still living in the past. Does he honestly believe shoveling horse manure this summer is going to give me character? This isn't some two-hour movie where I suddenly change my perspective and fall in love with the farm. I kind of hate it here."

Aidan tried not to chuckle. The kid looked miserable. Hell, Aidan remembered being his age, but in his world, if he didn't work, he didn't survive. Choices were limited, and he'd gotten used to doing what needed to be done. The result gave him the confidence and freedom to live life on his own terms. In his mind, it was a fair deal and nothing he bitched about. "Sorry to break it to you, but most people don't have money or indulgent parents to fall back on. I think your *granda* is trying to show you how to take care of yourself by taking responsibility as a man. I also think if he heard you whingeing all the time, he'd be disappointed. But that's your business."

Wild curls flopped into Owen's eyes as his head shot up in surprise. "Didn't mean to piss you off," he mumbled.

"You didn't. But I will say this. Harper and I are going to be busting our asses to try and make Phoenix a successful racehorse. Ever hear of the Triple Crown?"

"You shitting me?"

"Nope. That's our goal. If you start taking this job more seriously, we could use some help. But I got no time for bitching, slacking, or complaining. No one expects you to love the job, Owen. We just want you to have some respect for all of us, because we're doing something important here and it's a lot more complicated than shoveling shit. I better get back to work. If you want, you can take your break and call your friends."

He turned his back on the kid and kept his gaze on the track. After a few seconds, he heard Owen shuffle off.

Maybe he'd think about what he said. Maybe he wouldn't. Aidan was still glad he'd tried, though, for Harper's sake.

He got his stopwatch out, calculating the distance and the training schedule for the next few weeks. In the past few days, they'd signed the contract, he'd settled permanently into his room, and he'd spent every hour possible studying Phoenix. Slowly, he began to learn the horse's habits, tics, and vulnerabilities. He'd learned early on that training was mostly a mix of psychology, patience, and perseverance.

Harper appeared at the top of the hill, leading Phoenix by the bridle. Aidan studied the horse, his mind automatically filing away various facts that would help him train. The horse had a bit of a strange gait when walking, almost as if it wasn't as natural to him as running. Interesting. He'd also seen him favoring his left side. Harper mentioned it might have been where they'd whipped and beaten him. Aidan had always preferred his jockeys avoid the whip, unless it was a tap to let the Thoroughbred kick it to the final notch. He'd need to see how skittish Phoenix got. They might need to focus on the jockey's hands and feet movements, which he'd add to the training.

Harper stopped in front of him. The horse tossed his head, as if not wanting to be the first to ask for affection. It was a stubborn game he played, and usually Aidan acquiesced and approached Phoenix. But this time, Aidan wanted to wait him out to see if he'd make the first move.

"How do you like your new digs?" he asked.

Phoenix shot him a halfhearted glare, as if he understood the question.

Harper gave a long sigh. "We've had a few rough nights, but I think he's getting more comfortable. I never met a horse who didn't like so many other animals. Usually, they find comfort in companionship."

Aidan gave a half grin, still waiting to see if the horse would make the first move. "He'll be in a stall with noise, chaos, and numerous other animals on the road. If we don't get him more comfortable now, we'll lose before we even begin."

"Cryptic. You writing a book on philosophy or horse training?"

"You should know better. They're one and the same." He ignored her charming snort and tried to keep his attention on Phoenix. Unfortunately, every muscle in his body tensed the moment her scent hit him. If only she preferred expensive, musky perfume. Instead, her natural smell of soap and skin mixed with the morning breeze made him feel halfway drunk.

But the agreement had been struck. He'd die before he broke her trust or his word, and it was just too damn bad his dick strangled against the ridge of his jeans. He'd live with it. He had no choice.

"What's the plan for today?" she asked.

Phoenix finally broke, pushing his head against him so Aidan could rub under his chin.

"Mo chára," he crooned, reaching out to give him the affection most horses thrived on. "I knew you couldn't be pissed at me for long. But for now, you need to be limited on those oatmeal cookies. We're changing your diet to a healthier version to get you in shape."

Phoenix snorted.

He laughed and pulled back to grab his small spiral notebook. "I want you to take him around the course a few times. Get him warmed up, then when I give you the signal, open him up. We've kept his early morning workouts light, but we'll interchange them now with a few bullets. The seven-week mark isn't for several days before his official first race at Saratoga. You okay with that?"

She tilted her chin. "Of course. Did you contact your jockey?"

"Yeah, Elmo will be here tomorrow."

She blinked. "Elmo?"

Aidan rubbed his head. "Yes, Elmo. Before that red monster came onto the scene, it was a popular and respectable name. He agreed to meet Phoenix, check out the farm, and make his decision. He already has another offer in Saratoga."

She frowned and tapped a finger against her unpainted, plump lips, and he tried not to salivate. "He needs to be the right fit. I won't be so desperate for a jockey I'll compromise."

He couldn't help the laugh that escaped him and enjoyed her obvious surprise at his reaction. "Harper, I doubt you compromise on anything. Now get your ass in the saddle and go ride. I need to make sure I've got most of his quirks down before we introduce the gate or riding with a competitor."

She shot him a warning glare but donned her helmet and swung herself over the horse's back. Aidan watched carefully, looking for any signs of stress from being ridden, but Ethan and Harper had done their job right. Phoenix took the bit and didn't try to spit it out. Good. The horse was comfortable with getting tacked up. He was picky about who did it, but the biggest challenge for a green horse was getting them actually ready to ride.

Score one.

Harper took off, her gait graceful and comfortable. She was a true pleasure to watch in action, as if born to ride. Didn't hurt that her staggering height and perfect ass in those tight jeans made her a stunner.

Focus.

You're supposed to be watching Phoenix. Not the woman on his back.

Aidan took a breath, cleared his mind, and let his senses settle. He scribbled notes during the warm-up, then gave Harper the signal to begin stretching Phoenix out, pushing for speed. He hit the stopwatch. Then waited.

The horse took off and blazed a bullet path, his long black legs eating up the turf in front of him with blistering speed. Aidan clocked him at the far turn, saw him straighten out, then double up his efforts, as if imagining his own individual race where he always won, was always adored, was always accepted.

He looked at the time as he hit the final mark and snapped the button down.

Extraordinary.

Shivers broke through his body. His stomach clenched with excitement. The raw talent was all there. Phoenix was made for speed. He was made for the track.

Harper came riding up over the hill and stopped in front of him. "How'd he do?"

Aidan walked close and grabbed the bridle, looking into the horse's eyes. Right there. The lust and need to run. To win. It was something he couldn't teach, which made the indescribable element the living, breathing unicorn of the horse-racing world. With barely a sweat, he'd clocked in a staggering speed number and craved more.

Aidan locked down on the wild rush and focused on the issues. "He's sloppy with turns, which means he may struggle if he's boxed in with other horses or too far off the pace. This one's definitely no closer. He'll need to be up front, but our challenge will be keeping him fresh and on pace. I have no clue if he'll want to compete to beat the others or if his brain will fry out there and he decides to tell us all to fuck off. He's got a temper and he's emotional, so we need to work on him accepting shit without fighting us at every turn."

"That's his background. I thought you understood."

He raised his brow at her defensive tone. "Oh, I understand, but I don't have time to get him into therapy for a year to discuss his issues. We need to fix them. Fast."

She gave him a sneer. Yeah, she was like a fierce mama bear, protecting her own. Normally, it would be sexy as hell and he'd dream about securing her loyalty, but not in this time crunch. "We just started. He's sleeping in the main stable now."

"Who'd you put as his stablemate?"

"Flower. She's quiet and gentle."

He directed his next words at Phoenix. "That type of roommate is not going to help your cause, buddy. Let's go meet your new friend, Maximus."

Her eyes widened. "No way. He's way too alpha! They tried to tear each other apart the last time I put them together. I thought this was about easing Phoenix into the world, not ripping off the Band-Aid. He was abused."

"Yes, he was." Aidan stroked the horse's chin, saw the gleam in his dark, velvet eyes, and made his decision. "But he's a survivor. He needs to know that, and it's time we proved to him he can take anything we throw at him. We're done treating him with kid gloves."

Her gaze narrowed dangerously. "I disagree. We could break his spirit too early, and then this will all be for nothing."

Aidan realized this was the turning point. It came with all owners and trainers who had a vision but went about the goal with different tactics. Usually it came halfway through the process, but he shouldn't be surprised Harper would push him hard the very first week. Like this magnificent horse, she needed to know who was boss when it came to training her horse.

Aidan knew it'd be a brutal lesson for her to learn.

He gave her a cold glare and deepened his voice to get his point across. "Your disagreement is duly noted. And overruled. We move

Maximus in, and I want you to allow every single one of your farm animals to roam free in the barn. Especially Hei Hei—no more banning him from the stables. The more distractions and noise, the better. He can take it."

"He despises Hei Hei! He had a holy temper fit until we got the chicken out of there."

Aidan shrugged. "Let him have his tantrum. He'll be okay."

"No."

Aidan stilled. Cranking his head up, he stared at her long and hard. She looked like a disheveled queen in the saddle, green fire in her eyes, her body tight with tension. "Are you saying no because you really think I'm going to harm Phoenix by my decision? Or are you saying no because you don't like following anyone's orders but your own?"

She kept her gaze trained on his, refusing to look away or apologize. "Both."

He relaxed. She was truthful to a fault. He could work with that. "Understood. Now let me tell you where I'm coming from, otherwise we're going to have a lot of battles and disagreements over the next six months. Better to figure things out now, right? But first, climb on down."

Her mouth firmed, but she obeyed, standing in front of him with her shoulders thrown back, as if he were the Big Bad Wolf knocking at her damn door. He tamped down on the grin that threatened. He had a feeling if she thought he was amused, she'd coldcock him now and explain later.

Nothing like a hot Irish woman.

"Let me explain," he said in a gentler tone. "I promised in the beginning I won't make decisions that will harm or hurt Phoenix. But I said nothing about pushing boundaries or causing him some discomfort. We won't win by taking the easy road. Every single thing I do is deliberate and planned. I won't throw shit out there on impulse, but some of my decisions will be based on his behavior or what I see that day. This is a learning curve."

For a second, a flash of vulnerability ignited those jeweled eyes before her chin tilted up in pure stubbornness. "And you need to understand if he gets pushed too fast, he may think we're betraying his trust. That we don't care about his needs or wants. If that happens, we could lose him."

Aidan jerked back, surprised by her passionate explanation. But it was the wobble in her voice that hit him in his gut. He was missing something—something big. Trust was a huge issue with Harper, and her words hinted at a deeper meaning than Phoenix getting pissed off that Maximus was in his stall. Aidan was used to pushing hard when he believed he was right, but for the first time, he backed off and tried to explain. "Love, I'd never do that to Phoenix. I know you're trying to protect him, but sometimes too much coddling has the opposite effect. If I think Maximus is going to damage his psyche, I'll personally pull him out. This is a delicate balance for all of us. But we need to start somewhere. Trust is earned, right? But if you don't give me a shot, how can I prove I'm worthy of the gift?"

She chewed on her lower lip and glanced over at Phoenix. "I don't know."

He bit back a laugh and nodded. "Fair enough. We can work on that. For now, how about we move Maximus in but keep Hei Hei away? We'll let Phoenix deal with one obstacle at a time. Sound good?"

"I can live with that." She let out a breath, almost in frustration. "I don't do well taking orders," she admitted. "I'd flunk out of the military."

"So would I. But I'm not about to order you around like some lackey, Harper. We're a team. We need to listen to each other, but I also need to do what you're paying me for. That means being in charge when it comes to training. Can you accept those terms?"

He watched the emotions run across her face. She fascinated him—from her quiet, strong manner to her generous heart. But there was pain trapped beneath. He sensed it in the moments she believed no one was watching her, when she seemed to go away to another time and place and remember. He wished he had the right to help her or share the burden. He'd never wanted such intimacy with another woman, though he'd tried several times to try and feel something deeper. Now that he finally did, she was off limits.

Life was a bitch sometimes.

"Okay," she finally said. "I'll try, Irish. Is that enough?"

It seemed hard for her to be unguarded with a stranger, but Aidan bet her tries were worth more than the agreements people gave to make things easy. He imagined being the man she trusted with her heart. The idea shouldn't sear his heart like a brand or make his throat squeeze tight. It shouldn't mean anything but a way to get to the end—a way to win.

But it did.

"Yeah, it's enough," he said gruffly. "Now, let's go. It's time for Phoenix to meet his new stallmate."

She patted the horse's flank and shook her head. "I hope you know what you're doing."

"We'll soon find out, won't we?"

♥ ♥ ♥

"What the hell are you doing?" Ethan fired the question at Harper, but he was glaring at Aidan, who stood in the middle of two pissed-off horses trying to claim dominance.

The moment Phoenix had caught a glimpse of Maximus coming toward him, he'd gone nuts, rearing back and issuing snorts of fury. Of course, Maximus didn't take that shit, so he tried to bump him, and this started a round of the famous game played between males in the animal kingdom.

My dick is bigger than yours.

So much fun.

Tension twisted her belly. Watching Phoenix struggle with his fears and discomfort brought up old memories. Bad ones. She tried to remain calm and soothe her brother. "It's a long story. Let's just say it's part of the training."

"Why didn't you step in and put a stop to it?" he demanded.

She regarded her brother with a steady gaze, even though her nerves jumped. "Because I think Aidan may be right—we've coddled Phoenix. We need to see if he can handle conflict on his own without shutting down."

"We don't coddle Phoenix," he argued.

She arched a brow. "We gave him his own private stall. We bake him iced oatmeal cookies for rewards. We chase away all of the animals from the barn and pasture when he's around. And when he fusses, we all sit around his stall and try to soothe him until his tantrum has passed."

Her brother opened his mouth to protest, then snapped his jaw shut. "We have coddled him," he finally muttered.

"We're not used to training a racehorse. Our mission has always been to save them, then rehabilitate. Give them a quality life with an owner. Phoenix is different."

She watched the horse glare at his trainer and hoped she wouldn't discover a flare of betrayal in those brown eyes. It'd destroy her to think Phoenix would begin to doubt her intentions.

Suddenly, the past reared up and yanked her back in time. Her vision blurred while she fought the images, reminding herself nearly two decades had passed and she wasn't that girl any longer.

But God, sometimes it felt like yesterday.

She'd been awkward in her teens. Painfully shy, more comfortable in the barn than a school party. Was that why she'd been such an easy target for teasing? How many endless days had she been tortured? Why did she think something had changed on that day Lyndsey Belle approached her?

With her long blonde hair and curvy, petite body, the boys were crazy about Lyndsey, and all the girls loved to copy her clothes and her gestures and her cute southern accent since she'd been transported north. That fateful day, she'd asked Harper to join her for lunch. At the cool table. Harper had been wary the first day, but as a full week passed and she was still welcome, she had begun to believe everything would finally be okay.

She'd trusted Lyndsey. Trusted her gesture to be honest.

Stupid. So damn stupid.

The bliss hadn't lasted long. Five perfect, fake days. At the end of the Friday lunch period, finally relaxed enough to chat with the group and pick at her turkey sandwich, she'd begun to engage. Open up. Feel as if there were a chance for her to make real friends.

Then Lyndsey Belle had given the signal.

And Pete Ryan dumped a container of tomato juice over Harper's head.

The chants and laughter in the cafeteria sometimes haunted her. They'd said awful things. That she stunk like a skunk, so she needed a bath of tomato juice.

Harper had run out.

Lyndsey got detention along with Peter Ryan, which only made things worse. Harper's solitary confinement continued, and when her mother threatened to talk to the teachers and principal, Harper laughed it off, pretending it was just a silly prank that had gone wrong. She hated the idea of her mother feeling sorry for her. She didn't want to be *that* kid. The one pitied and clucked over and gossiped about. The outcast.

Even though she was.

"Harp? You okay?" Ethan asked.

She shook her head and refocused. "Yeah, sorry, my mind wandered."

"Well, let's hope his methods don't backfire. Once a horse loses trust, it's hell to regain it."

They both watched as Aidan played peacemaker but refused to lead Phoenix away, forcing him to decide. She held her breath and waited. Praying Phoenix would understand this was to help him and not a cruel joke.

Phoenix reared back on his hind legs and leaped at Maximus.

Maximus gave a furious scream and lowered his head to charge back.

Aidan firmly tugged both of their bridles at once and used his voice like a whiplash.

Both horses settled down, breathing heavily, glaring at each other.

Thighs braced, shoulders back, Aidan stood his ground with quiet authority. He had a talent for staring into their eyes and figuring out what they needed. Watching him work his magic was hypnotizing. The way his hands roamed the horse's body, as if able to find all the sweet spots. The way his gaze delved deep for endless minutes until he nodded, as if he'd discovered something the horse had tried to hide. The way his lyrical voice deepened like rich velvet and stirred all her senses. The way his eyes squinted when he grinned, and how his hair reminded her of crisp, bleached hay, fresh and clean.

She shut down her dangerous mental wanderings and tried to focus. "Jockey arrives tomorrow," she told her brother. "Name's Elmo. Can you tell Ophelia we need another room?"

"Yeah, about that . . . we have a bit of a residency problem, Harp. Ophelia double-checked the inn calendar, and she's almost completely blocked for the next three months. She could probably manage to squeeze in one of them, but not two."

Harper sighed and tucked her hair behind her ear. "I was afraid of this. I can call the local hotels, but they're a decent drive from town."

"I'd offer up the new room at my place, but it's not done, and Mia and I just can't deal with another guest. I'd suggest Aidan stay with you, but I know how you feel about your privacy."

The idea skittered through her brain, but it was too awful to imagine. No way could she have Aidan in her personal space. Yes, she had a spare room she could clean out, but like the farm, her home was sacred to her. Safe. She refused to share it with anyone, especially a man who offered a physical temptation on a daily basis.

Hell no.

"Let me make some phone calls. I'll figure something out."

"Okay. Chloe should be coming soon, and she'll be able to help out."

"Good, maybe she can keep Owen out of my hair. I'm at the end of my patience. I can try to—holy crap. I don't believe it." She stared at the scene before her.

The two horses had settled and were sharing space without trying to maim each other. Aidan had retreated, his leg propped up on the fence, elbow resting on the post, keeping his sharp gaze on the horses.

Damn, he was magnificent.

She must've said the words aloud, because Ethan nodded in agreement. "Yep. One hell of a horse."

Thank God he didn't realize she meant the man.

"Aidan's got something special," Ethan said thoughtfully. "A gift with horses."

"Like you. Remember how we used to call you *the horse whisperer?*"

He grunted. "Sure, I got the glory for stepping in at the right time, but you're the one with the real gift, Harp. You remind me of him, actually."

"Who?"

He jerked his head toward the pasture. "Aidan."

Her heart stopped, then resumed in a crazy rhythm. "Just because we both like horses?"

"No. Because you both see people and animals for who they really are. The only other person I know like that was Mom."

Surprise flickered. "Ophelia was always the most like Mom. She's the one who runs the inn and likes guests and bakes homemade scones."

Ethan grinned. "But you're the one who kept her real passion alive. Don't you know it was always about the horses? She would've done that full time, if possible." His cell rang and he glanced at it. "Gotta go. Have to meet Mia." He squeezed her shoulder in a quick goodbye and walked away.

Harper sifted through her brother's words. A faint smile curved her lips. Yes, she liked the idea of continuing her mother's legacy. Maybe Ethan was right. Mom had loved going to the barn late at night. Harper once caught her singing to the horses, and when she asked about it, her mother said she didn't want them to have bad dreams. She had loved to ride whenever possible and been fiercely protective of all the furry residents on the farm.

Maybe her mother had also dreamed of owning a racehorse.

Maybe they'd been more alike than Harper ever had believed.

The thought danced in her mind while she watched the horses graze in the pasture, finally at peace.

Chapter Eight

"I'm Elmo."

Harper dropped her gaze. She'd expected small—she'd been around jockeys before—but her height only made the contrast between them more daunting.

His hair was dark and cropped close to his head. Brown eyes regarded her steadily, slanted slightly at the corners, reflecting little emotion. His lips were firmed, and his legs and arms seemed to dangle next to his body. His cheek was swollen and bruised, like he'd just gotten into a fistfight before heading to the farm. He wore black riding pants, boots, and a short-sleeved red jersey.

Harper stuck out her hand. "Harper Bishop. It's nice to meet you."

He shook with a strong grip, nodded, and turned to Aidan. "Where is the horse?"

Aidan jerked his head toward the barn. "In the pasture, ready to meet you. Want to get settled in your room first? We can talk and grab some lunch."

"Not hungry." Without another word, he tucked his head down and walked out to the field with a determined stride.

She shot Aidan a look. "He's a chatterbox."

Aidan quirked a brow. "That was a big conversation for Elmo. Come on. It's all up to him now."

She trotted after Aidan. "How will he decide if he wants the job?"

Aidan snorted. "He's extremely . . . unconventional. It's all about the energy for him. If he doesn't like the aura around the horse, or if there's a negative spirit, he'll just leave."

"Negative spirit? Within the horse?"

"Yep. He's very superstitious and picky. He's difficult to deal with, but if he believes in the horse, he's one of the best. I think it will be a match."

Her mouth dropped open. "What if he deems poor Phoenix has a negative energy?"

Aidan shrugged. "Then we're screwed."

She blinked. "Tell me you're kidding." When he remained silent, she groaned. "Are you telling me you don't have another jockey on standby?"

"Elmo is plan A, plan B, and standby. There's no one I'd trust more with an emotional type of horse like Phoenix. We have to hope they like each other."

"Phoenix rarely likes anybody."

"Maybe Elmo will find him a challenge."

She blew out a breath in frustration. "It can't be that hard to find another jockey if Elmo says no."

Aidan shook his head. "Jockeys prefer to work with trained horses and build a name for themselves. Injury is always a possibility with a green horse, and Phoenix has a bit of a temper with an abusive past. Basically, he's got tons of baggage. You've never had a racehorse, so you have no reputation to sell. And though I'm well known, my wins have all been Irish horses. We don't have much to offer, love. Elmo knows me. He's patient, experienced, and he can usually reach a difficult horse. So start praying they get along."

She smothered another groan as their situation suddenly became violently, sharply, crystal clear.

Phoenix was grazing on his midmorning snack. The jockey approached, stopped a few inches away from the horse, and stared.

Phoenix curled back his lips in his legendary sneer, pricked up his ears, and went back to his food.

Elmo dropped to the ground in front of the horse, crossed his legs, and didn't move.

Harper expected some type of skilled approach, hand gestures, or anything that looked like he was bonding. Instead, Phoenix continued to ignore him, and Elmo continued to wait.

Owen walked over and did a double take. "Wow, a real live jockey, huh? What's he doing?"

"Bonding with Phoenix," Harper said.

Owen glanced back and forth between them. "Looks like he's taking a squat and doing nothing to me."

Aidan grunted.

Finally, Phoenix stopped chewing and began to check out his new visitor with a bit of pique. He took a few steps toward Elmo and pawed the ground, showing off.

Harper winced. Probably a bad sign. Maybe Elmo would mistake the horse's fiery personality for a demon, and they'd have to scramble to look for another jockey who wanted to take a chance on a green horse from an unknown stable with an owner with no previous races under her belt. Her palms began to sweat, and she wiped them down her jeans.

Elmo stretched out his legs in front of him. Rested his hands flat on the ground behind his back, propping himself up. And kept waiting.

So they all waited.

Harper had no idea how many minutes ticked by. Her nerves jumped, and she curled her hands into loose fists to keep from chewing on her thumb.

Finally, Phoenix seemed to be so annoyed by the visitor who made no sound and sat in his territory, the horse leaped in a menacing manner, as if to physically herd Elmo away.

The jockey never flinched.

After more time went by, Phoenix walked up close and sniffed, baring his teeth.

Harper's heart sank. She cupped her hands and raised her voice. "Umm, Elmo, if you give him a chance, you'll see he just needs time to get comfortable with you. I think—"

"Shush," Aidan whispered, grabbing her hand. "He needs silence."

Harper glared, especially from the jolt of electricity she felt at his touch. "For what?" she hissed back. "I think he needs a decent explanation to make an informed decision."

"Trust me, there will be absolutely no logic in this. Now, shush."

She went to snap at him for the chauvinistic command, but when she realized Elmo didn't bother to respond and remained silent, questions burned in her mind. Was this jockey actually good? Or was he crazy? And if he was crazy, did she want him riding Phoenix?

After a few more tense moments, Phoenix got brave enough to butt at Elmo's head but pulled back when the jockey didn't move.

"This is ridiculous," she whispered. "He's doing nothing!"

"He's examining the aura. Just be patient."

Elmo slowly stood, unfolding each part of his body with a deliberate slowness and grace. Phoenix stilled, obviously wary. They stayed in that position until the jockey seemed satisfied. Then, in a sudden challenging move, Elmo grasped his bridle and pulled his head close. Phoenix blew out his breath and bared his teeth in a creepy Halloween grin. Elmo leaned in way too far, until his nose practically touched the horse's.

Harper wondered if she had enough liability insurance for this upcoming claim.

Elmo blasted the words right at Phoenix, his voice echoing in the air. "I ride."

"What the hell is going on?" she asked. "Can he even mount without a block?"

"Just let him do his thing. We'll have a decision soon." Aidan didn't let go of her hand, tugging her closer toward the riding area.

Elmo made a move to mount, but Phoenix sensed it coming and began to buck. Moving in front of the horse, Elmo pushed his face close once again and began whispering something Harper couldn't hear.

Phoenix stilled. Cocked his head.

With a firm pat, Elmo moved back to the horse's left side, and in one graceful, dancer-like motion, he threw himself up and swung into the saddle.

And then they took off.

He rode a few laps, allowing the horse to find his natural stride, then pushed him to open up.

Harper watched horse and rider take off in the trademark speed she was used to seeing with Phoenix and waited patiently while Elmo finished his test ride. When he finally dismounted and walked toward them, Harper tried to stay calm.

"Horse has demon in him," the jockey stated.

Her heart sank. "If you just gave him another chance, you'll see he needs time to settle, and I know you'll change your mind."

Elmo furrowed his brow. "Don't need no more chance."

Aidan rubbed his head. "Is there a way we can release the demon?"

Harper almost laughed at the ridiculous conversation, but they were both desperate. "He's really quite sweet," she said.

Phoenix took that moment to jam his head into Elmo's side and practically knocked him over.

Elmo looked back and glared.

Phoenix bared his teeth in a sneer.

Aidan sighed. "Damn it, I'm sorry. I thought it'd be a good match. I can get you on the next train back to Saratoga, but you're welcome to 'stay the night. I'll take you to dinner."

"Not hungry. I go to room now. We start tomorrow."

It took her a few moments to register his words. Harper jerked back. "What? You're taking the job?"

"Yes. He good demon. We win."

With a curt nod and final glance at the horse, Elmo disappeared down the path on the way back to the inn.

Head spinning, she looked at Aidan. "What just happened?"

Aidan grinned. "We got ourselves a jockey."

Harper grinned back and slowly became aware of their still-linked hands. Her arm tingled pleasantly. When was the last time a guy had held her hand? Hell, when had she last snuggled up with someone on any type of intimate level? It was amazing how hand-holding could seem more intimate than sex. At least, in her life.

Trying not to show how his touch affected her, she dropped his hand. His gaze pinned hers, those glowing amber eyes swirling with a mixture of emotions she couldn't name. Her breath squeezed from her lungs. Intensity settled between them.

He cleared his throat, breaking the spell. "I'll take a room at the Hampton until a spot opens back up at the inn. Make sure to call my cell if anything happens and I'm not around. I'll meet you here at five a.m. for his morning workout."

"Okay." She turned away, then hesitated, remembering she'd promised her sister to have him over for dinner. "You're invited to dinner Sunday night." She hated the slight huskiness to her voice, but hopefully he didn't notice. She shifted her weight and tried hard to seem natural and not awkward. "Ophelia is cooking a big meal. Owen and Chloe are coming, and I'll invite Elmo now that he's decided to stay."

He cocked his head. "Thanks. But we can get something from town. Elmo and I are used to taking care of ourselves."

She frowned. "I know, but it's not good to live on takeout. Ophelia composed a meal schedule. Dinner will be served at the inn for everyone Sundays and Thursdays. The rest of the time, we're on our own. With everyone's crazy schedule, we decided this would be a good way to talk.

about Phoenix's training on a regular basis without trying to schedule meetings. Besides, connecting over a meal is important."

Was that a flash of longing on his face or just her imagination? "Sounds nice. What's your day to cook?"

She gave a half laugh. "Never. It's not one of my talents."

"Bet you have more important talents."

Harper knew it was meant as a joke, but by the end of his quip, a sexual heat laced itself through his words, inspiring images of darkened rooms, tangled sheets, and sweat-slick naked bodies. Particularly his. In her bed.

He stepped back the same time she did. The connection between them surged and punched with a power she still wasn't used to.

"Better get back to work," he muttered.

"Yeah, me, too." She shoved her hands awkwardly in the back pockets of her jeans.

He grasped Phoenix's bridle and led him over to the barn. "Come on, capalleen. Let's get you bathed and brushed and try a new companion. Maybe Stitch? She seems a bit sweet on you."

Harper listened to him until his voice faded away. She had to be more careful. No more touching, even casually. No standing too close.

And definitely no thinking of him naked in her bed.

A few nights later, Harper rubbed her eyes and tried to refocus on her laptop. Endless Excel spreadsheets, bank accounts, and a list of fees crowded her tabs and made her itch for another cup of coffee. This horse-racing business was expensive, especially the race-entry fees. She'd made the hard decision to not attend the last horse auction, knowing they had limited stall space until she placed two other horses. Plus, she needed to be careful with all the money being funneled into training salaries, equipment, and time.

Guilt assaulted her. The haunting image of horses who needed her seared her brain, but it was part of the business and she had to accept it. She couldn't save them all. Compartmentalizing her emotions helped, especially when she knew there was no other choice. Phoenix had been a gift, and she needed to put the effort and focus into his training.

Groaning, she stretched out in the chair. Bagheera and Baloo had given up on her hours ago, sprawling on the threadbare couch in a sleepy pile of fur. Figaro perched on the top of the recliner, occasionally raising her head to give the dogs a long-suffering look. Maybe Figaro would get along with Phoenix. They were both disgusted by their animal companions, preferring the beauty of their own company.

This past week had been a bit of a challenge. Seemed Phoenix still wasn't comfortable with any stablemates. Oh, he'd learned to silently suffer. He'd even stopped chasing Wheezy and Bolt away when they tried to come up and play. Yes, technically he could be around other animals now without reverting to fear or violent aggression, but she wasn't sure if he'd be able to transition yet to a fully stocked barn with other racing horses consistently around him, battling for space.

Aidan was trying different techniques and introducing various animals to see if any made a difference. So far, no success. She'd even gone to visit neighboring farms to borrow Esther the pig; a goat named Molly; and a trio of sweet-natured cats, Flopsy, Mopsy, and Cottontail. The horse hadn't been amused by his new visitors, and after Phoenix chased them out of the barn and tossed crap at them—hay, apple cores, and even water—Aidan was almost out of ideas.

Too bad Flower had gotten hurt by the horse's previous rejections to play. She was such a friendly little mare, frisky and always looking to make a new best friend. They shouldn't have moved her out of the stall until—

Harper shot up from the chair. *Shit.* Had Flower been properly locked up? She'd been so damn busy with other stuff and asked Owen to lock up. She'd meant to swing by and check on him—she still didn't trust Owen completely—but left to attack paperwork. Nibbling on her lip, she grabbed her phone and glanced at the time.

Past eleven.

She could text Ethan, but then she'd end up disturbing Mia. Aidan was at the hotel, and she wasn't comfortable contacting Elmo yet. God knew the man barely spoke, refused to text, and still had an ancient flip phone.

Damn it. She'd just go to the stable herself. It wouldn't take long, and she'd finish the bills tomorrow.

She moved to the door. The dogs' heads lifted in question. "I'll be right back. I have to go to the stables, and then we're going to bed. Okay?"

They flopped back down on the sofa.

It was a habit to tell her crew exactly where she was going and what she was doing. They were pretty much the best roommates ever—they never annoyed her with questions or comments.

She hopped in her beat-up black truck and made the two-minute drive down the path that led straight to the barns. Jumping out, she went into the first barn, giving a whistle to alert the horses. Flower was safely locked up in her stall and seemed surprised to see her. Good. Owen had finally followed through on a task. Maybe things were getting better.

She did a quick check on all the other horses in the first barn and was headed back to her truck when she noticed a light burning in the main barn ahead. She frowned and walked over.

Who'd be checking on Phoenix this late? Was Ethan having bad dreams again? He'd seek out the horses sometimes when the memories of his past hit him hard. But since Mia, his midnight visits had practically disappeared.

She pushed the door open.

Aidan lay in a pile of hay outside Phoenix's stall. Head propped up on his elbow, he was reading something on his phone, legs crossed at the ankles. A ragged flannel blanket lay beside him, along with a spiral notebook and pen. A battered olive-green duffel bag was open at his feet. When she stepped into the barn, his gaze rose and crashed into hers.

Golden light glowed so fierce and so bright, she stood still in shock. She caught the raw want in his eyes, which was usually carefully banked, and her body softened in response. An uncomfortable heat burned between her legs. She tried to rally, realizing she wasn't wearing a bra and probably had that fresh-out-of-bed look. "What are you doing here?" Her voice came out like a husky invitation, so she cleared her throat. "Is Phoenix okay?"

He sat up. "Yeah, he's fine. I couldn't sleep and figured I'd do some work. Check on the horses. You?"

She frowned, taking a few steps closer. "I asked Owen to put Flower in her stall and lock up the barn, but then realized I never double-checked. I live only a few minutes from here, so I figured I'd come back."

"Did he do his job?"

"Surprisingly, yes."

He nodded. "Good."

Her frown deepened. "Your hotel is twenty minutes away. You came all the way back this late because you couldn't sleep?"

His gaze swept to the side. The energy between them shifted and moved, and she sensed something important hovered on his lips—a secret she was both desperate and terrified to hear. "I don't do well in hotels," he finally said.

She closed the rest of the distance and leaned against the scratchy wooden post, looking down at him. She should mind her own business. She should nod politely, walk away, and go home to her bed. The question flew out of her mouth, refusing to be caged. "Why?"

He muttered something in Irish. "Let's just say I'm the most comfortable in a barn."

A short silence fell. She allowed the familiar sounds of the barn to wrap around her. The soft hush of horses' breath. The gentle creaks of wood. The occasional snort or shift of position. The brush of hay over the concrete. They mingled with the outside harmony of crickets and the occasional bright flash of light from the fireflies.

"This is my favorite place in the world," she admitted. "I love my home, but when I step into the barn, I feel like I'm returning to the best part of myself. A place where I'm completely understood and capable. I feel strong here. Silly, right?"

He regarded her in the dim light for a while. He rubbed his jaw, as if caught between his own desire to share and the walls he'd built high to keep everyone out.

She studied the beautiful lines of his face, the squint around his eyes, the firming of those perfectly defined lips. And she wondered if one of her biggest regrets in her life would be not knowing how this man kissed.

"I came from a big family. My father had left, and my mom tried to raise four headstrong boys. We learned early on there wasn't any money, and if we wanted to eat, we needed to work. So I cut out of school early and found work at a horse stable. We had a lot of racetracks and horse farms around, so it seemed like easy, plentiful work. I had no idea the moment I stepped into a barn, my life would change."

"How old were you?"

"Fifteen."

She sucked in a breath. "You were so young."

"Didn't feel like it. Each one of us left home looking for work the moment it was possible. I had no money for a long time, so my home was wherever I traveled. Sometimes I'd hook up with an owner or trainer who'd give me a bed or bunk for a few weeks. Sometimes not. I got used to sleeping in the barn. All I needed was a blanket and some clean hay, and I was comfortable." He shrugged. "When I began to study training, I slept by the horse. It was a bonding ritual for both of us."

Her heart ached, imagining a young boy on his own, not having a safe place to stay. She couldn't imagine being homeless. "You weren't afraid?"

His lips quirked up in a half grin. "Never. Nerves of steel." When she narrowed her gaze suspiciously, he chuckled. "Just kidding. Hell yes, I was scared. But I learned fast, about the job and myself. Of what I needed versus what I wanted. It all worked out. I relied on myself, so I was never disappointed. The horses gave me everything I really needed."

He spoke with a casual tone, but his eyes gave him away. It had been hard. Harder than she probably imagined, but he'd risen above and fought to make a name for himself. He'd ended up owning a business and winning the Irish Derby.

Harper stared at the lonely flannel blanket and stack of hay. What must it feel like to not belong anywhere? At least she had her family, who always supported her, and a home. Despite feeling alone and rejected at school, she'd always felt loved and a part of the bigger whole on the farm.

Ethan's suggestion rose up and taunted her. She hesitated, torn between her head and her gut. Inviting this man into her home was an important decision. If they didn't fit well together in a tight space or she felt uncomfortable in his constant presence, she'd regret the offer. And what if becoming roommates began to affect their working relationship?

But something about the hard lines of his face, disguising his own vulnerability from his past, touched her deep. She knew what it was like to search for a connection with others, only to find solace in the quiet of the barn. She'd also learned to rely on herself rather than offer her trust and be disappointed.

In that moment, Harper realized she didn't want him to feel like a hired hand who meant nothing to them but a way to win. Didn't want to think of him in a lonely hotel, unable to sleep, displaced and sent off like a spare part until another room opened up at the inn. She wanted him to know he could trust her, too.

She went with her heart. "You can bunk at my house."

He cocked his head. "What?"

"When Ophelia has some openings, you can stay at the inn. In the meantime, I have a spare room where you can crash. It's a short walk from here, so you can come to the barn whenever you'd like. Besides Bagheera and Baloo, I have a cranky cat named Figaro, but she'll leave you alone. It's tight quarters. I don't cook, it's always dusty, but I make a mean cup of coffee."

He rolled to his feet and came close. A tic worked in his jaw. "You feeling sorry for me, love?"

She shook her head. "No. I'm not offering up my home because I pity you, Irish. It just makes sense."

He seemed to be battling something deep inside. His eyes seethed with primal emotion. "Ask me if I would have changed anything," he demanded roughly.

Her breath caught. Dear God, he was fierce and prideful and strong. The intensity crackling beneath the surface tugged at her very soul. She tilted her chin in challenge. "Would you?"

"No. I may not have a bunch of stories to tell about chummy family dinners, but I got to live my life on my terms. I do what I love, and when my feet get itchy, I hit the road for the next big win. I learned how to not only survive but also thrive. Why would I ever want to change that?"

Her throat tightened. Her fingers curled into fists. Every cell in her body screamed to be close, to touch him, to feel the steady beat of his heart against her ear, to be surrounded by the whipcord strength and heat of his arms. She craved to give comfort; she craved to kiss him, part her thighs, and let him fuck her right here in the hay, in the place they both loved the most. She craved to let him really see her, and that was the most dangerous of all.

She closed her eyes halfway and fought her internal need like a wildcat. If she could walk away right now and not surrender, she'd be able to handle the next few months. If she could deny them both right now, the initial terms of their agreement would stay alive.

She crossed her arms in front of her braless breasts and stepped around him. "You're the last man I'd ever feel sorry for, Irish," she said lightly. "You can grab your bag and follow me."

"And if I don't?" His slow drawl gave her goose bumps.

She shrugged. "Then you don't. It's your decision. Your terms, remember? I'll wait in the truck for two minutes before I leave."

Harper walked out of the barn, got in her truck, and cranked the engine. Her slick hands tightened around the steering wheel as she waited. It'd be better if he didn't show. This whole invitation was pushing fate. Maybe bunking in the barn wasn't such a bad idea, after all. He liked it. He was comfortable. He was probably happy to stay. He—

The headlights illuminated his figure as he came out with his bag slung over his shoulder. He threw the latch and climbed inside the truck.

Without saying a word, she drove them both home.

Chapter Nine

Aidan sipped his Barry's Tea and looked around.

The moment he walked into Harper's home, familiarity surrounded him. The space was small and functional, from the well-worn smoke-gray lounging couch to the oversize chair situated by the large window that overlooked the woods. The coffee table looked handmade and built from tree trunks in a deep-red cedar. There was little clutter other than an overflowing bookcase, colorful braided throw rugs, and a few framed pictures. The only thing he disagreed with was the television. It was noticeably ancient. He would've upgraded so he could binge on Netflix or HBO on those rare occasions he had a rainy Sunday off.

The living room led straight to the kitchen with no walls blocking it off. He'd heard it termed *open concept*. She'd been honest about her limited cooking skills, obvious from the Spartan-like feel of the limited appliances and decor. A sturdy wood farm table and matching chairs held a vase full of wildflowers and some mismatched placemats.

But she clearly had her priorities. The counter boasted a fancy French press coffeepot, a red Keurig machine with expensive African blends, a coffee grinder, and a shelf full of every type of coffee bean he could imagine. Labeled.

The woman liked her coffee.

He'd gotten up at four thirty a.m., thrown on some clothes since he'd showered last night, and headed to the kitchen so he could at least have the coffee brewing and let the dogs out for her.

Of course, she'd already brewed a pot, the dogs had given him a standard greeting before settling back into sleep, and he heard the shower running. How much sleep did she really need? He'd always boasted he was good to go on five, but he had a feeling Harper had him beat. Another thing about her that turned him on. Nothing like a woman who was ready to go before the sun crawled up over the horizon.

Grinning, he rummaged in her kitchen, found some bread, and popped four slices in the toaster. The butter was fresh, and so was the blackberry jam, so he prepped breakfast in under five minutes. He ate at the table, waiting for her, his mind replaying the previous night.

He hadn't intended to tell her about his childhood. It was something he kept private, those endless days after leaving his mother and his fear of failure. He'd never questioned his mother's decision to kick them all out of the house so young, and hated to be judged. Mum had done the best she could on a limited income and with too many children his bastard father had abandoned. He'd meant every word uttered to Harper. He didn't regret a moment, because everything that had happened had led him right here.

Even the betrayal of his best friend.

His fingers clenched around his mug. Phoenix was going to get him back in the game. If he did his job and won, he'd be able to return to Ireland as a king. Pick his own horses to work with. Prove to his ex-partner he'd fucked with the wrong guy. Everything would fall back into place.

It all hinged on Phoenix.

He'd been surprised how easy it was to share his story with Harper. Even though he'd been wary that she'd offered her home out of guilt, he'd known it was the right move. He needed quick access to Phoenix at all times, and staying with her allowed them to work constantly on their goal.

The inner voice rose up in a taunting whisper. *Bullshit. You wanted access to her. You're smitten.*

He shot back his answer. *I've got this under control. There's too much at stake. I'm not going to screw up my only chance for a roll in the literal hay.*

The mocking laughter pissed him off. He shut down the voice with a ruthless control and took a bite of his toast.

Her scent hit him first. Clean soap and the faint hint of cocoa butter from her skin drifted to his nostrils. His muscles tightened with awareness as the energy in the room whipped up like a tornado gaining steam. He dragged in a breath, reset, and cranked his head around.

Then stared.

God, she was sexy. Hair damp from her shower, her powder-blue T-shirt and jeans could've been designer wear straight from Paris and couldn't have looked better. Those Amazon legs practically begged to be wrapped around his hips while he thrust into her. Those haunting sea-green eyes were meant to go misty and dazed when he drove her straight to the edge of orgasm and kept her there, just so he could drink in her gorgeous expression of need. Those pale peach lips cried out for his mouth and his teeth and his tongue until they were swollen and ripe and her taste was ingrained in every cell of his body.

She scowled. "Why are you looking at me all weird? You better not have drank all the coffee." She marched past him, grunting while she refilled her mug, and sat down across from him. She grabbed a piece of toast and began munching.

He decided not to respond and adjusted himself under the table. He had to stop mooning over her like a hormone-crazed teen. He was better than this.

The dogs immediately jumped down from the couch, sat by her feet, and gave her dual perfect pleading expressions. She automatically broke off two pieces of the crust and fed them. Then they trained the looks on Aidan, tongues lolling out, their begging like a well-rehearsed play repeated twice daily.

He shook his head and gave them some crust. "Guess you don't adhere to the rule not to give them table food?"

She snorted, which shouldn't be charming but was. "If you could only have one food for the rest of your life, wouldn't you get depressed?"

He chuckled. "Never thought of it like that."

"Life's too short. As long as it's nothing harmful and not too much, they should enjoy a varied diet. Baloo is a peanut butter fiend. Bagheera loves turkey breast. Figaro becomes halfway nice when I tempt her with tuna."

"That how you got Phoenix hooked on oatmeal iced cookies? Trying to give him some happiness?"

She winced. "Guilty. I didn't realize what a pig he'd become. It started as a way to tempt him to let us get close."

"I'll never forget that look he tossed me when I gave him carrots instead."

A laugh escaped her lips, and the sound warmed his chest. He wished he could make her do it more often. "Yeah, he's a bit of a handful. But that's also going to help him out on the track. Are we practicing with breaking from the gate today?"

He nodded. "Yeah. I'll combine practice with the gate and light racing against a competitor next week. We'll begin with Flower. He'll need to learn the right way to be paced. I don't want to throw Maximus at him so early, but we'll work up to it."

"Sounds like a plan." She popped the last piece of toast in her mouth. "Thanks for breakfast. How was the spare room?"

"Better than the Hampton." He grinned and put the mugs in the sink. "I'll stop in town and get some groceries."

"No need."

"Yeah, there is." He leaned against the sink. "We split the food bill, okay? What do you want me to pick up, or do you want to text me a list?"

She chucked the paper plates in the garbage and smirked. "Well, aren't you domestic? One night and already you're grocery shopping."

"I'll buy a vacuum when I'm in town, too."

Her eyes widened. "You're kidding."

He winked. "Yes, I'm kidding. I like dust."

She laughed again, and his chest swelled with pride. He could get addicted to her laugh.

The voice nudged open the box. *Told ya. You're smitten.*

He slammed the lid back down and refused to engage. The silence was blissful, but the damage had already been done.

He was terrified the voice was right.

♥ ♥ ♥

Aidan watched the jockey guide Phoenix into an easy trot around the track. His gaze assessed the way Elmo handled the horse, his body language, and the way Phoenix seemed to respond.

Yeah, he'd been right. Phoenix wouldn't have taken to just any jockey. Elmo had a talent for connecting with emotional horses. Aidan had seen him coax the best out of green-broke Thoroughbreds. Too bad Elmo wasn't as well received in the racing world as he should be. Many didn't agree with his unconventional methods regarding aura, energy, or using endless patience to break bad habits. Too many wanted a quick fix or a jockey who had big numbers, but Elmo sought out horses he could help or who needed him. He liked to sit in the pasture and read a book while Phoenix grazed. The jockey's presence seemed to soak into the horse's routine. He also knew the right time to challenge and claim control. Aidan loved watching a good jockey break down, assess, and build up a horse's stamina and skill. But for Elmo, it was all about the heart. His decision to stay with Phoenix confirmed Aidan's own instincts.

"They've bonded." He turned to find Ethan with one foot propped up on the fence, watching horse and rider become one.

Aidan nodded. "I sensed they'd be a fit."

"Your instinct was right." He let a few moments pass in comfortable silence. "Heard you spent the night at Harper's last night."

Ah, shit.

Refusing to react to the probing statement, Aidan nodded, his gaze still trained on the pair on the track. "Yep."

"How was it?"

"Good."

He waited some more, and Ethan finally broke. "My sister never lets anyone stay with her. Strangers in her personal space make her uncomfortable. She's very . . . private."

Aidan swiveled his head around and met the man's gaze. "Hoping I'm not a stranger for long. But I don't intend to make her uncomfortable. I respect our working relationship too much."

Ethan rubbed the back of his neck and cursed. "Look, I'm not playing overprotective big brother here. Harper would lose her shit if she knew I was mentioning this. I only want you to know she took a leap of trust by letting you stay. By letting you into her world. I hope you respect it. That's all."

Aidan relaxed and grinned. He was glad her brother looked out for her. He was a straight shooter who protected his family. "Got it. And I do. More than you know."

Ethan grinned back, and an alliance seemed to form between them—unspoken, but the type men shared around a woman they both cared about. "Good. Gonna try to break him from the gate today?"

"Yeah, he's definitely skittish, so I want to know how he does. Want to watch?"

"Would like to, but I have some things to take care of. I'll check in with you later." He tipped his head and strode off, his slight limp reminding Aidan he was a man who'd sacrificed for all of them without question. That was the type of man he could work with.

So far, the Bishop family was turning out to be his favorite client.

An hour later, he examined the starting gate, which was the key to getting Phoenix ready for a race. For the past few days, they'd been loading the horse into the gate and keeping him there. It'd been rough in the beginning, and Elmo had been challenged trying to keep the horse from kicking and breaking out in a frenzy. They'd gone from a few seconds in the gate to just under a minute now, and Aidan felt comfortable about trying the break. He'd already spoken at length with Elmo about the use of various techniques, but both of them decided to rely on the old-fashioned way.

The three of them stood by the track. "Each horse has a different reaction to the gate," he explained to Harper. "It may feel claustrophobic and put them into a panic. We need to get Phoenix comfortable with breaking clean and fast the moment the door opens. Coinciding it with a loud noise will help condition him."

She nodded, absently patting the horse's shiny black coat. "I've been conditioning him to be more comfortable around noises. Ethan used a cowbell, then paired it with comfort, so he's been less skittish."

"Good. I'm going to give you the signal, and then you hit the button to release the gate. I'll ring a buzzer at the exact time. Elmo, use your discretion for now on how you handle him, depending on his stress level."

They agreed, and Elmo mounted. Aidan guided the horse toward the gate. Phoenix immediately pulled back, trying to avoid the tight quarters, and Aidan took a few times circling until the horse began to relax. By the eighth retreat, they squeezed him in, and he quickly gave the signal, not wanting Phoenix to be enclosed for too long the first time.

The gate sprang open. He hit the loud, shrieking buzzer.

Phoenix reared up, rushing ahead with a drunken gait, then straightened out and began to run.

Harper shot Aidan a look. "That was rough."

"Yep. Definitely not his favorite thing to do, but most horses dislike the gate." He called out to Elmo, "Bring him back and let's do it again."

He praised the horse, who thought the torture was over, then began circling him again. It took the same amount of repetitions to get him locked in. The buzzer rang, and he lurched out, this time taking off pretty fast, but he was all over the track.

Elmo trotted back. "He likes to go left. Post position by rail could be big problem."

"Agreed. Harp, has the vet told you anything about his left side being weaker?"

She shook her head. "No, but when I rescued him, there was bruising. I think he may have been whipped and tries to protect it?"

"Okay, could be a mental thing. For now, guide him toward the outside and see how he straightens out. We can work up to running on the inside later on."

They did it again. And again. And again.

The sun grew hot and his T-shirt stuck to his back. He chugged water and called for a break. "Let's stop for the day. I don't want him to get frustrated or link the gate with punishment." He patted the horse's flank and slid out one oatmeal cookie from his pocket. The horse's ears pricked up, and he showed his teeth in his trademark macabre grin, waiting for the treat.

Aidan laughed and held it out. "Sugar addict. You get carrots for lunch."

Phoenix finished chewing, then bumped his head forward, knocking Aidan back a step.

"Oh, tough guy, huh," he crooned, rubbing under his chin. "Let's save that fire for the track." Grinning, he turned and caught Harper staring at him.

Slowly, his grin disappeared.

It was the longing in her eyes that almost slammed him to his knees. Her gaze roved over him almost hungrily, as if starved for his affection like the horse he now rubbed. With the sun glinting off her tousled dark hair and her beautiful face tilted upward, he ached to touch her. His gut clenched and he gritted his teeth, swearing under his breath. Then turned away.

"I take him in," Elmo said.

Aidan nodded, not trusting himself to speak. It was better this way. Ignoring the connection between them was the only way to move forward. It was the only way to keep himself sane.

He started back toward the barns. She fell into step beside him.

"How often will we practice the gate?" she asked.

"Every day," he said gruffly. He stuck his hands in his pockets. Probably better to keep himself from temptation. "I don't want him to burn out, though. A happy horse will give the best to the track. We're pushing hard, and at his young age, he needs plenty of play, sleep, and snuggle time."

"Consider this your invitation to the pajama party at the barn, then."

"It will be quite the *craic*, especially if you put Owen in charge of the planning." He tamped down a smile and shook his head. If only she weren't so damn fun to talk to. A physical attraction was easier to fight. Liking her?

That just sucked.

As they neared the barn, he noticed the crowd of people surrounding Phoenix. "He's got a fan club already, huh?"

Her face lit up. "Chloe's here! Come on, I'll introduce you." She ran the rest of the way, and he enjoyed the graceful swing of her hips and ass framed in tight, faded jeans.

When he reached the group, a young girl with long dark hair and piercing blue eyes stepped out in front. The tiny diamond nose ring she wore winked in the light. She was dressed to work—in old jeans, boots, and a purple V-neck top. It matched the lone violet streak in her hair.

"You're a real horse trainer!" she said excitedly, sticking out her hand. "I'm Chloe."

He laughed, shaking her hand. "Nice to finally meet you. I'm Aidan. And yes, I'm the one hired to get Phoenix ready for the track."

"That is so fridge!" she squealed.

"Totally fridge," Ethan repeated, giving Chloe a high five.

Mia frowned. "Huh? What's fridge?"

Ethan shot Chloe a suffering look. "She doesn't understand the lingo," he said sadly.

Chloe giggled. "It means *cool*, Mia. If you go to my IG, you'll see the meme with the word on it I used to describe the new car Daddy got me. Well, used car, but I love it."

"Hey, a Jeep is totally fridge, even with miles on it," Ethan said.

Mia rolled her eyes. "He doesn't know what that means! He's just pretending."

Ethan assumed a hurt look. "Do too. If you followed Chloe's IG stories regularly, you'd know more things." He turned to the young girl. "Can you show me how to do those puppy ears on Snapchat?"

"Definitely."

Mia groaned. "I give up."

Chloe laughed and turned to Harper. "I can help you out till mid-August, when I head back into Manhattan to hang with Dad. How's Chloe's Pride?"

"She's missed you." Harper squeezed her shoulder with affection. "We've all missed you, but I heard you got on the dean's list this semester. Way to go."

"Thanks." Her face lit up. "I'm thinking about getting into law. Specifically, animal protective rights litigation. There are so many rescues who suffer and need someone to fight on their behalf. You taught me that, Harper."

Aidan watched the emotions play over Harper's face. Pride surged. She was so damn special, but she had no clue. She was the type of woman to keep her head down and barrel forward, never thinking of herself. She needed to be told more often she was important. Chloe's words seemed to tug at something she kept carefully hidden—a longing to be seen or heard.

He wanted to be the man to give it to her.

But he couldn't.

Elmo dismounted and introduced himself with his usual one-word answers, but Chloe didn't seem to mind.

Owen strolled out of the barn with a confused look on his face. "Hey, guys. Did I miss a group meeting or something?"

Harper waved him over. "Owen, this is Chloe Lake. She's the one who helped us out last summer and attends SUNY New Paltz. She'll be helping us out again this summer. Maybe she can teach you a few things."

Aidan caught Harper's edgy voice and winced. Owen had been trying, but he was still sloppy with instructions, afraid of a majority of the horses, and distracted by his phone.

Chloe gave Owen a smile. "Nice to meet you," she said.

A strange look skittered over Owen's face. He stood stock-still, staring at her with his mouth half-open and a glazed look in his eyes.

Aidan watched him with a bit of worry. "You okay, buddy?" he asked.

Owen didn't move.

Chloe frowned and touched his shoulder. "Is it the heat? Summer is rough. You have to make sure you're hydrated."

A slow, dopey smile broke over the kid's face. Those crazy surfer curls bounced and brushed his cheeks. "Chloe," he whispered, staring at the girl.

Uh-oh.

Chloe stepped back, shooting him an odd look. "Uh, yeah. That's me. How do you like working at the farm?"

The dopey grin stayed put. "Love it."

Harper let out a humorless laugh, completely oblivious to what was happening. "I wish," she said with a bite of sarcasm. "He's been struggling, but Aidan is teaching him how to ride, and if we can surgically remove his phone from his hand, he may do better."

Chloe laughed, swinging her head, and Owen blinked, as if dazzled by a flash of lights. "I had some trouble when I first came here, too," she admitted, shooting a mischievous look at Mia. "But some great people straightened me out. Just let me know if you need help."

Aidan watched the poor schmuck crumble before him. Oh yeah, he had it bad. Lovesick after one glance at the lovely Chloe, his fate could go one of two ways: his work at the farm would suck even more because he'd be distracted by his new love interest, or he'd get his shit together and try to impress her.

Aidan hoped for the latter.

Owen glowed. "Thanks, Chloe. Maybe you can show me how to—oh, crap!"

A mad, shrill screech and clucking rose in the air. Hei Hei crashed down the path, his crazy head feathers bobbing, and hurtled straight to . . . Owen.

Aidan tried not to wince as the scene played out in rapid time. Owen screamed, seemingly too overtaken by fear to act cool in front of Chloe, and began to frantically back up. Mia and Ethan snapped out a command for the chicken to stop, but Hei Hei averted Mia's reach by inches and charged.

Owen stumbled and fell back onto the ground. Hei Hei began pecking with glee at his feet, fat jowls jiggling, while Owen squirmed and tried to crawl away like he was trapped in a Stephen King movie. Owen kicked, and Hei Hei backed up, apparently satisfied he'd made his presence known.

Then those beady eyes fastened on Phoenix.

Everything morphed into a shitshow.

Phoenix took one glance at the crazed chicken and went nuts. Shaking his head and pawing the ground, the horse tried to challenge the creature in an old-fashioned game of . . . chicken.

Elmo grabbed for the reins, but Phoenix twisted hard and advanced.

Hei Hei shrieked and charged back.

Mia yelled, and Harper suddenly jumped in the middle of the dueling pair, causing Aidan to have a fucking heart attack. With a dancer's grace, she pivoted, knocking the chicken off course, while she yanked hard on the horse's bridle just in time.

The two animals stared at one another in some type of alpha battle.

Mia threw her head back in temper. "Hei Hei! Bad chicken! I've told you not to bother Owen! You just like taunting him, and that's mean, and Phoenix had every right to trample you for your behavior. Are you listening to me?"

The chicken raced over to Mia and began rubbing his head feathers against her legs.

She shook her finger at him. "Sucking up is not going to help this relationship right now," she said sternly. "You're going in the pen, and I want you to think about this behavior of yours and how you want to change."

Hei Hei squawked.

"I don't care. Maybe by limiting your freedom for the day, you'll learn to appreciate the animals you share space with. Now, let's go. March."

Aidan stared at the bizarre exchange. But when Mia took off down the path with Hei Hei following sullenly, his mind was officially blown.

Damn. That was some chicken.

Chloe knelt in front of Owen. "Are you okay?"

He got up, brushing himself off, and nodded. "Yeah. Sorry, he never liked me."

"He has issues with men," Chloe said seriously. "Harper said it took a long time for him to feel safe because of how he was hurt, but he'd never truly harm you. He just likes the power of being in charge since he was helpless for so many years."

Owen stared at her with undisguised hero worship. "Wow. You're really amazing with animals. I never thought of stuff like that before. You must be supersmart."

"Not really. I have to study hard to get good grades, but I want to practice animal law one day," she said.

"That's a great field. Maybe you can teach me more about the animals on the farm. You know, so I'm not as afraid."

"Sure."

Aidan shared a look with Ethan. They both shook their heads at the problem blossoming before them.

Ethan cleared his throat. "Hey, Chloe, why don't you come with me to the inn and say hello to Ophelia? Owen, I need you back in the stables. Can you clean out the stall for Chloe's Pride so she can be ridden later?"

Owen's face fell. "Well, I kind of wanted to—"

"Oh, that's my horse," Chloe said, beaming. "She's a sweet little mare, isn't she? I really appreciate it."

Owen did a quick pivot, nodding with crazed enthusiasm. "Of course! Chloe's Pride is my favorite in the whole barn. I got it covered, boss."

Boss?

Ethan and Chloe took off, and Owen disappeared back into the stables. Elmo had taken in the whole scene without a word, and he kept his silence, trudging off with Phoenix, leaving them alone.

"That was kind of stupid," Aidan said.

Harper spun around and treated him to a level glare. "Excuse me?"

He squared his shoulders. "Jumping in the middle of two charging animals? Not. Smart."

Her gaze narrowed. "It was a chicken I know very well and a horse I was able to grab in time. It wasn't like I was in Spain with dueling bulls."

"You could have gotten hurt."

She studied his face for a while, then seemed to relax. "But I didn't. I can handle myself."

It happened so fast, he had no time to rein in his reaction. His hand shot out and gripped her upper arm. He felt the sleek flex of feminine muscle beneath him. "Not saying you can't. But I'm not going to apologize for not wanting you to get hurt." His grip gentled, his thumb brushing her soft skin. "Especially on my watch."

Her pupils dilated, and for endless moments, they stared at one another, locked in their own intimate world.

He liked the surprise on her face almost as much as the fleeting flicker of longing. She wasn't used to people giving a crap about her, other than family. She was a lone wolf, used to doing everything on her own without apology. Aidan didn't want to change that. But the primitive part of him needed her to know he was with her every step of the way, and damned if anything or anybody was going to hurt her. The protective instinct was new for him, but now that he'd felt it, he couldn't pretend the urge wasn't there.

Just another crazy element he experienced with the woman.

He waited for her to jerk away and snap at him for being overbearing. Instead, a smile touched her lips and she softened under his touch. "Getting all alpha on me, Irish?" she asked. "Too many males challenging each other for their turf?"

He grinned back, opening his fist so he could stroke her entire arm with his palm. God, her skin was like velvet. He could only imagine what she'd look like naked, sprawled out in her bed. His body shuddered at the thought. "Maybe." He paused, diving deep into those jeweled green eyes. "Or maybe I'm trying to put my own claim in."

She jerked, strangled out a breath, and stepped away. Yeah, she wasn't ready to hear that. He couldn't blame her. He'd just broken the strict rules she'd set up between them. Especially since he was now staying at her house.

Cursing under his breath, he rubbed his face with his hands. "Sorry. I was outta line. I'll meet you back here in an hour."

He turned and left her, refusing to look back.

Chapter Ten

Two weeks later, Harper stared out at man and horse and wondered why she still couldn't stop thinking about his strange declaration.

Maybe I'm trying to put my own claim in.

She'd spotted the regret carved on his face as soon as the words left his lips. His quick apology and even quicker retreat should have made her happy. Yet she kept going over the exchange, wondering what he would've done if she'd questioned him. Stepped closer. Whispered his name.

It was good she'd managed to stay in control.

After all, she was known for her levelheaded actions. Ophelia had been known for her temper when she was young, but age and Kyle had mellowed her. Harper had always been more like her brother. Able to shut down her emotions when threatened. The talent had gotten Ethan all the way into special ops. Her? Well, she was able to run a profitable horse rescue without falling apart each time she failed an animal. She was trained to shove down all those messy emotions and lock them away. It was the only way to not just survive but also thrive.

Lately, though, she'd been wondering if all that practice had put her soul into a deep freeze with little chance of thaw.

She pushed her sunglasses up her nose and hooked a leg over the lower fence post. The dogs were lined up, as if sensing a show, faces framed with longing as they watched Phoenix warm up in the field.

The horse was breaking better from the gate and had settled into a good pattern. After early morning workouts, he munched out and relaxed, then lounged in the sun by his favorite tree, running off any animal visitors. He now recognized the vet, who he had tried to chase away several times, but Aidan insisted on regular checkup visits, citing too many instances of early injuries from pushing a young horse too hard. Harper knew many critics believed racing equaled cruelty. But her heart told her Phoenix was born to run, and it was her job to keep him safe, healthy, and happy while pursuing a racing career.

It was funny how they had formed a quirky type of family revolving around daily routines. Afternoons were for gate practice and social interaction. Aidan had settled into his own routine at her house. Breakfast was quick and punctuated with the day's schedule, which blurred by in a steady cycle focused on Phoenix and regular barn work. Dinner was takeout, usually from the Market in town, maybe a shared beer and summary of the day, and then he headed to bed with a polite "good night" and an averted gaze.

He was a perfect roommate, careful about respecting her space. Since his slipup, he'd made no move to touch her. If they got too close and that intense energy roared up between them, he made an excuse to leave the room.

Things were perfect.

Things suck.

Harper sighed and tried to settle her uneasy thoughts. Why was she acting like such a girl? She hated when words contradicted action. Aidan wasn't playing any bullshit games. He wasn't trying to get her into bed for an extra added bonus. It should make her happy.

The voice slyly peeked out and rose up within. *What would it be like to be the woman he wanted? To be claimed by his rough hands and warm lips and demanding voice?*

Heaven and hell.

Orgasms and regret.

It'd be worth it.

She shook her head hard to rattle the voice and headed to the barn to get Maximus ready for the upcoming ride. The two horses tolerated each other's presence enough to test on the track. Aidan warned they needed to gauge how Phoenix dealt with competition in order to figure out the next steps to training. With his first race fast approaching, today would be the first time Aidan tried to pit Phoenix against a competitor. He had run with Flower a few times at an easy pace and didn't seem threatened by her presence. They all figured it was time to step up the experience so there were no surprises at Saratoga.

She tacked him up, seated herself in the saddle, and rode out, forcing her mind back into work mode. Elmo was ready, and Phoenix danced around in a spirited fashion, always happy when he got to run.

Aidan greeted Maximus with his usual warmth and raised his gaze. "You ready?"

She nodded. "Do you want me to let him set the pace or hold him back?"

"This is a practice, so just let him go. I'll be watching how Phoenix handles it, and we'll tweak later." A slight frown creased his brow. "Be careful."

Warmth flowed through her. She ignored it. "Always."

Aidan walked both horses around, loaded Phoenix in the gate first, then Maximus. Both horses eased in without a fight. Harper mentally counted it out, and then the buzzer screeched. She broke out in one clean jump, guiding Maximus to the right to give Phoenix a bit of space.

Clumps of dirt flew up over scrambling hooves, and she leaned forward, urging him with her squeezed legs as Maximus settled into his pace. Harper concentrated on her mount, glancing only once toward Phoenix in order to ground herself. The turn rose up, and she urged Maximus faster, sensing Elmo was ready to push Phoenix harder. The wind hit her face, and her body screamed with elation over the sleek, moving muscles flying over the track. At the next turn, she opened the horse up and hung on, letting Maximus run full speed, tightly focused.

Phoenix whirled past in a dizzying black cloud. And kept going. And going.

By the time Maximus crossed the finish line, Phoenix was already happily trotting, as if imagining a crown of roses around his neck.

Elmo turned. "We win."

Harper laughed, adrenaline pumping in a mad rush through her bloodstream. "Hell yes, you won. I didn't even see you coming."

Aidan walked over. Excitement etched the carved lines of his face. "That was incredible time. Seems he has no problem with a bit of competition. I think we're right on track to enter the August third race at Saratoga. He'll be matched with a bunch of juveniles who are all testing their limits."

"You think he'll travel okay?" she asked.

"I don't know," he said truthfully. "But we'll find out. I'll keep working with his limits to get him in the proper headspace." He gave each horse equal praise and motioned to Elmo. "How much did you have to hold him back?"

"Enough. He's a pacesetter. With more horses? Maybe a stalker. Didn't have to push when I asked for more. Won't like being boxed in."

Aidan nodded. "Yeah, and if we have too many battling at the front, he may get confused. Gonna have to see how he feels about the rail, too. We'll have to work with some different scenarios. Can you hot walk them for me? I need to talk to Harper."

Elmo led the two horses back to the barn, where iced oatmeal cookies waited as a reward.

She tilted her head. "What's up?"

"I'd like to run another practice with more competitors. You have any other horses we can match up with Phoenix?"

She ticked through the horses and their abilities. "Not to match him. He's way too fast."

"That's okay, I'm more concerned with quantity now. Your whole family can play jockey, right?"

"Sure, I just need to let them know when."

"Good. I've got to run out and get some supplies. Meet you back here in a few hours."

"Need any help?"

He hesitated. She recognized the sudden hungry gleam in his eye when he looked at her, but it was shut down so quickly, she might have imagined it. "No. I'm good."

She refused to acknowledge the disappointment. "Okay. See ya later."

"See ya."

She didn't look back and watch him walk away. It was too pathetic.

It was better this way, of course. Less to lose. He had proven to be a man of his word and did everything she'd asked.

Yeah, life was just great.

Aidan bumped along the narrow, twisty roads and tried to keep his mind off Harper.

He'd been good. Two weeks had passed without an issue, and he'd kept himself under control. No moony eyes or casual touches. No conjuring up new ways to make her laugh. He'd stuck to business and kept his distance and his promise. Ophelia had told him a room would be opening up soon at the inn, so he could eventually move back.

The problem?

He didn't want to leave Harper. He'd gotten used to seeing her face first thing in the morning and last at night. He'd grown attached to her animals and her crazy Herculean coffee. He liked being able to talk about racing and all the details of his training plan with someone as passionate as himself. He'd spent his whole life roaming the world, happy with his own company and freedom, only to succumb to a sweet summer crush on his boss.

He groaned and focused on the road before him. So stupid. They were both walking a tightrope, and if they weren't careful, one of them was going to crash. He just had to keep reminding himself the goal was too damn important. Phoenix had to win. His future depended on it.

He knew leaving Ireland had been a risky move. Walking away from a champion horse in his prime stirred up questions and doubts regarding his ability as a trainer. He knew gossip and rumors had ignited, and his ex-partner had exploited his departure. Shame burned at the idea his once-spotless reputation was now tarnished, along with a simmering frustration and need to prove his worth. If he could get Phoenix to the Triple Crown, everyone back home would realize Aidan was still a winner. His decision to train in the States would look like a brilliant move rather than a failed retreat. And he'd finally have something he'd itched for since that fateful day in the barn when his best friend betrayed him.

Justice.

Thoughts whirling, he tamped down on the surge of emotion and refocused. No need to travel down memory lane. He had one job to do now, and he'd focus all his energy on it.

He completed his various errands at the feed store and neighboring farm, then parked to head into the Market. It'd become one of his favorite places in town, offering fresh, home-cooked food for people who didn't cook.

Perfect for him and Harper.

Fighting a grin, he perused the prepared-food aisle, trying to decide between the lemon chicken and fresh cod, when someone tapped him on the shoulder.

"Aidan! Where have you been? I specifically told Jeff to make those magic bars you love, but they sold out too fast. Next time, I'll put some aside. How's Harper? How's Phoenix?"

He grinned. Fran owned the Market and had immediately introduced herself the moment he stepped into her place. He was used to Kildare, where everyone knew everyone else, so he didn't take offense at her probing questions and general gossip.

She had tightly permed dark hair, brown eyes, and a smile that was always genuine. Her regular outfit of jeans, a short-sleeved button-down white shirt, and sneakers was casual, but the big name badge declaring **MANAGER** pegged her as the one who personally greeted her guests, learned their food preferences, and made sure to deliver.

"Sorry, it got busy and Ophelia cooked, so I didn't need to come yesterday. We're all good and working hard." He shot her a sheepish look. "But I need dinner for tonight. How's the cod?"

"So fresh it may wriggle out of the bag."

"That sounds scary good. I'll take two fillets. Can you put that lemon-pepper sauce on it? It's Harper's favorite."

"Of course. I'd recommend the sweet potatoes with it, and the peas."

"Harper hates peas. How about the asparagus?"

Fran smiled, but it seemed smug and full of interest. "Perfect. How nice you know exactly what Harper likes. Does she come over to the inn with you to eat?"

"Oh, no, I'm staying at her house for a bit while I wait for an extra room to open up."

The moment the words popped out, he knew he'd made a terrible mistake. Those dark eyes lit with a mad glee that warned him the entire town would be gossiping about their relationship within the hour.

Crap. Harper was going to kill him.

"How wonderful!" Fran crowed, patting his arm like he'd done something truly magical. "You have no idea how happy this makes me! Harper has always been such a loner. So passionate about her animals and causes—the whole town admires her—but we've been worried. You're a perfect match!"

He refused to blush. Real men did not succumb to such weakness. "Umm, actually, we're not involved in a relationship. It's strictly for the benefit of Phoenix so I don't have to stay at the Hampton. I need access to the barn twenty-four hours a day."

Her smile got more zealous. "Oh, don't worry, I'll keep your secret," she practically whispered. "I'm just so happy! I won't tell a soul. This town is so gossipy, it's ridiculous. Why would anyone want to stick their nose into someone else's business?"

Aidan smothered a groan. "I appreciate that. Maybe you can throw some of those lemon tarts in for dessert, too?"

"Yes, let me get you all settled. Be back in a few."

The moment she disappeared, a deep, commanding voice rang out in the small market. "Aidan O'Connor? The one training Phoenix for the Triple Crown?"

He turned and faced an older gentleman with distinguished white hair and thick, black-framed glasses, dressed in a crisp suit, a tie, and a red carnation in his lapel. Even in the scorching summer heat, he looked fresh and pressed, as if going into the office, but he looked easily in his late seventies. "Yes. Sorry, have we met?"

The gentleman reached out his hand. "Judge Bennett. Seems you're working with my grandson, Owen."

Aidan shook the man's hand, admiring his firm grip. "Pleasure to meet you, sir."

"Pleasure's all mine. How is Owen doing, paying for his crimes?"

Aidan caught the glint of amusement in the man's gaze and realized, though he was being firm with his grandson, the judge also understood a young male's tendency to get into trouble. "He's doing well. Learning the workings of the farm."

"Has he managed to put down that accessory that's tattooed to his body?"

His lips quirked. "The phone? Well, we're working on that."

"Good. He's a bit of a whiner, and a pinch of lazy, but his heart is kind. I figured the Bishop farm has helped a lot of kids in the past, and my grandson could use some character. I heard about the monstrous chicken, though." A gray brow arched. "That creature won't really hurt him, right?"

Aidan laughed. "Nope, but he's good for a little intimidation now and then. I promise we're all looking out for Owen. Teaching him how to ride. Honestly, he's doing better."

Judge Bennett's face relaxed. "Thank you. So when I heard you're training a local horse for the Derby, I looked you up. Have a few solid wins behind you. Surprised you left Ireland." The narrowed gaze told him he'd switched to a bit of suspicion.

Aidan knew it was best to deal with the retired judge by keeping it simple and honest. "Won a few. Lost some others. Been wanting to find a horse in the States, so I took some time to explore various tracks. The moment I laid eyes on Phoenix, I knew I wanted to train him. He has something special."

"I'm glad. Harper has always been the one rescuing damaged souls. It will be nice to see one of hers be successful at the racetrack. Together, you must make quite a team."

And then, it happened.

Fran popped her permed head in the middle of them and hijacked the conversation. "Isn't it wonderful that they both fell for each other while training a horse?" She sighed deeply and offered Aidan the large bag of carryout. "So romantic."

Ah, shit.

Suddenly, the judge cut him a sharp glance. "You're with Harper?"

"No, we're just—"

"They're living together!" Fran announced. "Finally, Harper found someone who has the same interests. I'm so happy! I put some extra lemon tarts in there. Enjoy! Good to see you, Judge Bennett."

She floated away on a cloud of romance and left Aidan holding the bag.

Literally.

"Dinner for both of you?" Judge Bennett asked dryly, motioning to the bag.

"Yep, well, to eat in the barn. By Phoenix. With other people." Was he sweating? "I better get going. It was nice to meet you."

He left the Market, feeling various stares digging into him, and knew he'd be hearing about this later.

♥ ♥ ♥

Harper glanced down at the text her sister had just sent and caught her breath.

No. Way.

After a fabulous dinner, Aidan insisted on doing the dishes, so she'd gone to her room to change into sweats. Her body was sore from a long day, and she looked forward to kicking back on the sofa.

The message came at her in screaming caps: TOWN THINKS YOU'RE HAVING AN AFFAIR WITH AIDAN AND SHACKING UP.

Harper fumbled with her phone to shoot back a response. R u kidding me? Where did you hear this?

Bea from the diner heard it from Tony at the tattoo place who heard it from Fran.

. . .

R u?

Ugh, thank God she only had to face her phone screen. She tapped the two letters harder than necessary to make her point: NO.

K. :)

She dropped the phone on her bed and groaned. This was so humiliating. She hated the thought of the town gossiping about her and Aidan, but she probably should've known better.

Tugging her hair back into a ponytail, she changed into her extra-baggy gray sweats and a black tank. Best to try and ignore the buzz. Aidan would move back to the inn soon, and she'd squash the rumors when she went into town. Her plan firmly in mind, she headed back into the living room.

A prickle of pleasure shot through her. The small amount of dirty dishes was clean and dried. The table was clear. He'd gotten her a glass of ice water with lemon and placed it on the coffee table next to the shot of whiskey he liked to drink at night. He sat on the sofa with Baloo and Bagheera flanking him and Figaro curled around his head like a cobra. The ease and comfort he had with her animals warmed her blood. His large body dwarfed the room and ate up all the air and space, causing a shot of sensual awareness to shiver down her spine.

Aidan flicked on the television. "Hey. *The Curse of Oak Island* is on tonight. Wanna watch?"

Harper hated the slight resentment that ignited. Where were all the heated stares? The crackling sexual tension? The hungry flare in his amber eyes?

Right now, he looked at her like a beer buddy watching a football game.

She cleared her throat, mentally scolded herself, and sat down on the opposite side of Baloo. "Thought you said that series was stupid. Tried to convince me there was no curse."

He shot her a sheepish grin. "I think I was wrong. These guys are starting to convince me it's real. Plus, I love that you don't watch those high-drama reality shows or Animal Planet."

She wrinkled her nose and settled against Baloo's furry warmth. "I don't have the stamina for Animal Planet or any sad stories. Once, I caught one and almost jumped on a plane to save a beagle named Bagel in Arizona. Ophelia and Ethan had to stage an intervention, and now I'm on a restricted television diet."

He laughed. "Smart. Now, if I can only get you to upgrade to a bigger screen."

She arched a brow. "It's a thirty-two inch."

"Which is a crime. You need a fifty-two for this room."

"Bigger isn't always better, Irish."

"Oh yes, it is, love." A spark of mischief and the edge of something raw flickered from his gaze. "Whoever told you that didn't know what he was talking about."

"Actually, it was Ophelia." Her lips twitched. "Kyle was complaining about the small size of the meat she'd bought. She reminded him it was quality, not quantity."

He shook his head. "Kyle and his meat. Always obsessing."

Their gazes met and they burst into laughter. The dogs looked up to see what they were missing, then flopped their heads back down. Figaro gave a pissed-off hiss and curled herself tighter around Aidan's neck.

She loved that he didn't shake the cat off or complain.

She loved that he settled back and watched the show she'd gotten him hooked on and didn't find the need to chat endlessly during the episode.

She loved how he handed her the water every time he took a sip of whiskey because she couldn't reach the table without bothering Baloo.

The show ended. They discussed the pros and cons of the new discovery, and when he went to turn the TV off, the channel clicked and John Wayne filled the screen. They both gasped in pleasure.

"*The Quiet Man*," she breathed. "God, I love this movie."

"A classic. Damn, it's late. Should we do it?"

She nibbled on her lip. "What if we let ourselves sleep till five thirty? Just this once?"

He grinned. "Done. It's halfway through, anyway."

"We didn't miss my favorite part!" she practically squealed.

"The part where he pushes her against the door and kisses her, right? Women love that part."

A sigh escaped her. "Maureen O'Hara was so beautiful. She had Ophelia's hair."

"John Wayne was a complete badass. Always wanted to be him."

She leaned toward the right and he leaned toward the left. With Baloo snugly between them, their heads rested a few inches apart on the sofa. The lash of his body heat and smell of man and whiskey filled the air. The old-fashioned movie delivered all the story points she demanded, along with a burning romance with a man a woman could believe in. As the movie unfolded, Harper fought back the sudden urge to reach her hand over to touch him.

But that would be against the rules.

During the famous kiss scene, her body revved to life until the seeping sexual tension filled the entire room, and their harsh breathing mixed together. Neither of them glanced at the other. Neither of them was ready to cross the invisible line.

When the credits rolled, they were silent for a long time. "That's what I call a perfect movie," she finally declared.

"Agreed. Looks like they're having a John Wayne marathon this week. Maybe we can watch *True Grit* tomorrow."

"Yes." The thought of having a tomorrow together made her happy, but then she remembered that soon he'd return to the inn. "Guess it's time for bed." She went to get up.

"Harper?"

She stopped. "Yeah?"

"Something happened today. I think I screwed up."

She frowned. "What is it?"

"I was talking to Fran while I was ordering our food, and of course, she was shooting off a ton of questions. I ended up letting it slip that I was staying with you."

Her mouth dropped open. "That was you! Ophelia texted me and said it's buzzing in town that we're having an affair."

He groaned and shifted on the couch. "I'm sorry, love. I wasn't even thinking when I said it, and when I tried to explain, she didn't want to hear it."

"Sounds like Fran. At least now I know where the rumor started."

"You pissed?"

She sighed and shook her head. "No, this stuff comes with the territory. I'm just not used to it. I'm sure the talk will die down once someone else does something around here."

Aidan winced. "Judge Bennett was there, too."

"Ah, crap. That means Owen may be watching us more closely."

"Doubt the judge will tell his grandson." He peered into her face, studying her with those heated golden eyes. "Can I ask you a question?"

"Sure. We're an item, remember?"

This time, he didn't smile. His features set into a carved mask. "Are you embarrassed because of the gossip? Or is it because you wouldn't want your name to be associated with me?"

She blinked. "That's a strange question. Are you asking me if I'd be ashamed to be involved in an affair with you?"

His jaw clenched. She ached to reach out and touch him. Ached to see if his stubble felt rough against her fingertips or if his lips were as soft as she imagined. "Yeah. I guess that's what I'm asking." He paused, as if suddenly uncomfortable. "But you don't have to answer. It has nothing to do with our business relationship." The reminder stung, even more so because he began to shut down again, turning away from her.

She didn't want him to disappear into his own room and his own bed and leave her aching another night for something she didn't even understand. "Aidan?" His name fell from her lips.

He turned back, and she noticed his muscles tense and bunch. "Yeah?"

"A woman would be crazy not to be proud to call you hers."

The space between them heated, constricted, sizzled. Her breath caught in her chest, and time stilled and stretched, ready for one of them to make a move that would change everything. Sexual frustration and hunger gleamed in his eyes. He muttered in Irish and ripped his gaze away, his fingers clenching in Bagheera's fur, as if fighting for resolve.

His voice rumbled like silken gravel. "Thank you, love."

He got up from the sofa. Patted and said good night to the dogs. Took the cups back to the kitchen and then stood in the doorway of his room.

"Five thirty a.m.?" she asked.

"Yes. We'll pair him with a few other horses tomorrow. See how he does."

"Good."

"Good night, Harper."

"Good night, Aidan."

Figaro lifted her head, staring at both of them with half-slit eyes. Then she jumped gracefully from the sofa and stalked into Aidan's room.

Shocked, Harper stared at the cat's tail swooshing and watched her jump up on the bed. "Does she sleep with you?" she asked.

"Sometimes. I leave the door cracked, but she doesn't bother me." He gave her one long, hard stare. "I like the comfort. The night can be lonely."

With his words hanging in the air, he stepped back and disappeared into the room.

She sat for a while, thinking about what he'd said. Yes, animals helped when the night was long. But in that moment, she ached to be the one next to him, soothing his loneliness, wrapped in his arms.

When she stood up, she noticed her hands trembled. "Let's go, babies," she said.

The dogs jumped down and followed her into her own bed.

It was hours before she was finally able to fall asleep.

Chapter Eleven

Aidan finished settling Phoenix in his stall when he overheard Harper talking on the phone, her voice filled with worry. She clicked off, chewing on her lip in the trademark stressed-out gesture he now knew well.

"What's the matter?" he called out.

She swiveled her head, those lovely brows creased in a frown. "Sara just called. She's got a problem with a baby goat that was dropped off anonymously and never picked up."

He shook his head. "Vets get injured animals all the time. Sons of bitches out there seem to think they're a dump place that can solve all problems."

"Yeah, Sara has no room. She knew we were full, so she called some other rescue shelters but no one can help. She asked if I'd head over to take a look, but I have a prospective buyer coming to check out Bruce."

He locked up the stall, ignoring Phoenix's glare when he handed him a carrot instead of a cookie. "I can go for you."

"Oh, that'd be great. Can you assess the amount of care needed and let me know? I'd like to help if I can, but don't want to miss this appointment."

"Sure. While I'm out, I'll swing by and get the new delivery of hay, also."

Her face relaxed, and Aidan felt a rush of satisfaction. He liked helping her on the farm, even if it had nothing to do with Phoenix.

He'd become slowly invested in all the animals here, watching them thrive under Harper's care.

"Thanks, Irish." She looked like she was going to say more, but then her mouth snapped shut and she headed off, her loose-legged stride graceful and determined.

He watched her go and wondered what words she'd smothered.

Not that it made any difference.

Cursing under his breath, he got into the truck and drove into town. Each night he spent in her house made the hunger in his gut claw a bit deeper. Watching *The Quiet Man* in her company had been better than any date in a fancy pub, and those worn sweats had looked hotter than any expensive dress. Who would've thought he'd enjoy her company so much, camped in front of the TV with her animals surrounding them? Or that the scent of cocoa butter made him sweat? Or the glimpse of a hot-pink bra strap had the power to make him practically weep with the need to peek under her shirt?

Keeping it strictly business between them was getting harder.

His mind chewed on the problem as he parked in the vet's lot and went inside. He told the young brunette at the front desk he was here to talk with Dr. Beadle on behalf of Harper. She quickly settled him into a room painted sunny yellow and promised the doctor would be there shortly.

Aidan studied the cheery art posters of various animals with messages like DON'T FORGET TO BRUSH!, YOGA FOR YOUR DOG!, and GET YOUR FURRY FRIEND TICK-FREE! The aura was comforting, and the room held a large exam table, chair, and matching kids' seats with jars marked KIDS' TREATS and DOG TREATS. He smiled, liking the inclusion of the entire family in a vet appointment. He'd always believed kids should know all the steps required to take care of an animal.

The back door swung open, and Dr. Beadle emerged with her crisp white coat, pinned-up bun, and serious brown eyes peeking from behind black-rimmed glasses.

"Hello," said Aidan. "Harper sent me to check on the goat. She had a horse appointment she couldn't break."

"Good for her. It's getting harder these days to place the amount of animals coming in," she said with a sigh, sliding onto the chair by the large counter. She flipped open a pad and glanced at her notes. "This is a long shot even asking her to consider, but I know she'd want me to reach out. We received a drop-off of a baby goat. He suffers from severe malnutrition, dehydration, and several lacerations. One ear was halfway ripped off. He was unconscious but just recently woke up. We think he was dumped off a main road and had been wandering for several days. It's a miracle he's still alive."

Aidan gritted his teeth and pushed past the flare of anger toward the assholes who believed animals were garbage.

"He needs twenty-four-hour care. I can't find anyone in the area to take him in, and we're full. Even the staff is overbooked. Oftentimes if we have no space, we'll take them home, but everyone is at full capacity. I don't have much choice with this one unless I can place him today."

Nausea twisted his belly. He hated the idea of putting an animal down. "Can you tell me about the care involved?"

"He's in shock, so besides feeding him water with a dropper and slowly increasing his food, he'll need to be watched round the clock. He hasn't spoken, so he may be mute. He's half-blind. He needs rest for the next few days and then to slowly be introduced back into farm life. It's a lot to take on, and I know Harper has her hands full with training Phoenix."

He rubbed his head and groaned. There was no way they had the time to give around-the-clock care for a baby goat. Their schedule was already packed, and this was an abused animal that they couldn't just drop in a stall. If the goat didn't heal, they'd be faced with a difficult decision and endless guilt. Still, he didn't want to make a decision without talking to Harper first. "Let me call Harper and give her the details."

"Of course."

He called her and let it ring, but she didn't answer. After a few more tries, he shot her a text message and waited. "I'm sure she'll get back to me soon," he said. "What do you think about the situation? Does he have a chance?"

He caught a flicker of anguish in the vet's dark eyes, but it was quickly extinguished. God knew how many times she'd been forced to make decisions she dreaded. He knew most rescues were overburdened, underfinanced, and depended on people who also struggled to fund all their favorite charities. "They all have a chance," she said firmly. "But this one's a definite long shot. Do you want to meet him first before making a decision?"

Ah, crap. Meeting a broken animal took something from his soul, but the goat deserved to be seen. "Yes."

"Be right back."

While he waited, he tried Harper a few more times, then texted Ethan in case he was close. He still had no response by the time the vet walked back, carefully cuddling the small animal.

The goat was a muddled black and white, with tiny horns, wide-set closed eyes, and one ragged, bloody ear. Aidan stared down at the still animal while his gut churned.

Could they really take on a half-blind goat who needed constant supervision? What if the goat was suffering? Was it fair for him to try and save his life only for the goat to be alone and terrified of strangers? From the looks of him, he'd had a tough past. Aidan knew how difficult that was to overcome in the best circumstances.

Suddenly, the goat's eyes flew open.

Aidan stilled, holding his breath so he wouldn't freak the goat out even more. One amazing powder-blue eye with a long black slit stared back at him; the left eye socket was closed over and useless. The goat remained perfectly quiet, as if sensing his fate was about to be played out in this small examination room, under Aidan's assessing stare.

Slowly, Aidan neared. He spoke in soothing tones, stroking the small animal, feeling its sharp ribs and rough coat. The goat never flinched, an air of despair and surrender in its very aura that told Aidan he'd already given up.

Maybe this one wasn't a fighter like Phoenix.

Maybe this one was just too far gone to be brought back.

Then again, didn't he deserve a damn shot? Disabled did not mean disposable. Every single person had been roughed up at one time or another and got the opportunity to try again. Why should this goat not get his second chance?

"I understand it's a tough decision. I can wait till after you talk to Harper." A small smile played on the vet's lips. "I heard you're living together now. I'm so happy for you both."

Aidan opened his mouth to explain, then shut it. Stared at the goat. And made the only decision he could. "I'll take him. Just let me know everything I need to do."

She beamed and launched into a detailed description, promising to write everything down with some antibiotics, medicine droppers, and a few other pieces of equipment to help.

Guess he had a new goat.

♥ ♥ ♥

Harper finished up with Anabelle, who was now the proud owner of Bruce, a retired carriage horse. The horse had been in bad shape when he came to the farm, but he was one of the sweetest, most well-adjusted geldings in the barn. She'd miss him, but the Palmer farm was a perfect place for him to live out the rest of his retirement. Harper loved each of her horses so much, but seeing them go to a permanent home was always the true goal.

She guzzled down some water, and Chloe walked into the barn. "Hey, Harper, can I take Owen for a quick ride?"

The girl had become an excellent rider, but Owen was so nervous, Harper was a bit hesitant. "Aidan only took him out twice. I don't know if he's ready for a solo yet."

Owen came around the corner. "I'll be real careful and listen to what Chloe tells me," he said in a rush, face carved out in longing.

Harper bit her lip to keep from laughing at the overeager expression on the teen's face. Damn, he had a bad crush. And it looked like Chloe didn't have a clue.

"What if you get spooked?"

He shook his head and puffed out his chest. "Chloe's been helping me a lot, and I'm not afraid anymore. I can take Flower. She's real gentle."

Chloe smiled at him like he was a kid brother. "We won't go on the trail. I'll take him to the pasture and just do a simple walk. Chloe's Pride needs some exercise today."

Harper nodded. "Okay. Wear your helmet, and listen to everything Chloe says."

"I will, thanks!"

"Welcome." She headed toward the barn, suddenly remembering her damn phone. Cursing, she ran to her desk, where she'd forgotten it, and glanced at the screen.

Two missed calls from Aidan. One text:

Call me ASAP. Need to make decision on goat.

Nerves jangling, she responded quickly, waiting for the three dots of response.

Nothing.

She was just about to call Sara directly when the truck pulled into the driveway. Aidan climbed out, his hair mussed, his features settled into a hard, distant shell that made her pause in sudden dread. Her heart ramped up, and a bad feeling began to creep over her. "What happened? I'm so sorry, I forgot my phone when I was with Anabelle."

"Did she take Bruce?"

"Yeah."

His smile held a grim edge that made her heart beat even faster. "Good. At least something decent came out of today."

"Aidan, tell me about the goat."

He rubbed his head and leaned against the faded black truck. "The poor thing was in rough shape. Starvation, dehydration, half-blind with half an ear. Probably dumped off the road and wandering for days. Broke my damn heart."

She cursed. So many to save. Too many lost due to simple cruelty. Hei Hei had been dumped to wander around, his lavish head feathers almost frozen from the cold, and she'd practically had to steal a bunch of runt piglets from a monster who called himself a farmer. Many she managed to place. Many she didn't, but at least she offered them stable, happy lives here. "I wish they knew how it felt to be dumped to die. What was his prognosis?"

Aidan looked uncomfortable. "Not good. Sara said he'd need round-the-clock care, and even then, she's not sure he'll be able to be back on a farm with his disability. She thinks he may be mute from the shock, and he may not recover his voice. He's still fighting infection and needs a cocktail of meds. He's a mess, love." He paused.

It was the sad gleam in his eyes that froze her insides. As if he were getting ready to tell her something she didn't want to hear.

"To be honest, I thought it may be best to let him go—"

"Oh my God." She placed a hand over her mouth. The rage hit out of nowhere. Her body shook with pent-up emotion and frustration. Aidan had chosen the easy way, like so many others. Saving a goat who might not even survive would be too hard. Too expensive. Too messy. Much easier to put a broken animal to sleep and pretend it was for the best. After all, his only focus was on Phoenix and winning. He wouldn't want her distracted by playing nursemaid and keeping them from his real goal.

Fuck that.

"You killed him," she whispered furiously, fingers clenching into fists. She took a few steps forward and got in his face, unable to contain herself. "You didn't want any complications, but I would have taken him! Even if the odds were against him, I would've tried, but—" She broke off, and her heart shattered a bit at the cold lines of his face. "You just didn't care. Did you tell her to do it right away? Do I still have time to save him?"

"Harper—"

"I should have known you're like all the others. The only value you can see is money. I bet if something happened to Phoenix and he wasn't able to race, you'd be out of here so fast the door would slam you in the ass."

"Stop." His voice had gone dangerously low. The coldness was still there, along with a banked anger simmering like soup on a stovetop, ready to explode. "I'm trying not to lose my shit, but if you say one more word, you won't like the consequences."

She gasped. A red mist settled over her vision, and her heart hurt, so she fell back to some nasty habits she still hadn't been able to completely break.

She hurt back.

"I hope you see that goat's face in your dreams," she hissed. "I hope you wonder if he could have lived a happy life here on the farm with Hei Hei and the others. I hope you realize you were lazy and cruel and took the easy road out. Because that's what you know best, right, Irish? Who cares if you leave nothing behind? I bet you've never had a real connection with anyone, have you?"

In seconds, he'd lifted her completely off the ground, spun her around, and pressed her back against the truck. He leaned in, stealing her space, trapping her against his hard chest and the vehicle. His hands grasped her upper arms and his face settled inches from hers. She caught the rough scrape of stubble hugging his jaw; the defined, lush curve to his bottom lip; the hot fury in his cognac eyes; the stain of sunburn over his nose and cheeks.

"Don't you *ever* assume shit about me. You should be grateful I'm giving you a pass on this juvenile tantrum because I know you're torn up inside." His breath struck her mouth in tiny bursts. "I'll say this once, and you will never question me again. I don't quit because things get hard. I don't toss away people or animals because they're not easy."

"But—"

"I didn't put the damn goat down, Harper. I saved him. He's in the truck, sleeping under a blanket. I have no idea what we're going to do with him or if he'll be able to adjust to the farm with his disability, but there was no fucking way I was giving up without a fair fight. Do you really think so little of me after the time we've spent together? Do you really think I'd give up on anything or anyone so quickly?"

Her head spun like a careening Tilt-A-Whirl, and she automatically reached out to hold on to him, her brain trying to register his words that changed everything.

He had saved the goat.

"Now, I'm going to clear my head. You're going to figure out a plan. The care instructions and meds are in the glove compartment. Not sure if he'll be okay with the dogs, but if I have to, I'll sleep out here in the back barn with him, where it's quiet."

Slowly, his hands dropped. For one heart-stopping moment, he lifted his fingers and pressed them gently over her lips in a whisper-soft caress. For one perfect moment, their gazes locked and their breaths melded.

Then he muttered something in Irish—the same expression he'd used before—and pivoted on his heel in one lightning-speed moment. "His name is Captain Hoof," he said roughly. "I know you're obsessed with Disney names, and the only character I could think of was Captain Hook, so that will just have to do. I'll see you later."

He stomped off. She heard the slam of the trunk. The scent of hay and feed and raw male temper scented the air.

Slowly, she opened the front driver's side door.

The goat lay nestled in a sea of blankets wrapped securely around him. One ragged ear was scabbed over with blood. His eyes were shut and his breathing deep, with tiny little snorts emitting from his mouth. Two stubby horns poked out.

And right then, she knew everything had changed.

Harper just needed to decide what to do about it.

Chapter Twelve

Aidan squared his shoulders and opened the door to Harper's place.

Since their confrontation, he'd stayed away from her. She'd disappeared with the goat, and he'd thrown himself into work with Phoenix, not wanting to think of how close he'd come to kissing her. He figured she'd spent the last few hours stewing and plotting his demise. But damn, had she pissed him off. Assuming he'd put the poor goat down without a thought was a low blow. Even worse?

The shot of pain from her crappy views on him.

The woman was his own personal kryptonite.

The scent of lemon and garlic hit him first, and he briefly wondered if he'd gone into the wrong house. His entry was blocked by a mass of wriggling, happy canines, who attacked him with licking tongues and needy paws. He knelt to give them his attention, enjoying how they made him feel like a king entering his castle. Figaro strolled toward him, her nose in the air with disgust as she watched her companions lose their dignity and roll onto their bellies.

His lips quirked. "Want any of this?" he asked her, opening his palms to offer some petting.

The cat hissed and stalked away. Yep, the feline loved playing hard to get. Just last night, she'd been snuggled up in his bed, purring madly.

He pushed away the thought of another female purring in his arms and kept tight to his anger. He refused to forgive her too easily.

"She likes you."

He looked up. Harper studied him with hooded eyes. She'd changed into a fresh pair of jeans and a black V-neck T-shirt that screamed **Adopt, Don't Shop!** She'd stuffed her hair up in a clip. Her face was bare of makeup, and her feet were naked. The sight of those cherry-red painted toenails made him think she was hiding things. What type of sexy underwear was she hiding under those clothes? He had an instinct a peek would drive him to his knees.

"She runs hot and cold. Sometimes I think she hates me."

She surrendered a smile, and his heart did that ridiculous flip-flop in his chest. "If she hated you, she'd ignore you all the time. That was her personalized way of greeting. She doesn't want to give her trust too easily."

He stilled. Was there a double meaning in her last statement? "Yeah, I'm striking out with all the women in my life lately," he finally muttered.

"Not all."

The soft words hit him straight in the gut. He uncurled himself from the floor and regarded her thoughtfully. "I miss something?"

She shrugged. "Just an apology. I'm sorry I thought the worst of you. I'm sorry I yelled." A short awkward silence fell, and she forced her gaze to meet his. "Sometimes I forget not all people make the wrong decision. I forget some deserve trust."

His anger eased, and he nodded. "I can accept that."

"I made dinner."

"You made what?"

She turned her back and went into the tiny kitchen, where all those smells emanated from. "Dinner. Well, kind of. I went to the Market, and Fran set me up with an entire home-cooked meal. All I had to do was stick it in the oven. I didn't even burn it."

The pride in her voice was so adorable, he made sure not to show his amusement. He followed her into the kitchen and stopped short.

She'd set the table. Oh sure, she'd used paper plates, but they were laid out in a precise way that told him she'd tried. Mismatched silverware lay on perfectly folded paper napkins. Jelly glasses full of water and two open beers flanked the plates, which were filled with lemon chicken and green herbs, tiny roasted potatoes, and crisp, bright green beans. A small loaf of bread wrapped in foil lay open and steaming. Drool gathered in his mouth, but what was even hotter than this amazing meal?

Harper's expression. A bit wary. And a lot expectant, as if waiting for his approval. She shifted her weight back and forth on those long legs and chewed absently at her lower lip. He bet the woman wasn't used to trying to please many people, especially a man. The idea that she had worked so hard to back up a verbal apology told him a lot about her.

Stuff he really, really liked.

He smiled. Surprise flickered over her face, and then she smiled back. "If this is the way you say you're sorry, we're gonna be doing a lot of fighting," he drawled.

She laughed. "Don't get used to it. I truly doubt I'll be wrong again."

That made him laugh, too, as they sat at the small table, with the dogs smashed against their legs and heads tilted up just in case any scraps dropped. The first long sip of cold beer made him groan with pleasure. "Where's the Captain?" he asked, setting the bottle down.

"In my bedroom. I've been giving him some water and food every half hour like Sara instructed, and he woke up a few times and didn't panic. Seemed calm, as if he sensed he was safe. But he hasn't wanted to go out and explore yet. I'd like to try to get him out to potty, but at this point, I don't think his body has much to expel yet."

He nodded, cutting up the chicken and forking up a bite. So. Good. Fran was a master of food. If he and Harper stayed together, there'd be no real reason for either of them to know how to cook. They'd just schedule regular meal pickup from Fran and—

Wait. What was that thought?

No. Hell no. This shack-up was temporary, and he was moving back to the inn tomorrow. Time to get his thoughts back in order. "How are we going to work caring for him tomorrow?"

She took a sip of her own beer. He watched the muscles of her throat flex, and he imagined running his tongue over the sensitive flesh and downward. "I can take a day or two. Ethan and Chloe will pick up the slack on the farm, and I can work on paperwork from home. If he gets stronger, I can bring him to the farm in a few days. It'd be better for him there with the other animals. Goats like companions."

"You got these two goofballs," he said, jerking his thumb. The dogs shook in delight, and he fed them each a chunk of chicken.

"They're quite gentle, and Figaro should leave him alone, but I'd rather he get used to farm life. I've done some studying on the internet about goats and what they need. I can't leave him alone, so at least we can keep watch at work."

"I'll come relieve you in the afternoon, when Phoenix is resting," he said, cutting up his potato. Rosemary and olive oil clung to the skins, making them sheen. A groan of pleasure escaped. "We'll give it a few days and work from there."

"You don't have to," she said softly.

He drilled her with his gaze. "Yeah, I do. I'm just as responsible for his care as you, love. Deal?"

A smile bloomed on her lips. "Deal."

His heart squeezed into a merciless fist. Damn, she was beautiful. Did she realize it? He'd love proving it to her in a variety of ways.

She cut up her chicken in tiny squares and gracefully popped them into her mouth. He enjoyed the way she ate like a lady. He'd been around workers on the farm and admitted most of their manners were rough—including his. He liked how she took care with her meal, pressing the napkin to her lips in regular intervals, as if they were on a date.

He needed a distraction. Fast. "Has Ethan worked the farm his whole life?" he asked, the first question he came up with. But he was curious about the close bond she shared with her brother.

"No, he was a Special Forces paratrooper. He was in Afghanistan when his leg was shot up pretty bad. You probably noticed he walks with a limp."

"Yeah, I noticed. Knew he was military, but I didn't want to ask."

"He left about a year and a half ago and came home. Had PTSD. Took him a while to heal, but being on the farm and meeting Mia helped. He's always been a bit of a horse whisperer."

"Yeah, I noticed that, too."

"He shares a special bond with Phoenix. Got the horse to take a saddle and ride again. Spent nights in the barn, calming his fears. The name he picked symbolized both of them. They've flourished." A tiny sigh escaped her lips. He stared at her, fascinated by the sound that reminded him of faint longing. "Phoenix healed from Ethan. Ethan healed from Mia. Kind of beautiful, isn't it?"

He ached to slide his hand across the table and entwine his fingers with hers. Already the connection between them simmered like a low flame ready to rise. "It is. Your brother is a hell of man." He took another pull of beer. "All of you are. Bet your mom was pretty amazing."

"She was. A hard worker. A fiery temper like Ophelia used to have. A heart so full of love, there was enough for the entire world. Ophelia's husband, Kyle, had a hard time back in the day with his dad. He'd run to the farm and Mom always took him in. He was like another member of our family growing up."

"Was she as passionate about animal rescue as you are?"

He figured it was an easy answer for her, but when she hesitated, he studied her face. A flicker of pain glinted hard and deep in those sea-green eyes. She dropped her head and focused on her plate, as if afraid to show him too much. "Yes. I never knew why, though. Maybe it's just a calling to certain people. I believe God bestows certain gifts.

Ophelia has her singing. Ethan has his bravery. And I'm able to connect with animals."

Something was missing in her answer. She was a puzzle, and this piece was critical in peeling back those layers she kept tight around her. He made his voice sound casual in order not to spook her. "Did this gift start at a young age?"

Her fingers jerked. The fork dropped. He waited, silent, sensing an anguish swirling around her figure. She picked up her beer, but he noticed the slight tremble in her body.

Demons. They all had them. Some were forgotten with enough time. Some came at night. Some stayed buried.

Some lay in wait with a haunting presence, planning the perfect time to spring.

"Let's just say animals saved my life." She looked up, her face rearranged into a well-guarded expression, and the moment slipped by.

Aidan hoped he'd get another shot at the truth, because he sensed it made up the essence of who she truly was. For now, he decided to lighten the mood. "I really enjoyed this apology. But it feels a bit short. Maybe some dessert would allow me to completely forgive you."

She laughed and he drank in the way her face lit up and her lips softened and her eyes glowed like the Caribbean Sea. "I figured you'd insist on the full-course apology. I got bourbon pecan pie."

"You are officially forgiven."

"With vanilla bean ice cream."

"And you get a marker against any future insult," he added.

They laughed together, and he helped clear the dishes while he snuck more scraps to the dogs. She put on a pot of Rwanda Blue Bourbon coffee—one of his favorites now if he didn't choose tea—and they talked business while they feasted on pie.

Night crept in. The plates were scraped clean. The coffee grew cold. Aidan tapped an index finger against the rim of his cup. "Ophelia said I can move back to the inn for the next ten days," he said casually.

The energy shifted, expanded, heated. The dogs trotted away, as if sensing the growing tension, and flopped down near the door.

"Oh." She paused, lifting her gaze. "Do you want to go back to the inn?"

He considered his answer and chose the safe route. "Do you want me to?"

He caught the tightening of her muscles, the uneasy shift of her weight. She popped out of the chair, grabbed the rest of the dishes, and turned away. "Up to you."

"Actually, it's not," he said. His tone was mild, but this had to be her call. Sure, it was convenient to stay here, but for him, it was much more. He craved her presence: the sight of her face, the scent of her hair, the sound of her laugh. He'd miss her. Seeing her at the farm was different from sharing time with her at home. Eating dinner, watching television, shoulders pressed together on the couch while the animals encircled them—it had all become a routine he'd begun to savor. Every moment he seemed to discover another part of her that both fascinated and attracted him. And yeah, that was all sorts of fucked up, since they'd only been together a short time and decided not to cross over the blurred line between personal and business, but he didn't care anymore. "You offered out of sympathy and convenience. Now I'm able to leave, and I want to know how you feel about it."

She blew out an annoyed snort and whirled back around. A frown creased her brow. "It's no big deal for you to stay here," she tossed out. "Your choice."

He tried to back down, but frustration and want twisted inside and made him a bit ugly. Made him want to push. "I'll go. Unless you tell me you'd like me to stay."

Her mouth fell open. "What is it with you and my verbal assurances? You don't need anything from me to make your own decision."

A grim smile played on his lips. "Oh, but I do." Slowly, he unfolded himself from the chair and stood in the tiny kitchen, facing her. "I'm getting tired of ignoring what's going on with us. Pretending we don't want to forget about what's right and what's wrong and rip each other's clothes off. So I'm going to ask again. Do you want me to stay or go?"

Shock filled her eyes, but it was the quick flare of lust he was more interested in.

Aidan cocked his hip, rested his hand on the top of the chair, and waited.

♥ ♥ ♥

Feet rooted to the ground, Harper stared at the man a short distance away and battled back the urge to close the distance, yank his head down, and sink herself into the glory of his kiss.

Vision blurred, she watched him, waiting for him to move. Of course, he didn't. The man made sure every step he made was agreed to. Hell, she'd probably need to sign a contract to get him to take her to bed. So why was it so sexy? Why did his rigid control and refusal to push her on his terms make her knees wobbly and her pussy throb with seeping heat?

She'd always hated men who liked to steamroll a woman just because he judged himself bigger, alpha, or more important. Give her the ones who watched with a careful, heated eye to see what she liked or didn't, the men who actually respected a woman's strength of mind to make her own damn decisions.

Yeah, Aidan O'Connor *got* her. His ruthless honesty challenged her in a way no man had ever done before. Even now, he'd pack up his bag and go back to Ophelia's without a protest unless she asked. Even after stating he'd be happier to stay and rip off her clothes.

Oh God. What was she going to do?

Ignoring her tingling nipples and flip-flopping belly, she threw back her shoulders and rose to full height. "I clearly remember having this same conversation a few weeks ago," she said, trying not to let her voice wobble. "We agreed to keep it strictly business."

"We did. But it's getting harder for me not to touch you."

Her heart galloped in her chest. Sweat pricked her skin. She remained silent, tangled between her head and her heart.

A rough laugh escaped his lips. "This would be easier on my ego if you'd admit you're having the same problem."

She shook her head and pressed her fisted hands against her eyes. "You sure don't know the art of subtlety, do you?"

He shrugged. "No time for that shit. Well?"

She let out a half laugh, half groan. "I think this is the strangest conversation I've had with a man."

"Are you hot for me, Harper?" His voice was all grit and gravel and sexy as hell.

Lust speared through her, raw and hungry and demanding. "Yeah."

"Good. I'm obsessed with kissing you. So I have a proposal."

"Of course you do."

"One kiss. Let's try it out. Maybe it'll bomb once we give ourselves permission," he said.

"I'm swooning from your romantic intentions."

His lips kicked up in a grin. She wanted to trace her finger over his mouth to see if it was as soft as it looked. "Sorry. What do you think?"

"I think I've stepped into a new dimension. Tell me this, Irish. Do we want the kiss to bomb?"

He nodded. Eased closer. "I think it would be for the best. Neither of us wants a complication in our solid business partnership. We have a long road ahead of us. Sex makes things messy."

Her brow shot up. Oh, he was good. Pretending to be all rational and cool while he stalked her like a graceful panther. Her blood grew thick and heavy, and the throbbing between her thighs raged. The real problem revolved around one simple, plain fact.

She was dying to kiss Aidan O'Connor.

Just once.

The tiny voice inside her flared to life and whispered a warning: *One kiss will never be enough. Not from this man. Not with the way you already feel about him.*

God, she didn't want to listen to reason right now.

Harper tilted her head. "True. If the kiss fails, we can get back to work without all this bullshit. Move on and focus on the real relationship here."

"Phoenix," he said.

"Exactly. Can you promise one thing?"

He took a few more steps. His scent wrapped around her like a silken cloud, spicy and clean and addicting. The leashed heat from his body practically ripped a purr from her throat. She curled her fingers, digging her nails into her palms to try and hold back from jumping into his arms.

"What do you need me to promise, love?"

A shiver worked down her spine. She imagined that lilting brogue whispering dirty commands in her ear while he thrust deep inside her. "If the kiss sucks, no hurt feelings. We move on and don't talk about it. I can't take any weirdness between us."

"Agreed. I hate weird."

He was right there, face close, inches from her body. The last time he was this close, he was angry. This time, his eyes crackled with hunger. His powerful thighs braced hers, and when he leaned in, his hard erection pressed against the seam of his jeans so she felt every glorious inch of promise. She licked her lips in anticipation, and slowly raised her arms to hook around his shoulders.

"Just once," she whispered in warning.

He cupped her cheeks with rough, calloused palms. His amber gaze locked on hers. "Yes."

"We'll get it out of our system and move on."

"Harper?"

"Yeah?"

"Shush."

His mouth closed over hers.

Once, Harper had gone sleigh riding down the back hill of the farm. She remembered every moment of the thrilling trip, from the first slow slide of the rudders over slick snow to the steady acceleration growing faster and faster until the icy wind whipped her cheeks and stole her breath, and her body flushed with the high of adrenaline, power, and the tiniest spark of fear. Fear she'd go flying and hit a tree. The ride was short, fast, and hard. Afterward, she realized she was addicted to those moments of total freedom. The risk was worth the reward.

Just like Aidan's kiss.

Soft, firm lips molded to hers, applying the most perfect pressure, the shocking heat of his tongue thrusting in male demand, urging her to open wider to let him completely in.

She did.

Her fingers dug into hard muscle as her knees weakened. He pressed her against the wall for leverage and took the kiss deeper, exploring every slick crevice of her mouth, nipping at her bottom lip, soothing with his tongue. Those thumbs stroked her cheeks, then moved up to bury in her hair and clasp her head, holding her still.

She drowned in the primitive, masculine need he unleashed on her mouth, her skin, caught up in a firestorm shattering through all the resistance she'd carefully built over the years to keep the unknown out. And now she knew why she'd been so afraid. Why she'd avoided any type of overwhelming demand to give over her body completely.

Because now she knew what had been missing.

Now she'd be unable to settle for less. Not after kissing him.

A whimper caught in her throat, and he stroked and soothed, whispering her name over and over like a beautiful mantra as he kept kissing her, that glorious, tempting mouth taking tiny bites and licks and thrusting deep until she twisted and reached for more, her body practically weeping. Arching her hips, she hooked one leg around his hips and tilted her head back.

He cursed, his tongue tangling with hers in a passionate game, and his hands finally moved up under her shirt to stroke her back, coasting around to cup her small breasts, his thumbs dragging over her tight nipples. She cried out and nipped at his rough jaw, sucked on his bottom lip, and then his mouth was back on hers and she sagged helplessly against him under the devastating intensity of the savage, needy kiss.

The barking rose to her ears in a sluggish crescendo, cutting through the fuzziness of her head. Suddenly, he stepped back, breaking the contact, and the surge of loss took her by surprise. As if her body recognized its other half and now refused to live without it. Eyes wide, lips swollen, she stared at him with rising horror, recognizing what they'd just done.

They'd ruined everything.

She'd be haunted by that kiss for the rest of her days and, God help her, all the nights. Barely able to swallow, she ripped her gaze from his face and focused on why the dogs were barking.

Captain Hoof was in the doorway.

Swaying a bit on his feet, he swiveled his head back and forth, as if trying to focus and register the barking. Bagheera and Baloo seemed to sense the goat's tentativeness, and they transitioned to happy whimpers of greeting, sniffing noses, and even a gentle lick on the goat's cheek.

She reached deep and rallied her strength. "Look who's up," she said, her voice a tad unsteady. Determined to break the shattering tension, she walked slowly over and sat on the floor in front of the goat. "You feeling a bit better?" she crooned, petting him and the dogs. "Don't be afraid of these guys, they're very sweet and protective. And I think you need some of that, right?"

Captain Hoof focused on her, that long, narrow pupil opening only in the right eye, his body beginning to stop shaking under the warmth of the dogs and her affections. She heard Aidan's footsteps disappear, and then he was sitting on the floor next to her, until the goat was surrounded by a tight circle of affection.

"Let's get you some water, buddy," he said, holding the dropper to the animal's lips. The goat drank, his tongue lapping slowly, then more urgently. "Better. Maybe we'll try a little more food. Get you a bit stronger."

The goat stared back at his audience and remained silent.

"At least he's not afraid of dogs," she said, stroking him. "He seems to like affection."

"Definitely a plus."

They fell quiet. Spent the next few moments comforting Captain Hoof. Tried thinking about anything other than that kiss that had blown away the last of their resolutions and illusions. Tension grew. Her breath got stuck in her lungs. Desperate for some space, she began to rise. "I'll get some food and take him out for a bit. Just in case he needs to go."

"I'll take him."

She shook her head. "You don't have to. I know you had a long day, so—"

"I want to stay."

The words pinged through the room like a gunshot. Her body sagged with relief. The idea of him leaving hurt her too much. She didn't know what would happen, or if they'd both decide to take a risk together. But God, she wanted him close.

"I want you to stay," she said softly.

His gaze searched her face. "It didn't suck."

She laughed and tried to ignore the joy squeezing her silly, traitorous heart. "No. It didn't suck at all. But I'm not ready to decide about . . . us. Not yet." She pulled in a breath. "I'm scared. And you made me feel more than I was ready for."

Vulnerable, halfway terrified, she waited for his response.

Slowly, he reached out his hand. She took it. He entwined her fingers with his, each deliberate motion as if he were tying her to him. "Me, too. We'll let it settle. For now, we move forward with Phoenix. No weirdness."

Her smile felt lit from within. "Deal."

When their hands dropped, separated, she felt the strength of his fingers in hers for hours afterward like an imprint.

Just like the one on her heart.

Chapter Thirteen

Aidan stared down at Harper and said the only thought currently jumping in his head. "You're fucking with me, right?"

Harper shook out a furry chicken costume from its packaging. It was egg-yolk yellow, with a bright-red hood that mimicked head feathers. He stared in astonishment at the ridiculous getup and wondered if it was a joke. The animals gathered around her as if this were a viewing party, including Figaro, who sniffed curiously at the outfit.

"I know you're freaking out, but I just want to try it."

"Try what? Getting him to think he's not a goat?"

They'd spent the last week caring for Captain Hoof and switching up responsibilities at work. Harper insisted on taking on the bulk of care, preferring Aidan and Elmo work with Phoenix while she stayed home. The goat had gotten stronger, now able to eat and drink on his own, and was comfortable around his animal crew. They'd both agreed it was time to take him to the farm to reintroduce him to his roots. Unfortunately, when neither of them was in sight, the poor thing went into an anxiety attack. He'd also taken up a habit of becoming dependent on the beat-up red-plaid blanket Harper had placed in his bed. He consistently tried to wrap it around him or drag it around wherever he went. Right now, it trailed behind Captain Hoof in tattered glory as he lined up with the dogs to see what Harper had unwrapped.

Harper kept talking while she smoothed out the costume. "I read on this Instagram account that goats with anxiety issues like to be wrapped in something protective. This woman at Goats of Anarchy put a costume on her baby goat, and immediately the goat calmed down and was able to allow her to leave the room."

"Are you sure she's not just doing that for more followers?"

"No, her nonprofit is incredible. She takes care of abused animals and has a ton of goats. I'm surprised I didn't know about her organization sooner, but she popped up when I was researching goats with anxiety. I know it seems silly, but we need to try."

Aidan rubbed his scalp. He'd seen some weird shit when it came to caring for animals, but this might win the prize. Of course, it wouldn't work, but he'd just let her see for herself so they could move on to another tactic. "Fine. Go ahead. Put him in a chicken costume. Hei Hei will attack him, Captain Hoof will have a nervous breakdown, and we'll all be one happy, dysfunctional family."

She ignored him and pulled the costume over the goat's head. The Captain allowed her to tug it over his body and through his legs without struggling. She slipped up the hood to cover his tiny horns, then sat back on her heels and examined the goat.

Aidan felt as if he were tripping out on psychedelic drugs. The image before him was so bizarre, he could only stare at the goat-chicken creature in front of him. The Captain's tiny head poked out from the hood sprouted with fake red feathers, and his whole body was covered in fuzzy yellow.

"No," he ground out, changing his mind. "Just . . . no."

"Let me poke a hole in the back for his tail," she said. Grabbing scissors, she chopped at the costume until a stubby tail stuck out from the rear.

Captain Hoof got up and began walking around while the other animals swarmed him, trying to figure out what the strange thing was about. Aidan held his breath, praying the goat would begin to shake it off or communicate his irritation with being transformed into a Halloween chicken.

Instead, the goat began to prance, as if testing out his new clothes. The dogs got into the dance party until Aidan realized with rising horror that the Captain actually liked it.

Harper stood up and beamed. "Look, he's happy."

He shot her a disgusted look. "I thought this was supposed to help with his anxiety problem."

"Let's test it out. Come with me into the bedroom."

"No thanks, I'm not in the mood right now," he grumbled.

She laughed, yanking him through the door and closing it. They each pressed an ear to the thin frame, waiting for the scramble of hooves and butting of his head against the door. Instead, there was divine silence.

"Not possible," he said.

She cracked the door an inch and they peeked out. Captain Hoof was fine with them out of his sight. He stopped dancing and cuddled up next to the dogs by the sofa, snuggling into that ridiculous costume. "It's working," she whispered in glee.

He wasn't ready to accept such an atrocity. "He's just testing it out. Just wait; within the hour he'll hate it. Then we can take it off and never discuss this incident again. Agreed?"

Mirth bubbled up from her figure. If he weren't so pissed, he'd find it adorable. "Agreed. Let's eat dinner and see how it goes."

"It had to be a damn chicken?"

"It was the only thing left in the party store besides Elmo. And I just couldn't do that to our jockey."

Their eyes met. He fought hard but it was too late.

He burst into laughter, and she joined in, laying her head against his shoulder. They held each other and watched their goat happily snoozing in the living room, dressed like a chicken.

And Aidan wondered why he felt happier than he ever had.

♥ ♥ ♥

The next day, Harper lifted the goat out of the truck and placed him carefully on the ground. He pivoted his head around, studying the landscape with his one eye, but remained pressed against her side.

"You're going to like it here," she told the goat.

Silence.

Harper didn't know if he'd ever speak, but maybe once he was settled and happy, he'd discover his voice again. Right now, her job was to find him his animal tribe. She might need to get another goat for him to play with, but for now, he'd have his pick of dogs, chickens, and horses.

It was time for the Captain to relearn how to be a goat.

Problem was, he seemed terrified, and she worried it had to do with that costume. When she'd tugged it off before placing him in the truck, he turned mournful and began to shake. Had she done a terrible thing like mothers did with their babies' Binkies?

Cursing under her breath, she snatched the chicken costume from the truck. "Okay, it's early enough, but you can't wear it this afternoon. It'll be too hot."

She quickly fit it over his body, and immediately the goat perked up, his huge slanted eye filled with happiness.

Harper sighed. "Aidan's going to kill us. Look, here comes Wheezy and Bolt!"

The welcoming committee came hauling ass down the path and bounced around their new friend. Sniffing noses and licking tongues welcomed, and Harper watched the goat's reaction carefully. The Captain was very still at first, then began to relax under the affection.

Harper let out a breath.

"Hey, Harper, when is Chloe coming?" a voice called out.

Her gaze narrowed thoughtfully on Owen. She had a ton of work to do and needed a babysitter. He'd gotten better since Chloe arrived. Maybe he wanted to impress her, or maybe she was really making a difference in how the kid viewed a horse farm. Either way, she'd just found her solution.

"She'll be here around ten. Owen, I have a task for you today."

He brightened, then stilled when his gaze dropped to the goat. "Umm, Harper? Is that a goat dressed as a chicken?"

"Yes, it's a security blanket for him. He was abused, so he needs to feel safe."

"Okay. Wow, never saw anything like that before. But he's sorta cute. Can I ask you a question?"

"Sure."

"I know Chloe said she broke up with her boyfriend a month ago. What an asshole, right? I mean, was he blind? She's the coolest chick on the planet. And I want to ask her out, but do you think it's too soon? I don't want to be friend zoned, so I—"

"Definitely too soon," she interrupted. "I think you need to show her you're a man, not a boy. That means impressing her with work. Good work. Then you ask her out."

She refused to experience guilt when Owen nodded with enthusiasm. "Yeah, makes sense."

"Here's your first task. I need you to watch Captain Hoof today."

Owen blinked and stared at the goat. Unease gathered on his face. "Umm, I'm not sure. I don't really like goats. Can't I do paperwork or computer stuff?"

"Chloe will be impressed when she sees you caring for a rescue animal. The Captain is very sweet; he won't hurt you. But he's half-blind and needs to be watched until he gets the layout of the farm. And be careful when he's meeting the horses. He's fine with the dogs, but keep an eye on him. If you bring him into the pasture, make sure he has plenty of room to explore safely."

His face fell. Harper tried not to laugh. Seemed his idea of dazzling Chloe was fading in importance. "I still think I'd rather—"

"Owen. I need you to do this."

He gave a deep, regretful sigh. "Okay. What do I feed it?"

"Hay from the pasture, and grain, but only a fourth of a cup for now. How's Phoenix?"

"Elmo and Aidan are working with him now."

"Great, thanks." Harper knelt down. "I need you to go with Owen, baby. Wheezy and Bolt will keep you company in the pasture. It's safe here, I promise."

She walked away. The goat followed her.

Owen threw up his hands. "What do I do?"

Wheezy and Bolt raced around, sensing a fun game about to commence. "Pick him up and bring him out by the oak tree, where Phoenix likes to rest. The dogs will come with you and keep him company. Come get me if he panics or doesn't settle down."

This time, she left without looking back, even though guilt swamped her. The Captain needed to trust, and forcing the issue sometimes helped. He couldn't hide with Harper in her home forever.

She glanced at her watch. She'd give Owen fifteen minutes and then check on them.

Heading out to the practice track, she met Aidan halfway. "How'd he do?" she asked.

His lopsided grin stole her breath. "Was gonna ask you the same thing. Please tell me you took off the chicken costume before you came."

She ducked the question and touched his nose. "You need to put on a hat, or sunscreen. You're getting burned again."

He ran his fingers along the back of her hand before she pulled away. Chemistry crackled between them, bright and hot and alive. It had only grown more intense since the night of their kiss.

Oh, that kiss.

How it haunted her day and night, but especially at night, when her subconscious relived every sweet, luscious slide of his full lips, the demanding thrust of his tongue, the wicked hunger licking her nerve endings as he took and gave and mastered all at the same time.

They'd both taken a step back to regroup, but the air between them still sang with sweet, agonizing awareness. But Harper wasn't ready to change the dynamics yet. Too much still hung in the balance, and if they fell into bed and things blew up in a week, she'd be out a trainer and an opportunity for Phoenix. For now, it was better to keep things neutral.

Her body, of course, didn't take to her decision well. But for now, her mind was a tad stronger.

At least for today.

"I'll reapply," he said. "And you didn't answer."

"I had to leave it on. Just for a little while, until he gets used to the farm."

"Harper, I swear—"

"He was shaking, Irish. I had no choice. I left him with Owen. Wheezy and Bolt are playing with him, though, so he already has two new friends. How's Phoenix?"

He blew out a breath. "Still has a bit of a temper. It'll be nice on the racetrack if we can funnel it. Unsure of how he'll take to the travel, though." His gaze sharpened, assessed. "His first race is in four weeks. It's time to see how he competes on the track."

Nerves prickled. She knew the speed was there, and the heart. The unknown factors were running with other horses and the stress of travel. They'd been working hard on desensitizing him to animals, crowds, and noise, but Saratoga would be a real test. "I'm ready. I think Phoenix is, too."

"Good. I want to load him in the trailer to get him used to the confinement. Take him on a short trip so it's not a shock, even though it's not far to Saratoga. We've pushed hard this week, so he needs a relaxation day." He shook his head. "That horse likes his me-time. If he were human, he'd be binge-watching Netflix and getting fat on the couch."

"A horse after my own heart."

Aidan snorted. "Woman, you are a born and bred workaholic. If I didn't know better, I'd think you were at the farm twenty-four seven."

The words hit her hard, a sharp reminder she pretty much had no social life. Mia and Ophelia regularly recruited her for a girls' night out, and she had some casual friends in town she'd dine with, but no other deep connections. No lover. Was she strange? Lacking in some way? Was it wrong she didn't really miss trying to be someone she wasn't?

"Hey." The soft whisper of sound jolted her out of her thoughts. "Where did you go?"

She turned, desperate to hide her sudden vulnerability. "Sorry, just daydreaming."

Gentle fingers closed over her chin and forced her to meet his gaze. Those piercing amber eyes refused to let her hide. "I didn't like that expression on your face. What were you thinking?"

No one asked her such questions. She moved through her life with such deliberate purpose, it probably never occurred to anyone that she'd question her path. She opened her mouth to give him her standard answer that she was fine, but instead, the truth tumbled out.

"I am a workaholic, but I like what I do. How I choose to spend my time in this world. But when people stare at me with sympathetic looks because I'm not married and have no children and don't bitch about wanting more, I start questioning myself." Heat seeped into her cheeks. She forced out a laugh, embarrassed at her outburst. "It's nothing. Forget it."

"No." His face set in serious determination, he shook his head hard. "No, I won't forget it. You're a rarity, Harper, and people don't understand how to deal with a person who claims her life on her own terms. Everyone is so used to excuses, and regrets, and questioning every step taken, wondering if it's right, wondering if it'll be judged, always looking for the right answer outside, rather than inside." His thumb pressed against her lips. His eyes darkened with a seething intensity, captivating her. "I like who you are, Harper Bishop. Don't ever question yourself

172

based on a bunch of nameless society groupies who live to lump you into a category because it's easy. You're too big for them to label. And God, that's sexy as all hell."

She sucked in a breath, shattered by his words and the truth ringing in his lilting voice. Shattered that he seemed to see right into her soul like no one ever had. Shattered because every day, she wanted him a bit more, and damn the consequences.

The sound of horse hooves behind them broke up the moment. His hand dropped, and she stepped back and stared up at Elmo. The jockey glanced back and forth between them, and Phoenix must've sensed the tension, because he tossed his head and butted right in between them, diving into Aidan's pocket for his end-of-workout oatmeal cookie.

Aidan stumbled back, laughing. "Fine, fine, take your cookie, mo chára. But you're on a diet for the rest of the day. I want you lean and mean for the race, but not cranky. Think you can work with me on this?"

Phoenix blew out a snort, then closed his teeth around the treat.

"Good ride. Ready for Saratoga."

Aidan patted the jockey's leg. "Yes, we are. We're gonna win. I can feel it."

"Me, too. Demon settled. He run fast."

Harper grinned at the jockey, whose speech was as Spartan as his movements. But she realized his true affection lay in what he gave his mount. The way he looked at Phoenix as if seeing into his soul. The complete dedication and focus when he rode, as if honored by the gift of the horse rather than trying to embellish and dominate with his own human power. It was a rarity in a jockey she treasured, and Aidan recognized the gift because he had the same type of heart.

"Let's get him familiar with the trailer later. For now, he gets a few hours of laziness."

"I take him into pasture," Elmo said. With a touch of his heel, he eased Phoenix to a gallop and shortly disappeared.

"I'm so glad you targeted him as our jockey," she announced. "It's like you knew he'd be a fit for Phoenix."

Aidan nodded. "Elmo's unusual, which makes him special. He has a colorful history. Came from Sardinia and rode in the Palio di Siena."

Her eyes widened. The famous Italian horse race that took place in Siena was dangerous, and one of the fiercest competitions in history. Jockeys rode bareback, and most standard racing rules did not apply, allowing the crowd and riders to experience a primitive tradition like the bull fighting in Spain. "How did he do?"

"Got knocked off and broke a few ribs but lived to tell. He's traveled all over, from Spain to Ireland, and the States." A grin curved his lips. "Did you see Owen's face when he spouted out that Shakespeare sonnet at dinner Sunday night, then stalked away?"

Harper laughed. "I couldn't believe it. Who would've thought he spoke so eloquently when he wanted to? Chloe said it was the best moment yet, and Owen can't stop talking about it."

"Elmo once told me he refuses to waste words on a world that cheapens them. He made a decision to base everything on action, deciding to only speak what's necessary." He cocked his head, deep in thought. She enjoyed the spill of sun over his figure, turning his hair to gold-spun straw and illuminating the laugh lines carved around his mouth, the pinch of sunburn sprinkled over his nose. "I think he enjoys holding back from people, allowing them to judge. I guess the three of us make up the perfect team."

"Why?"

"We all know who we are," he said simply. "And we don't give a shit."

She laughed, and he grinned down at her, and she savored the few moments on a hot summer's day with a man she was beginning to care deeply about.

"How about we go check in on the Captain?" he suggested.

Suddenly, her hand flew up to cover her mouth. "Oh no. He's in the pasture. I forgot to warn Elmo to be careful with Phoenix around him."

"Crap, let's go."

They hoofed it swiftly up the hill and careened around the stables, toward the pasture. The scene unfolded as they got closer, and Harper quickened her pace. Wheezy and Bolt had taken off at the first sight of Phoenix, not wanting to risk a kick or charge. Captain Hoof was alone in the pasture with Phoenix a few feet from him. His bright-yellow costume was like a beacon. The horse was staring straight at his prey.

Elmo and Owen were nowhere in sight.

Aidan cursed and sprang past her, ready to grab the horse, already yelling at Phoenix to try and distract him.

The little goat approached the horse, sensing another companion. With each step, he moved faster, stumbling a bit over the grass, ears perked, intent on greeting a prospective new friend. Phoenix looked as if he were shocked at the aggression—the intrusion of his personal space a crime that deserved worthy punishment. He pawed the ground, lowering his head as if to charge the strange creature he couldn't even recognize.

This was going to be a disaster.

Aidan wasn't going to make it. Harper said a quick prayer Phoenix wouldn't hurt the goat, who had no clue about the horse's picky distaste with all other animals. With one last desperate cry, she waited for the collision.

Captain Hoof reached the horse and began butting his tiny horns against the massive beast in an awkward gesture of affection. Phoenix curled his lips back, ears pinned, and—

—dropped his head and gently bumped the goat away.

Captain Hoof moved drunkenly around the horse's legs, as if he wasn't used to running in so much space and still needed to gain his goat legs. Phoenix stood perfectly still. When the goat made his way back to the front, Phoenix nudged him gently, blew out a breath, and stared with suffering patience at the animal who didn't seem to listen.

Aidan stopped running. So did she. They stared, unable to move, and watched the scene unfold.

Three times, Captain Hoof circled the horse, trying to play. Phoenix carefully retreated a step, probably thinking he'd remove himself from the situation, but the goat stuck close, trying desperately to rub his chicken costume–clad body against the horse.

Finally, the horse stopped. Glanced around as if looking for help. And lowered his head once more to nuzzle the goat.

Harper's jaw dropped.

His job done, Phoenix turned and headed toward the hay bale and began to munch. The Captain stayed tight on his heels, prancing madly, maneuvered himself close, and began to pull hay from the bottom bale.

Aidan retreated from the scene to stand beside her. "What just happened?" he asked. "He hates goats. We tried Mike and Molly from the Bakers' farm, remember? Whenever they came near, he threw a temper tantrum."

Harper studied horse and goat eating together peacefully and shook her head. "I don't know," she said faintly. "Did he think he was a chicken? Or a new animal breed?"

Elmo strode toward them from the barn with Owen trailing behind. "They friends?" Elmo asked with a jerk of his head.

Harper let out an exasperated breath. "Owen! I told you not to leave the Captain alone!"

The kid's cheeks reddened. "Sorry, I had to go the bathroom. It's gated, with plenty of room, and the dogs were fine with him. What happened?"

"That." She jerked her thumb at the scene before her. "But it could have gone very differently. Sorry, Elmo, I should've told you the goat was fragile. I didn't trust Phoenix with him."

Elmo popped a sunflower seed in his mouth and chewed. "Why not? Wounded souls recognize one another. I take break now." Elmo disappeared, still munching on seeds.

Owen turned to face them. "I'm really sorry," he said. "I wasn't trying to slack off."

She softened. "It's okay, I can't expect you to watch a goat twenty-four seven. It worked out for a reason. They were destined to meet. Maybe they can both help each other's anxiety." She studied the pair. "We could bring Captain Hoof to Saratoga with us. That way I don't have to worry about someone watching him."

"Hey, I'll do anything to get him out of that ridiculous chicken suit," Aidan said.

"Sorry, Irish. I don't think we'll be getting rid of that anytime soon."

"Fuck."

♥ ♥ ♥

"I can't believe we're here."

She looked out at the scene before her. The freshly raked dirt of the track curved in a large, graceful arc, sandwiched between lush green grass and white fences. The scoreboard lit up in neon with the entries, odds, and calculated prices of the possible wins based on current odds. The early afternoon was clear, bright, and hot, but the breeze cut down the humidity and brought crowds to the rail, to get as close as possible and watch the horses charge over the finish line. People squeezed together, drinking lemonade and draft beer, eating hot dogs and pretzels, and clutching rolled racing forms. Pencils were tucked behind ears, and discussions regarding the current crop of picks for the upcoming race were loud and lively.

Harper breathed in the energy and glory of the moment. Nerves twisted in her belly and batted like butterfly wings. "Want a beer?" Aidan asked her. Today, he wore a gray hat threaded with purple, slanted low on his head. His short-sleeve button-down shirt was a dark purple. Jeans and boots completed the outfit, making him look masculine and virile. He walked the track like he owned it, cutting a path in the crowds with an easy power that made her mouth dry. This was his world, and she loved being introduced to the behind-the-scenes of one of the most famous tracks, where American Pharoah and Secretariat and Cigar once ran.

Harper shook her head. "No, I'm too nervous. After. When we celebrate."

He nodded. "When we celebrate. Let's get back to the stables. It's almost time."

They'd taken a quick break to walk the front grounds and mix with the crowds. Right now, Phoenix was going off at 45–1, but most of the horses were unknowns, looking to begin competing for future gold. Harper couldn't care less what anyone thought her horse was worth on a bet. Today was important to test not only his stamina, but his thirst for competition. Some horses naturally had competition in their blood. Others, even though they had speed, just couldn't kick it to the next level in a drive to win.

Weeks of training had gotten them this far. Now it was time to test the racetrack waters.

When they reached the stables, a different excitement buzzed in the air. One of jockeys and owners, horses and companions, with last-moment nerves, commands, and disasters waiting to unfold. There had already been one scratch for a young filly who bruised her foot. Elmo was dressed in his silks, the white and bright robin's-egg blue reminiscent of the inn's colors. Harper had been able to register the colors and sketched design of the inn with the Jockey Club, and they were set for future races. The jockey's features seemed cold and distant, but Aidan informed her that was his game face to transition into racing.

"He seems to be calm," she said, rubbing under the horse's chin. Resplendent with the same bright colors as Elmo, his black coat gleamed and showed off lean muscles, the reward of all the hard weeks of work. She peered into his eyes, noting the bright awareness and the charged energy that buzzed around him. Almost as if he knew what was about to happen and was getting into the same mode as Elmo.

"He did well with the trip," Aidan said. "So did the Captain."

The goat was currently resting in Phoenix's stall, tired from the bustling activity, his chicken costume securely around his body. From the moment they shared hay, the horse and goat had been inseparable. Phoenix allowed the goat into his stall, where they happily rested and snoozed together. They played in the pasture, and the horse had even reluctantly decided to allow Wheezy and Bolt to join in on the games. A new, more peaceful energy seemed to settle around the horse when Captain Hoof was around.

Harper believed in fate, and God, and prayer, and knew there were no coincidences. Captain Hoof had been sent to them for a reason. They had been meant to be healed by each other, and it was another reason why she loved her job so damn much.

"It's time," Aidan said.

Elmo saddled up, nodding at her, and they began to fall in line to walk the horses down the historic path to the track. "I'll meet you by the stands," Aidan told her. "The handler takes Elmo and Phoenix down for now."

Her throat tight, she pressed a kiss to the horse's nose. "Good luck," she whispered in his ear. She said the same thing to Elmo and headed to her seat.

The minutes seemed to crawl as she waited for Aidan to join her. She peered through binoculars until she spotted Phoenix walking in a line of horses, toward the starting gate. Her heart galloped in her chest. Moments later, the scent of spice and Irish Spring soap rose to her nostrils. Aidan's hard body pressed against hers, and his hand reached out to squeeze her fingers. She tilted her head to look at him. His eyes shone with a rock-steadiness and warmth that allowed her to take a shaky breath. "Does this get any less nerve racking?" she asked, reluctant to let go of his hand.

"No," he said. "But you get used to it. And honestly, once that excitement fades and you're too burnt out to enjoy the show, it's time to quit."

"Makes sense."

The horses were guided to the gate, and one by one, they were locked in. Phoenix had drawn post number four, which wasn't terrible, but they'd been hoping for an outside post. He was able to make up the speed, but the crowds and getting boxed in were the real trouble. Of course, Harper had better get used to luck being a factor in the long game anyway. Better to experience it early so it wasn't a surprise.

The final horse was loaded. The gate snapped closed.

Harper held her breath.

The shriek of the alarm boomed in the air. Ten gates flew open.

"And they're off!" the announcer shouted.

The six-furlong race seemed to take centuries as she watched Phoenix break cleanly from the gate. They'd discussed their strategy multiple times, all agreeing to let the horse get toward the front, then settle into the pace depending on the front-runner. They didn't want him to burn out too quick so he could save some juice for the final stretch.

Phoenix tore ahead, and multiple horses fell back, giving him the space he needed. Glacier Pike got to the front and squeezed alongside Tom Tom, leaving Phoenix to settle into close third.

"He's in the perfect position," Aidan said.

The three horses stayed at the front through the first corner turn and into the second. Phoenix began to edge closer to the front-runner, Glacier Pike, and Tom Tom shifted over so Phoenix was sandwiched in between both horses. Hooves pounded in furious pursuit of the finish line. Dirt flew, people screamed, and the announcer boomed loudly over the speaker.

Her focus narrowed to Phoenix, his physical grace and beauty mesmerizing when he was at full power.

Suddenly, the cavalry charge pounded up behind them, the closers making their final run for the win. Phoenix held the lead, but as the final turn came around, Glacier Pike and Tom Tom hovered close, pulling Phoenix's focus from the finish line.

Harper watched the scene unfold in slow motion.

The horse began to slow, drifting, as if confused, and Tom Tom and Glacier Pike began to pull ahead. The closers threatened, and she watched Elmo try to spur the horse on, knowing he had plenty left in the tank. Instead of speeding up, Phoenix slowed even more, as if his hooves were stuck in mud rather than dry dirt. A rush of horses came up from behind and whooshed past him.

Phoenix passed the finish line in second-to-last place.

Harper closed her eyes.

She heard the softly muttered curse from Aidan. Disappointment crashed through her, along with a rage of doubt. Maybe she'd been wrong. Maybe they'd all been wrong.

He didn't have the heart and soul of a true racehorse. At least, not enough to go on for the epic Triple Crown.

They lapsed into silence while the crowds cheered and Glacier Pike pranced to the winner's circle.

She chewed her lip and glanced at Aidan. His profile was carved in granite. "What happened?"

"Don't know. But I'm going to find out. Let's go."

Chapter Fourteen

They'd lost.

Aidan tried to beat back the ache of failure and focus on the problem. He'd been so damn sure this time. He'd experienced plenty of setbacks and failures from horses, but he'd never been so hopeful. Anger nipped at his nerves. It was his fault for letting everyone get in his head. He'd never been so attached and bonded with a horse, let alone an entire family.

He'd gotten weak.

They were back at the stables. Phoenix had been properly cooled down and settled back in his stall to munch on hay. Captain Hoof ate beside him, oblivious to the heartbreaking loss.

Aidan barely contained the bite of his words as he addressed Elmo. "What happened out there? It was a clusterfuck. You didn't push him enough."

Elmo faced him. His dark eyes were cold as he leveled his stare. "I did. Had plenty left in him but refused to give me it. Other horses looming spooked him. He got in his head. Couldn't focus."

"You're an experienced jockey. Why didn't you touch him with the whip to focus him?"

The jockey's stare grew icier and matched his tone. "We agree no whip. Only hand ride. He knows my signals. He chose to ignore me."

Aidan spun around, rubbing his scalp, too pissed off to think straight. He knew it wasn't Elmo's fault. The jockey was right. He'd had the perfect position and break from the gate. Phoenix should've been there. His workout this morning had been blistering fast—faster than he'd ever seen before. Aidan had gotten cocky and relied on the horse's raw natural talent to get him to the finish line.

But Phoenix had gotten distracted.

The overwhelming sense of failure sank onto his shoulders. He turned back. "I'm sorry. I didn't see this coming."

"None of us did," Harper said firmly. She leaned against the stable door. "He'll be better next time."

Aidan remained silent. So did Elmo. They both knew it could be a sign the horse wasn't cut out for the track. He tried to remind himself it was the very first race, and there was plenty of room to grow and tweak. But the doubts were nibbling fiercely inside of him, and like a frayed cord, his confidence threatened to snap.

Phoenix was supposed to be his big comeback.

Aidan needed him. Needed to show he could win on his own, with his natural talent to pick the right horse. Needed to return to Ireland a champion.

This couldn't be all for nothing. He must be missing something— a crucial piece of the puzzle that would allow Phoenix to rise to his potential. What the hell was it?

"I think we're all tired," Harper said, her husky voice soothing his ears. "Let's take a break and get something to eat."

"I go eat with jockeys," Elmo said. He gave Phoenix a pat on the head, nodded, and strode out of the barn.

Aidan let out an irritated breath. "I acted like an asshole," he muttered. "He didn't deserve it."

Harper touched his shoulder. "We weren't expecting this," she said quietly. "Let's regroup. There's no need to rush back when we have a hotel for the night. Have dinner with me. We'll come back to check on them later."

She was right. He needed to clear his head and figure out his next step. Maybe Phoenix just needed to become more familiar with the circuit. He pushed his spinning thoughts aside and tried to focus. "How does Mexican sound? The cantina in town has good food and strong tequila."

Her lips curved in a faint smile, but just the dim light of it soothed his soul. Gave him space inside to breathe. Usually, when he lost a race he isolated himself, picked over his mistakes, and got stinkin' drunk. Today, he wanted her company.

"Nothing a good taco can't cure, Irish. Come on."

She offered her hand. He stared at it for a moment, surprised by the gesture, then tangled her fingers within his.

And things felt . . . right.

The cantina was dark and cool. The margaritas were heavily spiced with jalapeño, offering a stinging bite that soothed his wounds temporarily. The crunch of the tacos paired well with the shredded pork and black beans, and he attacked his third with zeal, as if eating like a champion could eventually make him win like one.

He felt her stare on him in the shadows. He fell into silence, into his old patterns of going deep to analyze every motion and decision that could have made a difference in the race. Doubts assailed him, pushing him to wonder if, for the very first time in his life, he was wrong about a horse.

"Do you always torture yourself like this?" she asked brusquely, leaning forward.

His gaze snapped to hers. "I don't like to lose," he said. "You hired me to win. Not fumble spectacularly at the first challenge. And if you're in this for the right reasons, you should be pissed, too."

"Oh, I'm pissed, all right." Stubborn fury burned from those sea-glass eyes, sucking him into a twist of hunger and fascination. "Because

I think you forgot our long game here. I did hire you to lose, Irish. I'd rather you lose spectacularly now before we face some of the most talented horses in the world at the Derby."

He frowned. "Look, I know you're not used to this. But when a horse with that kind of speed can't cross the finish line before poor closers, we have a problem."

"Did you think it was going to be easy?" she challenged, tipping her chin up. "Did you think this was some type of movie where you waltz in and start winning from the get-go? That Phoenix was magically going to beat all of his issues because he suddenly became friends with a goat? Or because he had stellar workouts in the safety of his own farm? Because if you did, I may have hired the wrong trainer."

He blew out a breath and challenged her back. "I'm trying to be real with you. If I don't figure this shit out, we're done. We've been working our asses off for months, and I—"

"Expected more?"

He muttered a curse. "Yeah. I expected more."

Her features softened. She took a long sip of her margarita, nibbled on a chip, and regarded him with a hard stare. "Well, we didn't get more. He has another race coming up here in a few weeks. We have time to retrain and identify the problem. I still believe in him. Do you?"

He rubbed his head and gave a short nod. "Of course."

"Good. Remember what you said after you saved Captain Hoof? You told me you don't quit when things get hard. And you don't toss away people or animals because they're not easy. You still believe it?"

A chuckle rose up from his chest and escaped. She remembered his exact damn words. Where had she come from? How was she able to rip the same emotions from him and spin it so he understood? He was a cranky son of a bitch when he failed, but she didn't seem to care, and she wasn't intimidated by his temper or distance. "Yeah, I do."

"Good, then we're on the same page. Let's get the bill and go back to the hotel. We need some sleep before we regroup tomorrow. Deal?"

"Deal."

He got the bill, paid, and walked back to the Hilton. He walked her politely to the door and watched her use the key card to open it. "Hey, Irish."

"Yeah?"

"I still believe in you, too. I hope you haven't lost faith in what you do, because without it, we'll never win."

Then she stepped into the room and shut the door softly behind her.

Aidan closed his eyes. Pressed his forehead to the door and wondered what he'd do if she opened it up, invited him in, and offered to ease the doubts and pain of the day with her sweet mouth and generous heart.

Smothering a groan, he gritted his teeth and backed away.

Then went to his own room, alone.

A week later, Aidan watched with frustration as Phoenix took the last turn and slowed down rather than speed up. The other three horses barely had enough run in them to threaten, but Phoenix was so distracted by their movements, it was almost as if he wanted them to catch up.

To prove he could win? Or did he simply not care enough to push?

Phoenix finally crossed the finish line, but his time was so poor, a dozen horses in a normal race would've blown by him.

This wasn't working.

He shot a look at Harper. She watched the field, biting down on that lower lip, a concerned frown marring her brow. If Aidan couldn't figure out the horse's real problem, the racing season would be over before it even began. Phoenix was fine one-on-one, but the moment he joined a group of horses, he became anxious and unresponsive to Elmo's signals.

Muttering a curse, Aidan waved Elmo over. The jockey looked just as pissed off at the poor performance. Aidan studied the horse, noticing he'd barely broken a sweat. There was so much more in the tank ready to burst. How did they tap into it? What was he missing?

"Any ideas?" Aidan asked.

Elmo's face was set in stone. "He fight demons in his head. He don't give me enough gas at the end."

Aidan glared at him. "Well, is there a fucking voodoo spell we can do on him for those demons? Come on, Elmo, I'm asking for some damn help here."

Elmo glared back. "I give you help! Silence demons first, then he runs."

"Great, maybe I'll serve up Hei Hei on a spit and offer his corpse to the voodoo gods!"

"Do not disrespect the voodoo!"

"Guys, cut it out." Harper stepped in, shaking her head and patting the horse's flank. "This isn't helping. Our next race is coming up, and we need to figure this out."

Ethan and Chloe rode in on Maximus and Chloe's Pride, followed by Ophelia on Scar. The horses hadn't even been decent competition for Phoenix, but it didn't matter. Too many other horses surrounding him got Phoenix distracted. Aidan could keep running him in big groups, desensitizing the horse until he was able to concentrate, but it might not be enough to win.

Ethan shook his head. "Not sure he's comfortable with horses running up on him," he said. "The blind spots are a problem. He loses focus."

Aidan nodded. "Good point. I think we need to get him comfortable with running the track with other horses until he realizes he won't get hurt."

"May take a while," Harper said. "But it's a solid plan."

"Then let's do it. We schedule intermittent practice races and rotate the other horses."

Ophelia and Chloe shared a concerned look. "I'll send Kyle to ride in the other sessions. He needs a break from his writing, anyway. Some fresh air will do him good."

"I'm free to race every day this week," Chloe said. "I have to leave next week, though. Back to the city to be with my dad."

Aidan smiled at the girl. "Thanks, Chloe. You've been a great help." He'd been impressed with her work ethic and ability to sense what the horses needed. She'd also been able to whip Owen into shape. The kid now ran around the farm, doing extra duties in the hunt to dazzle her.

"Let's take a break and get them cooled down," he said. "Harper, let's talk."

They strolled over to the barns.

He couldn't help but stare at her. With the sun glinting in her short, shiny hair and the faded denim cupping her magnificent ass, she was a sight to behold. Her small breasts pushed against the cotton of her powder-blue T-shirt, and those jeans emphasized her long, lean legs. The same legs he'd dreamed had been wrapped tight around his hips as he thrust into her hot, wet heat. The hunger had only grown since Saratoga, when she'd challenged him with her sharp words and brilliant mind and stubborn heart. He ached to touch her, stroke her hair, murmur her name. He looked forward to the end of the day, when they returned home, ate dinner, and settled in for a cozy night together. He loved how she settled close on the sofa while the dogs and Captain Hoof clustered around them. In a short time, they'd begun to form a unit. Kind of like a family.

Temporary, of course.

He buried the slight sting the reminder gave him and concentrated on the present. "I'm worried," he said bluntly. "We have a grade-three stakes race coming up, and I can't seem to reach him. We'll have some big competition from owners looking to prove their two-year-olds, and we need to score some points."

She tucked a stray tendril of hair behind her ear. "I know. I keep trying to think of a way we can make him feel more secure. Kind of like Captain Hoof and his chicken costume."

He couldn't help but grin. "At this point, I'd try anything. Chicken costumes. Voodoo. Hell, I'd dance in a tutu if I thought it'd help."

"You do have nice legs."

He laughed. "Least I'm good for something. Ah, looks like we got company."

Captain Hoof peeked his head around the barn, obviously searching for them. He spent most of his days at the farm and then went back to Harper's house at night. He was usually with Phoenix, but when the horse was racing or being bathed, the Captain liked to wander and play with Wheezy and Bolt and the other horses. He still had some minor bumps from navigating his surroundings, but it was amazing how the other animals seemed to sense his disability and helped guide him. Especially Phoenix. The horse nudged him out of the way of danger, and consistently checked on him to make sure he was safe.

Aidan had never seen such an extraordinary change in a horse before. Phoenix still disliked other visitors, but Captain Hoof was his buddy. Somehow, they'd built a bond of trust that allowed them both to feel safe.

He leaned down and stroked the goat's face, which peeked out from his chicken costume, and he nestled in for a hug. He was still silent, but Aidan was hopeful one day he'd speak. It just needed to be in his own time.

"Let's grab something to eat first, and do rounds," he said to Harper, rubbing the goat's ears. "Phoenix should be done by then, buddy, so you can nestle in for a long nap. Maybe without the costume for a few hours."

They both walked out of the barn with the goat trotting behind, then stopped.

Hei Hei stood in the path before them, beady eyes trained on the goat, massive head feathers swaying in the breeze. A hushed silence fell over the farm as Captain Hoof met the Polish chicken for the very first time.

"Don't you even think of it," Aidan said firmly, his finger jabbing in the air at the chicken. "If you scare him, I'll take it up with Mia."

The goat suddenly swerved around them, prancing right toward Hei Hei.

And then it happened.

With a massive squawk, the chicken dragged his clawed feet against the ground, and charged.

Captain Hoof stayed put, his head cocked in curiosity, completely calm under the direct attack.

Aidan made a move to block the chicken, but it was too late.

In midadvance, Hei Hei suddenly screeched to a stop a few inches from the goat, pure confusion radiating from his figure. He shrieked again in warning. Captain Hoof remained still.

Slowly, the chicken closed the distance, studying the creature before him, and began pecking experimentally at the goat's costume. Captain Hoof allowed the exploration until the chicken rubbed his feathers against the goat, as if trying to figure out what type of animal he was dealing with. The goat responded with eagerness, nudging his nose at the chicken, trying to butt with his tiny horns, until they were locked in a strange fowl-goat half embrace.

"I don't believe this," Aidan muttered, taking in the scene before him. "What is going on?"

Harper spoke in pure wonderment. "I think Hei Hei is shocked he's not afraid. Most animals retreat or charge back. And I'm sure he's never seen a goat in a chicken costume before, so he may think it's a new breed of animal, just like Phoenix."

The animals kept trading affectionate gestures until Hei Hei finally pulled back. Captain Hoof pranced around him with an innocent happiness that put the chicken in shock. Without another word, the chicken shook out his feathers in irritation, pivoted on one clawed foot, and stalked away.

Captain Hoof followed him, prancing happily.

"Umm, Captain, maybe you should stay with us," Aidan called out.

But it was too late. The goat was intent on following his brand-new friend. Chloe came running up, her mouth dropped in astonishment.

"Did you see that?" she squealed. "That is the cutest thing ever! I gotta put this on YouTube and IG. It'll go viral." She fished out her iPhone and followed them. "Don't worry, Harper, I'll keep an eye on the Captain."

"Thanks, Chloe."

Aidan shook his head. The most unlikely of friendships seemed to bloom around the Bishop farm. Maybe there *was* voodoo in the air. The good kind. The kind that brought teen crushes and strange animal bonds and the magic of possibility.

The cynic in him sneered at the unicorn thought. The only reason Captain Hoof had no fear of Hei Hei was his blindness. Probably couldn't see the chicken charge, so he remained calm. Sometimes ignorance is bliss. Sometimes—

The realization slammed through him and knocked him breathless. *Phoenix.*

He'd been looking at this scenario all wrong. If the horse couldn't see . . . he couldn't be afraid. Or distracted. He could focus on only what was right in front of him.

The finish line.

Excitement slithered through his veins. He turned toward Harper. "I got it," he said.

She tilted her head. "Got what?"

Laughter exploded from his chest. He picked her up, swinging her around in a tight circle, enjoying the easy way she leaned in and allowed her body to trust his. "The answer to our big problem! I can't believe I didn't think about it before. We don't use them in Ireland, but in this case, it could make a huge difference."

"Use what?"

"Blinkers." He let her go and stared down into her face. "Blinkers, love. I think they could help Phoenix focus and not be distracted by the chaos around him."

Her eyes widened. "It could be a game changer," she breathed in wonder.

"Let's hope so. I'll talk to Elmo. I may be able to get my hands on some today. Come on, we'll tell the others."

Aidan prayed this was the answer they were all looking for.

♥ ♥ ♥

The next day, they all gathered around the track.

Phoenix had been fitted with blinkers, and so far, the horse had easily accepted the change. The headgear was a black nylon hook with plastic eyecups attached, forcing his vision to focus ahead of him and blocking out any distractions.

Ophelia, Kyle, and Ethan were all mounted on their horses. Harper decided to join them on a strong stallion named White Knight, a temporary boarder from the farm down the road until they finished their barn addition. He was comfortable racing and would be a nice pacesetter for Phoenix.

Her belly fluttered with excitement. If the blinkers worked, they'd be able to attack the next Saratoga race with confidence. If not, they'd run a few more experiments and try something else. Taking a deep breath, she settled her horse next to the others and waited for Aidan's signal.

The buzzer screeched.

The horses leaped.

White Knight had a smooth, graceful gait and battled Phoenix for the lead. They flew over the track, quickly leaving the others behind after the second turn. Attention on her own mount, she managed to glance over and check Phoenix, noting this was the location where he usually began to slow, as if frustrated by the other horses looming up behind.

Not this time.

She urged her horse into a full extension, guiding him with her body and her words, wanting to give Phoenix a decent competition. As the final turn loomed, she watched Phoenix kick into full gear, his body a flash of black as he flew ahead and left them in the literal dirt.

Phoenix passed the finish line in record time.

White Knight crossed six lengths behind.

A complete blowout.

She pulled her horse up, easing him into a trot, then a walk, and met Elmo's gaze. The jockey pumped his fist in the air, patting Phoenix as the horse seemed to almost prance with pride, as if sensing he'd won on his own terms.

The blinkers had worked.

Kyle, Ophelia, and Ethan rode up to them. "Looks like we solved our problem," Ethan said with a grin.

Ophelia shook her head. "Harp, that horse was on fire! Did you see him kick it up at the finish?"

Aidan walked to meet them at the finish line, face carved with a deep satisfaction. "Elmo, did you push him hard?"

Elmo grinned. "Nope. Gave me a pure breeze, not even a race."

"That's what I thought. Which means we have a champion on our hands." He stared at Harper with pride. "Just like you always believed."

Surroundings faded away under the sting of those golden eyes. He'd believed, too. Believed in her and Phoenix, enough to drop everything to stay and train him. Slowly, he'd become a fixture here at the farm and in her daily life.

Slowly, he'd become a man she deeply cared for.

"Come on, capalleen, let's get you some cookies," Aidan said. "You deserve a reward."

Harper watched man and horse walk away, and she wondered when the stakes had become so much bigger for all of them.

Chapter Fifteen

"And they're off!"

The announcer's voice rang over the speaker system, and a shout rose from the crowd. Tingles crept down Aidan's spine. It never got old. There was a piece of his soul buried in the dirt of the racetrack, now being pounded by dozens of horses' hooves. Aidan watched Phoenix break clean and head to the front. With his newly fitted blinkers and a solid breeze under his belt, he was ready to tackle Saratoga one more time.

Harper clutched his hand and stared through the binoculars. She realized how important this race was to indicate the horse's skill. There could be no more excuses. After months of training, and with fall closing in with big stakes races ahead, coming in last was no longer an option.

Aidan raised his own binoculars and watched the horse career smoothly around the first turn. No lack of focus yet, but that's not where his problem usually peaked. It was all about that final stretch and the cavalry ready to threaten the horse's lead. The pace was unusually fast for such young horses, which told him the season might hold strong competitors. Still holding solid, Phoenix completed the final turn and headed down the backstretch.

Aidan's gut clenched with the familiar nausea and adrenaline. His gaze held tight to the fast-moving horse and jockey, bonded together as one as they raced down the backstretch and toward the finish. Elmo scrubbed his hand up and down the horse's neck for a final push, and Phoenix gave it to him. The other two horses threatened, then died five and a half lengths back. The lone closer never fired. As if it were just a normal workout session, Phoenix breezed over the finish line and won the race in a stunning upset.

Oh yeah. His odds were 50–1, and Phoenix had just made some long-shot lovers very, very happy.

Harper turned to Aidan, eyes wide with joy. "He won," she breathed. Gripped his shoulders. "He won!" she screamed, shaking him while he laughed and spun her around.

"Yes, he did. And damned if he isn't going to get a whole packet of cookies."

She laughed, hugging him tight, and a sense of rightness settled inside of him. The lure of the win was like a drug, always calling horse trainers to the road, to the next horse, to the next possible victory. He'd celebrated a few, and mourned many, but nothing felt as good as being with Harper during both.

They visited the winner's circle and posed for pictures. Phoenix mugged for the camera, sensing he'd done his job well and happy to revel in the pride of the win. When Aidan rubbed under his chin and praised him, he caught the look in those soulful brown eyes that stared back into his.

Let's do it again.

Yeah, the horse was hooked. He had the Thoroughbred heart pounding loud and true, and now that he'd gotten a taste, he wanted more. Emotion rose up and squeezed Aidan's throat. How many obstacles had this horse battled through to stand here? How much hurt and pain had he suffered, somehow never losing hope there'd be something more if he could just hang on? He was a beautiful spirit and survivor who made Aidan believe in all the good things in the world.

Like Harper.

He relished her smile and the light dancing in her mineral eyes. "I think he likes the attention," she said, laughing as Phoenix bobbed his head with a haughty delight.

Elmo snorted. "Champions like to win."

"He looked good at the final stretch," Aidan said. "What about the shake-up? Did you have to push him hard?" God, that was the most important. A horse couldn't make the Belmont if he didn't have the staying power of a marathon.

Elmo grinned. "He had more in him."

Excitement fluttered his nerves. He did the calculations in his head and whistled. "You sure?"

"'Course I'm sure." Elmo gave him a frown. "Blinkers remove demons. No more distraction. Now we go win more."

Aidan looked at Harper, who kissed the horse's nose. "Hear that, boy? This is only the beginning. If you want it, you can take it. We all believe in you."

He was transfixed by the sheen of tears in her eyes and the conviction of her voice. He had just stepped in a few months ago and was hopelessly attached to the horse's success. But Harper had been the one to rescue him and heal his battered soul step by slow step. She'd been the one to save him. To give him a chance to leave his past behind and live in the light.

His gut stirred. Harper's complete bond with the animals she saved fascinated him, and he sensed another battle going on beneath the surface, as if her own past was one she'd fought through and conquered on her own. The questions burned in his mind, but he knew it would take a lot for Harper to bare her secrets. Maybe he'd never know what truly drove her.

But now wasn't the time to linger on the past or painful secrets buried deep. It was a time to celebrate Phoenix and his victory.

Sensing his thought, Phoenix nibbled at his mistress's hair, bumping her cheek, and they all laughed together, feeling like anything was possible.

♥ ♥ ♥

Later that night, they all gathered around the laptop in the hotel room. The minibar had been raided, and bottles of liquor lay scattered on the glass-top table. Room service was burgers and fries and chocolate-mousse cake for dessert. The television blared low in the background. Papers and charts littered the excess spaces.

"After this win, he'll be watched," Aidan said, rubbing his temple. "We'll need to rest him enough before the Champagne."

Elmo flipped through the printouts. "Not sure yet where competition will lie." He pointed to a massive chocolate-brown horse that seemed regal, even at two. "This one dangerous. Wicked Wind. Won last week. Much power."

Harper tapped her finger against her lip. "Intimidating, but Phoenix has a speed and agility that can overwhelm sheer power. If he can't see him directly moving up on his right or left, he'll focus on getting the job done."

"Agreed," Aidan said. "Phoenix is a speed runner, but he also flips back and forth from a stalker to a pacesetter. It's a great talent to be flexible." He frowned, his brain ticking through the endless competition. "We keep stats on all the potential threats. Famous trainers Pletcher and Baffert will be in the mix; they're always trouble. I think we're smart to tackle the Champagne at Belmont rather than the American Pharoah. First, we don't have to travel to Santa Anita Park, and he needs the experience at Belmont. We work on building his stamina slowly and rest him."

Harper nodded. "I'm comfortable with that. I'd rather keep him fresh."

"Me, too. We attack the Champagne in October, then the Breeders' Cup Juvenile in November."

One of the biggest race days of the year was the Breeders' Cup— an all-day feast for gamblers and racetrack aficionados, along with the occasional betters who liked to win a pretty penny. A strong showing in the Juvenile would put Phoenix on the map straight toward the Triple Crown, and it was less than two months away.

"We win the Champagne," Elmo said firmly.

Aidan laughed and shook his head. "Dreaming big, huh? You know how hard that is."

"Aren't they all hard?" Harper asked.

"The Champagne is one mile, and the competition is ruthless. It's a challenge race. Whoever wins gets their fees automatically paid to compete in the Breeders' Cup. It's called the 'Win and You're In.'"

Her gaze narrowed with a ruthless intensity that simply turned him on. "Then we win it."

"Yes," Elmo said. "He fastest horse I ever seen. He can do it."

Aidan loved their confidence and belief, but the real problem was the hope. It scratched at him from deep in his gut, clawing its way upward with an agonizing fierceness and strangling his breath. He had so much at stake on Phoenix. They all did. But at the end of this whole road was just a flesh-and-blood horse who'd try his best. Sometimes Lady Luck got pissed and shit all over a hopeful. Bad weather. A bad post position. A bad break from the gate. A bad mood. The numerous obstacles were overwhelming, and it all came down to two lousy minutes and one shot at victory.

Maybe that's why he loved the race world so much. It was like entering the lottery on a regular basis and getting close enough to try again. And again. And again.

"Elmo, what do you want to do when we win the Triple Crown?" Harper asked.

The jockey gave a half grin. "I see Fiji."

Aidan cocked his head. "Huh? Figured you'd want to build a big house somewhere and invest in your own horses."

"Don't need stuff. Want to sit on beach and drink rum from coconuts and watch sunset."

Harper reached out and took the jockey's hand. And damned if Elmo didn't treat her to a gentle smile and return her grip. "I love that. What about you, Aidan?"

Return to Ireland like a king. Take his pick of training any horse he chose. A new challenge. A new farm. A new road to travel.

The words floated in his brain but wouldn't transfer to his tongue. It all felt . . . false. Instead, he shrugged. "Anything I want. On my terms."

She nodded, but her gaze dropped from his and she busied herself with the endless folders. Had he hurt her by his smart-ass answer? And why did that idea hurt him? "And you, Harper? If Phoenix wins the Crown and you come into big money, what's your dream?"

Elmo leaned in with curiosity, waiting for her answer.

She lifted her gaze, and Aidan's breath seized in his lungs. He tumbled deep into an ocean of sea green and sank below the surface, seeing the truth gleaming bright and true. "This," she said simply. "Don't you see? I'm already living my dream. We've won, even if we lose. Phoenix is healed, I got to go on an incredible journey, and I met you both. What more could I want?"

He remained speechless. There was nothing he'd be able to say— not when she so clearly spoke from her heart. He sat silent, mulling over her words, not wanting to show how much she affected him.

Finally, he said the only thing he could. "Bullshit."

Elmo cut him a hard glare. Harper narrowed her gaze.

"You'd save a hell of a lot more animals."

Elmo and Harper shared a glance and began laughing.

"When you're right, you're right, Irish," she said.

Elmo got up and stretched. "I go to bed now."

They said good night. The soft click when the door closed behind him echoed in the sudden silence.

He looked at her, but she was staring at the laptop with a mad focus. Her hand trembled slightly over the mouse. A touch of red heated her cheeks. Did she ache for him as bad as he did for her? Or was she just tired and overheated, and he was the only one with this raw hunger? Pissed off at the surging need chopping through his body, he stood up. "I guess I should go, too. I'm next door."

"Good to know. If I need you for anything, you won't be far."

He arched a brow. That line had been cryptic. Had her cheeks flushed brighter? He cocked his hip and gave in to impulse. "Did you need something?" he drawled.

She ducked her head, then looked up. Her voice was tentative. "I thought maybe you could stay for one more drink. To . . . celebrate."

Shock got him for a moment. She chewed her lip, looking like it was no big deal, but Aidan realized it was a hell of a big deal. She'd just asked him to stay. And damned if he wouldn't let wild horses drag him away from this fragile opportunity to follow her lead.

Slowly, he smiled. "I'd love another drink."

Chapter Sixteen

What was she doing?

The inner voice screamed a warning she was heading into the danger zone. Yes, he lived with her, but there was something different about tonight. The hotel room seemed extremely . . . intimate. The looming presence of the king-size bed behind them distracted her. At least in a suite, the bed would be safely hidden behind closed doors. Now she'd have to sip a cocktail alone with him with the monstrosity close by, mentally torturing herself with all the things he could do to her in that bed.

She shouldn't have let Elmo leave. He was an excellent chaperone.

"You okay, love?"

She pinned on a false smile and nodded with way too much enthusiasm. "Yep, I'm great. If you refill the glasses with ice, I'll grab the last two bottles."

Did his gaze skew slightly to the left, past her shoulder, to stare at the bed?

Refusing to think about it, she grabbed the Jack Daniels and handed them over. He doctored the drinks. The ice clinked. The amber liquid spilled into the glasses, reminding her of the stinging heat of his eyes. He lifted the glass and handed it to her, raising his in the air. *"Slainte."*

She savored the sound of his Irish on his tongue. *"Slainte."*

The liquid burned, then warmed her throat. She licked her lips and let out a throaty purr. When she looked up, his gaze was hooded, and a dangerous spark hung thick in the air. Her body surged to life. A throbbing ache settled between her thighs. Her breasts grew heavy and ripe, as if anticipating his tongue and lips and teeth on her nipples. She spun around and dropped in the red chair, desperate for space.

Was she tempting fate? Or was she finally ready to admit having him for one night might be worth the risk?

The silence pulsed with unspoken emotion and unfulfilled lust. She fell back on the only topic she was comfortable with. "Wasn't his performance amazing today? Between Captain Hoof able to calm him down and the blinkers, he'll be unstoppable. I was thinking he's more of a pacesetter than a stalker, though."

She glanced over. His muscles were tight with tension, and his fingers shook the glass, making ice cubes move and clink together in a happy melody. His gaze probed hers. She waited for his assent. Waited for him to dive into the topic they were both obsessed with.

Phoenix.

When he didn't answer, she continued. "Captain Hoof hasn't worn the chicken costume as much—have you noticed? We may be able to wean it off of him in the next month. Or allow him to wear it strictly in the house when we leave him alone."

Silence.

She gulped the rest of her drink and put it down on the table. The loud crash made her wince. Guess she'd used a bit more strength than she thought. But he was making her nervous. She shouldn't have invited him to stay. She sucked at this stuff, and she didn't even know what she wanted.

"I think you should go," she finally said.

Nothing.

When she risked another glance, he was staring at her with a predatory hunger that smashed the breath out of her lungs. "You want me to leave?" he finally asked, his voice like rough gravel and sand.

A shiver shook through her. "I don't know what I want," she said truthfully. "Do you?"

"I want you."

A gasp escaped her lips. The stark words fell between them like hard stones dropping into water. Confusion swamped her. "For a night?"

"No. That kiss proved to me I couldn't give you up after one night."

She began to pace furiously. His words swarmed her ears with sweet promise and crippling panic. Men weren't this direct. Men liked to seduce and play pretty games, didn't they? Why was he choosing to push her tonight after all this time of fighting their attraction?

"Is this because Phoenix finally won?" she challenged. "You want to complete your victory by having me fall into bed with you? Control both the horse and owner?" The stinging words peppered out of her mouth before she could swallow them back. "If he'd lost again, we'd never be having this conversation."

He placed his glass carefully down on the table. Put his hands on his hips. And regarded her with a savage intensity that made everything stop. "Yes, we would. We've been building up to tonight since the moment we met. I'm just deciding to call you out on it now." His voice came out rough. "Do you want me?"

She blinked. "I—I—"

"Simple question. I need a yes-or-no answer."

"Yes." Her cheeks burned and fear bubbled in her veins, but she wasn't going to lie. Not about this.

His face softened. "Good. Time for a few truths. I've been hard since I laid eyes on you. Been dreaming about you every night. So I'll tell you what I want, and you can decide if you want me to stay."

Eyes wide, she stared at him, helpless under the primitive male energy swirling around him. She'd never craved a man this badly before.

Her whole body turned to high alert, waiting for the signal to cross the room and step into his arms.

"I want to take off your clothes, lay you out on that bed, and make you scream with pleasure. I want to claim you tonight and every night after this, until there are no barriers between us. I want to be your man, Harper, for however long this journey lasts." His eyes dimmed with a flare of frustration. "I can't offer you marriage or promise I'll stay. After the road to the Derby, I plan on returning to Ireland. You need to know that in order to make your decision. And if you say no, I swear to God, nothing will change between us. You mean too much to me at this point to screw around with our relationship or what we have with Phoenix. I can handle the rejection like an adult." He let out a breath. "That's all of it. I can go back to my room, right now, if you want."

His intent was plain and stark. He wasn't sticking around. There'd be no false promises or words of love between them. But maybe there would be something bigger. The opportunity to experience everything this man had to offer, a chance to dig deep and push herself to really make a connection with a man, past the physical surface of a temporary attraction. Maybe this was what she'd been waiting for, and Aidan O'Connor was her gift. She was so tired of being alone. Wasn't she entitled to a great love affair, even with the end clearly known?

"I don't want to get married," she admitted. "Or have children. And I understand you want to go home to the land you love."

He took a step closer, then stopped. Sizzling energy pulsed between them. The silence screamed with unspoken, raging lust. Fascinated, she watched his jaw clench and every muscle in his body tighten. The rough command ripped from his throat. "For God's sake, Harper. Help me out here. I fucking promised not to touch you, and I won't, but if you want to do this, I need you to say so."

"I say so."

Naked lust shot out from across the room at her. She shivered at the dark promise in his eyes, a promise that warned he wasn't going to hold back. Not with her body. Probably not with her heart.

Harper didn't care.

"Come to me."

Her breath shuddered in her lungs. Every step was a deliberate reminder she was choosing him. When she finally stood close, the lash of his body heat struck her hard; the scent of soap and skin and spice surrounded her. His hands wrapped under the line of her jaw, holding her still, and his gaze delved deep, probing all the way to her secret, lonely soul. Vulnerability hit, but his slightly shaky hands told her she wasn't the only one affected.

"You're so damn beautiful," he said gruffly, his thumbs stroking her cheeks. "I'm afraid I'll be too rough. I've wanted this for a long time."

His admission soothed her nerves. She wrapped her arms around his shoulders and tilted her head back, giving him full access. "I don't want gentle," she whispered back. "I want hard and rough. I want dirty."

An Irish curse blistered his lips. She caught the low scrape of his chuckle before his mouth paused an inch from her own. "That I can give you."

His mouth took hers, and her entire body sighed. His lips were supersoft and his tongue hot and delicious as he claimed her, drinking every drop, and her nails bit into his shoulders while she pressed close, her breasts cradled against his muscled chest, teasing her hard nipples.

He groaned, ripping his mouth from hers only to tug off her T-shirt. The buttons of his shirt scratched against her skin, and her fingers clumsily began pulling at them, desperate for full contact. They kissed in between wriggling off clothes, kicking off shoes, until finally they were in their underwear, and he scooped her up to lay her out on the bed.

She shivered under his blistering gaze, remaining still as he devoured her with his eyes, his pupils darkening in savage satisfaction. "I knew it," he murmured, tracing the line of her purple lace bra strap. "I had an idea you were a seductress under those clothes. Do you know how many sleepless nights I spent imagining this moment?" He tweaked her nipple through the lace, ran his hand over her trembling stomach, and raked his fingers over the matching delicate panties.

A surge of wetness dampened the lace, and she bowed her hips, offering more. "Funny, I've been sleeping fine," she managed to get out, the lie evident in her needy body practically weeping for him.

A devilish smile rested upon his lips. "Oh, I'm gonna make you pay for that remark."

She arched up and tried to drag him onto the bed. "Good, I'm waiting. Do you have a condom?"

"Right here." He reached down and grabbed one from his pants.

A husky laugh escaped her lips. "Planned to seduce me this weekend, Irish?"

"I've been carrying them around since I met you, love. Leave a man to his dreams, okay?"

Her second laugh died in her throat when he peeled his briefs over his hips. Harper took in every inch of solid muscle, earned the old-fashioned way, with hard labor and sweat. Hair dusted golden skin, lighter in the places shielded by his clothes. His thighs reminded her of sturdy tree trunks, braced apart, emphasizing the hard, swollen length of his thick cock. A low moan cut through the room. She didn't even realize it'd come from her until he shook his head in warning.

"Keep looking at me like that, we both won't last long."

"I'm just admiring the view. There's no curse here."

He stalked toward the bed again and stared down at her with a touch of greed. "What curse?"

Her lips curved in a mischievous grin. "The Irish curse."

Recognition hit. One brow quirked, and he joined her on the bed. "Oh, you're really in for it now, love. Let's see how loudly you can apologize." Hard hands lifted her hips and tugged down her lace panties.

Her eyes widened. "I was just kidding! Aidan—"

Sliding her thighs open, he positioned his shoulders in between them. "I love how you say my name. I can't get enough of it. Can't get enough of you."

His head dropped.

Oh God.

He worshipped her with his tongue, licked and sucked and teased, holding her open with his thumbs and humming in pure satisfaction with every motion. Her hips rotated in demand, helpless under the deft ministrations of that delectable mouth, until the orgasm shimmering in front of her hit full force. She writhed on the bed and cried his name, her fingers twisting violently in the sheets, riding out the exquisite release that shook every inch of her body.

He kissed the backs of her knees, her hip, her belly button. He slid back up, running his tongue between her breasts, then quickly snapping open the front closure of her bra to free her aching nipples. "You taste so damn sweet, Harper," he murmured, sucking gently on one swollen tip. Her hands found the back of his head, sliding through the crisp straw-colored strands and holding him tight to her. "I can't wait much longer. I need to be inside you."

"Yes." She tried to focus, halfway drunk from his touch and smell and taste. Wrapping her legs around his hips, she opened herself up and invited him in.

He rasped out something in Irish, his breath hot in her ear. Fitting himself quickly with the condom, he rose up, grasped her knees, and surged inside.

Fullness. Stretching. Heat.

Pleasure.

Her body squeezed him tight, even as she fought for breath at the complete and utter invasion. Buried to the hilt, he took a ragged breath, his gaze raking over her face. "Stay with me, love," he murmured, patient as she adjusted to his girth. She rocked her hips a bit as the tension eased and her muscles relaxed, and he groaned, pressing his forehead to hers. "God, you feel so good. Tight. Perfect."

"And you're so damn . . . big."

His laugh was low and intimate, and he took her mouth in a deep, drugging kiss as he began to move. His hands reached across and grasped her fingers, entwining them together and bringing them up beside her head. Slowly, ever so slowly, he pulled completely out. Paused.

Then slammed fully inside.

She gasped at the electric sensation, her sensitive clit pulsing, ready for the perfect pressure to detonate. But he kept up the rhythm, moving a bit faster each time, until she became trapped within the searing agony of sensual tension, hanging on the edge of the void of orgasm.

"Aidan," she pleaded, digging her nails into the back of his hand. "Please."

"Don't want it to end." His golden eyes glittered with savage intensity. "Want it all."

She groaned with frustration and did the only thing left to do.

Squeezing her legs tight around his hips, she lifted up and, using the pressure of her body weight, forcibly flipped him over, with him still deep inside her. Climbing on top, she sank down fully, bowing back her body.

"So perfect," he breathed out, his hands cupping her small breasts. "Take what you want, Harper."

With a savage growl, she did. Moving her body to her own demanding pace, she found the angle that hit the shimmery spot, her clit scraping against his dick as she chased her orgasm, getting closer, until—

His name ripped from her lips. She threw her head back and let the release wash over her in waves, riding it out for endless moments that stretched forever in glorious, brutal pleasure.

He grasped her hips, bucked upward, and surrendered to his own release.

Her muscles shut down one by one until she slumped over, stretched on top of him. Legs entwined, his breath on her cheek, her hair spilled in a mess over the pillow, she let her mind go blank and her limbs limp. Sated, she relished the floaty sensation of complete bliss.

He pulled her close, wrapped his arms around her, and relaxed into a full snuggle. They were quiet for a while, as if they both sensed the moment was bigger than any words. The scent of sex and sweat and musk lingered heavy in the air.

He spoke first. "I don't want to hide this from your family. Is that a problem?"

Her heart swelled. She pressed a kiss to his carved jaw. "No, I don't want to hide this, either. We're adults. We know exactly what we're doing." She pushed the image of her brother and sister aside, knowing they'd ask a billion questions, but she'd deal with it later. Her path was different from theirs. She'd never been one to dream about white wedding dresses or babies or promises of forever. Aidan would give her all of himself for the time they were together.

It was enough.

Sleep threatened. She snuggled deeper into his warmth, her eyes beginning to slowly close. "What was that Irish term you said?" she whispered. "A curse?"

He hesitated. Then his hand came up to stroke her hair back. He pressed his palm against her cheek and met her sleepy gaze with eyes the color of gold. *"Mo stór."*

"What does it mean?"

He kissed her, slow and deep and gentle. Then smiled. "It means *my treasure.*"

Warmth heated her blood. She smiled back. "No one's ever called me anything special before."

She closed her eyes, rested her head on his shoulder, and slept.

Chapter Seventeen

Returning home from Saratoga was different this time. There was a new excitement buzzing around Phoenix and his impressive win, and the town was already twittering about the upcoming Champagne Stakes. But the biggest change was her relationship with Aidan. Now that they were lovers, there was an intimacy difficult for anyone to miss, from the shared glances and occasional touches to stolen kisses in the barn. Sure, they were still professional, but their new connection was practically visible. Every night, they spent hours making love, talking long into the night, greedy for every moment stolen together.

Her tummy flipped at the erotic images burning behind her lids.

She'd told both her siblings about their affair in a calm, cool manner and asked that they respect her privacy. Both agreed, as if they'd suspected the relationship all along. There seemed to be no suspicion or judgment from either of them, which was a sweet relief.

A few days after they'd settled back into their routine at the farm, Ophelia shot her a text to meet her at the inn.

Harper looked down at her dirty clothes and groaned. Her sister liked to keep the guesthouse ruthlessly neat and organized, and she usually sought Harper out in the barns for a chat. She was tempted to tell her she was too busy, but her sister rarely asked for her company unless it was important.

Dragging her palms down her jeans, she stuck the loose, sweaty tendrils of hair under her baseball cap and took the walk over. The woods were cool, and the musty scents of earth, leaves, and wildflowers tickled her nostrils. Her mind cleared, and she fell into the stark beauty of nature. Twigs snapped under her bootheels. Birds flapped their wings and screeched in song from the tops of trees. A tangerine butterfly took flight, floating in front of her as if bestowing a gift, then disappeared into the brush. By the time she reached the inn, a smile rested on her lips.

Ophelia sat in a rocker on the front porch. Harper climbed the steps, frowning at the pitcher of sweet tea and the blueberry scones set out as if she were a guest. "Do you have something bad to tell me?" Harper demanded, dropping into the rocker next to her sister.

Ophelia laughed. "No, I just wanted a few minutes of your time."

"You didn't have to bribe me with your bakery goods to snag my attention," she said, grabbing a scone and relishing that first bite. So good. Just like their mother used to make, with the sweet tang of berries amid the firm crust and soft center.

"I wanted to. I feel like everything's happened so fast these last few months. Kyle and I getting back together. Phoenix transitioning into racing. Mia and Ethan planning a wedding." Her sister's bright-blue eyes flickered with worry. "I feel like we don't spend any quality time together. I miss you."

The declaration startled Harper, and emotion rose up and choked her throat. Damn, what was going on? She loved her sister, but they'd never been sappy with each other. Harper had never been comfortable with words of affection—she preferred action. But the way Ophelia looked at her caused an answering surge of sentiment to squeeze her heart. "Are you okay?" Harper demanded. "You and Kyle?"

"Yes, we're fine. I actually wanted to talk about you, Harp."

She blinked, confused. "What about me?"

Her sister shook her head. "You really have no clue, do you? I want to talk about you and Aidan."

She took another bite of her scone and frowned. "I already told you about Aidan. We agreed to engage in an affair while he stayed to train Phoenix. He'll end up returning to Ireland once we take Phoenix as far as possible, and I'm completely okay with that. There's nothing to worry about."

"Bullshit."

Harper jerked. Her sister rarely lost her temper anymore, but when she did, it was quite spectacular. She didn't sport red hair for nothing. "Now I pissed you off? Why don't you tell me exactly what you'd like from this conversation so I can give it to you and go back to my barn."

Her sister jabbed her finger in the air. "Cut it out, Harp. Oh, I know you think this whole thing with Aidan is simple and straightforward. Hell, you probably believe you'll engage in some great sex, then tell him goodbye and move on with your life. He'll be a lovely memory you treasure, and you'll throw yourself back into the farm without a hitch. How am I doing so far?"

Harper's own temper rose, but she kept her tone crisp and cool. "Sounds good to me. You have a problem with that?"

"You're lying to yourself. Aidan is different from the other men you've been with. I see it every time you're together. I see it in your eyes when you look at him. And I'm scared shitless that if you don't stop pretending this is some type of sophisticated, fun affair for sex, your heart is going to get broken."

Her sister's accusation arrowed straight dead center, tearing down the careful wall Harper liked to hide behind. Her siblings rarely pushed her on any private matters, knowing she preferred to deal with them in her own time and isolation. But this was different. Ophelia was ripping through the surface and searching for the real truth. A truth she'd been trying to deny since she first met Aidan.

"I'll be fine."

213

"Listen to me, for God's sake. Just this once. I went through the same thing with Kyle. Believed I'd be fine because my heart was barricaded behind a defense mechanism that matched the Great Wall of China. I pretended it was just sex, and an itch I needed to scratch and get out of my system. But I knew the truth. It took me a long time to finally admit my feelings, and when I did, everything changed. You see, I was taking the coward's way out. Too scared to step forward and declare I still loved him. It worked out for us, but it may not for you. Do you understand? If you deny what this man means to you, you may let him walk away and lose the love of your life. And you'd lose him with a lie. To me, that's the worst way to lose anything. Don't you agree?"

Harper put the rest of the scone down with shaky fingers. This intervention was horribly intimate, and even though she knew her sister had good intentions, she wasn't ready to tackle those type of truths.

She just . . . couldn't.

Her sister's gaze was fierce, and all mama bear. Harper reached out and took her hand, squeezing it tight. "Thank you for talking with me. I know it comes from a good place. But I can't do this right now, Ophelia."

Her sister's shoulders slumped in defeat. She blew out a hard breath. "Shit. You're not ready. I get it. But I won't apologize for trying. You're my sister, and I love you, and I—" Her voice broke. Pain flickered over her face. "You've always been harder to reach. I know something bad happened to you a long time ago. When we were young. I never asked about it because I was afraid if I did, I'd lose you. But I'm here for you, Harp. Anytime you need me. Okay?"

The memory reared up and swallowed Harper whole.

Blinking fast, she rose from the chair and dropped her sister's hand. "Okay. I gotta go back."

"Will you do me a favor? I'm singing at Crystal's on Friday night. Will you come? I want to invite Aidan and Elmo, too. We want to have a bit of a celebration for Phoenix's win."

"Sounds good, I'll let them both know. We could probably use a bit of downtime away from the barn."

Harper climbed down the stairs, then paused. Keeping her back turned, she spoke to the woods, though she knew her sister heard.

"I love you, too, Ophelia."

Then she went back to the barns—the one place she always felt safe.

Aidan glanced around the restaurant and wondered if the romantic atmosphere was casting voodoo spells on his heart. Crystal's was a fancy place decorated in dark wood and rich burgundy, with a glittery chandelier and real china. Tonight, he was glad he'd dressed up and looked nice.

Or maybe it had nothing to do with the restaurant at all.

Maybe it was just Harper Bishop.

He sipped at his IPA and tried to focus on Kyle's entertaining account of working in Hollywood. It wasn't as if the man lacked the skill for telling an amazing story. It had more to do with the woman sitting next to him.

She was dressed in her usual jeans but had paired them with a sexy beaded camisole that revealed more than it concealed. Her heeled black boots put her at his exact height. She'd foregone all other makeup except for red-painted lips.

Instead of asking him if she looked good, or if she looked fat, or if he liked her new top, she'd strutted right past him without a second glance and announced she was ready to go.

God, she was glorious. A total sexpot who didn't give a crap what anyone thought. And now he found himself completely distracted by a million details he wanted to study. The way her dark-brown hair brushed the top of her shoulders. The way her eyes looked almost emerald against her dark lashes. The smoothness of her endless bare skin and sleek muscles revealed for his hungry gaze. The barest brush of her nipples pressing against the flimsy top. The delicious, familiar scent of cocoa butter drifting to his nostrils, making him want to howl like an alpha wolf.

He heard his name uttered from a distance and tried to refocus. "Yeah?"

"Ever think of writing your accounts into a book?" Kyle asked. "Horse stories sell pretty well. The public has always been fascinated by the racing scene."

Aidan grinned. "I love to read, man, but I despise writing. Besides, my life isn't all that glamorous. Sure, my last horse won the Irish Derby, but most of my days consisted of boring, routine training methods. Let's just say I've never had a Seabiscuit or Secretariat before."

"I'm surprised you didn't stick with Kincaid's Crown," Ethan said curiously. "That horse has a lot of wins still in him. What made you want to leave when he was at the height of his career?"

The question brought a tingle of panic. He refused to lie, but hell, he didn't want to go into the details of why he'd needed to leave. Harper knew the most, which still wasn't much. He took another sip of beer and shrugged. "It was more of an administrative thing than my personal choice," he finally said. "The owner decided on another trainer, and I took the opportunity to explore my options. I always like to take on new challenges. It worked out well, or I would've never met Phoenix."

Ethan nodded. Aidan relaxed in his chair. It was a fine line to walk between hiding the real truth without outright lying. Was it time to tell Harper the entire truth of what had happened in Ireland? She trusted him now. He'd be able to explain his side of the story. Now that they were sleeping together, she deserved to know the last of his secrets. He'd just have to take the chance that she'd believe him.

Uneasiness stirred. What if she still fired him? Or believed his ex-partner over him? It was a possibility.

His gut clenched. Maybe it was best to wait, at least until Phoenix won another race. Until he was sure their bond was strong enough for her to truly listen.

Elmo interrupted his thoughts. "Aidan good trainer. He connect with horse's heart."

"Where'd you guys meet?" Harper asked. He caught another whiff of her scent and thanked God the tablecloth was long enough to hide his burgeoning anatomy.

"We have bar fight," Elmo said.

"Oh, I gotta hear this one," Mia squealed, propping her elbows on the table, as if waiting for a bedtime story. Her sleek black dress and burgundy hair screamed trendy city girl, but Aidan had learned she was more comfortable with Ethan on the farm than anywhere else. "Who won the fight?"

"I did," Elmo said.

"No, I did," Aidan said. He gave the jockey a pointed glance. "I knocked out your tooth, remember?"

Elmo glared. "Only loosened it. I gave you black eye."

Everyone burst into laughter. "What was the fight about, and how did you end up friends?" Kyle asked.

"I met with the owner of a prospective horse I considered training. The guy suggested Elmo as the jockey. I told him Elmo wasn't tough enough, from what I'd seen and heard around the track, and referred him to a different jockey. Fast-forward a few days later. I was in this dive bar, trying to mind my own business and get fluthered, and Elmo strolls in, asks if my name was Aidan O'Connor, and when I say yes, he belts me in the face."

"No," Harper breathed, those red lips pursed in fascination. She must've been wearing some type of gloss, because her mouth looked wet and shiny, like a freshly washed ripened apple. His dick pulsed with discomfort, and he shifted his weight, trying to ease off the pressure.

"Yep. So I hit the floor, get up, and start swinging. The bartender throws us both out in the street, and we beat the crap out of each other until neither of us can move."

"I tell him never talk bad stuff about me again," Elmo said.

"After we got done bleeding, I gave him the job. Elmo was able to get that horse to place in a big stakes race. No other jockey was able to manage that fiery filly."

"'True friendship can afford true knowledge,'" Elmo said seriously. "'It does not depend on darkness or ignorance.'"

Silence fell.

"Thoreau," Elmo said.

Aidan grinned. Ethan and Kyle shared an understanding look. "It's all about the respect, man," Kyle said. "Nothing says respect like a black eye. Remember I gave you one after you found out Ophelia and I were secretly sleeping together?"

Ethan grunted. "Dude, I beat your ass and barely allowed you to keep your pretty face."

"Fine. We both did good and beat the crap out of each other. Okay?"

"Damn right," Ethan agreed. They high-fived, raised their drinks, and sipped in a silent salute.

Harper groaned. "Men are bizarre."

Mia sighed. "But the bromance thing has always fascinated me. Reminds me of those old Muppet men. You know, the grumpy ones?"

Harper snapped her fingers. "Yeah! They sit in the audience and complain about everything, but you can tell they really love each other."

"They're mean, too, but together, they're kinda sweet, so you can forgive them," Ophelia added.

Aidan lifted his hand in the air. "No. You did not just take a good bar-fight story and warp it into the Muppets."

"We're not fucking Muppets," Kyle muttered in irritation. "We're virile alpha men who settle our differences with our fists."

"And manage our women with old-fashioned seduction," Ethan said.

Uh-oh. Aidan half closed his eyes at the slipup and hoped it wasn't too late.

It was.

Mia narrowed her gaze. Her voice dropped to a dangerous softness. "Did you just say the words *manage* and *seduction* in the same sentence?"

The realization of the depth of trouble he was in registered on Ethan's face. A touch of panic flickered in his tone. "Nope. You must've heard wrong."

Aidan winced. Not a good defense. It was about to get worse.

Harper sipped at her wine. "You guys are meatheads," she muttered. "Anyone here at the table know about the Me Too movement?"

Kyle threw up his hands. "I didn't say it, and I wholeheartedly support that movement."

Ethan shot him a look of disgust. "Really, bro? You're the suckiest wingman I ever had."

Kyle patted Ethan's shoulder. "Sorry, man. But I really want to get some tonight. Have you seen how hot my wife looks?"

Ethan must've realized he'd be celibate for a while, because he sucked it up and turned to Mia. "Sorry, babe. Didn't mean it—I got all caught up in the bar-brawl story. A testosterone thing. I couldn't manage you if I tried. And I could only seduce you if you wanted me to."

Aidan pressed his lips together, desperate to keep the belly laugh from escaping. Damn, he liked these two. Why was he so comfortable around their banter and the way they publicly adored their women? Usually, he felt left out when he was taken in to train a horse. Kind of like that uncle everyone tolerated around the holidays but couldn't wait to get rid of. But here?

He felt like he was home.

Mia shared a glance with Ophelia. Both women gave their men matching smiles that made Ethan and Kyle slump in their seats with relief, but Aidan knew something was coming.

"Apology accepted," Mia said. "Oh, I forgot to tell you. Ophelia and I decided it would be fun to have a little sleepover. Some strictly girl time. You understand, right?"

"Of course," Ethan said. "Sounds like fun."

"It will be. So we're good for tonight, right, Ophelia?" Mia asked.

"Definitely," Ophelia said.

Harper choked out a laugh.

Shell shock crawled over Kyle's and Ethan's faces. "Huh?" Kyle asked. "What do you mean tonight? I thought we'd be able to have some alone time," he added in a harsh whisper.

Ophelia never missed a beat. With simple grace, she pushed back her chair and pressed a kiss to the top of her husband's head. "So did I, but seems like plans have changed. Pity. You can sleep over at Ethan's tonight, babe. Have some bonding time. Now, I have to go sing."

With a wave, she disappeared.

Kyle groaned and drained his glass, but unfortunately, it was seltzer, so Aidan doubted it helped much. "I'm an idiot," he muttered. "Should've seen that coming."

Ethan still looked hopeful. "Maybe you can reschedule your girls' night?"

"Don't think so, horse man. How about you, Harper? Want to join us for a little girl time? Watch some chick flicks and drink some pink cocktails?"

Aidan held his breath. He'd been looking forward to laying her out on the bed, stripping her naked, and spending endless hours giving her so much pleasure, she'd never think of another man without remembering his face.

Primitive, yes. But he didn't feel like analyzing it. Unfortunately, Ethan and Kyle had screwed him in the process. Odds were high Harper would be joining the women in their collusion to teach their men a good lesson.

Harper put down her glass and regarded the table with a measured glance. "No, thanks. I intend on getting laid tonight, but you and Ophelia have a good time."

Stunned silence fell.

And then Aidan laughed. He laughed so hard and so deep, something eased in his chest and released, a tight knot he'd never even realized existed until it was gone.

And just like that, something truly awful happened.

Aidan began to fall in love with Harper Bishop.

♥ ♥ ♥

"Did you have a good time?" she asked when they were driving home.

"Yeah. I've never heard Ophelia sing before. Her voice gave me chills. What was that song she sang?"

"'Always Remember Us This Way.' Lady Gaga sang it in *A Star Is Born*. My sister's obsessed with musicals, and that's her new favorite."

"Why isn't she on Broadway or touring?"

"When she was young, she ran off to Hollywood with Kyle to become a star. Unfortunately, she realized her love of singing wasn't enough. She was urged to turn herself into a pop star with a certain image, and she was never comfortable."

"The Bishop sisters know who they are," he commented.

She smiled. "Damn right. She came home, brokenhearted, and lost Kyle to his new career as a hot screenwriter. He returned last year after he realized he'd never stopped loving Ophelia. They had a rocky road, but I'm glad they ended up back together. They're soul mates."

"Too bad Kyle couldn't write that love story."

"Actually, he did. And it's being turned into a movie next year. There's this company called LWW Enterprises that bought the manuscript, and they think the movie will be a huge hit."

He shot her a surprised look. "Crap, that's pretty amazing. So now Ophelia is singing again?"

"Yes, but on her own terms. Because she loves it, not because she wants to become a star. And Kyle's happy to be back home helping her run the inn and writing. They got their brand-new ending after all."

He seemed to ponder her words, his fingers tapping against the steering wheel. "I think your family is incredible. They're nuts, but maybe that's why I like them so much."

Harper laughed, relaxing back into the seat. "I think Elmo had a good time, too."

"He did. Hell, he spouted Thoreau tonight. That proves he's in a good mood."

Harper shook her head. She adored the jockey, who spoke in broken sentences deliberately and fell into the most poetic pieces of literature and philosophy when everyone least expected it. "I can't believe that fight story—it was epic."

He pulled up to the house and cut the engine. "Know what else was epic?"

Her skin tingled under his hooded gaze. The air in the car thickened and sizzled. "What?"

A slow, sexy smile curved his lush lips. "The way you announced you were going to get lucky tonight."

Heat seeped into her cheeks. The words had popped out of her mouth without apology, but the way Aidan had laughed made her confession worth the embarrassment. She tossed him a teasing glance. "Am I in trouble for assuming? Are you going to join the ladies' sleepover to teach me a lesson?"

He leaned in. His finger trailed down her cheek, and she shuddered. His amber eyes glinted with satisfaction. "Only lesson I'm going to teach you is what happens if you make me wait too long." He paused, letting the tension linger. "All evening I've fantasized about getting you out of these clothes."

Seduction wasn't part of her skill set. She didn't flirt or tease or own the ability to make a man weak with desire. She'd always been more comfortable with the direct approach, mostly stripped of romance or flowery sentiments, centered straight on sex.

But Aidan made her feel like a goddess. The way he stared at her with open lust and kissed her with such possessive passion, as if trying to claim her. For the first time, she embraced her body with feminine power and confidence gained directly from the way he treated her.

For the first time, she was connecting with her sexy side, and she adored every moment.

With a low chuckle, Harper grabbed his tie and yanked him forward. Her lips paused inches from his, and she spoke each word with deliberate precision and tempting promise. "Then we better get inside fast, Irish."

He growled and reached for her, but she'd already pulled back with a naughty wink, slipping out of the truck.

Unfortunately, instead of ripping at each other's clothes, they had an animal menagerie to take care of first. Aidan volunteered to take them all out, and she used the time to brush her teeth, recheck her lipstick, and light some candles in the bedroom. By the time he'd reentered, she had bones ready for the dogs, tuna for Figaro, and special treats for Captain Hoof.

Aidan grabbed her hand, pulled her inside the bedroom, and shut the door.

His eyes burned like golden fire. "We've got about an hour before they try to bust down the door."

She stepped close and began working at the knot of his tie. He was sexy in working clothes, but when he'd walked out of his room in a charcoal suit and red tie, she'd almost jumped him. "We can do a lot in an hour. You look smoking hot tonight."

"And you're fucking beautiful. When I caught sight of this beaded top, I almost cried. In a manly way, of course. But real tears."

She choked on a laugh and began working on the buttons of his crisp white shirt. God, she loved the way he weaved humor into their physical intimacy. How could she be ready to combust from his talented fingers playing with her tight nipples, yet want to laugh with him? He seduced not only her body but her mind.

She curled her nails into the hard muscles of his abdomen as he slipped down the beaded top and played with her breasts. She was so sensitive and swollen, every tug, scrape, and teasing caress twisted her stomach in delicious knots. She managed to yank off his shirt, an appreciative groan spilling from her lips, and busied herself with touching every carved, defined muscle. Crisp chest hair tickled her fingers, and she raked her nails gently down, causing his arms to tighten around her and drag her upward, forcing her into an arch.

His hot, wet mouth closed on her nipple.

She fell into pure sensation, helpless under his ministrations. He licked at her, gathering her taste, sucked hard, then tugged carefully with his teeth. "I love your breasts," he murmured. "Like a perfect gift just for me."

"They're small," she said, hooking her leg around his hip to grind against him. A sharp tingle of pain cut through her, changing quickly into a hot stream of pleasure. "Ouch. You bit me."

He picked up his head and gave her a hard stare. "Don't ever talk bad about your body. It's perfect. Just like you."

Her chest ached with a need that practically seared her like a brand, but then his mouth took hers and there was nothing left to do but hold on for the ride.

Clothes dropped off. They fell on the bed, limbs entangled, skin to skin. His tongue buried deep with an animalistic possession she only encouraged, and she climbed on top of him like a madwoman, desperate to touch and taste every inch of his hard body.

With a groan, she yanked her mouth from his and began to work her way lower. Every hiss of his breath, tug of her hair, and curse from his lips urged her on, until she cupped his throbbing erection, stroking and squeezing the hard shaft, drunk on power and pleasure.

Her tongue snaked out to slide over her bottom lip. Her head lowered. She blew a warm breath over the tip, teasing him.

"Fuck," he groaned, his hips thrusting up. "I need you, Harper. I need your mouth on me."

His words held a hint of vulnerability, and she was lost. Opening her lips wide, she took him inside, sucking and licking with an urgency and tenderness she'd never experienced with a man. He buried his fingers in her hair, guiding her head, and she fell into a delicious rhythm meant to bring him to the brink.

Sensing he was moments away, she dragged the edge of her teeth down his shaft, and he exploded up from the bed, flipping her over, parting her thighs, and surging inside her in one hot, deep, perfect thrust.

His golden eyes glittered like a provoked tiger's. Her head arched into the pillow at the complete invasion, her body squeezing tight and welcoming him back. He stayed buried to the hilt, his gaze raking over her face as if memorizing every flicker of emotion, satisfaction oozing from his pores like he'd claimed her as prey.

She reached up and pulled him down for a long, drugging kiss. "I need you," she whispered against his lips. "Please, Aidan."

A broken litany of Irish sang in her ears, and then he was moving, each roll of his hips and thrust of his cock shoving her to the edge of orgasm. She clung to him and begged, and then she was breaking apart and shaking with the raw, almost agonizing bliss that took over every inch of her body. He chanted her name like a mantra, teeth gritted, eyes mad with lust, and then he let himself go, pressing his forehead to hers and never breaking his gaze while she watched him orgasm.

The intimacy was too much.

A piece of her broke off and the hole widened, letting in so much light it was almost blinding. She held him tight and prayed making love with Aidan O'Connor hadn't just destroyed her.

♥ ♥ ♥

Minutes later, he raised his head, every muscle tight with tension. "I forgot to put on a condom."

Her fingers were tangled in his straw-colored hair, and she paused in her caress. Dear God, she was so stupid. There was no excuse for not being careful. They weren't a couple of sex-starved teens fighting out-of-control hormones. Her cheeks heated. "I cannot believe I did that. But I just had my yearly physical, and I'm on the pill for my period. Have been for years."

His breath left his chest, and he tucked her back into his embrace. "I got tested right before I came to New York. I'm sorry, Harper. That's on me, I should've been more careful."

The close call woke sleeping demons inside. All the reasons she never wanted children whispered in her ear, and she squeezed her eyes shut, shivering slightly.

"What's wrong?" he asked.

The past and present shimmered together, merging in a blurred memory that demanded her attention. She hadn't thought about it in so long. Buried the truth under so much rubble, she'd thought it was dead forever.

But it wasn't. Her talk with Ophelia had stirred the monsters up. And they had never been far from the surface. Here in the dark, in his arms, feeling safer than she ever had before, she realized she wanted to tell one person what had happened.

Just one.

"I was bullied when I was young."

His arms tightened around her. She waited for his questions, but he settled into a silence that told her he'd spend the whole night listening. She felt like a ravaged animal, not sure if she was ready to take the leap into trust, but his hand gently closed around hers, as if trying to give her his strength.

"I was always ridiculously tall for my age. At fourteen, I looked like a freak, towering over everyone in the school. I'd been teased for years because I was pretty shy and awkward. I never felt like I fit into any groups. There was one girl I hung out with who was supersmart, but she was a nerd and that didn't really help my popularity."

She forced a half laugh, desperately trying to lighten the mood. Her palms began to sweat, but when she tried to pull away, he held her tight, refusing to let her do it alone.

"A few new girls started at my school. They seemed to have everything—money, beauty, and an ability to dazzle any boy they wanted. Everyone loved them. Begged to be part of their group, or sit with them at lunch, or be invited to their after-school parties. It would have been fine, I think, if they hadn't focused on me. This girl named Lyndsey was the leader of their crew. For some weird reason, she hated me immediately."

Her heart beat off-key, and she dragged in a breath, trying to push through. Panic edged her nerves, but damned if she wasn't going to finally say it aloud. Just this once.

"At first, they were really mean. They'd gather around my locker to taunt me and make fun of me in the cafeteria. I started to dread school. But then one day, they started being nice to me. Invited me to sit with them at lunch. Asked me to hang out after school. I was so damn relieved; I actually believed they liked me. Until they sprang this awful prank in front of everyone, and I realized the whole thing had been a setup."

She clenched her fists but kept talking, desperate to get through it. "Then the torture really began. Every day, they did something to make my life miserable. They got the entire school in on the action, until I felt like every morning, I was entering a battlefield. I began to have anxiety attacks, so I isolated myself from my family to hide it. I spent most of my time around the horses and the barn to keep my distance. I was humiliated. Ophelia and Ethan loved school. They had friends and social lives and everything seemed so easy. They always hung out together with Kyle and did stuff. They were talented. I felt like . . . nothing."

She paused. Took a few more moments to settle. Then finished.

"I knew I had two more years left of high school. Two years of isolation, and mocking, and pain. I didn't think I could survive it. So, one day, I made my decision. My mom hated taking meds, so she'd shove her old bottles into her bathroom cabinet, unused. She'd had mouth surgery, and I knew there was a full bottle of Percocet. I took it as a sign, so one day after school, I swiped the bottle. Ethan and Ophelia were in after-school activities. My mom had gone to the horse auction. I'd have several hours before anyone would find me.

"I went to the barn. I decided it was the only place I ever felt good about myself, so it should be the place I say goodbye. We'd gotten a fairly new rescue called Jiminy Cricket. A white mottled gelding. He'd been quiet and withdrawn. Mom had been steadily working with him, but he wasn't responsive. Anyway, for some reason, I decided to take the pills in his stall. Not really sure what I was thinking, but a part of me almost believed he'd understand. He had this look in his eyes, a look that said he'd met a lot of bad people in the world. I sat down in his stall, on a fresh pile of hay, and opened the bottle. I shook out the pills and stared at them for a long time. I thought about leaving a note, but I didn't know what to say. I thought about how many pills would do the job and decided on all of them. I was sitting there, thinking through the details, and suddenly, Jiminy Cricket came over and began nudging me.

I patted his nose, not really thinking about how it was the first time he seemed to respond to anybody, and then he got a bit crazy."

The image of the horse was ingrained in her brain. The desperate glint sparking from his big brown eyes. The almost-panicked air as he butted and nudged her body, trying to get her to focus on him for attention. The soft whinnies from his mouth.

Harper cleared her throat. "He just started nipping at my hair and butting me like he was trying to tell me something. I petted him at first. Then tried to ignore him. Then pushed him away. But he kept getting worse, so I put the cap back on the bottle and laid it down beside me. And the strangest thing happened then. That horse just lay down right in his stall and put his head in my lap." She shook her head. "Horses don't do that. He acted like some oversize lap dog and just plopped himself as close as possible, and his neighing was like whimpering, and all I could do was stroke him and kiss his head and tell him everything was going to be okay.

"That's when I realized he knew I was going to kill myself. And he didn't want me to. I think Jiminy Cricket knew if I quit on life, there'd never be hope for him, either. In that moment, we were connected. He'd been sent to me with a message. And I made my decision not to let those girls win. That I was worth living a big, beautiful life. That I wasn't ugly, and stupid, and useless. I cried for hours in the stall, with my arms wrapped around Jiminy Cricket, and he never moved. When I was done, I returned the bottle of pills to my mother's cabinet. I told no one. But the next day, my mother told me Jiminy Cricket had become a different horse. He was responding to her, and had begun to eat, and play in the pasture with the other horses, and became happy again."

A smile curved her lips. "He was adopted six months later by a family who fell in love with him at first sight. I visited him all the time, and he finally had the perfect home, just like he was meant to."

"And you?" His voice came out like rough gravel. "What about you?"

Her smile grew bigger. "I decided I'd spend my days making sure as many animals as possible get their second chance. Just like Jiminy Cricket gave to me. I still had a tough two years. Not much changed about their behavior, but I had changed my reaction. I knew I was trapped in a tiny droplet of time, but there was a massive ocean of years out there, waiting for me. I just needed to do the best I could until things changed, and they did. I graduated high school, and I never looked back. I decided not to have children. The world is too painful, and I feel like I could do better taking care of animals who needed me. Maybe I lost a few things along the way. But overall? I love every moment of my life. And I owe it to that horse."

She didn't realize she was crying until he cupped her cheeks and wiped her tears away with his thumbs. His eyes were so warm and bright, she fell into them, and oh, there was understanding and so much tenderness. No pity. No judgment. Nothing but the man's heart shining just for her.

"Mo stór," he whispered. "You humble me. Thank you for giving me the gift of your trust. Thank you for being brave enough to live."

His lips brushed hers. Whisper soft, and as fleeting as a butterfly's wings. And because there were no words worthy of a response, she reached for him, and he made love to her slowly, shattering the last defense of her heart and rebuilding it whole.

Chapter Eighteen

"Hey, Harper. Something's wrong with Flower." Owen stood in front of her, brows lowered in a frown.

She hung up the last stack of bridles on the hook and wiped her hands on her jeans. "What happened?"

"She's acting funny. And there's this gross stuff coming out of her nose. Looks like she has a cold."

She motioned for him to follow and headed to the mare's stall. Giving a quick whistle in greeting, she opened the gate and stepped in. Flower usually jumped to greet her, extremely affectionate and playful, but she just stared sleepily at Harper, as if unable to use up the last of her energy. "What's the matter, sweetheart?" she murmured, stroking her while she did a quick examination. Owen was right—there was mucus coming out of her nose, and she weakly swayed in her stall. Flower rarely liked to lie down, preferring to sleep standing up, but in a matter of minutes, the mare sank down in the hay in surrender.

Crap. She was really sick.

"Is she okay?" Owen asked, staring at the horse. "Why is she lying down?"

"We need to get the vet over here. Thanks for letting me know, Owen. Can you finish hanging up all the equipment for me? I don't want to leave her."

"Sure." With one last worried glance, he trudged out of the barn.

Harper plucked her phone from her pocket and dialed her vet. Thankfully, Sara Beadle was able to get to her quickly, and within two hours, she'd given her diagnosis.

"It's equine flu, I'm afraid," she said, standing up and dusting off the hay from her knees. Sara always looked coldly professional, but she had strong hands, a gentle heart, and an iron will to do the best for her clients. She'd been working with Harper for years, and they'd become friends. "Caught it early, but there's not much I can do. I'd advise quarantine, especially since Phoenix may have come in contact. Keep a close eye on the others."

Harper rubbed her temples to ward off the impending headache. With the stress of the upcoming Champagne Stakes less than a month away, now she'd have to keep a careful eye on the poor mare and pray none of the other horses got sick. "Anything I can do to speed up her recovery?" she asked.

"The usual. Lots of fluids and rest. Keep a close watch for worsening conditions. The next few days are key to make sure there's not another type of infection going on. Call me if there's any concern."

"Thanks, Sara. I appreciate you coming out here so fast."

"Are you kidding? I owe you. You saved that poor baby goat. How is he doing?"

"Thriving. Loves farm life and found a best friend in Phoenix. He's part of the family."

"So nice to hear a happy ending for a change. I knew the moment I looked at Aidan he wouldn't leave the goat behind. He's so like you."

Harper tried not to blush at the vet's pointed gaze and led her out of the barn. After thanking her, she headed back to the sick mare and stroked her head. Those joyful brown eyes now filled with exhaustion. "My poor baby. We'll take care of you."

She sighed, making a mental list to rearrange tasks in order to be on call for Flower. She'd move her to Phoenix's old stall, scrub this one down, then move Stitch, who'd just recovered from a bruised foot, in here. Aidan was gone for the next few hours doing errands, Ethan had trail rides booked all day, and Chloe had returned to the city to be with her father. Which left . . . her.

And Owen. But he'd be leaving shortly after she announced the big news.

After Chloe left, Harper had expected his work ethic to suffer again, figuring most of what he did around the farm was to impress his new crush. He'd gotten her number, and Harper was sure he texted her regularly. She'd caught him taking selfies next to Chloe's Pride.

Maybe he wasn't as clueless as she'd originally thought. The kid knew the way to a girl's heart was through her animal companion.

The subject of her thoughts walked into the barn and stood by the stall. "What'd the vet say about Flower?"

Harper leaned an elbow against the scratched wood. "Equine flu."

"Does she get medicine?"

She shook her head. "Unfortunately, no. She's got to ride this out. Sometimes it takes a few weeks to get back to normal. It's also contagious, so I have to move her into Phoenix's old stall, sanitize everything, and watch her round the clock for the next few days."

"That doesn't sound good." He walked in and stroked her mane. "What if she doesn't get better?"

"She will. She's strong, it just may take some time." Harper tucked a stray tendril of hair behind her ear and smiled. "I do have some good news for you, though, Owen. I'm sorry I have to announce it when no one's around, but you're officially free."

He blinked. "What do you mean? Free of what?"

A laugh escaped her lips. "Of us—the farm. You've done all your community service hours. I contacted your grandfather, and he signed off on the paperwork, so if you're done sorting the equipment, you're free to go."

He was silent for a while, as if trying to process. "You mean I don't have to come here anymore to work?"

"That's right. I know you don't have much time left before the fall semester is in session, but you can hang with your dudes for the few days and party." She regarded him thoughtfully and was able to utter the truth. "You did well. Not at first, but you learned, and I've seen a huge progression these past few weeks. Thank you for all your work and kindness to the animals."

Owen grinned, pride flushing his sunburned cheeks. A wave of affection washed through her at the sight of his bouncy surfer curls, blistered hands, and new air of confidence that surrounded him. As much as she bitched, watching the kids grow up and mature over a summer made the program worth it. "Welcome. And thanks for not getting too pissed off at me when I screwed up."

She laughed and squeezed his shoulder. "I know Aidan and the crew will want to say a proper goodbye. Maybe you can swing by later in the week for dinner? Or at least a cake?"

He ducked his head. "Wow, cool. Yeah, I'd like that."

"Good. Okay, I gotta get to work. Get the hell out of here and have some fun."

She waited for him to grab his phone and text his buddies or sprint out of the barn with a celebratory shout. Instead, he stayed where he was, petting Flower, and regarded her a bit cautiously. "Umm, Harp. I got nothing really going on yet. Can I help you get Flower settled? She doesn't look too good."

Gratitude flowed through her. "Owen, that's the nicest offer I've had in a while. I would love some help."

He threw back his shoulders. "I'll get Stitch moved out so we can swap."

The rest of the day passed quickly in a flurry of activity. By the time Aidan returned, she and Owen had managed to switch stalls, sterilize everything, and get Flower settled with fresh hay and water. The other horses were content, munching on dinner, and Captain Hoof was napping with Phoenix. She told him the details with Flower.

"Crap, we have to watch Phoenix carefully. Let's not push him this week. Give him plenty of rest with easy breezes to keep him limber. What do I need to do with Flower?"

"Actually, Owen was a great assistant." She laughed at his stunned expression. "It's his last day, and when I tried to send him home, he asked if he could help me with Flower. I guess this summer did make a difference."

"Told ya. Chloe didn't hurt, either. It's amazing what a boy can manage to do in the quest to impress a lady."

She leaned in and stole a long, lingering kiss, enjoying the delicious fullness of his lips skating over hers. She pulled back and gave him a naughty wink. "Interesting. Looking forward to you impressing me later."

His brow arched and a low growl escaped his throat. "You flirting with me, love?"

"You up for it, Irish?" A fizzy pleasure bubbled in her blood at the look of darkening hunger on his face. She'd actually learned how to flirt without feeling like her actions were forced or contrived. With Aidan, the banter was fun and natural.

"Always. What color today?"

The man had become officially obsessed with her underwear. She pursed her lips and pretended to think. "Hmm, don't remember. Was it the hot-pink boy shorts? Or the peach thong?" She shrugged. "Sorry, maybe you'll find out later."

She tried to walk away, but he grabbed her around the waist and tried to steal a kiss while she laughed, playfully fighting him off. After a few more kisses and giggles she'd swear never happened, they took a look at the schedule for the rest of the week.

"Let's swap turns to stay with Flower for the next few nights," he suggested.

She nodded. "I'll take tonight."

He didn't fight her, which was a complete turn-on. The man respected her decision to take care of her own. He gave her the space to be who she needed to be and never tried to change her.

She'd finally met a man who had no desire to rescue her. He knew she'd slay her own dragons, but he wanted to be there in case she needed an extra sword to borrow.

It was a heady combination.

After a late dinner, she headed back to the barn and settled herself in. Flower had a bit of a wheeze in her breath, but she'd been drinking water at least. She hated being in isolation, though, and was definitely one of her most needy companion animals. Harper laid out her sleeping bag on a fresh pile of hay as close as she could to the stall, so at least Flower knew she was near.

The creak of the barn door alerted her to company. Definitely Aidan. She opened her mouth to tell him to get his ass home and that she had things covered, but Owen walked into the barn. He carried a backpack and a rolled-up blanket.

"Owen! What are you doing here?"

He stopped a few inches in front of her. "I want to sleep here tonight. I'm worried about Flower."

Surprise flickered. She narrowed her gaze and studied him. "Listen, Owen, you don't have to do this to impress Chloe. I'll be sure to mention you were amazing today with her. There's no reason to stay—I've got it covered."

A mulish expression flickered over his face, but she caught the faint blush her words had caused. Still, his mouth firmed with determination. "I think Chloe is the bomb, but I'm not here for her. Flower was the first horse to teach me not to be afraid. She's sweet, and she takes care of everyone else on this farm. I want to help take care of her."

Ah, crap.

She blinked back the sting of emotion from his declaration and sighed. "Fine. You can stay. I guess she wants all the company she can get, don't you, girl?"

Owen dropped his stuff, unlatched the stall, and sank down next to the sick horse. Even through the vats, Harper watched the sweet mare press against Owen, as if sensing his strength of will to get her better. Owen crossed his legs, getting comfortable, and Harper pulled the blanket over her and closed her eyes.

A smile played on her lips.

Score another recruit for the Bishop farm.

Harper rubbed the back of her neck and tried to stretch it out. She'd spent the last two nights in the barn with Owen, watching over Flower. Thank goodness the horse was feeling better. Harper craved her own bed.

Specifically, with Aidan in it.

She opened the door, praying there were buckets of fresh coffee awaiting, and stilled at the scene in front of her.

Figaro lay sprawled out on Aidan's lap, purring madly. He stroked her back while the dogs wrapped around his feet in a snug bundle of fur. Captain Hoof snoozed on the side of the couch, his head smooshed against Aidan's hip, his tiny horns poking through the chicken costume. The scent of coffee hung in the air, along with eggs and greasy bacon.

His words drifted to her ears with a touch of his lyrical Irish brogue.

"I don't know why cats have such a bad reputation. Is it so wrong to demand trust is earned rather than give it freely, without thought?" Figaro flipped over to her belly and stretched. Her paws batted in the air, demanding more petting. "You're a big mush, but I promise not to tell. As long as you don't tell Mom I fed you extra tuna today. Deal?"

The purring resembled a chainsaw in action, rumbling through the room with pure feline satisfaction.

He laughed. "Yeah, I love you, too."

And then it happened.

Harper realized she was in love with Aidan O'Connor.

Her heart leaped, and her sweaty hands closed around the knob. She sucked in a ragged breath as the realization rolled through her. So stupid. She'd done everything they'd agreed not to, yet her heart had gone AWOL.

Damn him. Damn him for recognizing her inner heart and understanding her secrets and loving her animals and saving a disabled goat on his own.

Damn him.

Harper closed her eyes and fought for composure. At least he'd never have to know. She'd keep the words locked tightly inside. It wasn't his fault she'd broken the rules, and she refused to make him feel guilty or ruin the next few months hoping he'd feel the same way.

Decision made, she schooled her features into a calm mask and shut the door hard behind her.

The dogs jolted and jogged sleepily over for their greeting. Figaro shot her a disgusted look at interrupting her nirvana, leaping gracefully out of Aidan's lap to rub against her legs for a quick hello, then retreated back to her favorite place on the chair. Captain Hoof joined the group, butting his head against her, and she got down on the floor to give them her attention.

Aidan slid off the couch and headed toward the kitchen. "Hey, how is she doing? I've got your coffee ready, and a big breakfast. Not that I cooked it. But I made a special stop to Bea's Diner, and all I have to do is heat it up. Sit down, I'll get you set up."

Her throat tightened with emotion. She stared at him and wondered how many other women had experienced his tender side. The way he nurtured the people and animals he cared about. The man had a gigantic heart buried under a bit of Irish gruff. He was everything she'd ever wanted, and she needed to try and savor every single moment he was hers.

She rose and walked toward him. Jeans rode low on his hips. His T-shirt was stretched out and faded from too many washings. His feet were bare. His jaw was covered in rough stubble.

Harper rose on her tiptoes, fisted his shirt in her hands, and yanked his mouth to hers.

He growled with pleasure, hitched her high up in his arms, and carried her to the bedroom. "Good, I wasn't ready for breakfast, either," he muttered, his tongue diving deep and claiming her in the thrilling way that made her toes curl. He laid her on the bed, stripped off their clothes, and slowly pressed his lips over every inch of her body. With slow, teasing kisses, nibbles, and strokes of his tongue, he journeyed from the curve of her collarbone to the swell of her breasts and worked his way downward. She felt practically worshipped as he sucked on her nipples, dipped into her navel, and settled his hot mouth right over her sensitive clit to lick and pleasure, his fingers curling and plunging deep inside until she cried out his name and begged for him to take her.

He lifted her hips and slid home in one perfect thrust.

Buried to the hilt, he pushed back her hair and stared deep into her eyes.

"Watch me, Harper. I want to see your face when you come."

She shuddered. He moved. With graceful, deliberate strokes, he surged deep, rolling his hips to hit that magic spot that shimmered with electricity, then slowly pulled out.

And slammed back inside her.

Again.

Again.

Her nails bit into his back. Her heels dug into his ass. She writhed and reached and still his gaze locked on hers, refusing to allow her to hide, and the raw vulnerability of the intense connection broke down the last barrier. The orgasm shattered through her, breaking her apart with agonizing pleasure, and he saw it all.

His lips took hers, his tongue plunged deep, and he came, his body jerking as he gave himself to her. She clutched him tightly, limbs wrapped around his, and knew her heart had been waiting all this time for the man she was meant to love.

Tears stung behind her lids. She buried her face in his shoulder and prayed she'd be strong enough to let him go.

When it was time.

Chapter Nineteen

The Champagne Stakes held at Belmont Park was a highly anticipated race in the quest toward the ultimate Crown. Harper wasn't a person easily impressed by either celebrity or money, but when she caught Todd Pletcher, William Mott, and Bob Baffert—with his trademark gray hair—wishing her good luck on the race? Well, she almost lost it.

Aidan didn't bother to hide his amusement at her sudden starstruck, temporary muteness meeting the famous horse trainers. He'd called her cute, and the insult was enough to snap her out of the fog.

Now, she was ready to watch Phoenix race.

The fall afternoon was crisp with the perfect bite of chill in the air. Elmo looked striking in his robin's egg–blue silks, and Phoenix was in good spirits, prancing toward the starting gate with his blinkers wrapped snugly around his head. Harper's belly jumped with nerves, but it was the other gut feeling that threw her off the most.

The instinct that Phoenix was going to win the race.

She snuck a glance at Aidan and studied his profile. He'd been comfortable greeting all the players in an industry that was known for a sharklike ruthlessness among gentle beasts. The television crews, reporters, and announcers brought a certain chaos she wasn't used to. Aidan had warned her beforehand, schooling her appropriately on the proper responses to specific questions, drilling her like a lawyer with a witness about to take the stand.

She'd hated every moment, but today, she was grateful for his lessons, knowing if Phoenix did what she hoped, there'd be only more press and craziness to deal with.

The announcer broke into her thoughts. "And they're in the gate."

Aidan reached out and took her hand. Seemed he didn't give a crap who knew about their relationship, even in public. He refused to hide her as a dirty secret, even if they did have a professional working relationship.

Good. She didn't care about gossip, either. After all she'd been through, she'd emerged stronger. Hard lessons had been learned in the battleground of high school. They'd serve her well now.

"And they're off!"

The field was big this year, and talented. The well-known trainers had a few entries, with a mix of unknowns from various barns, but she was probably the most green of all. At first, she'd devoured the newspaper stories, trying to handicap the field, but when the majority of analyzers threw Phoenix out as a poor choice and a "lucky onetime winner," she stopped reading.

Action was better than words any day.

Gaze glued to her binoculars, Harper watched the one-mile race, which took place on a fast, dry track. Phoenix had a good break, and Elmo got him to the front without much fuss. She could tell the ride was easy, and Phoenix was comfortably breezing past the first-quarter pole, his legs eating up ground and space like he was meant to fly rather than run.

The announcer's voice echoed over the loudspeaker. "Phoenix takes the early lead in the twelve-horse field, but Lacey's Due and White Cliff are right behind. In the Money is three and a half lengths back, with Dangerzone on the far outside, and Wicked Wind, the favorite, is trailing behind."

"He's running like a champion," Aidan muttered, his voice full of excitement and a touch of fear.

She couldn't answer. Nerves shredded, she nibbled at her lip and prayed while Phoenix battled for the lead as an entire field of horses chased him.

"Phoenix, Lacey's Due, and White Cliff barrel around the far turn, with Dangerzone falling back, and In the Money at the rail. Steve's Sad Sister is now four lengths behind and beginning to challenge for the lead, but it's still a tight race as they head to the backstretch."

Nausea mixed with excitement in a cocktail she doubted she could handle. The impulse to close her eyes was strong, but she battled through, forcing herself to watch every tension-filled second as Phoenix barely maintained the fragile lead that she prayed he'd be able to hold.

"Down the backstretch they come! Phoenix is still in the lead with Lacey's Due and White Cliff a length back, and here comes Wicked Wind making his move! Wicked Wind passes Dangerzone and In the Money, and they're thundering down the final stretch! It's Phoenix still in the lead, with White Cliff a length behind. Lacey's Due is two lengths back, but Wicked Wind is closing the gap in a spectacular move! White Cliff falls behind to make way for Wicked Wind, and Lacey's Due can't keep up. Here comes Wicked Wind, the closer, as they near the finish line. Phoenix is hanging on. Wicked Wind is now two lengths back in the final challenge, and it's . . . Phoenix! For the win! Wicked Wind is second, and White Cliff is third, in the official running of the Champagne Stakes!"

Her heart stopped.

The crowds roared, and cameras flashed. She watched as Elmo stood up in the stirrups, kissing his fingers and putting them up to the sky in his trademark thank-you, and that beautiful, perfect, gorgeous horse with a fierce heart and temper pranced down the track.

"We won," she said. Her hands shook fiercely, and shock crawled over her body, making the entire scene feel like a dream. "We're going to the Breeders' Cup. On their dime."

Aidan looked down at her, grinning, then threw back his head and shouted with triumph. He seemed to soak up the spotlight, charming reporters and smiling for the camera while she hid on the sidelines. Watching him take command with a sense of pride etched in his features made her realize he was born for the winner's circle.

Just like Phoenix.

♥ ♥ ♥

"So the Breeders' Cup Juvenile is in November at Churchill Downs," Ophelia said, handing Aidan his bowl filled to the brim with Irish beef stew.

He almost wept but didn't want to do it in front of Kyle and Ethan. The chunks of flavorful meat mixed in the perfect broth and set off the crisp potatoes and carrots, and dear God, was that stout?

"Yes, we'll need to be in Kentucky in about three weeks," Harper said, grabbing a chunk of French bread and dipping it in the broth.

"How did it feel watching him cross the finish line?" Mia asked in wonderment.

Pride and joy shone from Harper's face. "It felt like Mom was right there smiling and cheering with us. It felt like Phoenix was telling his previous owners a big *fuck you*. It felt damn amazing."

"Amen to that," Mia said, raising her glass of wine. "You may be going to the Derby, guys!"

Aidan smiled. "We plan on it," he said. "But the next hurdle is crucial. We want him to make a decent showing to keep focused on the road to the Derby. I'm mostly concerned with the amount of travel for this race. We've been racing him in New York, but out of state may be a challenge."

"We need to get Captain Hoof a passport," Ophelia said with a laugh. "Damn, we wish we could go with you."

"I know, but it's so important you stay to handle things here," Harper said. "I appreciate you all doing so much to allow us to get this far."

"What do you need to do with Phoenix next?" Kyle asked curiously.

Aidan managed to lay down his spoon for a moment. "Keep him engaged and fit, but he needs a lot of rest. He just turned three, and it's a delicate balance when racing at this age. My goal is to keep him healthy and happy. So less iced oatmeal cookies for a while."

Harper lifted a brow. "Like Rocky in training, huh? Are raw eggs next?"

Mia groaned. "Ugh, gross!"

Elmo frowned. "What is Rocky? They make movies I never heard of."

The women at the table shared a dangerous look. Then they shrieked all together in perfect unison. "Movie night!"

Kyle and Ethan groaned. "Not again. We watched *Coco* with Chloe, and I couldn't stop singing that song," Ethan grumbled. "Plus, she cried. I hate when she cries."

"'Remember Me.'" Ophelia sighed, her eyes a dreamy blue. "So beautiful. It won the Academy Award, you know?"

"I loved *Coco*!" Mia said. "Crying at Disney movies cleanses a woman's soul. It's like a purity ritual, and we come out stronger."

"Count me out, too," Kyle said.

"Guys! Elmo and Aidan need to see one of the newest Disney movies. It's our responsibility to introduce them to greatness," Harper said.

Aidan stared at her, amused at her passion over these cartoon movies. Sure, he'd seen the classic *Peter Pan* and various Mickey Mouse, but weren't they for children? Why was his fierce warrior woman so enchanted with Disney? Was it all those cute, cuddly animals?

"I will do it," Elmo announced. "Pick a good one."

Kyle and Ethan shot Aidan a look. But once he registered the excitement on Harper's face, he was doomed. "Okay, I'm in," he agreed.

"Shit," Kyle said glumly. "There goes *Road House*."

"Again?" Ophelia squeaked. "I love Patrick Swayze and Sam Elliott, but I just don't get the appeal of that movie. The plot is lame."

"Great movie," Aidan said.

Kyle and Ethan glared at him, still unforgiving for the Disney fail.

Harper practically jumped in her seat, and it was worth being out of the men's club for a while. "I vote for *Moana*," she said.

"Yes, it's perfect," Ophelia agreed. "They can see Hei Hei's namesake."

Mia nodded, and just like that, movie night was official.

"Ophelia, this stew is amazing," Aidan said. "Is the recipe from your mom?"

"Close. We had to make a few changes," she said, her eyes flashing with mischief.

Harper frowned. "What changes? Tastes just as good as Mom's. Better, even. What'd you do?"

Ophelia sighed. "Well, the original recipe calls for kid goat, but I swapped it out for beef. Now if we can only give up eating chicken, we may be okay around here."

Harper's jaw dropped. "Mom used goat?" she whispered in horror.

"I'm sure she didn't," her sister rushed on. "It was written down in the original recipe, but Mom used the grass-fed beef from Kiernan Farm. It was just a bit startling when I riffled through her recipes and found it."

The table fell silent. "Poor Captain Hoof," Mia said mournfully. "Can you imagine?"

And then it happened. Ethan broke first, a tiny grin cracking the corner of his mouth. Kyle pressed his lips together, hard. Mirth danced in Ophelia's eyes. But one by one, the grins won out, and everyone burst into laughter.

"You're all sick," Harper announced, but Aidan caught the humor in her sea-green eyes before she was able to hide it, and he ended up laughing harder.

A few hours later, after the dishes were washed and the table cleared, they settled in the rear sitting room with the giant flat-screen television and a comfortable, large sectional to accommodate everyone. Shoes were kicked off, blankets were passed around, buttered-popcorn buckets distributed, and Aidan held an ice-cold IPA in his hand. The women drank Prosecco in delicate glasses of colored crystal. He had no idea an at-home movie night could feel like a red-carpet premiere.

Settled into the cushion, with his arm slung around Harper's shoulder and her head resting on his chest, a sense of contentment and peace rippled through him. The night she'd confessed her intention to commit suicide, something had changed between them. It had gone beyond sex into an almost soulful connection. She'd spilled her innermost secret, trusting him to keep it safe, and the gift only made him want to share more of himself. He'd finally met a woman strong enough not only to match him, but challenge him to push harder, take chances, and do more.

Be more.

For both of them.

Temporarily.

The warning voice inside told him not to get too comfortable or settled or happy, because at the end of the road, he was leaving. His journey had only one good ending for both of them: win the Triple Crown. That's it.

But he had eight months left. Eight months could be an entire lifetime to enjoy Harper Bishop. He didn't intend to miss a moment.

Usually, he heeded the voice. It kept him sharp and focused. It kept him on task and protected.

Tonight, he'd shut it down, lock it up, and watch *Moana*.

♥ ♥ ♥

"What are you humming?"

Aidan continued kissing each of her fingers, marveling at the beauty of her hands. Long, tapered fingers. Square, short, unpainted nails that showed off perfect half moons. Palms rough, a few old blisters still lingering. Graceful and strong, just like the woman. Who was currently in bed, naked, and trying to grill him. "Nothing." He slipped each finger into his mouth and sucked, scoring the pad with his teeth.

She pulled in a breath, and he hid a smile from her heated response. She was such a pleasure in bed—easy to please, giving and creative and passionate. Hours flew by like seconds. He'd begun dreading the sunrise because he had to finally release her from his arms. He figured he'd finally distracted her, but he should have realized his woman was too savvy for such a simple diversion.

"Lie. You're singing 'You're Welcome' from *Moana*. I saw you tear up at the end."

"Ridiculous. Real men don't cry." He nipped at her palm in punishment, extending her arm to begin trailing kisses upward. "But it was definitely a kick-ass movie. The sailing, and the adventure, and those cool tats on Maui. Plus, Hei Hei. Doesn't get much better than that."

"Told ya."

He refocused, tugging down the sheet to study her small, defined breasts. He licked her peach-colored nipple, watching with satisfaction as the tip grew hard and swollen under his ministrations. Her muscles tightened underneath him, and a low moan escaped her throat. "Irish? What are you doing?"

"Investigating."

She laughed, tangling her fingers in his hair, arching upward. "You just did a thorough investigation less than a half hour ago."

"I need more evidence of my amazing prowess in bed."

She laughed again, then stopped when his fingers slipped into her warm, wet heat. He watched her face as she began to fall apart, completely giving under his touch. She made him feel like fucking Superman with one look. She'd bewitched and captivated him, and he now knew he was completely in love with her.

A piece of his heart crumbled, so he gave her what he could—pure pleasure from his body and mouth, slipping down to taste her spicy essence, until her screams as she fell apart under his tongue rang in the air and erased all other thoughts.

Later, he held her in the dark and stroked her hair.

"What's your favorite part about Ireland?" she sleepily murmured.

"The Irish stew." She tried to playfully smack him, but she was too tired. He laughed, pressing a kiss to her forehead. "Kidding. I'd say the land. The mix of raw rock and vivid green. The thickness in the air when it rains, and the clean scent when the storms pass, as if it's washed away all your sins. The tainted glory of stone castles, half-broken, climbing up from the valley, as if still battling the past. The glassy, cold surface of the lakes reflecting towering trees. The sprawl of endless horses grazing in the pasture under a weak sun." His mind turned to all the good things about his home, ignoring all the empty, lonely hours that had taken up his days before he'd met her.

"God, that was so beautiful," she whispered. "I saw it in my mind better than a picture."

"Reminds me of Gardiner. Small town where everyone knows your business, but you're family. Mountains and greens, lakes and pastures. Horses. Polish chickens and baby goats dressed in costumes." His fingers drifted over her lips and found her smiling. He breathed in the scent of cocoa butter on her skin and wished the moment never had to end.

"Are you glad you stayed?"

The question—asked hesitantly—was so much more than he'd ever be able to answer. His chest tightened at the idea she could doubt how much she meant to him. So he held her closer and gave her what he could.

"Every day I get to hold you, work with you, laugh with you, I'm happy, Harper. I'm not glad. I'm fucking humbled and grateful you gave me the opportunity to work with Phoenix and eat with your family, and that you welcomed me into your bed. You have to believe that."

A soft breath whispered in the air. "I do. And I feel the same way about you."

Her words hit him directly in the gut and shattered his defenses. He squeezed his eyes shut, craving to tell her the ridiculous confession that he'd fallen in love with her, but he bit it back, knowing it didn't matter. He'd leave. She'd stay. There was no future for them.

Better to keep it this way.

But the Irish expression rose up and escaped his lips in the only way he could tell her how he felt. "Mo stór." *My treasure.*

Silently, his heart screamed another endearment. *Mo grá.*

My love.

She relaxed in his arms. And they didn't talk again for a long time.

Chapter Twenty

Home to the Kentucky Derby, Churchill Downs was the Vatican out of all the churches of the racing world.

People from all over the world dreamed of putting their feet on the same hallowed ground where the most famous Thoroughbreds and jockeys had walked.

From the moment she entered the gracious white-and-green gates, Harper had been struck by a rich sense of history and southern charm that was bred into every particle of dirt and blade of turf in the track. The twin spires added character, and the overwhelming crowds filled the space with a burgeoning excitement that was almost tangible.

She'd made it to the big time.

Emotion choked her throat as she gazed at her team. Elmo was dressed in his silks and meditating in a corner. Phoenix had done surprisingly well with the travel—maybe because they'd left early to give him time to settle in. Maybe because Aidan had been smart enough to take some longer road trips to get the horse used to the feeling of being transported. Captain Hoof helped soothe Phoenix's nerves, and they'd kept him in a strict routine so he knew what was coming next.

The only real problem seemed to be the press.

Aidan had warned her it'd get harder, especially after winning the Champagne Stakes. Phoenix was hot news in the racing world. He'd scored the golden ticket to advance without worry about points or excess fees, and many didn't seem happy. Gossip zinged through the papers and blogs, and her private life was suddenly cracked open for opinion. She'd turned down interviews and remained solitary, relying on Aidan to take care of the social media aspect, which he did with a deft charm and knowledge, impressing more with each day. Even now, when Harper wanted to steal a few moments bonding with her team, a reporter shoved a microphone in Aidan's face. Instead of getting pissed off, Aidan smiled and calmly answered questions. The public seemed to devour Phoenix's rags-to-riches tale, while the insiders of the world seemed to scathingly dismiss the horse as a one-hit wonder.

Harper studied the regal Thoroughbred waiting to set the track on fire in front of her. He'd changed in the past few months—there was a new maturity and a bit more calmness, as if all their hard work had finally paid off. He was beginning to accept the track and its limits, all in the pursuit of being able to run.

She rubbed under his chin, smiling as Captain Hoof spent the last few moments pressing his body against the horse's hooves. "You're quite regal-looking in your silks," she said, giving him some extra pressure that he loved. His gaze locked on hers, and for a little while, she was back in the barn when she'd first rescued him, looking at a broken, bruised horse with fire in his eyes and a *fuck you* snarling from his lips.

God, he was magnificent. A fighter.

Hers.

"We're ready." Aidan's gravelly voice echoed close to her ear, and she shivered, her mind whispering the same mantra when she looked at him.

Hers.

She shook her head to clear it. "Hear that, boy? It's time to show them what you got. We love you."

She kissed his nose and stepped back, letting him exit the stall under Aidan's capable hands. Captain Hoof knew the drill and settled back into his pile of hay to wait for his buddy's return. Elmo finished his meditation, and they all stood together beside Phoenix. Harper had figured she'd be jumpy with nerves and fear, but instead a peaceful strength flowed through her, and when she met each of their gazes, they shared a smile. Clasped hands for a few precious seconds. And believed.

It was everything she'd wished for. They sent Phoenix out to race in the Breeders' Cup Juvenile Sprint with positive energy, love, and acceptance.

Twelve minutes and three seconds later, he stood in the winner's circle as a champion.

♥ ♥ ♥

Aidan lifted his hands up in front of him.

He was shaking.

He stood in the bathroom stall in the greatest racetrack on Earth and tried to get his shit together before he went out to face the crowds again.

Phoenix had won the race, setting an all-new record for speed. The horse had stood like an Arabian king as bulbs flashed in his face and a crown of roses was placed around his neck. There was none of the skittish fear. None of the fiery temper. He'd brought his battle straight to the racetrack and he'd won.

For the first time since Kincaid's Crown had crossed the finish line at the Irish Derby, a sense of purpose filled Aidan. He'd been born to nurture, train, and watch a horse mature into a winner. But sharing the experience with the woman he'd fallen in love with?

Fucking priceless.

He needed to focus on the next few hours of madness. He didn't want Harper alone for too long with the vultures. Now that the big win was behind them, things might get nasty. They'd made a name for themselves from nothing. An abused horse. An unknown farm. A foreign trainer. A jockey with no grade-three stakes wins under his belt.

America might love an underdog story, but the insiders who lived and breathed within the world of horse racing might decide to do whatever was possible to stop them.

Good thing Aidan knew that nothing was stopping Phoenix.

He grinned, left the stall, and washed his hands. Swiping his fingers over his face, he stared into the mirror and reminded himself he was finally getting everything he'd ever wanted.

Redemption.

He headed back to the stables. Phoenix was happily settled, munching on iced oatmeal cookies while Captain Hoof attacked the hay. Harper was talking animatedly to her phone, so he figured she had her siblings on FaceTime to go over every last detail. He grinned and began walking over when he heard his name called.

The voice sounded too familiar. Crisp and clean, with a slight Irish brogue. Dread pooled in his gut. Trapped in a nightmare he never saw coming, Aidan slowly turned and faced the man who'd betrayed him.

Colin Flynn.

His best friend. His surrogate brother. His business partner. A man he'd drunk with, cried with, laughed with, and dreamed with. A man he'd put his trust in, only to have it ripped apart.

Even now, his blue eyes held not a shred of regret or pain. Just stared back with a cool resolve, his face chipped in stone. Money looked good on him. He'd upped his game and wore a custom-cut gray suit. His stylish hat was tipped low over his brow. With a stocky build, red hair, and pale skin, he was a favorite in Ireland—a true homeboy who brought fame and esteem to Kildare with each win. But Aidan knew the truth. Colin cared about nothing but himself and how big his name could get with his stables. His plan to become one of the most famous trainers in Ireland had taken precedence over something Aidan couldn't have sold.

His soul.

Aidan refused to pretend to be civil and didn't want this man near Phoenix. "What are you doing here?" he clipped out.

Colin rocked back on his heels, his sharp gaze narrowed. "Is that how you greet an old friend and partner?" he asked.

"You're neither of those now."

"But I was, until you made the decision to leave."

Aidan shook his head, his laugh full of bitterness. "You always did like to rewrite history. Just tell me what the hell you're doing here."

"I've come to congratulate you, of course." He spread his hands out in a gesture of surrender. "Only you'd be able to take an unknown horse and get him all the way to a Breeders' Cup win. Plans for the Derby?"

"No."

Colin chuckled. "Liar. Just be careful. You don't get to the Triple Crown by playing it safe. That's what ruined you before. I tried to help, but you always were stubborn. Are you sleeping with the owner? She's quite fresh. Different than your usual type. Rachael still asks about you, by the way."

Rage battered his body, but Aidan kept it under a tight lock. Colin knew every weakness to poke at, and for some reason, he was intent on making his presence known. But why? What was his goal?

Aidan pretended like he didn't give a crap and assumed a bored expression. "Get tired of Ireland already? Decided to slum it for a day in the States, or do you have your eye on a new recruit?"

Those blue eyes revealed a glint of greed. "Maybe. Can't say yet, but I received an interesting call. I decided to make the trip to research the possibility. Imagine my surprise when I find your name blowing up the papers. I guess I did a favor letting you go."

His mind spun with the possibilities. Could Colin be stepping in to train another horse for the Derby? Or was he just trying to mess with him? Aidan opened his mouth to tell him to get the hell out, but Harper stepped up beside him with a smile on her face.

"Sorry, Ophelia and Ethan had a million questions. Hello, I'm Harper Bishop." Assuming they were friends, she extended her hand,

and Colin shook it. Aidan had to bury the primitive howl that almost burst from his chest at the idea of the man even touching her.

"A pleasure. Colin Flynn. I'm an old friend from Ireland. We used to work together."

"You did?" Harper glanced back and forth between them, obviously catching the swirling tension. "Well, this must be a nice surprise. Do you have a horse entered?"

Aidan couldn't take another second. Grabbing her wrist, he forced a tight smile. "Sorry, we better get going. We have an interview scheduled soon, and Phoenix needs some time." She shot him a puzzled look but allowed him to lead her away until his chest finally loosened and he was able to drag in air.

She lifted a brow, her face amused. "Gonna assume that guy was not a friend of yours?"

"Not anymore."

He opened his mouth to tell her they needed to talk, but a swarm of press surrounded them. Within minutes, he'd be forced to deal with them, so he turned on the smile and nodded with enthusiasm. The social blitz was important in the horse-racing world—as important as it was in any sport where sponsors, networks, and potential owners could sway odds, report stories, or a hundred other minor details that were critical to get ahead of. He motioned for Harper to step away, giving her some space, and swore to himself to tell her the entire story of him and Colin tonight.

She deserved the truth.

It would all work out fine.

♥ ♥ ♥

"Congratulations on your win."

Harper turned, her gaze narrowing at the stylish Irishman who'd claimed to be Aidan's friend. It was obvious he had sought her out and had something to say. Her instinct told her to walk away and ask Aidan about their relationship, but her curiosity took hold and kept her feet locked to the floor.

Curiosity, it seemed, did kill the cat.

"Thanks." She crossed her arms in front of her chest and waited. She refused to ask questions or tempt him to confess his truths. If he wanted to say something specific to her, it'd be on him to make the effort.

A smile rested on his lips. "You're involved with Aidan, aren't you?"

She quirked a brow. "Why do you want to know?"

His smile grew. "I bet you've been good for him. He seems to lose himself in the thrill of the chase."

She nodded. "I'm not the jealous type, Mr. Flynn."

He chuckled. "Sorry, I meant for horses. Always on the hunt for the next possibility. He thrives on the unknown." When she remained quiet, he continued. "Of course, his last lover, Rachael, was also a horse owner, but she didn't involve herself in the mechanics like you do. She just liked to show up at the races in a pretty dress and hat and take her place in the winner's circle. At least you love the industry as much as he does. I'm sure it's a special bond between you."

"I don't love the industry," she said. "I love the horses."

"Hmm, a quality to be respected. Especially in today's times. Too many people are focused on the win, no matter what the consequences."

"You building up to something of interest, or can I politely take my leave now?" Her clipped words came from a deep sense of foreboding. She didn't trust this man, but so far, she couldn't seem to pinpoint exactly why.

His face changed. Assumed a trace of grief and disappointment that threw her off guard. Colin took a step closer, creating an intimacy that made her uncomfortable. Not from a physical threat. No, this was worse. This was an emotional attack she'd never be able to forget.

But she was too late.

He began talking.

"I thought about keeping my silence. But if I did, I'd regret not giving you the option of deciding for yourself. Phoenix is an amazing horse. Aidan's trained many talented horses in his career, but I can tell this one is special. Reminds me of Kincaid's Crown."

Harper kept her voice cool. "Aidan got that horse to win the Irish Derby. He'll do the same for Phoenix."

"Let's hope he doesn't use the same tactics." Colin rubbed his head. Regret carved out his features. "I'm sorry, but you need to know. Aidan and I were business partners for many years. Not only partners, but close friends. Almost brothers. We trained horses together, built our business from the bricks up, and grew our reputation over time to be one of trust. Reputation in the horse business, you see, is everything, and ours was stellar." He paused, as if caught up in the memories. "When we got the opportunity to train Kincaid's Crown, we both decided he could be our turning point. I sensed something was off, but I never wanted to dig deeper. I was afraid of what I'd discover, but after he won the Derby, I couldn't pretend any longer." His blue eyes filled with sympathy. "Aidan was caught doping the horse in order to improve his performance. I found out he'd been doing it regularly."

She shook her head, not even allowing the unease to hit. "Aidan would never hurt a horse."

"Of course not! I'm not saying he did—he loves every horse he trains. But the need for a win became too strong for him. Kincaid's Crown began slipping. Losing power. Lost a big stakes race. Aidan believed he was helping everyone by giving him the drug. When I confronted him, he defended his actions. Looked me dead in the eye and explained he'd kept the dose low. Low enough not to get detected. Low enough to enhance the horse's natural talent, he said."

"This is impossible," she said. "I don't believe you."

Colin nodded. "I understand. I wouldn't believe me, either. Aidan's not only passionate, but charming, and focuses completely on the horse he picks. Did he tell you he had a gut instinct that shows him his next horse? That Phoenix picked him, and they were meant to train together?"

He must've caught the surprise in her expression, because he nodded again.

"He's quite careful who he chooses. The horse has to own natural speed but also be adaptable to a drug that's not easily detected. When I found out, I threatened to expose him and our business unless he stopped. We had a blowout—things were said that couldn't be taken back—and I forced him to leave. I didn't want Kincaid's Crown to suffer for his actions. The owner agreed with me, and Aidan decided to head to the States."

"He's not a cheater," Harper clipped out. "Why are you telling me these lies? What do you get out of it?"

"I'm very sorry I upset you." He ducked his head. "I just don't want the same thing to happen to you. Watch him, Ms. Bishop. In his mind, it's not cheating or hurting the horse. It's helping the horse be the best possible—a racing machine who will win at all costs. He will choose the win every time. Please don't forget it."

He tipped his hat and disappeared into the swallow of the crowds.

Harper tried to calm her wildly beating heart. Of course, she believed nothing the man said. Knew it was lies, because she knew Aidan O'Connor and the man he was. He'd never dope a horse or rely on drugs to win. That was obvious.

The real problem Colin had hit on?

Aidan's voracious need to win.

She'd spotted the gleam of hunger in his eyes when he watched Phoenix run. The almost-drunken sheen of greed as he stared at the winner's circle. The thirst for the spotlight and flashing cameras and reporters screaming his name. The stinging failure and anger directed at himself in Saratoga after their first loss.

Aidan craved the win. It was as if his entire sense of worth was built around the horse's success. How could a woman hope to compete?

The man she'd fallen in love with had a need to win at all costs.

Just like his ex-partner had stated.

The flare of hurt bothered her the most. Just because they were sleeping together didn't mean they were required to share their secrets. Yes, she'd told him about the bullying and her attempted suicide, but it'd been her choice. Aidan must not have wanted her to find out about the doping scandal, or the details of the breakup of their partnership. She remembered one conversation at the barn, when she'd asked what had sent him running from Ireland. His answer danced in her memory, and all the pieces clicked together.

"Something did happen back home. I got my heart broken, so I came here to put myself back together again."

Rachael? Or his old partner? Why hadn't he told her the truth? He'd looked her family in the eye when asked about the business he'd left behind and lied. Oh, not technically. He'd been clever to blur the line so he could claim he hadn't lied. But it came out all the same, didn't it?

He'd covered up his past, lying by omission about an important part of his life that reflected his goals and priorities when training a horse. By refusing to trust her enough to listen and make her own judgments, he'd stripped the choice from her, leaving her ignorant and exposing Phoenix to someone who might not be who she would've chosen as his trainer if she'd had all the information up front.

Anger stirred and simmered. The confrontation had tainted the glory of Phoenix's win. She refused to let any further races happen until Aidan told her the truth. All of it. Then she'd make the decision that was right for both her and Phoenix.

Swallowing past the lump in her throat, Harper squared her shoulders and headed toward the circle of reporters.

Chapter Twenty-One

"Who's Rachael?"

Aidan stilled. Pivoted on his heel and stared at Harper, who regarded him with a raised chin and cold eyes. Ice slithered down his spine, along with the sting of regret.

She knew.

The day had been hectic, so they'd decided to skip a public dinner and order room service. She'd been distant, but he'd figured she was exhausted. But now he knew Colin had found her and spun his lies.

Aidan had been such an asshole to withhold the truth. And now he was going to pay for the mistake.

His gut clenched, but he remained calm as he removed his jacket and headed to the minibar. Without a word, he poured them two glasses of whiskey, added some ice, and handed one to her. The memory of the first time they'd made love assaulted him. It seemed so long ago, and then again, just like yesterday. In a hotel room, after their first win, he'd gotten to touch her, taste her, claim her. And he'd never been the same afterward. She'd changed him, but he'd played the most dangerous game of all with something even bigger than her heart.

Her trust.

"Rachael is the owner of Kincaid's Crown."

Her eyes widened as the implication hit her full force. She drained her glass with one tip of her hand, then slammed it on the table. When she spun on her heel, refusing to allow him to see her face, raw pain punched him straight in the solar plexus. He was about to hurt the only woman he'd ever loved, and it was all because he'd been a selfish prick who refused to share the parts of his broken past.

"Do you sleep with all the female owners?" she asked lightly.

He cursed, took a step forward, then stopped. "No. Rachael's nothing like you. She was . . . convenient. I cared about her, but it was mostly a physical relationship. She didn't love the horses like you do. She was extremely wealthy, and her father set her up with her own farm. She liked the trappings of the world, and I was considered one of them."

"Convenient, huh? Such a distasteful word," Harper said. There was no emotion in her voice. "Why don't you tell me your side of the story? I've already had the pleasure of hearing Colin's version of events. Would be nice to play a game of comparison."

He let out a vicious curse and clenched his fists. "I fucked up, Harper. I know you won't believe me now, but I wanted to tell you many times what happened back in Ireland."

"Why didn't you?"

Shame burned but she deserved his truth. "I was scared. Scared you wouldn't believe me. Scared to own up to the decisions I'd made that led me to that moment. Scared to be a man not worthy of you and Phoenix."

She turned to face him. "Scared I wouldn't let you train Phoenix?"

He winced, but he deserved it. "Yes."

"You never gave me the opportunity to prove you wrong."

Regret was a bitter companion. God knew he'd dealt with it before, but he'd never experienced this wave of panic he was feeling at the idea of her walking away. He cleared his throat. "No, I didn't. Rachael isn't the one who broke my heart. Colin was. He wasn't just my business partner, he was my best friend. We came up in the ranks together and became close. When we decided to start our own business, all of those hard years of being homeless and a nobody were finally behind me. We began to take on bigger clients. We began to win."

The images of him and Colin celebrating their first big stakes win tore through him. He refilled his drink, then continued. "Colin took care of the business, and I took care of the training. When Rachael approached us with Kincaid's Crown, I knew in my bones the horse was going to change things for all of us. I knew he was a champion. For that year, I worked day and night to get him ready. Rachael and I fell into an affair. And Colin did his magic, until our names were synonymous with victory. We were the hot new trainers on the block. It was as if all of my dreams were coming true."

"What happened?" she asked softly.

He took a sip. The burn slid down his throat and calmed his nerves. "I caught Colin doping the horse. I lost my shit. Kincaid's Crown didn't need any help making it past the finish line. He'd lost a big stakes race before the Derby, and it sent Colin into a tailspin. He was obsessed with us losing all our momentum, so he'd taken it on himself to guarantee we didn't lose the next one."

Aidan set down his empty glass and tunneled his fingers through his hair. He still dreamed of that one moment where everything had crashed down around him. The shock of betrayal cut deep. The ensuing dialogue with the man he'd loved like a brother had almost destroyed him.

"Let's just say we had a difference in opinion. I told him I was bringing the information to Rachael, and he just laughed. Said she already knew."

Harper sucked in her breath. Then held out her glass.

Wordlessly, he gave her a refill and began to pace, feeling like a caged tiger, trapped in the past. "The Derby was coming up. I told him I refused to enter the horse with any type of illegal shit going on, and we had a blowout. Finally, he agreed to back off and let me do my job. Our relationship had taken a hit, but I was still hopeful. I told myself they'd panicked. Reminded myself how hard it'd been before, and he'd made a mistake he wouldn't repeat. I was vigilant with the horse. I slept in the barn, hired someone to watch the horse round the clock, and made it to the Derby. We won."

Oh, how the victory made his blood sing and his heart ache with emotion. Seeing that beautiful horse in the winner's circle gave him joy. He knew some horses were born to run, and Kincaid's Crown was one of them. He'd loved the horse with every breath in his body and been excited about his bright future.

"I thought everything was back on track. Until I headed to the farm, and Rachael and Colin were waiting for me. They informed me they had proof I was doping the horse."

He felt Harper's intense gaze, but he headed toward the window. Placing his palm on the cool glass panes, he stared sightlessly out at the parking lot.

"They wanted you out," she said, her voice filled with pain.

"Yes. Colin had told Rachael I'd expose them. Convinced her to flip the situation on me and get me out. I tried to fight it, of course, but they said if I left quietly, they wouldn't go to the press. Colin would take over the business and give me a small buyout to start over. When I told them no, that I'd fight them all the way, they said my decision would end Kincaid's Crown's racing career, along with mine. Colin said they'd never race the horse again. That their ultimate revenge would revolve around me watching the horse I loved stuck in a stall, knowing he'd never run again. They said he'd be ignored and never sold—an unending reminder of my failure."

She fired off a litany of expletives that was pretty impressive. "I'd kill them both," she muttered.

"I wanted to. But when I looked at all my options, I realized we could never work together again. I'd lost not only my partner, but my best friend. And the thought of Kincaid's Crown never racing again? I couldn't live with myself. So I made them a deal. Told them if anything happened to the horse, I'd spend my last breath taking them both down. Colin believed me. I have a close friend who's a trainer who lives near, and he checks on the horse regularly. Two weeks ago, Kincaid's Crown won a stakes race and broke a new speed record."

"Do you think they doped him again?" she asked in a hard voice.

"No, even Colin admitted the horse was a natural talent. He knows I'd tip off the racing authorities if I suspected any tampering. My friend knows the signs to look for." He turned away from the window and met her gaze. "Rumors spread about why I left. Some said I got itchy feet. Others said I wasn't good enough and was replaced. I decided to come here for a break and begin fresh. I always wanted to train in America, so it was a good place to start."

"And you met Phoenix."

He nodded. A piece of his heart crumbled at the touch of sadness in her sea-green eyes. "And you, Harper. I met you."

Her lips firmed. "But your plan is the same, right? To return to Ireland? Prove to everyone back home that nothing changed—you're still a winner?"

No.

Nothing would be the same ever again, because when he returned to Ireland, she wouldn't be with him. Yet she was right. His dream to return home to the land he loved as a winner and prove to Colin no one could break him hadn't changed. He wouldn't allow himself to be distracted from that one main goal, no matter how deep she'd carved herself into his heart.

"Yes."

The word exploded through the room like a bullet. She winced slightly, but he kept his gaze pinned to hers, knowing he owed her the last shred of truth he could give.

"But you're not Rachael. You're not an extra side benefit or a pleasurable distraction. My heart recognizes yours. For the first time in my life, I know what it's like to crave a woman night and day. To look forward to sharing a meal, or a conversation, or sitting in front of your tiny television surrounded by animals. You changed my life, and I won't let this story make you believe you don't mean everything to me."

She wrapped her arms around her middle. Pain and want pulsed in her aura, but he remained still, knowing she needed time. Harper liked to process things in her own space. He refused to power through or use their physical intimacy to push her.

"I need some time to think."

"I know." He picked up his jacket. "I'm going to go out for a while. Make sure you eat. Text me if you need me for anything. And Harper?"

"Yeah?"

"Thank you for listening to me. I fucked up. I never wanted to hurt you or your family, but I swear to God I won't make that mistake again. I can only hope you can forgive me."

He didn't wait for her answer.

He left.

♥ ♥ ♥

She heard the door softly close and rolled over.

Harper stared at the ceiling and listened to the sounds out in the suite. She'd been up the whole night, unable to sleep. Combing through each one of his words and looking for an answer.

The jealousy was the worst. She hated thinking of him with Rachael and had to fight not to compare herself. A good hour was spent torturing herself on all the things they'd experienced together, including winning an Irish Derby. Maybe she was just another chapter in his book. Another tool in his belt. Another notch on his bedpost.

But her heart told her no.

She sensed he'd held nothing back with his story. Aidan wasn't the type of man to bestow platitudes or flowery words on a woman just to work with her horse or seduce her into bed.

You changed my life . . .

Within all the mess, those were the words that stood out. He'd been just as scared. Scared to open up to another person and be vulnerable. Scared to admit there might be something more between them than a winning horse. She still worried about his obsession with winning, but it was a part of his very soul she'd never be able to change. Somehow, she needed to trust he'd do the right thing if ever faced with a decision.

Yes, he'd hurt her, but after hours spent analyzing his story, she came to one startling conclusion.

It didn't matter.

Her heart and body still craved him.

She still wanted him to train Phoenix, because she believed he was the best for her horse.

And God help her, she still loved him. She'd never say the words, but she could let her body tell him in her own way. That way, when he finally left, she'd have no regrets.

She slipped out of bed, opened the door, and padded softly over to the couch.

He sat up, a shadowy silhouette of hard lines tangled in a blanket. He'd shed his jeans and shirt, but it was his scent that hit her first, a mixture of whiskey and hay and musk. Silently, she knelt in front of him and put her hands on his knees. He leaned forward. His lips brushed her cheek in reverence, and his gravelly voice raked across her nerve endings, bringing shivers.

"Mo stór. Forgive me."

She reached for him, not needing any words for tonight. When his mouth closed over hers, her soul sighed with pleasure, and his tongue gently stroked her lips, savoring her taste before slowly thrusting inside.

He dragged her onto his lap so she straddled him. Her lacy boy shorts were no barrier to the hard, silken thrust of his cock against her most sensitive core, the fabric rubbing over her swollen clit to tease and tempt. He swallowed her needy cry, his fingers stabbed into her hair, holding her still while he devoured her whole.

She fell into his kiss like Alice fell into Wonderland. Time softened and blurred, and then he tore off her shirt and palmed her breasts, lifting them up like a present meant for his mouth and tongue and teeth. He suckled her nipples, and she rotated her hips in greed, her hands running over his hard muscles, enjoying the feel of rough body hair against her palms, then edging his underwear to the side while she cupped his throbbing erection, squeezing with just enough pressure to force a groan from his lips.

He reared up, golden eyes burning with a mixture of tenderness and lust, and he pressed a gentle kiss to her swollen lips the same time he ripped her underwear aside and surged into her wet heat.

The edge of lovemaking melded into fucking, a thrilling combination of nurturing care and savage possession. With each brutal thrust, he pressed a soft kiss to her lips, his palms cupping her cheeks, and she gripped his shoulders, helpless under the command of his body.

The orgasm grew closer with each roll of his hips, and the sheer tenderness of his caresses only fanned the flame. She begged in between each kiss, but he controlled every deliberate thrust, until finally he arched and slammed her onto his cock, and she cried out and shattered into orgasm.

She collapsed onto his chest. He wrapped his arms tight around her body, still inside her, and pressed his lips to her temple.

"Don't leave me alone in this," she finally whispered.

"I won't. Never again."

She dropped a kiss on his bare shoulder and snuggled into his embrace. They stayed like that for a long, long time, no more words needed.

Chapter Twenty-Two

They fell into a routine as gracefully as fall turned into winter.

It was a time Harper enjoyed and looked forward to at the farm. When the mountain peaks glistened with ice and snow, and a blanket of white covered the trees and grass, a hush came over the world. Even the animals enjoyed the new quiet, huddled in the barn under cozy blankets and sleeping nonstop. When they went for the occasional ride, they nipped and galloped with a mad glee in the bite of cold, and Harper laughed at their play and friskiness.

The guests at the inn slowed, and the holidays passed in a blur of cheer and cherished moments. Elmo took off for a few weeks to visit his family for Christmas and decided to stay until February.

The shorter days and longer nights lent themselves to intimate snuggling with Disney movies and a herd of animals always ready to hibernate and howl at the screen when they caught sight of a character that resembled themselves.

And Aidan became an important part of it all.

He was now sewn into all seams of her life, a partner not only in business but also in her day-to-day routine. With the victory of the Breeders' Cup Juvenile, they'd become just as famous as Kyle in Gardiner, and Phoenix became their new hero. Fall had brought an influx of visitors who lined up to catch sight of the celebrated horse, but in the midst of winter, everyone drifted away to do their own hibernating and left Harper, Aidan, and Phoenix blissfully alone.

For now, they'd safely passed Valentine's Day—her most hated holiday of all time—and decided to take an evening and hang out with Mia and Ethan.

Harper whistled at the transformation of the once-dilapidated bungalow the couple lived in. "Guys, this is amazing," she said, walking through the space. They'd pushed out the back wall to add an office for Mia and an extra bedroom and bath. A special mudroom off the entrance was now heated and held Wheezy's, Bolt's, and Hei Hei's equipment and feeding bowls. A new sectional in sleek silver with matching oversize chairs had replaced the battered secondhand stuff. They'd added a fireplace with a colorful throw rug, and the dogs were making good use of it by currently snoozing in contentment. The kitchen, which had once been a tiny space like Harper's, now boasted an open galley with gorgeous butcher-block counters and tables in rich reddish cedar and brand-new stainless-steel appliances. "Is Ethan finally going to cook?"

Mia laughed. "Well, we both decided to take cooking lessons together," she said, shooting a glance at Ethan.

Harper tried not to laugh at the look on her brother's face.

"There's only so much takeout we can depend on," he muttered.

"Kyle and Ophelia could have taught you," Harper said.

"Hell no," Ethan said, shaking his head. "My goal is to take a few lessons at the Culinary Institute, invite him to dinner, and blow his mind. We don't want them to know a thing."

Mia rolled her eyes. "His idea, not mine. But it would be kind of cool to see their faces when we come up with a dazzling dinner."

Aidan laughed. "I love it. Make sure you beat his meat, though. That's where he's the most sensitive."

Harper gave him a playful punch on his shoulder. "You're just as bad as they are."

Hei Hei came running out of his special room with Captain Hoof on his heels and shot them a long-suffering look. Aidan knelt down and the chicken shrieked, rubbing his feathers against his knee.

"I know, dude. But Captain Hoof loves you. You're gonna have to suck it up and learn how to babysit."

The goat slid from behind, and Hei Hei automatically blocked him from bumping into the large coffee table. Captain Hoof looked up in pure hero worship at his friend and licked him in thanks.

Mia watched the exchange, shaking her head. "I still can't get over it. It's the first time an animal bonded with Hei Hei, and the first one my chicken doesn't want to kill."

"At least we finally got him out of that ridiculous chicken costume," Aidan said. "I can't believe the press snapped a picture that went viral."

"It was cute," Harper commented. "People began sending Phoenix stuffed goats and chickens."

He glared. "Not cute. Humiliating. I refuse to be known as the trainer with the goat-chicken companion of a famous racehorse."

Ethan chuckled and handed them each a beer. "What's the plan for the next two months? The Wood Memorial is April sixth, right?"

Aidan settled back on the sectional and took a sip of IPA. "Yes. Harper and I agreed it'd be best to keep his spring season focused on that one race. The problem with racing them at this young age is the high percentage of injury and burnout. I want Phoenix to be fresh for the Derby and not push him into any other big races beforehand. The Triple Crown is really demanding, with only a few weeks in between all three races. It's important he enjoys just being a horse away from the track for now."

"Good idea," Mia said, taking a spot on the chair. Dressed in black leggings and a crocheted black sweater with elaborate silver pieces of jewelry, she looked both comfortable and fashionable in her home. "How important is the Wood Memorial?"

Harper sighed. "Very. We need him to try and place in the first three slots to be prepped for the Derby."

"We still have a long road ahead," Aidan added. "Elmo gets back next week, and we'll begin light training again." He gave her a glance full of intimacy and took her hand. "It's been a great winter, though. I feel like we all needed to take a breath."

Mia smiled at them, and Harper tried to keep a blush at bay. Aidan was part of the family and was accepted as such. For the past few months, the Derby had become a distant thought. She was fully engaged in every moment spent with Aidan and refused to think of the future.

But, soon, the future wouldn't be delayed any further. Phoenix would try to win the most important race in the world. And it would be one step closer to Aidan leaving.

She squeezed his hand, emotion tightening her throat, and pushed away the thought.

There was still time. Plenty of it.

She'd enjoy every last second.

"How's the wedding planning going?" she asked.

Mia sighed. "Good, we're all set for August twenty-fourth. I think the setting at Mohonk Mountain House is perfect. I'm glad we decided not to go with some fancy place in Manhattan."

"Me, too," Ethan said, giving her a smile. "There's just one thing I'm worried about."

"Kyle being best man?" Harper teased.

"Nope, bigger than that. In fact, we have an important question to ask you."

Harper frowned. "What?"

Ethan and Mia shared a pointed look. "Would you give us the honor of having Captain Hoof accompany Hei Hei down the aisle at our wedding?" Mia asked seriously.

It took her a few moments for the words to process, but it was Aidan's belly laugh that finally sank in. They laughed together, and emotion stung her eyes, and Harper realized she'd never been so happy in her life.

Six weeks later, Phoenix won the Wood Memorial at Aqueduct Racetrack and officially qualified for the Kentucky Derby.

And Harper knew that everything was about to change.

♥ ♥ ♥

"You gotta be kidding me."

She watched the parade of townsfolk pile out of their cars, arms filled with platters of food, flowers, and balloons, as if they were attending a wedding. The mass bore down on her precious barn, and she watched with as much dread as if confronting the terrifying clown from *IT*.

"What the hell is going on?" she whispered, peeking her head around the post.

Aidan walked over to see what was going on. "They're here to see Phoenix."

She blinked. "Why? He didn't win the Derby yet!"

He shrugged, shading his eyes from the sun as they approached. "It's nice. They're excited. When I got lunch at the diner yesterday, Bea asked if it was okay if some of them stopped in for a visit."

She glared. "And you didn't tell me? I would have told them hell no."

He winked. "I know. You're definitely not a people person. But Phoenix and the farm are important to everyone in town. They want to be part of it. Let's go say hello."

Her jaw dropped as she watched him stride over to the welcoming committee.

Oh, this was bad. As if the reporters and press and internet weren't enough, now she had her own town taking up her time. Still, she knew Aidan was right. It was sweet, even though such vintage small-town meddling was both overwhelming and annoying. She'd just have to suck it up and be nice.

She pasted on a smile and walked out of the barn.

"Harper!" Fran screeched, running over with a fresh bouquet of flowers. "I can't believe we'll have a Kentucky Derby winner from Gardiner! We'll be famous!"

"Well, we're not winners yet, but hopeful," she said. "Those are so pretty, thank you."

Fran yanked the bouquet back before she could take them. "Sorry, these are for Phoenix. For his stall."

"Oh, right."

Bea from the diner stepped up and shoved a platter of hamburgers at her. She'd owned the local diner in town for years, and like every teen in Gardiner, Harper had spent endless hours sitting in her red cracked-vinyl booths. With her beehive of gray hair, hot-pink lipstick, and blue shadow, she was like a blast from the past. Her fuchsia leggings and matching T-shirt were covered by a lacy half apron that was part of her uniform. "Hello, sweetie, how are you? I brought Phoenix some burgers to keep up his strength! I read that protein is very important for energy, but I wasn't sure if horses liked ketchup, so I left them plain."

Harper nodded, her brain already foggy from all the endless dialogue.

"Tony brought cookies, though, for dessert as a reward. Oh, and we didn't forget Captain Hoof!" She pulled out a small stuffed chicken and pressed the belly. The toy gave a clatter of squeaks from his tiny mouth. Bea and Fran burst into laughter. "Isn't that adorable? Where are they?"

Aidan stepped to her side, as if he sensed she needed support. "In the pasture taking a nice rest. You're welcome to go visit them. Elmo's out there, and he'll make sure Phoenix greets his guests properly."

Fran clapped her hands. Tony from the tattoo place handed Harper a pile of cookies carefully wrapped in plastic. With his shaved head, ink crawling up both arms, and mulish expression, he was sometimes cranky and hard to deal with, but he was part of the family, like one of those grouchy uncles who came over for Thanksgiving and bitched about everything but never left. "Those are for the horse," he warned. "Was thinking of creating a design of Phoenix for the customers, but I need your permission. It'll be good publicity." He handed her a crumpled stack of papers from his pocket. "Sign those."

"I'll look it over later today and let you know," she said.

He glared. "You think I'm trying to cheat you or something? Ever hear about branding? Don't you want my shop to make money, or you think you're the only one who can get rich?"

Bea sighed and flapped her hand in the air. "Cut it out, Tony. She needs to read the legal stuff before signing. Leave her alone."

Tony grunted.

Aidan clapped him on the shoulder. "I'm sure it's fine. I'll make sure to deliver it to you tomorrow, okay? Why don't you head to the pasture?"

"Yeah, okay."

Harper watched them head out with gifts and dealt with two more large groups who worked in town and attended SUNY New Paltz, all showing up to squeal and gossip and praise the magical horse. She accepted gifts—all for Phoenix or Captain Hoof—accepted congratulations, answered endless questions, and played the personal agent of her horse.

Un-fucking-believable.

When she finally got rid of them, Harper stacked up the gifts in the barn. "Is this normal?" she asked Aidan, shaking her head. "Because this seems a bit ridiculous."

"The Derby is a big deal. Speaking of which, I need a favor."

Her instincts flared to life. Something about his hesitant expression told her she wasn't going to like the favor. "What is it?"

"ESPN wants to do an interview with you for a behind-the-scenes piece on Phoenix. They can be here Friday with a camera crew and wrap up by midafternoon."

She groaned and spun on her heel to pace. "I'm sorry, Aidan, but my answer is no. I told you I hate this stuff. The cameras, and stories, and poking in my own damn business. I'm not going to put on a show for the camera for a bunch of people I don't even care about."

His jaw clenched. "I swear it'll be easy and quick. I have a list of questions already cleared. They'll take some video of the farm and the barns, and then you'll sit down for the interview." Waves of frustration shot out from his body. "It's important, love. Press is part of the success of a racing career. I've let you stay in the background until now, but they want to know about the owner who rescued Phoenix. It's a great opportunity to have publicity for the inn and the rescue farm. This could get you a ton of social support and money. Maybe even investors down the line."

"I don't care." Her nerves tightened, and her skin felt hot and itchy. She despised being put on camera. Being judged for her appearance or language or beliefs. She had no social media accounts other than for the businesses, and insisted Aidan did all the talking for the team. "Money and investors aren't worth giving up my privacy. There's no need to tell my story when you've already told it. Don't you see that all they want is a human-interest piece to grab ratings? The Derby is about Phoenix. Not me. Tell them your story—that's just as good."

"You're wrong." His voice came out hard, making her jerk back. "To have a successful racing career, you need to play nice with the press. People want to know you—the extraordinary woman behind a champion. You can inspire the world with your story, Harper. Stop being so damn stubborn. We all have to sacrifice for the team sometimes. Just do it this once. For Phoenix."

In that moment, as she stared at the man she loved, her heart squeezed with pain. That mad gleam flickered in his golden eyes, the one that told her his career would always be more important than anything else. He was willing to sacrifice her comfort and need for privacy in order to make Phoenix a star. Maybe she could have dealt with that type of intention if it had been truth.

But it wasn't.

Because she knew he was the one who wanted to be a star.

If she did the interview, he'd be an even bigger celebrity, thrust into the spotlight he always wanted. He'd be able to prove once again to Colin that he was a winner. God knew she'd never deny him that right. But not at the expense of using her.

Disappointment crashed deep. She turned away, heartsick, and tried to find the words to explain why she couldn't do what he asked. Her voice remained strong and steady when she finally spoke. "I'm sorry, Aidan. I really am, but we have a difference of opinion on this. I won't bitch about letting them follow me around, and take pictures, and shout questions. I've handled the endless articles tearing Phoenix apart, and my lack of expertise as an owner, and the other so-called horse experts gleefully awaiting our defeat so they could laugh and poke fun at our dreams. But getting on camera to ask the world for their approval, to basically beg them to like me and my farm and my family? No. Once, I wanted so badly to be liked and accepted, but the rejection made me almost lose myself. I swore in that barn all those years ago I'd never do that again."

She faced him, chin tilted high, and locked gazes. "Please, don't ask me again. Now, I'm going to check on Flower and get Phoenix settled in his stall. He has a big week coming up."

She waited for him to say her name. To stop her from leaving. To apologize and explain he understood.

But he was silent as she left the barn.

♥ ♥ ♥

Aidan watched her leave, the words he wanted to say stuck in his throat and forever trapped.

Over the past weeks, she'd been ruthless about her restrictions on interviews and cameras. At first, he'd accepted her decision, but with the Triple Crown upon them and the buzz going on with Phoenix, he'd figured she'd break down and do just one interview.

Guess not.

He uttered a vicious curse and strode out of the barn. Yes, she revered her privacy, but he'd never imagined her fear of the camera would go so deep. He'd been a total asshole to push that hard. But in the racing world, no one wanted to hide. He was used to the competitive, sharklike hunger for press and exposure from the owner, trainer, jockey, and everyone in between. His attitude toward her continuous denial of the public spotlight had turned from respect to frustration. Television was the crown jewel during racing season, with everyone fighting for the camera.

Except Harper Bishop.

He sought out the path twisting through the woods, trying to clear his head. It made more sense now—how the endless bullying would have caused a distrust of the public spotlight. He knew personally how easy it was to be a hero one moment, then be ripped to shreds the next.

America adored thrusting someone onto the pedestal of success, but they liked yanking them down even more.

The vulnerability in her sea-green eyes had shredded his heart. She had so much damn pride—what had it cost her to admit she needed her privacy for her own peace of mind? Yet he hadn't gone to her. Hadn't pulled her into his arms like she deserved to tell her he understood and accepted.

No. Instead, he'd let her go without a word.

The question taunted him.

Why?

He walked, crunching over twigs and grass and leaves, letting his gaze trace the edge of mountain and sky just turning a hazy shade of blush pink, ready for sunset. The spring air stirred his nostrils and brought the musky scent of earth and florals, reminding him of the woman who'd stolen his heart.

You know why, the inner voice taunted. *You just don't want to admit it.*

The answer unfurled from the depths of his soul.

Because you want to return to Ireland like a king. A champion. And you'll do anything to accomplish it.

Just like Colin.

He stopped walking, breathing hard, looking up at the mighty pine tree towering above in a quest for peace. No, he wasn't like that. He was nothing like Colin.

His mind spun, and the jagged pieces of reality attacked.

He might never dope a horse, but he'd push hard. Push Phoenix to the edge of competitive training even in his youth. Push Elmo to be the perfect jockey. Push Harper to fall in line and do the television interview. Push the family into mortgaging and paying the high fees associated with the glory of the Triple Crown.

When did it really stop? The lines were blurred. Maybe he'd never realize how much he would sacrifice unless he was faced with a monumental decision—a decision he prayed he'd never have to make.

He stayed in the woods with his tangled thoughts for a long time and then went to find Harper.

She was leaning on the gate to the pasture, watching Phoenix and Captain Hoof. Her hands were clasped on top of the rail, one bootheel hooked in the bottom rung. Aidan watched the animal couple with amusement. The horse would grab a few bunches of hay, then drop some on the floor for the goat. In between munching, Phoenix would nicker and rub his face against the goat's small body. In return, the

Captain would push back into those magical racing legs with pure affection.

"You taught them both to love."

Her shoulders stiffened, but she turned to meet his gaze. There was a wariness in the depths of her eyes that caused his gut to twist. He settled next to her, close but not touching. "No," she said softly. "It's what Elmo once said. Two wounded souls recognize each other."

He let out a breath. "I was out of line. I'm sorry."

She nodded, her gaze sliding away. "Apology accepted."

Her generosity at forgiving him so easily made him feel even more ashamed. "This is bigger than a simple apology, love. I needed to take a deeper look at some of my intentions. See, this is the only world I've ever known. I really had no idea you could live in it any differently. But you're teaching me. I'm truly sorry."

This time, her eyes were clear, and she reached for his hand. The warmth and graceful strength of her fingers wrapped in his brought him a sense of peace he used to get only from being in a barn, alone, or with an animal companion. Now, he'd reached a new level of intimacy, and he never wanted to go back.

"I know press is important. I just don't want them to take anything that doesn't belong to them. Does that make sense?"

He smiled and squeezed her hand. "Perfect sense. I'll tell ESPN no. Was also thinking of getting some bodyguards to man the gate. Just to keep out unwanted visitors."

She smiled back. "Sounds good. Ethan used to work as a bodyguard, so he has a bunch of friends who can help. I'll speak to him in the morning."

"A bodyguard, too, huh? Good to know." He tucked her hair back behind her ear. "Let's go home, Harper."

Chapter Twenty-Three

Phoenix seemed to know he was back in Churchill Downs to win.

The trip had been smooth, and he settled in his stall like a returning king. Harper sipped a mint julep and wore a fancy Derby hat in white and robin's-egg blue to match her jockey's silks. Her designer dress was the same bright color and custom fitted to her body, and her heels were too damn high, but Mia had insisted she wear the ensemble, threatening her if she dared try to step out in work boots at the Kentucky Derby.

She smiled at endless television cameras and watched her horse's journey streamed live on television for the entire world to share in, without a personal interview. She shook numerous hands of important, famous trainers and owners and jockeys, along with various celebrities who wished her luck. And the whole time, the only things she truly cared about were Aidan and Elmo and Phoenix and if they were doing okay.

The unforgettable walk to the gate was an image that would be forever burned into her memory. The strains of "My Old Kentucky Home" filled the air along with voices raised in celebration, and the horses began walking down the track in the post parade. Phoenix looked regal in his splendor, prancing down with his blinkers keeping him on point. Elmo seemed completely focused on his job ahead, his lips set in a thin line, and she knew he'd already sunk into his safe place. He meditated before every race, and had once explained it was like wrapping himself and Phoenix into a protective bubble where no one could hurt them. Aidan stood tall, fingers linked with hers, smiling as the horses began to advance to the gate.

Nerves jumped in her belly, but she savored the precious moment of victory for all of them—making it to the historic Kentucky Derby was an opportunity few horses ever experienced.

"We got lucky with our post position," Aidan whispered to her. "The nine slot will give him every opportunity to break clean and get to the front."

"Elmo knows what to do," she whispered back, squeezing his hand in reassurance. "We need to let them both do their jobs."

He winked at her and bulbs flashed. Though she hated that their private moment would be splashed all over for the world to assess and judge, there was a new sense of acceptance and ease within. Yes, she'd always protect her privacy, but she didn't need to hide any longer. She'd fought and claimed her life on her terms, and she wasn't afraid to let the world see who she was. Phoenix had taught her that.

So had Aidan.

She watched Phoenix circle twice, then easily get loaded into the gate. Her skin prickled and her gut clenched, and she said a quick prayer while she waited for the announcement. Down the line they went until each horse was locked and loaded.

Silence fell upon the packed racetrack.

The clang of the buzzer shrieked, and the crowd roared.

"And they're off!"

Phoenix broke clean and quickly made his way to the head of the pack, setting the pace. Three horses roared from behind and crowded around him. He let Tom Tom get ahead of him and began to stalk while White Cliff and Sandy's Son flanked him from both sides. The pace was fast from the onset, and the worry was always that Phoenix would run out of gas before the final push to make way for the closers.

Holding her breath, she watched the group of horses thunder past the first turn and into the backstretch. Positions shifted. Wicked Wind made a move toward the inside and settled by the rail, taking fifth. Dirt flew and hooves pounded. Tom Tom began to die, falling back, and made way for Sandy's Son and White Cliff to close in, but Phoenix still held on.

"He's waiting for the blowout," Aidan commented, voice shaky with excitement. "Elmo has the perfect ride so far."

And it was. In slow motion, the race ramped up and narrowed to the focus of the final stretch. Tom Tom began to gain ground, and Sandy's Son faltered, stumbling back. Elmo gave Phoenix the signal, and the horse picked up speed at the same time the closers near the middle kicked it up.

She held her breath as White Cliff drew near, head to head with Tom Tom and challenging Phoenix.

The well-known closer, Wicked Wind, exploded in a burst of energy and began passing horses in a blur of speed, nearing the front.

Harper began screaming her horse's name, over and over in a war chant as the finish line drew near and Phoenix was three lengths ahead. Wicked Wind came closer in a blistering rush, squeezing Phoenix's lead to two lengths, one length, and—

Phoenix crossed the finish line.

The stadium exploded.

Throat raw, Harper threw herself into Aidan's arms, tears leaking from her eyes as the reality rushed over her.

Phoenix had just won the Kentucky Derby.

Cameras rolled, mics were pushed in her face, and Aidan held on to her for a few more precious seconds, his hug relating all the emotions that could never be formed into words. When he pulled away, his eyes were damp.

They pushed their way through the thickening crowds toward the winner's circle and took their place alongside the memory of the most famous horses of legend.

It was one of the greatest moments of her life.

Chapter Twenty-Four

One week later, they sat together in the pasture and watched Phoenix and Captain Hoof laze in the sun.

Harper's head lay in Aidan's lap. He stroked her hair, munching on sunflower seeds, and watched the clouds float by.

She lifted a hand and pointed to the periwinkle sky. "Look, a turtle."

He squinted. "Looks like a naked woman lying on her side."

"Really, Irish? You got a boob out of that?"

"Sorry, guess my head's not in the right place." His burgeoning erection under her cheek made her laugh. "Or maybe it's the other head that's giving me the problem."

"We just had sex this morning."

"Hours ago. I'm starved for affection." He pressed a kiss on her lips, and she sighed with contentment. "How does it feel being a Derby winner?"

"Ask Phoenix."

They grinned and stole a glance at her champion. He lay stretched out on his side, eyes closed in bliss. Captain Hoof squeezed in tight beside him, always needing to touch, with his head resting on top of him. Bolt and Wheezy circled around, barking occasionally, but the two of them refused to budge.

"I don't think he cares much," Aidan commented, lifting strands of hair and combing through them. The motion made her sleepy. "He's definitely not a diva."

"Not his style. Nor mine. How many interview requests have you turned down?"

"Too many to count."

"Did you see the camera crew parked outside the gates, trying to get a glimpse of Phoenix working out?"

Aidan groaned. "Yeah, Ethan's buddy has been amazing. Said he'd take care of it. He'll be at the Preakness viewing party they're holding at Bea's Diner. Don't want the press to overrun the town's celebration. We have a few more days before we have to leave and dive back into the chaos."

"Are we ready?"

"What do you think?" He grinned, lowering his head, and kissed her. She kissed him back, reaching up to hold on to him, falling into his embrace like a young girl with her first crush. He gave her both the butterflies and the sense of rightness. How had she gotten so lucky to find him? "You're not nervous, are you?"

"About the second leg of the most difficult circuit in the world? Nah. Not a bit."

"His workouts have been stellar, and he's had plenty of rest. The Belmont is the one that concerns me the most. It's the longest, when closers can finally catch up to him, but we'll worry about that later."

"Maybe our horse should be running laps instead of napping."

"It's called a *power nap*." His teeth nipped at her bottom lip. "Maybe we should take one. Want to take a stroll in the barn?"

Her almost giggle still surprised her. She didn't think it was possible for her to create a giggle. "That's called a *roll in the hay*."

"Semantics, love. The barn is ours for the taking. John's on break. Chloe and Owen are in school. Ophelia and Kyle are running the inn, and Ethan and Mia are in town for the next few hours. And I promise Flower won't tell."

"Race you to the barn."

He rolled over and chased after her.

♥ ♥ ♥

The second leg of the Triple Crown, the Preakness, was run at the Pimlico Race Course in Baltimore, Maryland, and began just like the other big races had. Phoenix had another good travel trip and was safely installed in his space amid a stall befit for glory. People had sent him gifts—from roses to iced oatmeal cookies to stuffed-goat toys. He was no longer considered a lucky one-hit wonder and had turned into America's sweetheart. With his rescue backstory and cranky temper with other animals besides a disabled goat, the blinkers he proudly wore, and the way he pranced on the field as a bit of a show-off, the country obsessed and dreamed he'd be the next winner of the Triple Crown. His speed was breaking records, and even critics had a hard time betting him down for the Preakness.

"The morning line odds are three to one," Harper announced, throwing the paper on the table. They were eating breakfast in their room, nibbling at fruit, croissants, and a platter of crispy bacon. She'd bitched about the subpar coffee on their last trip, and now he carried coffee beans and a grinder with him so they could make their own brew.

He grinned, tipping his cup to take another sip of tea while she drank her extra-strong coffee. "Odds will jump all over the place today, especially as we get closer to post time. Don't get attached."

"I think his odds should be two to one. He's coming in strong."

"But was almost beat by Wicked Wind. It was close enough to make the handicappers doubt. Tom Tom made a strong rally also, and got a post by the rail. We pulled an outside position, where it's not easy for a pacesetter to break and get ahead."

She waved her hand in the air and snorted. "Phoenix likes a good challenge. Why are you being a Debbie Downer?"

He laughed. "I'm just reciting what I heard on TV. I better get dressed and ready." He stood up, grabbing his phone as it buzzed frantically. He glanced at the number and swiped with his thumb. "Elmo, we're getting ready and will be over in a bit. I think we should—"

"Aidan. You need to get over here."

He froze at the sound of his jockey's voice. Instantly, his heartbeat ramped up and a cold, clammy sweat broke out on his skin. "What's the matter?" he asked calmly.

"It's Phoenix. Something's wrong with his ankle. Call the vet."

Aidan closed his eyes and dragged in a breath. He couldn't lose his shit now—it was too important. For everyone. "I'll be right over."

Harper sensed his unease and stood up from the table. "What is it?" she asked worriedly.

"We need to get to the track. Elmo noticed something wrong with Phoenix's ankle. I'm calling the vet now."

They shared a glance. His gut clenched at the look on her face, but she quickly got dressed, and they sped over to the track.

Elmo was waiting for them. "Noticed swelling round the right ankle. No heat, but there's some stiffness."

"Hey, boy," Harper cooed, rubbing under his chin. "You got some pain?" She knelt down and Aidan joined her. They both ran their hands over the sore spot, probing gently. "Seems like there's definitely inflammation," she said. Her teeth tugged at her lower lip. "Let's see what the vet says."

As Aidan looked at Phoenix, a voice whispered from deep within, rising up, the words slithering out with glee.

He's not going to run today.

You lose.

No. There was nothing wrong with Phoenix. He'd kept his training deliberately light. Been cleared by their own vet right before they traveled. The horse had put in a perfect morning workout, was in high spirits, and seemed on top of his game.

He had to run.

When the vet came, there was already a nervous energy buzzing in the air around them. Phoenix tossed his head, trying to buck away from the vet, probably in response to their gloom and doom and tension. Captain Hoof pressed against his legs, and the horse began to calm. Finally, he allowed the examination.

After what felt like an eternity, the vet straightened and shook his head. "Don't know."

Aidan gritted his teeth. "What do you mean you don't know?"

"There's no fracture or break. He seems to have full movement. There's a bit of inflammation, which tells me something is going on in the joint, but it may not be serious. Did he have a particularly challenging workout?"

"Short breeze. No issues," Elmo said.

"Walk him around for me," the doctor advised. "I want to study his gait and reaction."

Aidan opened the stall and took him out, walking him slowly back and forth.

"Okay, there's definitely minor stiffness, but he doesn't seem to be in pain."

"So he can run?" Aidan asked.

The vet gave them a shrewd glance, took off his glasses, and rubbed his eyes. "He can probably run, but you're taking a chance. Unless I give him an X-ray, I can't completely rule out a bone or cartilage issue. It could be a possible infection, but I can't rule that out, either, unless I collect synovial fluid and run tests. He could have landed a bit hard on a turn, and it just started bothering him now. Problem with ankle issues is it could be a cocktail of various things, but I don't have the time to get a diagnosis."

Silence descended. The words were like a gathering storm that grew power slowly but built up to a hurricane. Aidan's mind ticked through a hundred different scenarios, all with different outcomes.

"If it's something more serious, and he races, what can happen?" Harper asked.

"He could damage the leg, maybe permanently."

"And if it's nothing but a minor sore-joint issue?" Aidan asked.

"I'd suggest ice packs, some stall rest up for a few days, and maybe some inflammatory meds. I've seen these issues many times before. I've watched horses run with minor injuries and become lame. I've also seen horses scratched from a race for what looked like an upcoming infection that turned out to be nothing but a bad mood and temperament. He's clear to run if you decide to keep him in. I know it's difficult with the stakes so high, but at this point, it's truly a personal decision. I'll be around awhile longer. Here's my card if you have any further questions."

The vet handed Aidan the card and disappeared, leaving them all in shocked silence.

He stared at Phoenix. They'd come so far. He knew the racing business was full of hard turns and bad breaks. Scratches happened all the time, for various reasons.

But God help him, he had to think of all the players here.

"What do you think?" Harper finally asked, searching his gaze. Those sea-green eyes were filled with anguish, hope, and a raw emotion. "My instinct is to scratch, but it may be nothing. If we pull him from the race, there's no longer a shot at the Triple Crown."

Elmo muttered a curse and stroked the horse's flank. "No demons this time," he said quietly. "Did I take him too hard round turn?"

"No, Elmo," Aidan said quietly. "You did nothing wrong. In fact, you were the one who caught it. All of us could have missed the signs, it was so subtle."

"I think he do it," Elmo said. "I think he win if he runs."

Aidan did, too. It was in the horse's liquid brown eyes, the determination and spirit that drove him forward to give everything he had. Even now, the horse exuded confidence with every toss of his head, the prick of his ears when he heard his name. He'd fought his demons and won. It was an ongoing battle, but they'd done it together, and he deserved the shot at the Crown.

How could Aidan rip that away?

Because if something happened to Phoenix out there, he'd never forgive himself.

And neither would Harper.

"Aidan? I trust your opinion. What do you think?" she asked.

Trust.

That little word meant everything to her. The word he'd once broken by not telling her about his past, then slowly rebuilt each day they spent together. The word that made him vow to always put Phoenix first, no matter the stakes.

He could scratch him for nothing, and they'd regret it for the rest of his life. There'd be anger in the racing world for not being able to celebrate a possible Triple Crown. History wouldn't remember Phoenix as a winner but as the horse who'd been scratched, and handicappers would gleefully proclaim he'd never had a chance to win anyway. Aidan would return to Ireland with a mark on his record, questioned and doubted by owners because he was too scared to race against the odds. Colin would win.

Aidan could let him run and take his chances. If Phoenix won, he'd be one step closer to the Triple Crown, and Aidan would be one step closer to his goal of showing everyone back home he was still a successful trainer and avenging the betrayal of his best friend.

But if Phoenix ran and became permanently injured, they'd lose everything.

Aidan closed his eyes and went inward to the part of him that had once whispered he'd found his next champion.

And found his answer.

He slowly opened his eyes. Then took Harper's and Elmo's hands in his. "We have to scratch. It may be nothing, but if we gamble and lose, I'll never be able to live with the decision. Can you?"

A sob choked Harper's throat, but she nodded. "No."

Elmo was stoic, but his other hand closed around the horse's mane, as if trying to gather strength. "No."

"Then we scratch. We get the X-ray and the tests and take it from there. If it's minor, we rest him up and see if he can run in the Belmont."

Elmo looked to the gathering crowds swarming the barn, ready to pounce when the horses exited. The buzz of gossip had already broken, and everyone was frantic to know if Phoenix would still run. "They believe in him. We break America's heart."

"They'll still believe in him, Elmo. Whether or not he wins another damn race, he got a taste of the big-league glory. We all did." He smiled, though underneath, a soul-sucking grief at the loss threatened to overwhelm him. But not now. He needed to lead his team, and the next few hours were crucial. "We're going to inform them of the news with our heads held high because we already won. Understood?"

Harper put her arms around Aidan and Elmo as Phoenix moved close. "Understood."

He stood with his makeshift family and the horse who had changed him and gathered his strength to face what lay ahead.

Chapter Twenty-Five

A week later, Harper walked into the barn and found Aidan sitting with Phoenix. The lilting brogue in his voice rose in the air, and she leaned against the door to listen.

"Don't get too attached to those cookies, mo chára. Tomorrow, we'll get you back in action and see how that ankle holds. I should've known you'd love to bring a bit of drama to a Crown race. Also should've known you wouldn't make it easy. What fun would that be?"

His chuckle told her Phoenix had butted his head when Aidan stopped stroking him.

"Vet cleared you, buddy, so no more lazing around. Let's get you some fresh air. Come on, Captain, you need some, too." The gate unlatched and he stepped outside. Her heart broke at the wary glint in his eye when he spotted her. "Hey. Didn't hear you come in."

She walked over, giving the animals a pat in greeting. "I was eavesdropping. I'm glad he's ready to work out and there was no issue with the ankle."

Shadows chased his face, but he nodded. "Yeah. Me, too."

"Are you?"

He jerked back. "What kind of question is that? Of course I am. I didn't want him to be hurt."

Since he'd made the decision to scratch, Aidan had withdrawn into himself. He engaged in conversation, made love to her at night, and pretended nothing had changed. He spoke about winning the Belmont and moving forward, but a spark had died inside of him, and she didn't know how to get it back. Frustration raged and wiped out her patience.

She'd given him distance. When the vet had confirmed there was no infection, tendonitis, or serious issues, everyone was obviously relieved. But Harper caught the guilt glinting in Aidan's golden eyes along with the regret. He'd been torturing himself daily over his decision to pull Phoenix from the Preakness. Somehow, he blamed himself for all of them losing the possibility of a Triple Crown. Harper sensed if they didn't work through it, he'd be endlessly caught in a loop of guilt and regret that would affect all of them.

She tilted her chin and kept her voice steady. "I know you didn't want him to be permanently hurt, but let's be honest. If the vet had found something concrete, the decision to scratch would have been justified. Horrible, but easy."

He shook his head, his lips firmed. "I still didn't want that. Phoenix and I don't need easy."

She softened, stepping toward him. "I know, Irish. But you're forgetting something important. If I didn't agree with your decision, I would've changed it. My gut told me to scratch. If you had tried to push me, I would've pushed back. I could have agreed, then changed my mind right before the race. You did exactly what I had you promise me when we began this partnership—you chose my horse over the win. You not only did your job, you proved you're a man of worth and trust. A man I happen to love."

Something broke; a wall shifted and crumbled, allowing her to finally reach him. So she did. She reached out and took him in her arms, this beautiful, strong man who held her heart and chose the well-being of an animal over a country's obsession with glory.

She squeezed him tight, and then he was kissing her. Their bodies melted together, and the heat surged between them, hot and true and sweet. She kissed him with her whole heart amid the hay and the horses, in the barn that had always been her real home. And suddenly, Harper wasn't afraid anymore. Not about him leaving or eventually losing him. Not of Phoenix losing. Not of giving her love and trust to a man who could hurt her.

None of it mattered, because she knew she was strong enough to handle it all. Strong enough to risk love and give her heart on her own terms. For the first time since she'd considered taking her life, she realized everything had led to this moment, and a half life filled with security wasn't a life she wanted any longer.

She wanted so much more.

His big hands cupped her cheeks. *"Mo grá,"* he whispered against her lips. "My love. My everything—I love you, too. I just didn't want to disappoint you, not after everything we've fought for."

"You would've disappointed me if you had him run," she said truthfully. "Don't you know that?"

He gazed at her with gentle amber eyes full of emotion, and slowly nodded, pressing his forehead to hers. "Yes."

Phoenix snorted and butted them with his head, trying to break them apart. Captain Hoof bounced around their feet, as if asking if they were done with the silly kissing so they could go play in the pasture.

Aidan laughed. "Goofballs," he said affectionately. "Let's go. We have one last race to tackle."

Harper smiled and rubbed Phoenix under the chin. "Ready to go win the Belmont Stakes, sweet boy?"

The sound exploded to the rafters of the barn and stunned them into silence.

She looked down, her heart paused midbeat.

Captain Hoof stared up at them, his proud, honking bleat released into the world in pure goat fashion. Phoenix nuzzled him with his nose, as if surprised at the sound that emanated from him, and Harper grabbed Aidan's shoulders to steady herself.

"He talked," she breathed. "Oh my God, he talked."

Aidan laughed with delight. "Yes, he did. I think the Captain has finally found his voice."

Another bleat blasted out, the rough, loud, glorious sound better than any Mozart or Beethoven.

They knelt down and hugged him, and Harper knew that sometimes, hope and love and care were enough.

♥ ♥ ♥

Phoenix won the Belmont Stakes in Long Island, New York, two weeks later in a stunning victory.

The entire family made the trip, and Ethan, Mia, Kyle, and Ophelia crammed together in the stands, cheering him on. Wicked Wind barreled in three lengths behind after winning the Preakness, and Tom Tom performed a heart-stopping close to challenge, but it was Phoenix who was draped in roses, filmed by more than a dozen television cameras, and called one of America's most-loved horses for his grit and spirit.

They celebrated with a steak-and-champagne dinner, taking the party to their private suite at a fancy hotel. Phoenix got to eat gourmet iced oatmeal cookies from one of New York's premium bakeries, and Captain Hoof chowed down on organic goat treats flown in by one of his Instagram sponsors.

When they returned to the farm, they were dubbed major celebrities. The town shut down Crystal's and hosted a huge reception. The cake displayed the winning photo from the Belmont Stakes, with Phoenix mugging for the camera, his face peeking out from lush blooms.

Two weeks later, the chaos began to settle. Normal life took over, driving everyone back to work and school, still filled up from the amazing story that had captured each of them in its spell.

Elmo was the first to leave.

"I'll be so sad to see you go," Harper said when the jockey announced it was time for him to move on.

They'd decided to give Phoenix some well-deserved time off before making the next decision. The Travers Stakes in August was a possibility, and she'd received some solid inquiries about breeding. Either way, Elmo craved the next ride, even though the purse money had been substantial enough for him to take a long reprieve. Like Phoenix, he was in it for the love of the game.

"I stay in New York awhile," Elmo said. "You decide to race him again? Call. I drop everything."

She hugged him, and Aidan had slapped him on the back before the jockey went off to say a private goodbye to Phoenix.

His departure stirred up the bees' nest of emotion ready to sting. She hadn't spoken with Aidan about his own plans. Right now, she had the option of expanding the horse-rescue operation and making a true difference.

But Aidan might need more.

For the first time, she knew she might have to face the truth.

She might not be enough for him.

His fingers gently cupped her chin and turned her to face him. "You okay, love?" he asked, his gentle eyes lit with a golden flame. "I know it's hard saying goodbye."

She nodded, too choked up to speak. "He'll always be family," she said simply. "But he needs to do what he was born to. Race."

He smiled, but his hand dropped. The air felt suddenly cold, even under the sting of the summer sun. "Yeah. I have to go into town for a few hours. Need anything?"

"No."

"Not even those special lemon tarts from Fran?" he teased.

The cloud lifted, and she pushed away the sense of foreboding. Aidan wasn't in any hurry to leave. Not yet. She smiled back. "Okay, maybe."

He chuckled and kissed her, his lips lingering on hers.

♥ ♥ ♥

Aidan walked back to the truck with a few lemon tarts for dessert and thought about surprising Harper with a weekend away. Their schedule had been overrun with horse racing, and it'd be nice to steal a few days away from the animals. God knew he loved the menagerie, but they were like children. He just had to help her line up a sitter.

Whistling, he set the lemon tarts safely on the seat. His phone rang, and he glanced at the number, frowning. Ireland. One of his brothers? He hit the button and slid in the driver's seat. "Hello?"

"Aidan O'Connor?"

"Not interested."

He went to hang up, but the male voice rushed on. "This is Brian Keane. I own Gale Farms in Kildare. We've run into each other many times on the circuit."

"Yes, of course. Sorry, there's been a lot of calls lately."

A chuckle. "I bet. Congratulations on your win at the Derby and Belmont. Hell of a horse."

His heart began to pound, and the familiar gut instinct flared to life. Keane was a power player in the racing world, and owned one of the most prestigious breeding-and-horse farms in Ireland. He worked with a variety of trainers from all over the world and always had an entry in a big stakes race. Colin had always insisted once Keane noticed them, their business would explode. They'd stalked him for years, and though he was polite, he'd never seemed interested in the small local partnership.

"Yes, he is. It's been a pleasure to train him."

"I was surprised at your decision to scratch at the Preakness. Most trainers would've pushed."

His mind flickered to that life-changing moment in the stalls. For so long, he'd regretted not waiting longer, or trying to ice the ankle first, or retaining a second opinion. But he knew deep down it didn't matter. It was one of those decisions that was made with no guarantee of right or wrong. Finally he'd realized, after speaking with Harper, that he'd done the only thing he could at the time. And he'd do it again. It was the difference between him and Colin and maybe some other trainers who focused so completely on the win, they forgot their most important job of all.

The horse.

He'd finally proved to himself winning wasn't everything. Finally, the taunting inner voice inside him had gone silent.

"Yes, I'm sure they would have. I don't regret it. Pushing a young horse too far and too fast is dangerous. I'm not that kind of trainer."

"That's what I was hoping." Brian paused, as if gathering his thoughts. "I have a new horse I've been personally keeping a close eye on. A spirited filly named Run for the Roses. She's sired from Hal's Prince. And I think she's special."

Aidan whistled. Hal's Prince was a legend, with speed and power all packed into a relatively small body. Watching him run the track was a gift. "Who's been working with her?"

"No one. Just me. This one is . . . different. Ever get a gut feeling about a horse? Like you just know something big is going to happen?"

He chuckled. "Yeah. I lived my whole life looking for the next hit."

"I have an impressive roster of some of the best trainers in the world, and no one seems to fit. And then I watched you with Phoenix this past season. After you made the decision to scratch, I realized you're the one I want to train my horse. I need a trainer with heart, because this little filly has it. I think you're the perfect match."

Shock filled him. Yes, he'd known his wins with Phoenix had finally put him on the map. Yes, he figured one day he'd return to Ireland and have his pick of decent horses to train. But he'd never imagined Brian Keane would give him an opportunity to work with him. His mind clicked over the options and settled on the most important question of all. "When would you need me?"

"Right away. I'll send you some videos to help make your decision. I want you on my team, Aidan. I think we can make history together. I'd love to set up a meeting. Are you still in New York?"

"Yeah, I hadn't made any plans to leave yet. I'm humbled by the offer. Let me take a look at the video, do some thinking, and get back to you."

They clicked off. Aidan waited, staring at the phone for a while until the file arrived. He opened it up and watched.

A beautiful gray filly raced down the track. The camera angles moved to catch each side of her as she did a full loop. Legs moved like the wind. Her silvery coat caught the glint of the sun and shimmered over her like a diamond in the rough. But it was her face that stopped his breath. Oh, the joy and fierceness as she lowered her head and ran free, her entire focus on the road ahead and how fast she could get there. Shivers broke out on his skin. His throat tightened. And the voice deep inside his gut, which had been silent for more than a year, rose up inside and whispered that he was looking at his next horse.

With shaking hands, he threw the phone down and grasped the steering wheel.

No.

He wasn't ready to go back. Harper and Phoenix had quieted the raw edges of his soul and made him happy. He wanted endless time to enjoy the farm and help her expand the rescue portion. He wanted to watch Phoenix grow and see where his path led—whether it be competitive racing, breeding, or a combination. He wanted to help with the new volunteers for the summer and train them properly. He wanted—

Harper. It all revolved around Harper.

He groaned and rubbed his face. Funny, he'd never seen this coming. Didn't expect to find an opportunity that called to his sense of challenge and purpose in the horse world. But he'd warned her about his wandering spirit. Had it only been temporarily silenced while he was here? Was it just a part of his heart that even love couldn't tame? And yet . . . the idea of leaving her behind battered his very soul.

What was he going to do?

He sat in the parking lot for a long time, going over the options, but was able to make only one important decision.

He'd tell her about Brian Keane and his offer. He refused to hide anything under the guise of not wanting to hurt her. She deserved the truth, even if it broke him apart to tell her. Because he was terrified that if she asked if he wanted to go, he'd say the wrong answer.

Yes.

Chapter Twenty-Six

Harper stared at her clasped hands resting on the table.

He had to leave.

The admission curled through her body like an actual pain, but she made sure it never showed on her face. He'd been honest. She knew he loved her. But after she watched the video, she realized the man she loved didn't just belong to her. He belonged to the road he'd chosen to follow—a road that led him to nurture and care for horses. Phoenix wouldn't have accomplished any of it without Aidan. The care, patience, and love came from his very soul.

He was so like her. Only her path had stopped right here, on her mother's land, with the animals she saved every day. She couldn't run off to Ireland with him. She'd chosen differently. She'd always sensed he was a temporary gift in her life, and he'd never pretended to be someone he wasn't.

And in that moment, Harper realized she loved him enough to let him go.

"Irish, this is an opportunity of a lifetime," she said, finally able to look up and gaze into his beloved face. "This past year with Phoenix has taught you so much. You're ready. She has the same fire and drive that makes a winner. How can you not go?"

His gaze narrowed, and she caught a flash of temper. "Well, I can give you a ton of reasons, but how about I stick with just one?" He leaned forward. She caught the lines creasing his eyes and mouth, the rough edge of stubble clinging to his jaw, the sharp blade of his nose and flaring nostrils. "You."

Emotion choked her, but she fought through. If he stayed, she'd always wonder if he had regrets. God knew she could live with anything but the what-ifs, especially with the man she loved. "I know. I'm not going to lie and pretend I want you to leave, Aidan. When you get on that plane, my heart will break, but I also know this is who you are. Just like you once told me. My life is here, at the farm. I can't ask you to stay."

"Yes, you can." That glorious male temper was him fighting for her—for them.

She rose from the chair and went to him, sliding into his lap and burying her face against his neck. He held her tight, and they stayed locked together for a while before either of them was able to speak. Finally, she lifted her head and ran a finger down his rough cheek. "You have to go," she whispered. "If you don't follow your heart, you may regret it and blame me down the road. I'd rather die than have that."

"I don't know if I can leave you."

His broken voice almost destroyed her. She tipped his chin back and forced him to look at her. She smiled and kissed his beautiful lips, drowning in his scent. "We had a hell of a run, Irish. I'll always love you. But you have to go."

With a growl, he picked her up and carried her to the bedroom. They made love with a fierce tenderness. Each thrust held the rough edge of desperation, fueling the intensity between them, and when they shattered together, they held each other through the long hours of the night, refusing to part.

♥ ♥ ♥

A week later, Aidan stood in the barn, prepared for his final goodbye.

He now realized why he'd refused to become attached to anyone, why he refused to share his true self with anyone other than a horse.

It was too damn heartbreaking.

Ophelia had hosted a farewell dinner with enough food to last him for days. Afterward, they'd all gathered in the living room to watch *Coco*, and when he heard the haunting strains of the song "Remember Me," he'd almost lost his man card.

Disney was no joke.

Now he stood in the damp interior with the scents of hay and wood and mud, and made his final trek to Phoenix's stall.

The horse pushed his nose out.

"Hey, mo chára, I got something for you." He unlatched the gate and walked inside. The horse gave him a nice bump, raising his chin automatically for the love. Aidan laughed and gave him the affection he craved, rubbing all the spots he adored, then waited for him to detect the treat.

A few moments later, he nosed toward his pocket, those lips curling back to retrieve his iced oatmeal cookie. Aidan watched him eat, as he'd done a thousand times before, every movement and breath a part of his daily routine that he cherished.

His voice came out a bit hoarse. "I gotta go, champ. But I have something important to tell you. Something I hope you can understand and always remember."

The horse finished his treat, and then those liquid brown eyes searched his. Tiny snorts emitted from his nostrils.

"You changed my life. You made me believe again—and it wasn't by winning the Champagne, or the Cup, or the Derby, or even the damn Belmont. It was your heart. You never gave up and you never will."

The horse cocked his head, as if considering.

Aidan studied his face and felt something break inside of him, a pain and gratitude that humbled him to his very soul. He rubbed under the horse's chin, stroked his nose, and leaned over to kiss him. "You were always a champion, but now the world knows it. You did it on your terms, just like your mama, and every damn second with you was a gift. Do you understand, Phoenix? A gift."

The horse pressed his large head against Aidan's chest, as if sensing this was a goodbye. For a few precious seconds, Aidan closed his eyes and opened his heart to this horse who had made him a different man—a better man—one worthy to be the trainer of a victor.

"Love you, mo chára. Take care of your mama, okay? She needs you to stay strong."

Captain Hoof let out a bleat, signaling he wanted in on the lovefest.

Aidan leaned down to pet and soothe, studying his sweet face with the little horns and thick, healthy fur. The chicken costume was no longer needed, but Aidan admitted he almost wished he could see it on him again. "Take care of Phoenix, Captain. You both need each other."

His eyes stung. Slowly, he straightened, unlatched the gate, and walked out of the barn one last time.

♥ ♥ ♥

"Call me when you get there," Harper said, her hands entwined with his.

"I will."

"Ophelia gave you some blueberry scones for your trip."

"That was nice of her."

"I know you'll have some fancy digs, but don't forget to sleep in a bed sometimes, okay? You were having back problems last week."

He laughed, but it came out choked. "Damn, I'm not that old. It was just a kink."

"Well, it could get worse if you keep bunking on barn floors."

"Okay."

They smiled at each other. He'd tried to convince her to do an official long-distance relationship, but she'd refused. They both knew he wouldn't have the time to take many trips to the States, and she wouldn't be able to visit him in Ireland. She'd explained she was afraid if they clung to each other, their relationship would wither and die while they watched. God knew he couldn't handle that, so they'd agreed to make a clean break.

He kissed her. Savored her sweet taste and the scent of cocoa butter. Memorized the smoothness of her skin and the silkiness of her hair. When he stepped back, he stared at her for a long time, greedily devouring every inch of beauty.

"*Mo chroí. Mo grá.*" His voice broke. "My everything."

Her lips trembled when she smiled. "I love you, too, Aidan O'Connor."

The words rose and danced in the air. He turned and walked down the dirt path, refusing to look back.

If he did, Aidan knew he'd stay.

♥ ♥ ♥

"You okay?"

Harper glanced at her sister. They were sitting on the front porch. Iced tea and cookies were set out. The memory hit her hard. It'd been almost a year since her sister had given her the advice to lead with her heart and let herself be open to Aidan. Right now, as the pain crippled her, she wondered why she wasn't angry.

"Not really. I feel like I want to crawl into bed and sleep for a month."

Her sister smiled, reached over, and squeezed her hand. They rocked together in silence, staring out at the sprawling expanse of land. It was that special in-between time when the inn was mostly empty, the guests gone on afternoon adventures. "When Kyle left, I thought I'd die. I know how bad it hurts, Harp, but I'm proud of you."

"For having my first broken heart?" she joked.

"For trying," she said quietly. "For being human. Aidan loves you; it's so obvious. Did you ask him to stay?"

"I couldn't. I know how it is to feel called to do something in your life no one else understands."

"Yeah, that was the big thing with Kyle and me. Even Mia and Ethan. Odd, all of us picked soul mates who were meant to leave."

Harper choked out a laugh. "That's fucked up."

Ophelia laughed with her. "Yep. What are you going to do next?"

She shrugged. "Concentrate on the rescue farm. I'm going to expand and build new barns. Hire some help. There's so many more animals I can save now because of Phoenix."

"Mom would be so proud of you."

She sighed, and pride surged, soothing the ache. "Yeah, I think she would."

"I know she would. You're going to be okay, Harp. And something wonderful is going to come your way again. Aidan allowed you to see who you really are—who we all see every time we look at you. Now that you recognize it too, you're going to be unstoppable."

Touched by her sister's words, she smiled and rocked in rhythm beside her, thinking about her past, her future, and the man who had changed her forever.

Chapter Twenty-Seven

"She's doing well," Brian commented, standing beside Aidan. "I think you made a breakthrough. Rosie always hated the saddle, but she's taken to it well."

Aidan smiled and watched the spirited filly ease through a light breeze. "She's come far. You gave me a great foundation. She takes to the track like she was born for it."

They both studied the beauty of the filly flying over the dirt, but Aidan was seeing another horse in his mind, a fierce black beauty with fuck-you eyes and a rebellious fire in his soul.

God, was the pain ever going to go away?

It'd been almost two months. Two months of working with a horse who was talented, sweet, and born to run. Run for the Roses—a.k.a. Rosie—was all the things he looked for in a horse to train, and he'd grown to care deeply about her. His relationship with Brian had also grown, and Aidan deeply respected the man for not only his work ethic but also the love he had for every horse in his stables. They'd paired Rosie with a jockey Aidan knew by reputation, and they got along easily. Even Gale Farms was something out of a Hollywood movie, with its sprawling acres, gleaming white fences, and endless crisp apple-red stalls scattered in organized rows.

They employed hundreds of people for every task. Staff raked the dirt on the track to fine sand, while others cut the lawn so it never grew past a certain number of inches. His room was huge and located right by the barn for convenience. There was a full-time chef who cooked three square meals a day. Finally, he'd reached the big time. He had everything he'd ever wanted and dreamed for as that young, dirt-poor boy who fantasized of making it big on the racetrack with a horse he believed in.

He was a respected trainer who had the opportunity to work with the very best. He'd heard Colin hadn't gotten that last job he'd been sniffing around for at the Breeders' Cup, and that he'd split with Rachael. Kincaid's Crown had been sold to another farm, and Aidan was now able to regularly visit him.

His partner was failing, and Aidan had it all.

So why was he miserable?

He'd given it time. He knew he'd be haunted by her voice, her scent, her memory, but he pushed through and put all his focus into Rosie and his brand-new start in Ireland. He had fun hanging at the pubs with old friends and sinking back into the familiarity of the world he'd been raised in. He figured in a few weeks, the imprint of her on his soul would begin to fade.

It didn't.

Aidan looked out to a different pasture but thought about the one he was missing. He was haunted by the life he'd chosen not to take for the only one he'd ever known.

And every day that passed, he understood with a panicky realization he'd made a big mistake.

He wasn't happy. He felt as if he were missing a piece of himself, and though he went through the motions, his heart was hollow through every beat. He thought of his future, perfectly mapped out, and wanted to howl with misery. Everything had changed, and he couldn't go back to the man he'd been before.

He didn't want to.

He wanted to be the man he'd become with Harper.

His hands shook with the enormity of his decision. And then he closed his eyes and saw her face.

"Aidan? You okay?"

He opened his eyes. The knowledge sank into every pore of his skin and settled in deep. This wasn't home any longer. It was time to accept it and claim his new one.

"No, I'm not, Brian. We have a big problem, and I hope you can understand."

His silver brows drew into a frown. "Tell me and let's see if we can work it out."

Aidan shook his head. "You see, there's this amazing woman . . ."

Harper led the new mare out of the truck. She kept her motions slow and deliberate, sensing the horse had a serious case of trust abuse. The hoarding situation had been a nightmare, but thank God the authorities had closed the farm and moved all the animals to local rescue shelters. She'd been able to take two.

Next year, she'd take them all.

Harper glanced at her new charge, noticing the slight shake. Poor thing reminded her of a scared little deer, flinching at loud sounds as if a hunter were going to shoot at her.

"It's okay, sweetheart," she crooned, gently stroking her flank. "I think we're going to call you Bambi. Wait till you meet Flower, your stablemate. I think you two will be perfect for each other."

Ethan walked up behind her. "What a pretty little mare," he commented, slowly holding out his hand so the horse would catch his scent. "Flower will love her."

"I just told her the same. I'm going to name her Bambi."

"Sounds perfect. Don't forget the wedding rehearsal is Friday. Are you all set to run everything while Mia and I are gone?"

She smiled. "Money is a beautiful thing. I just hired a new full timer, Jared, so we'll be fine. And I don't want you worried about anything here while you're in Costa Rica. You going to zipline?"

"Hell yes. Mia's looking forward to it. And I'm looking forward to the red string bikini she just packed."

She rolled her eyes. "TMI, bro."

"What about you, Harp? Will you be okay while we're gone?"

Her heart pulsed at the concern in her brother's eyes. Everyone had rallied around, inviting her to endless dinners, helping her out at the farm, and keeping her occupied. She appreciated the attention, but once again, she found her animals soothed her wounds the most. Spending quiet time in the stall talking with Phoenix and Captain Hoof. Watching all the dogs play and run in the pasture. Riding Maximus through the trails down to the creek.

It was hard. She missed him every day, every moment. She still cried at night. But every day, she got up with a new purpose and embraced the woman she'd become because she loved him.

"I'll be fine. I'm meeting with the architect to draw up plans for the additional barns. I think it may be nice to add a place our employees can stay in case they want to remain close."

"Good idea." His gaze probed hers. "You talk to Aidan lately?"

His name pierced like an arrow, but she loved hearing it at the same time. "No. We figured it'd be better this way, but it's hard. Elmo texted, though. He's got a mount in Saratoga for the Travers. Wants me to come and watch him run."

"You regret not entering Phoenix?"

She shook her head. "No, I want to give him some time off. I think he may be ready to run in the Breeders' Cup again in November, so we'll see."

"A solid plan." They smiled at each other. "Let me take Bambi in and get her settled. Will you call Mia? She asked me to tell you she needs help with the bachelorette party."

She groaned. "Crap, why isn't Ophelia helping?"

"Don't know, I'm just the groom." He winked and strolled off, speaking to the mare in his usual magical voice.

Cursing under her breath, she wiped her muddy hands on her jeans and fished out her cell. She refused to deal with strippers, or anything else creepy. Maybe she could convince Mia to do a spa day? Much better getting naked with smelly seaweed all over her than sticking dollar bills down G-strings of oiled-up men.

God, she was lame. But she wasn't about to apologize for her . . .

Her thoughts trailed off and stilled. Her gaze narrowed on the figure ahead. She was seeing things again. She imagined seeing the man around every corner and figured it'd go away one day. Funny, though, the guest looked so like him, from his staggering height and solid muscled build and his—

The phone dropped lifelessly from her fingers.

Aidan.

His name trembled on her lips, but she wasn't fast enough. In a rush of fur and excitement, Wheezy, Bolt, Bagheera, and Baloo took off toward him, leaping with joy. He knelt down, giving them the love, folded into their canine embrace, and she moved a few steps closer, hoping it wasn't a dream.

A duffel bag lay at his feet. Battered jeans, work boots, and a navy-blue T-shirt stretching across his broad chest. His straw-colored hair was longer and blew in the wind, covering his brow. Her belly dropped to her toes, and she swayed on her feet, still speechless.

"Did your mother forget me already?" he asked the dogs, their bodies wriggling with delight. "Or does she need to smell me first?"

"Aidan?" She blinked furiously. "Wh-what are you doing here?"

He brushed off the dirt on his knees and stood. "Ireland wasn't what I imagined."

The shaking began deep inside and shivered to every muscle in her body, but she didn't move. Not yet. "It wasn't as green as you remembered?"

"Nope. More like an artichoke green. Quite dull."

"And the pubs?"

He wrinkled his nose. "Guinness everywhere. Not a decent IPA in sight."

"How about the horses? I heard Rosie was a champion," she said softly.

"She is. And she'll have a stellar racing career with or without me. It just so happens that I can't stop thinking about a certain horse who rose above the ashes to capture my heart."

Harper met his gaze head-on and asked her final question. "And Rosie's owner? Will you regret leaving?"

A smile tugged at his lips. "I'm not in love with him. He's not my type."

She choked on a laugh, but then his face turned serious and he took a step forward.

"You told me to follow my heart. Every road I've ever walked has led me to the next town, the next barn, the next horse, and the next piece of my soul. But then I met you, Harper Bishop, and I was ruined." Slowly, he closed the distance and stood in front of her. She caught the sexy squint of his eyes and the light sunburn on his nose. The blazing intensity of his amber gaze locked fiercely on hers. "You're my heart. And every damn road I ever took had one purpose. It led me to you."

Her eyes stung, and her hand trembled as she reached out, almost afraid to believe. "What about your dream?"

"I had to leave in order to come back. I had to realize you changed me. You're my dream, *mo grá*. I want it all, and I want it with you, right here." He pulled her into his arms and cupped her cheeks. "I want to stay. Help you expand the horse rescue, take on more community service volunteers, be a part of Phoenix's life. And I want to marry you."

She gasped. "What?"

"I know you once told me you're not the marrying kind, but God, I hope I can convince you to let me love you for the rest of your life. Here, I got a ring. Wait."

He reached into his pocket, dug out a box, and clasped it open.

The elegantly cut round diamond glittered in the sun.

"Aidan," she breathed in shock. "Oh my God."

"I didn't want any sharp edges like a marquis cut, and I know you wouldn't want it too big to wear under your gloves, so I—crap, I forgot to ask, didn't I?" He sank down in the muddy ground and looked up at her. *"Graim thu. An bposfaidh tu me?"*

She stared blindly at the ring. "Huh?"

A lopsided grin curved his lips. "Harper Bishop, I love you, and I'm begging you to marry me. Walk with me on this road together?"

There was only one thing left to say for a happy ever after she'd never seen coming and never believed she'd have.

"Yes." She reached for him, blinking away tears. "Oh yes."

Epilogue

"I now pronounce you man and wife. You may kiss the bride."

A roar rose from the crowd, and Harper watched her brother kiss Mia, wrapping his arms around her and lifting her high up. Mia laughed, obviously not caring about her designer gown or crushed veil or smudged makeup, joy pumping from her aura.

Harper glanced over and saw Chloe and Ophelia outright crying. It had been a long journey, and seeing her brother so happy made her feel the presence of their mother pressing down upon them, offering her eternal blessing.

Her gaze sought out Aidan in the crowd. Dressed in a sharp black suit with a red tie, he was devastatingly handsome. He caught her stare and lifted his hand, pointing at the happy couple and then back at her. A smile bubbled from her lips. The weight of the ring felt warm and secure around her finger.

Yes. They were next.

After the traditional receiving line and an hour of photos, they settled into the reception. The oversize windows overlooked the amazing view before them. The mountains surrounded them with a kingly authority, soaring edges and peaks squeezing the clear, crystal lake, where boats lazily rowed and guests fished.

Harper sipped her champagne, nibbled on appetizers, and melted into the tight group where her fiancé stood. "Hey, Irish, you may get lucky if you can score me more of those crab cakes."

He slipped his arm around her waist. "If that's your fourth champagne, I think I'm getting lucky tonight anyway, love."

She laughed and playfully punched his arm.

Kyle groaned. "You need to read my books, Aidan. Your lines are terrible."

"Well, we're all going to see your movie at the premiere," Ethan said, looking distinguished in his custom tuxedo. "When is *A Brand New Ending* coming out?"

"A few months. Presley Cabot at LWW is a godsend. Besides handling all the publicity shit, she's already got me producer credit after years of me begging to no avail."

"Sounds good. Maybe Aidan can gain some pointers."

"You need them, too, dude. A little romance goes a long way."

Ethan snorted, pressing a kiss to Mia's mouth. "I'm the king of romance. Plus, I'm an alpha. You've always been the beta in this relationship."

Kyle glared. "I'm not a beta," he retorted. "I'm as alpha as they come."

"When you were doing the best man toast, you cried."

His glare darkened. "I was not crying, just trying to show some emotion to get the crowd engaged in the story."

Ophelia shared a laughing glance with Mia, and they both grabbed their spouses' hands. "Let's go dance. Battle it out on the floor!" Mia yelled.

"Is that Prince? Oh my God, I love this song!" Ophelia shrieked.

Ethan and Kyle looked scared but allowed themselves to be flung into the center of the action.

Aidan looked at Harper and lifted a brow. "Don't even think about it."

"I hate dancing. I only like the slow songs."

"And that is why you're the love of my life," he said simply.

"You are so getting lucky," she whispered, pressing a kiss to his lips. "Oh, look, there's Owen! I haven't talked to him yet." She waved at him over Aidan's shoulder, and the boy strolled up with a grin.

"Hi, Harper, Aidan. How are you?"

"Great, I'm so glad you could make it to the wedding," Harper said, taking in his sleek black suit, crisp shirt, and yellow tie. He'd cut his hair—the bouncy surfer curls were gone. With his shorter hair, his face became more defined, and his blue eyes sparkled with an engaging light. "You look so handsome."

A slight blush colored his cheeks. "Thanks. How's Phoenix? Flower? And the Captain?"

"Thriving. Make sure you visit us. Flower always looks forward to seeing you, and we just got a new little mare named Bambi."

"I'll come by next week. I've been working at the bookstore in town. Grandpa Bennett gave me his wedding card. He's sorry he couldn't make it, but he's out of town—"

"Harper!" a female voice interrupted. "Dad won't dance with me, and it's Prince and—oh, Owen! Wow. You look . . . great."

Harper bit back a smile as Chloe took in the new, improved Owen.

The boy lit up under her scrutiny, but this time, he didn't babble. He just nodded and smiled. "Thanks. It was time to cut the locks. You look beautiful. How's your summer going?"

"Fun, but I took on some volunteer work at a local law firm. I thought I'd learn a lot, but I'm really just fetching coffee and doing crappy errands."

Owen laughed. "Gotta pay the dues first, right? Eventually, they'll learn how smart you are and let you start doing stuff."

"Yeah, maybe. Thanks." Harper noticed Chloe hadn't once glanced at her or Aidan, her focus completely on Owen. "Do you like Prince?"

"He's a guitar genius. How could I not?"

"Want to dance?"

"Definitely." He took her hand and headed to the dance floor.

Aidan whistled. "The boy got some moves," he said. "Maybe there *is* romance in the air tonight."

"Anything can happen," she said, stepping into his embrace and entwining her arms around his shoulders. "Want to dance?"

"To Prince?"

"We can make up our own tune. A slow one."

He grinned and held her tight, his hips swaying to hers, locked in a circle of intimacy just for them.

She closed her eyes, pressed her ear against his beating heart, and looked forward to the winding, ever-surprising road ahead.

Together.

AUTHOR'S NOTE

A shout-out to the rescue organization Goats of Anarchy, who inspired the character of Captain Hoof. You can find this amazing nonprofit on Instagram at @goatsofanarchy. Give them a follow and a donation!

And thank you to Devon Hensley, who helped me make sure I was using all the horse terminology correctly. Thanks to Michelle Mcloughney for helping me with Irish terminology and to avoid the trap of using *lass* for everything—LOL! Any errors I made are all my fault.

Any mistakes made with the road to the Derby and racehorse training are truly mine and mine alone.

ACKNOWLEDGMENTS

My dear readers, this book was so different from any other.

Let's just say I was surprised at how many rescue animals popped up along the way with a demand that their story be told. This was truly a labor of love and a tale that has been burning in my mind from the moment I wrote *The Start of Something Good* and dreamed of telling Phoenix's journey as powerfully as Harper's.

Thank you so much for going on this path with me.

I want to give special thanks to Maria Gomez and the entire savvy team at Montlake for all they do. My developmental editor, Kristi Yanta, who helped me polish this book to perfection—during the holidays no less, LOL! A hug to my agent, Kevan Lyons, who is a cherished guide and support in my writing career.

Finally, a special shout-out to my amazing family. If my husband didn't cook every night, and my two boys didn't understand the seriousness of the word *deadline*, I wouldn't be writing these acknowledgments! Love you guys to pieces.

I can't wait to see what comes next.

ABOUT THE AUTHOR

Photo © 2012 Matt Simpkins

Jennifer Probst is the *New York Times* bestselling author of the Billionaire Builders series; the Searching For series; the Marriage series; the Steele Brothers series; and in the Stay series, *The Start of Something Good* and *A Brand New Ending*. Like some of her characters, Probst, along with her husband and two sons, calls New York's Hudson Valley home. When she isn't traveling to meet readers, she enjoys reading, watching "shameful reality television," and visiting a local Hudson Valley animal shelter. Follow her at www.jenniferprobst.com.